MASTERS OF ILLUSION

Dragon studied Lea, his eyes hooded slightly. He said, "Me think you speak with forked tongue, pale face."

She tried to buy some time. "What do you mean, I speak with a forked tongue?"

He laughed again, softer this time.

She used his laugh to move closer to him.

He smiled at her then and turned his face directly toward her. "Let me show you a forked tongue," he said.

Lea gaped as Dragon opened his mouth and a long muscular forked tongue the color of snakeskin writhed out and wrapped itself around her throat.

She gagged, startled into immobility.

Fold upon greenish fold of stringy-wet tongue slithered out of Dragon's open mouth. Fold upon fold wrapped itself about her and drew her closer to him.

She wanted to scream, but the tight, contracting snakelike flesh about her throat wouldn't let the sound out.

Then she wanted to laugh.

The joke's on you, you bastard, she thought. *On you!* The hallucination he'd created was going to be the death of him...

Also by Mark Manley

THROWBACK

Published by
POPULAR LIBRARY

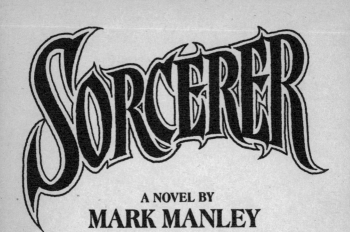

SORCERER

A NOVEL BY
MARK MANLEY

POPULAR LIBRARY

An Imprint of Warner Books, Inc.

A Warner Communications Company

POPULAR LIBRARY EDITION

Popular Library® and the fanciful P design are registered trademarks of Warner Books, Inc.

Cover design by Don Puckey
Cover illustration by Lisa Falkenstern

Popular Library books are published by
Warner Books, Inc.
666 Fifth Avenue
New York, N.Y. 10103

W A Warner Communications Company

Printed in the United States of America

First Printing: July, 1988

10 9 8 7 6 5 4 3 2 1

To my mother, Inez,
and
In memory of my father, Duane—

She taught me to dream and explore,
And to fill my sails with wind.
He taught me to chart my course by the stars,
Then set the tiller in my hand.

Prologue: A Warning

Cassadaga, Florida

Michael rang the doorbell and waited, one hand resting on his nine-year-old daughter's shoulder.

A woman opened the inside door and looked out through the screen door, smiling. "Yes?"

"We were given your name and address by a friend," Michael Dragon said. "You *are* Marie Fiero, the psychic?"

"Yes, but..." A frown creased her features. She edged closer to the screen door, squinted out at Michael and his daughter, Jenny. "I...I'm afraid I'm not really up for doing a reading today." Her smile was gone.

"My friend said you were very good," Michael said.

She backed away from the screen door, one hand reaching for the nearby heavy oak inner door. "I appreciate that. Please, tell your friend 'thank you' for me. But I'm sorry. I'm just not up for doing a reading today. I...can't, not now. Not today."

She started to close the inner door.

Michael put a hand up to her screen door. He noticed the woman stiffen. "We've driven all the way from Tampa. I'm a psychologist, and I wanted to learn a little about what you do, and about Cassadaga in general."

"Go away," the woman said, her voice suddenly containing a shrill note. "I can't do a reading for you."

"But we've driven all this way. We understood that the psychics in town were usually willing to take people without an appointment."

She shook her head with stubborn force, eased the heavy oak inner door further closed. "We do, yes. But . . . I can't. Not today. I . . . I'm not not feeling well. And if I can't do a good reading, I don't want to do one at all."

"What about Sylvia Danner?" Michael asked as the inner door closed to a crack beyond the screen door.

"I can't speak for Sylvia," the woman said through the crack. "Good day."

The oak door closed softly with a muted *shush* and a click.

A dead bolt slid home.

A safety chain rattled into place after that.

"What was wrong with that lady, Daddy?" Jenny asked.

Michael glanced down at his daughter. Her dark hair was catching the Florida sunshine and reflecting it back with deep auburn highlights. She looked so much like her mother, it was amazing.

That thought spawned a vague lightness in Michael's chest.

He didn't want to think about it, but he and Angie, Jenny's mother, hadn't been very close lately. For maybe three . . . four months. Longer than that, actually, but he hated to admit it. It seemed they could seldom get their schedules to coincide. They were drifting apart, Michael knew, and he wasn't sure why—wasn't even sure it mattered to Angie . . . anymore.

"I don't know, honey." He took her hand. Together they left the front stoop of the well-preserved frame home and made their way to the Buick.

An odd, dulling, prescient sensation tugged at his mind. *What was wrong with Marie Fiero?*

He dismissed the thought *and* the feeling.

The woman was ill. That was all there was to it.

Or maybe the feeling didn't have anything to do with Marie Fiero.

He dismissed that thought, too, not wanting to follow it to its conclusion.

As he slid into the driver's seat, Jenny crawled onto her knees and looked out the rear window. "This is a pretty town. I like the big old houses."

"So do I."

He pulled away from the curb and checked the second of two addresses he had scribbled on a scrap of paper in his shirt pocket.

Cassadaga was not a large town. He drove leisurely through the quiet streets, enjoying the pleasant, timeless feeling of the place. It was an old town, old for Florida, and in many ways did not look like a Florida community. It contained a mixture of Spanish- and small Cape Cod-style houses. Well-tended lawns and gardens slipped past beneath sheltering live oaks that reached up to tickle the underbelly of the sky.

Glancing at the scrap of paper in his hand, Michael pulled to the curb once again. He hoped to hell this trip didn't turn out to be a complete *fizzle*. He'd thought about visiting the famous town for nearly a year, and now that he'd taken the effort to do so, he didn't want to be disappointed.

"Wow," Jenny said. "Is this the place?"

"It is."

"It's pretty fandabulous."

The huge, two-story, turn-of-the-century frame house sat on a perfectly manicured lawn. Towering live oaks turned the grass into a sun-dappled carpet. To one side, surrounded by geometric flower beds, stood an ornate, whitewashed gazebo.

"I'd like to live in a place like this," Jenny said. "Do you think we could, sometime, Dad, huh?"

Michael smiled at his daughter. "Maybe," he lied, not wanting to put a damper on her enthusiasm. He and Angie had been through their old-house craze. They'd completely restored two of them, room by room.

But never again.

The work never ended on one of those old beauties.

Michael and Jenny stepped from the cool interior of the Buick into the furnace of a hot Florida summer day. Their shoes scuffed softly on the uneven flagstone walk.

A sweeping veranda formed a U around the front and sides of the house. A double porch swing hung motionless in the still, humid air. It was the kind of porch made for families, lemonade, and checkers.

"Don't you just love it, Dad? Mom would *really* like this place."

Michael smiled as he led his daughter up the front steps. "It is beautiful."

Their footsteps echoed dully on the wooden porch floor. Michael let Jenny ring the doorbell. It was one of the old-fashioned kind you had to twist.

"Neat," she said, giving it a second twist.

Doilied curtains framed the etched-glass, oval window in the center of the old door. For a moment, a sleepy bee buzzed around a flowered cushion on the nearby swing before flying off in frustration.

The front door opened.

"May I help you?" The woman had a soft, slightly gravelly voice, rich with sensuous undertones.

The woman was younger than Michael had expected. Thirty, maybe thirty-two. Only a couple of inches shorter than he was. Maybe five-eight or -nine. A bit too thin, although certainly well within the tasty category. Creamy skin. Her soft, honey-blond hair had a lot of body and was cut medium-long. She had beautiful, deep, emerald green eyes. It was odd, but they didn't seem to focus cleanly on his face.

"Sylvia Danner?" Michael asked.

"No," she said in that same remarkable voice. "I'm Carol Lewis. I've been helping Mrs. Danner recently. You might call me an apprentice, actually." She held her hand out.

"Is Mrs. Danner in?" Michael asked, moving to shake the woman's hand.

"She is."

The woman's hand was soft and warm. She had long, strong fingers, the fingers of a pianist.

She moved her head this way and that while their hands remained in contact, as if alert for something.

Those remarkable eyes still didn't seem quite on target.

"A friend gave me her name."

"Are you here for a reading?" There was a different note in the voice now, a . . . *note of caution?* Is that what he was hearing?

"Yes, if possible."

"I'm sure it is." The woman's smile, though controlled, was still dazzling. "Follow me, please. I'll tell Mrs. Danner you're here."

Michael and Jenny followed Carol Lewis into a foyer from yesteryear. The beautiful old house had either been maintained in its original grandeur, or had gone through a remarkable restoration somewhere along the line. Chandeliers, ornate natural woodwork, and inlaid hardwood floors were offset beautifully by the subtle shades of the wallpaper and soft Persian carpets.

"This is a pretty neat house," Jenny said out loud.

"I'm glad you like it," Carol Lewis said, pausing at a set of French doors. She gestured through the single open door. "If you'll wait in here, Mrs. Danner will be with you in a moment."

"Thank you."

Michael followed his daughter into the room. As he passed Carol Lewis, he was conscious of her putting out a hand to touch his bare arm, as if trying to fathom something about him by that simple act.

He glanced at the sharp angles of her face, wondering what she was thinking. His eyes caught the emerald sparkle from her eyes, and it was with some surprise that he realized she was blind. She hadn't caught his glance; rather, was reacting to something far off in the silent reaches of her mind.

In the next moment, she turned and strode deeper into the house.

Michael shook off his thoughts about the woman and shifted his attention to the room. He was surprised at its brightness. He'd expected a dim room dominated by candles and heavy draperies, with maybe even a crystal ball in prominence. Instead, he found himself in a long sun porch with a full wall of lead-framed north windows. Rich green foliage and white wicker furniture highlighted the dark flagstone floor. The room seemed to revolve around the muted colors of a soft Persian rug in the center of the room. The atmosphere was light and airy. The colors of the carpet were picked up in the cushions on the wicker couch and chairs.

"Ooo," Jenny said, running her hands gently along a wall of thick ferns near the windows, "Mom is going to be sad she missed this place. I bet she'd love to have a chance to sell this."

Michael chose one of the wicker chairs and sat down to wait. Angie *would* love to get her realtor's hands on this place, he knew. It was the kind of place that would generate a lot of interest. In the right neighborhood, a house like this would go for a mint.

Jenny took a seat finally in one of the other chairs.

Mrs. Danner entered the room a moment later. "Hello," she said brightly. "It's nice of you to stop in to see me."

As she crossed the room, Michael was aware of the congruence between the woman and this room. There was something very alive and vital about the woman. She was in her mid- to late forties, attractive, bubbly, with an intelligent and curious expression on her face.

"You're here for a reading, Carol tells me," Sylvia Danner said, reaching out to take Michael's hand.

Michael rose, extended his hand. "Yes. A friend gave me—" Their hands met, and the conversation took a bizarre turn.

"You," Mrs. Danner said.

"Pardon me?"

"You."

Michael frowned.

"You . . . you . . . yooooooooooooooooooo . . ."

Then Sylvia Danner snapped.

There was no other word for it.

She *snapped*.

She came bolt upright, as if some force had suddenly straightened her spine. Her mouth gaped. She went silent. Her eyes saucered open. Her rosy complexion went suddenly ashen and bluish. Her skin filmed with moisture.

"Mrs. Danner?"

She didn't blink. Didn't move. Didn't do anything for a moment.

Michael found himself torn between a sudden concern for the woman, and a scientific skepticism. Was this part of her psychic act?

Sylvia Danner's mouth began to work then, mechanically. Open. Close. Open. Close. Open.

Without sound.

Without intelligent intent.

Her eyes had gone blank.

"Daddy . . . ?"

Now the sound returned.

Pure sound. No meaning. No words.

It was a jittering, wailing, echoing fit of sobs and gasps that built rapidly to a glass-shattering crescendo. Tremors shook the woman's frame, growing more violent with the same uncanny speed and nerve-racking staccato tempo of her ululations.

"Mrs. Danner!" Michael said loudly.

No response.

Her broken wail continued to spiral maddeningly louder and higher.

"Mrs. Danner!" Michael yelled.

"Daddy, what's wrong with her?"

Michael pulled away from the woman.

Her fingers wouldn't release his hand.

He jerked backward.

The fingers still held him in their grip. They were like talons. Drawing blood now. Her long, lacquered nails were sunk deep into his flesh, scraping on bones in the back of his hand.

He felt the pain now.

And a strange sense of panic.

And he smelled something strange in the woman's scent, a salty, bitter smell he'd never experienced before.

This was no act.

"Mrs. Danner!"

He shook the woman with his free hand.

Her lips and nostrils were turning blue.

Her ululating shrieking had risen to a fever pitch. It was within decibles of becoming inaudible. It made Michael's skin crawl away from his flesh.

"Daddy! God, Daddy, what's she doing?"

Mrs. Danner's eyes had rolled up into her skull, exposing only the veined yellow underside of her eyes.

"Sylvia!"

It was the other woman, the blind one. She was at the doorway now.

"Help me!" Michael yelled at her. "Help me get her to the floor!"

"What is it?" the other woman asked, advancing into the room. "What's happening?" She had to yell to be heard above Mrs. Danner's breathless, squealing wail.

"She's having a seizure of some sort," Michael said, aware even as he spoke that Mrs. Danner was in the grip of something more violent than any *grand mal* seizure he'd ever seen, and he'd seen his share of bad ones.

Carol Lewis was beside them now. She reached out blindly, feeling for a good hold on her mentor.

Out of the corner of his eye, Michael saw Jenny edging her way into the far corner of the room. The poor kid was frightened to death by the scene.

"Jenny, go out in the hall!" he yelled at her.

She didn't move. She stood stock still with both hands held defensively in front of her, as if she didn't want to accept what she was witnessing.

"Out in the hall, Jenny! Now!"

"I have her shoulders," Carol Lewis said. "What now?"

"Help me lay her on the carpet," Michael said above the keening wails issuing from Mrs. Danner's wildly twisting lips.

They tilted the woman sideways.

Mrs. Danner's entire body was snapping now, firing with an eerie regularity, as if responding to spurts of controlled electricity. Her voice was growing hoarse. The wail grated out between her clenched teeth. A trickle of blood welled from the corner of the woman's mouth, trickled down her chin as Michael and the blind woman wrestled the spasming psychic to the carpet.

The wail continued.

But it began to degenerate.

They placed her on her back on the carpet. Michael kicked a chair out of the way, ignored the sound of it toppling over backward into something glass, something that shattered on the stone floor.

He still hadn't managed to free his hand from Mrs. Danner's claw. It was as if she had a hold of some incomprehensibly powerful electric current and couldn't free herself.

Blood burbled out of the woman's mouth now, flew in a fine spray, and bubbled as if a severed main artery were feeding the awful pool building within her mouth.

The wail metamorphosed into a gurgling. Blue veins and cartilage stood out in deep relief along the woman's neck and forehead. They looked like knotted ropes twisted beneath the fragile, blueing skin. For a brief instant Michael had an awful vision of seeing the blue veins bursting like leaking, overburdened fire hoses, spewing their dark blood every which way in the bright room. Mrs. Danner's eyes bulged nearly out of their sockets.

"Call an ambulance," Michael said with a gasp.

"But she's still—"

"Call a goddamn ambulance!"

The blind woman nodded, started to rise from her knees, then hesitated, as if sensing a sudden change in her friend.

Mrs. Danner stopped her snapping spasms.

The wail ended.

Silence.

No final gasp. No slow relaxing of strained and bulging muscles. Just a simple end to it all. Instant flaccidness.

No more blood burbling from her mouth.

Her eyes still stared at the ceiling, glued open and unseeing.

"Oh, no . . ."

"Call the ambulance," Michael said softly.

"But . . . she's . . ."

Michael nodded.

"I think you're right."

". . . dead."

He was already moving, shifting position, crouching above Mrs. Danner on his knees.

"But I'm going to try to keep her going until the ambulance crew gets here."

"You're what?"

"Call the ambulance."

He ignored her then as he steeled himself for what he had to do. He raised Mrs. Danner's skirt up and wiped at the thick gore that had bubbled from her mouth, then took a deep breath. He pinched Mrs. Danner's nose, tilted her head back, reached a finger into her mouth, held her tongue out of the way, then pressed his lips to her slack mouth and exhaled down her throat. Her breast rose slightly. Shifting quickly, he pressed the heels of his hands to her breastbone and pumped sharply downward on the woman's chest. He shifted back to her slick mouth, breathed deeply into her. Then back to her chest and another quick and forceful pump on her rib cage.

He blocked out everything else for a long, timeless moment, became a simple machine. Inhale. Exhale forcibly. Shift. Pump. Shift. Inhale. Breathe out . . .

A machine.

Repetitive.

Mind-numbing.

The only way to deal with the coppery taste in his throat and the ungodly exertion of unassisted CPR.

Exhale . . . shift. Breathe. Pump. Shift. Inhale. Blow it out. Back again. Pump . . . ignore the lightness in your head . . . ignore the tiny stars revolving in your vision . . . ignore the crying from the corner of the room.

"They'll be here in a few minutes." The woman's deep voice added to the impression that he was moving underwater.

Exhale. Press. Shift. Inhale. Expel. Shift . . .

Ignore the crying.

Sirens in the distance.

The woman's chest rising. Falling.

Halting for a moment, Michael watched the woman's breast. His eyes swam. She was still. Like a corpse.

She was a corpse.

He breathed life into her again.

And again.

And again.

Heavy, running footsteps. The house shook.

"Okay, buddy, we've got her."

He rolled back, blinking, exhausted. Trembling. Two men. Oxygen and defibrillator pads. One of the men ripped open the neck of the woman's blouse and stabbed a needle directly into her heart.

Within seconds, assisted by the marvels of modern science, Mrs. Danner began to snap again.

Snap.

Pause.

Snap.

Heartbeat.

Snap.

Snap.

Snap.

"Daddy?" It was tentative. "Daddy? Are you okay?"

Tear trails glistened down Jenny's pale cheeks. He wondered if she might be going into shock.

She reached out for him, but hesitated. Her face scrunched up. "Daddy, your mouth—it's full of blood." Tears welled out of her eyes. "What were you doing to the lady, Daddy?"

A thin arm encircled Jenny's shoulders. It was the other woman. Carol Lewis knelt on the carpet beside them.

Michael wiped at the gore spread across his face.

"Your dad was trying to save my friend," Carol Lewis said.

Michael's gaze fell on Mrs. Danner. She snapped one more time, her back arching upward against the flow of electricity. Then she fell still. Her hair lay about her head in wet tangles. Her face was streaked with red, some of which was already drying and cracking. Her staring eyes had turned yellowish and opaque.

One of the men from the ambulance shook his head at the other one. The second one turned his attention on Michael.

"What happened?" he asked.

Michael shrugged. He was beginning to wonder *that* himself.

1

The Concorde hit an air pocket. For an instant, Caine felt himself go weightless. His stomach tickled his throat.

The first-class-section stewardess two seats in front of him, at the very front of the plane, actually came off the floor. She spilled tomato juice on two elderly American women with blue hair and dangling jewelry.

Someone squealed.

Just a little squeal.

The fast plane caught the air again. Its wings bit into the solid atmosphere, and the flight smoothed out.

Caine swallowed.

"I hate airplanes," Helen said. Her English accent gave the simple phrase a harsh ring.

Caine glanced at his longtime compatriot, Helen Locklear, and smiled. Her face was pale. Her long, rich, red hair accentuated the whiteness of her even features and the blueness of her eyes. He patted her hand. "Nothing to worry about," he said. His accent was European, its country of origin indeterminable. He'd lived too many places for too long to have retained the speech pattern of his homeland. "Mile for mile, they're the safest means of transportation devised by man." He sounded like an encyclopedia, he realized. But if it soothed Helen's nerves, what the hell.

The sleek airplane abruptly bumped around roughly for a

few seconds, with all the smoothness of a rickety jeep on a rocky mountain logging trail.

"Hummph," was all Helen could say by way of response.

The plane caught once again and sailed on smoothly.

Caine licked his lips. He glanced out the nearby window. He could see nothing but darkness. Even if it had been daytime, he knew he'd have seen nothing. They were in mid-Atlantic by now. Nothing below them but mile after mile of cold, uncaring, undulating water.

Actually, he hated airplanes, too. He was at his most vulnerable in them. Everyone was, of course, but he more than others. More, that is, than all but two others like himself.

Mahafed and Eleanor.

A smile touched Caine's lined features.

He'd covered his trail well, was certain that the other two had no idea where he was at this moment. He'd set a simple plan in action in order to convince them that he was somewhere in the Dodecanese on a yacht. An appearance or two in Athens. A quick trip to Crete. A rented yacht leaving Rhodes in the middle of the night with a matching couple on board. The woman, with deep red hair and Helen's magnificent figure. The man—older, thin, tall, graying, of indeterminate age. By night, both mysteriously leaving the whitewashed villa Caine had rented overlooking the Aegean. He'd made certain that the couple had been seen along the waterfront. Eleanor and Mahafed must surely think that he and Helen were on that yacht, taking their pleasure.

But one never knew for sure, did one?

Mahafed and Eleanor were not fools. It was possible they had discovered his duplicity.

Possible but doubtful.

But the doubt itched unbearably in the back of Caine's mind.

He didn't like airplanes.

He rarely used them.

Except when he had to.

And this time, he'd been forced to.

Mahafed and Eleanor . . .

Bastards!

He was certain that Mahafed was in Egypt. Eleanor, his sources told him, was in Turkey. The two of them had banded together, were tracking him, trying to corner him. Europe. Africa. Asia. All were too close to the two of them. Caine needed to get farther away, needed to buy time without their interference.

Fortunately, he was always prepared for such a situation. The world had been his bedroom. There wasn't a continent he couldn't go to for protection.

Caine smiled ruefully to himself. It was an old story. As old as mankind.

Power.

As simple as that.

And he'd slipped out of their net this time. With a little luck, it would take them a few days to pick up his trail in the States. By then it would be too late for them.

Too late.

They wouldn't expect his next move, couldn't possibly be aware of his contingency plans, and by the time they realized what he was up to . . .

Too late!

"What are you thinking about?" Helen asked, pulling him out of his reverie.

He waved a hand amiably. "Nothing. Nothing at all."

"I heard you chuckle."

"I was simply musing, my dear. Thinking about—"

The supersonic jet took a sudden nosedive.

Caine felt his stomach slide grudgingly toward his throat. One of the stewardesses tumbled to the carpeted aisle floor. There, she held on for dear life to the legs of the nearest passenger seat. Caine could see her breathing deeply to calm herself. He could sense her barely controlled panic.

God, what a job, he thought. To fly on one of these damn things every working day of your life.

What a horror.

The vacant sound of the airplane's intercom clicking into life caught Caine's attention.

"*This is your captain speaking,*" the slightly metallic voice said. "*We have been encountering some unexpected turbulence that the radar didn't pick up earlier. For your safety, I've turned on the seat belt light and the no smoking signs. Please extinguish all smoking materials and buckle your seat belts at this time. We may be in for a brief period of rough air. But, please remain calm. We are in no danger, I assure you. This announcement is being made simply to ensure your safety.*" The empty air disappeared as the intercom was switched off.

Caine felt Helen's fingers reach over and take his hand. Neither he nor Helen moved to buckle their seat belts. They didn't have to. They had never unbuckled in the first place.

If man were meant to fly, God would have given him . . .

Stupid thought. Where had that come from? But it was true, wasn't it? Had he ever stepped onto an airplane without feeling apprehensive? Every time he experienced a takeoff he felt his sphincter tighten up out of fear of losing something important—like his innards. Every time he landed in an airplane he waited fearfully, listening for the godawful telltale sounds that would give him a split-second warning that oblivion was about to snatch him violently and unpleasantly from the world of the living. Every time an airplane he was in hit an air pocket he wondered if this wasn't the time the bottom would drop out of the sky and he'd be turned to pink mincemeat against the side of some mountain, or end up being scattered fish food for the toothy and tasteless denizens of some dark sea. To others, the glistening lights of nighttime cities seen from the air resembled gleaming baubles and gems scattered over black velvet. To him, the twinkling lights resembled millions of votive candles offered up for the souls of the dead or soon to be departed, and seemed to be a personal omen.

He hated flying, with a passion.

The captain's voice echoed back through the compartment again. "*Will all staff please return to their seats.*"

The air buzzed for several seconds as the intercom remained open, as if the captain were debating whether to share some more of his comforting words with passengers and crew. When the intercom finally clicked off, Caine was left with a rising sense of apprehension and a sinking feeling in his guts.

"I hate airplanes," Helen said softly.

"You said that before," Caine reminded her.

"So I did. So I did. Do you mind if I say it again?"

Caine smiled weakly. He slipped an arm around Helen and kissed her once, cleanly on the lips. "We'll be okay."

"I know," she said.

He leaned over to kiss her again.

This time her teeth slammed into his face and split his lip. She cried out and he groaned. The wings had fallen off the plane, he was sure of it. From somewhere behind them someone started crying in loud, whimpering gasps. The plane continued to dip, rocking roughly from side to side, turning, it seemed, on end, aiming itself straight downward like an arrow falling to earth. From outside, the air howled across the useless wings. Somewhere behind them, a kid started screaming. Someone's illegally stashed carry-on luggage bounded down the aisle and slammed into the door of the pilot's cabin, just beyond the front seats. It spilled open. A woman's pink curlers bounded out and rolled willy-nilly around the front aisle. Plastic drinking glasses and miniature glass liquor bottles rolled toward the front, clinking and rattling as they went.

"Aaron!"

Caine pressed himself back against his seat as well as he could. He tried to keep a hand on Helen's lap.

"Aaron!"

"Just hang on," he said softly.

Now was not the time to panic. There was, he knew, nothing he could do.

Goddamn airplanes.

A woman was shrieking now, and a sporadic number of other people were talking in loud voices and yelling in even louder voices. Most of the passengers were silent. Praying. Stunned. Or simply trying to keep themselves from flying into useless panics.

The fuselage of the airplane started to vibrate. Caine had an immense sensation of speed, vertical speed, straight-down speed. Plastic and metal screeches wailed through the cabin. Caine felt his entire body vibrating, being shaken loose, bone from bone. The entire plane thudded, jittered, racketed up and down as if being shaken in the hands of some gigantic, angry two-year-old. A fat man's seat belt gave way, and the rotund man cartwheeled through the cabin. He "oooffed" once, then bounced off the aisle floor, smashed into the backs of two seats, and bounded up. He hit the ceiling, dropped to the aisle floor, and skittered past Helen's aisle seat, leaving a trail of blood. His silence was horrible. It would have been less frightening if he had been screaming. A particularly violent toss slapped the fat man against the cabin ceiling again. He landed amid the curlers and the open overnight case, leaving a gruesome trail of blood across the ivory plastic panels of the plane's interior. The violent buffeting ceased. The unbelievably steep dive continued unabated.

A chorus of screaming followed the fat man's performance.

Aaron Caine forced his mind to heel.

If this was his end, so be it. He would not go out begging and wailing like some superstitious and gutless peasant regretting the loss of his daily bread and misery. His fate may be out of his hands at this point, but he would not give in to—

Or was it?

He swore at himself.

Stupid.

Stupid.

Stupid.

He closed his eyes and concentrated on the pilot's cabin, now set at almost a sixty-degree angle below him. The pilot's fear was real. Caine read it clearly. The man was strong, but he was confused, disoriented, unsure of what was making the plane dive as it was, unable to make sense of his instruments. The copilot was out cold, a victim of one of the plane's first violent thrashings. And as Caine concentrated, he sensed the violent movement of the pilot's limbs, felt the huge plane respond by twisting savagely to the side, shearing at a mad angle to the forces threatening to tear the plane apart.

There was something else there, too.

Caine stiffened. His eyes opened. He concentrated on the spiking brain waves emanating from the terrified pilot. *Not real! No turbulence! An hallucination! All under your control!*

He sensed the pilot's turmoil, confusion, and indecisiveness.

He couldn't wait for the pilot to regain his senses, not while there were two other forces battling for control of his senses.

Caine unbuckled his seat belt. He had to grab the seat in front of him to keep from falling forward into it.

"Aaron, what are you doing?"

"It's not real," he said. "It's in the pilot's head."

"What?"

"Eleanor and Mahafed," was all he said. He said it bitterly. He was a fool to think he could have escaped the two of them so easily. He wondered if they hadn't, somehow, set him up to take this flight in the first place.

Damn!

"No," Helen said with difficulty. "They can't know where we are."

"They do. And *goddammit,* they're nearby! Probably on another plane."

Caine edged past his redheaded companion. At the aisle, he let himself down onto the steeply angled floor. By gripping the legs of the passenger seats, he guided himself toward the nearby door to the pilot's cabin. He had to make the last few yards without the aid of anything to hold on to. If the plane thrashed, he would meet the same fate as the fat man, he realized. He'd be slapped off the ceiling like a spongy Ping-Pong ball.

When he reached the fat man, he tried to shove the leaden bundle of limp flesh aside. The fat man would not budge.

He was a dead weight.

Dead . . . weight.

His head lolled on a neck lacking the strength of an intact spinal column.

Screams and crying and the groaning, tortured shrieks of the airplane filled Caine's ears.

He edged to the side, into the angle made by the floor and the front bulkhead. With his back braced against the bulkhead, he propelled the obese corpse to the side, using the power in his legs. Rising to his knees, he tried the cabin door.

Locked.

He rattled the door, felt it give, but only slightly. Brute strength was not about to open it.

He closed his eyes and concentrated on the copilot beyond the door. *Wake up! The door! Open the cabin door!*

Caine felt the sweat coating his body, felt the racked synapses in his brain firing with all the power he could muster. *Concentrate!*

The door! Open the damn door! Wake up!

He felt the groggy mind of the copilot churn to life. He willed the man's rubbery limbs to ignore the pain in the man's head, to unbuckle his belt, to clamber, hand over hand, up the steep incline of the diving cockpit to the door. The images of what the pained copilot was seeing quavered and shifted in Caine's mind. The man was on the edge of collapse again. Caine willed it otherwise, pressed his thoughts into the copilot's fevered brain, felt other powers there, other minds directing from a distance, other minds who had once been Caine's friends, his compatriots, even his lover, other minds directing the copilot to *sleep . . . sleep . . . sleep.* Hypnotically powerful. Insistent. Irresistible.

Caine knew he had them beat. They were too far away to overpower his commands. They'd been waiting for him over the Atlantic. They were out there now, in the darkness, in some other plane. But he'd caught on to their tricks in time. If he had his way, it wouldn't be long before the Concorde was beyond their control.

He furrowed his brow, squinted, and then, forcefully, *exploded* his commands into the head of the copilot beyond the door. The man was so close it was impossible to resist the command, even with the wills of Mahafed and Eleanor interfering.

THE DOOR! OPEN IT! NOW!

The cockpit door opened immediately. No fumbling. No hesitancy.

Caine elbowed his way into the cockpit, aided toward his goal by the insistent presence of gravity. He nearly fell past the copilot.

The copilot's face was pasty, drenched with sweat, swelling along one temple. Caine eased off on his commands, and the man sagged to the floor, slid into a crumpled pile at the back of his empty seat.

Caine braced himself at the rear of the pilot's seat, reached around, and laid a hand on the back of the man's neck, already firing his commands into the man's skull, directing them through the medulla, at the base of the most primitive centers of the brain. He didn't want to say a word, didn't want any record of his entering the cockpit to be picked up on the black box, the in-flight recorder, which he knew would be examined after this flight.

Turbulence gone, he willed. *Instruments fine. Pull the plane level*.

The pilot tried to glance around.

NOW! Caine willed. *NOW!*

The pilot shifted.

Caine felt the huge plane leveling off, heard the pinging, screaming, crying stress of tortured metal, heard it fade ... fade ... fade to nothing ... fade to the soft roar of a powerful aircraft doing what it was supposed to do: fly.

He felt his own heartbeat slowing, returning to normal.

The terror and cries form the passenger section diminished. Sanity was returning, the madness of panic already being forgotten, being tucked into deep recesses of those minds and buried beneath any neuroses strong enough to control it and keep it under check. Bury that fear, ignore it, we all do, we have to in order to step into one of these hellish winged things, Caine thought. Block it off, wall it up, forget it until the next time a plane dips and shudders and threatens to rip the raw earth off that tenuous grave and expose the rotted, horrifying, uncontrollable reality of that all-too-human quality: panic.

Still touching the back of the pilot's neck, Caine willed, *You will forget me! You will recall only that you saved the plane and all aboard. You will feel a wild, excited exhilaration, an adrenaline rush, and you will know that you are a hero. Forget me.*

He let his fingers leave the back of the pilot's neck.

He knew he would have to make the passengers forget him, too, in the next moments. But once he had a moment to collect himself, that would be child's play.

He wiped at the trails of sweat dribbling from his forehead into his eyes. He had a headache.

But he was *alive!*

Alive!

A smile spread across his lined features, across that face that had seen so much, seen so many years come and go.

Beneath him he felt the steady thrust of the jets, the even, smooth, supersonic flight of a magnificent machine. He felt the huge bird turn upward, clawing its way back into the stratosphere, and he started to laugh. It was a soft, merciless, bittersweet laugh that sounded hollow in the confines of the pilot's cabin.

Next stop, the United States.

And he knew, now, that people were going to start dying.

He thought the fat man in the passenger cabin had been the first.

He didn't know about Sylvia Danner.

2

It was growing dark by the time Michael and Jenny crossed the Tampa city limits. It was after 9:00 P.M. Traffic on I-4 was still heavy. The anonymous cars flashed along beneath stark streetlights without concern for the speed limit.

Originally, Michael and Jenny had planned on spending the night in one of the Disney hotels just outside Orlando. But Sylvia Danner's untimely death had put a damper on the fun.

They'd eaten dinner in Orlando.

It had been uncomfortable.

Jenny broke into tears twice during the meal. Mrs. Danner's death had frightened Jenny something fierce. Even an hour and a half of psychologizing with her hadn't brought any great relief to the kid.

Jenny was asleep now, curled against the Buick's passenger door, rocked by the swaying car and serenaded by the hypnotic humming of the tires on the pavement.

Michael guided the car through the freeway traffic without paying much attention to the other cars on the roadway. He was lost in thought, pondering Mrs. Danner's sudden death.

When she touched me . . .

That thought had been a constant refrain for him since the death.

When she touched me, she died.

It sent an eerie shiver through his body.

He knew he couldn't blame himself for the psychic's death, but it bothered the hell out of him. Had she sensed

23

something—horrifying—when she touched him? Or had it simply been time for her string to be pulled?

A picture of the other psychic, the blind one, Carol Lewis, formed in his mind. He'd had the discomforting sensation that she had been trying to *look* at him, to study him with those brilliant, dead, green eyes, all the while the ambulance crew had been at the house. She hadn't touched him again, but she'd been very inquisitive, and she'd cocked her head dozens of times in that odd way she had that almost gave the impression she could see into his gourd, or was at least trying to pry the lid off.

She had been holding something back from him, he was sure of it. Something she knew, or suspected, something she had sensed.

A warning, perhaps?

He didn't know what it was, but he knew she had been very guarded and cautious with him.

He swung the Buick off the freeway near the airport and wound his way toward the bay. The car rocked to a stop at a stoplight.

The sudden deceleration jerked Jenny from her sleep.

She came awake with a scream.

"Daddy!"

Michael put an arm around his daughter's shoulder and slid her closer. She was whimpering. "Everything's okay," he soothed. "We're almost home."

Jenny was breathing heavily. Her dark hair lay plastered across the side of her face, damp with perspiration. Pink pressure lines on her cheek resembled the pattern of the upholstery fabric.

"I dreamed about you with all that lady's blood on your face," she said. Her eyes stared straight ahead, trancelike.

Michael rubbed his daughter's back, drew her to him, encircled her with an arm. If only there were some way to protect kids from the world, he thought.

"You'll stop thinking about it in a couple of days," he said gently, giving her a gentle pat on the leg.

She yawned. "I know. I'm not *real* scared anymore." She snuggled into him, started to say something else, and fell asleep in the middle of it.

Michael grinned ruefully to himself. "Kids," he said softly.

Within a few minutes he eased the Buick through the brick gateway at the entrance to the housing development in which they lived. He waved to Bernie, the evening guard stationed in the lighted security office, and crept through the quiet neighborhood at fifteen miles an hour. He drove past numerous residential streets interspersed with canals to his left. The area resembled dozens of half-mile—long fingers reaching out into the water of Old Tampa Bay. Houses lined the sides of each finger, overlooking the canals, while a single dead-end road ran the length of each finger, ending in a cul-de-sac.

Michael swung down Ivy Lane and pulled into the drive of their house. It was a split-level plan, with the back of the house facing the canal. Large, billowy hedges fronted the house and drive, while tall palm trees lined the road.

Jenny moaned and snuffled as Michael slid out of the car. She didn't rouse when he shook her, so he lifted her in his arms and carried her. Getting his key into the front door was a juggling act, but he was used to it.

The house was dark. Soft music was coming from the rear of the house, from the screened-in pool. Michael hauled his daughter to her bedroom and laid her on top of the bedspread. He'd tuck her in later. First he wanted to sit and talk with Angie, to let her know that he and Jenny were home, and why. She'd flip over the story about Mrs. Danner's death.

Michael headed for the pool.

The French doors off the great room were open. The music was louder back here. He stepped through the doors, into the patio end of the screened enclosure. The underwater pool light gave the undulant blue pool a surreal effect.

There was Angie, just as he'd expected. Yup, there she was, in all her petite majesty. Naked as a stripper, and dripping wet, her dark hair slicked back and falling in wet curls halfway down her thin back. Skinny-dipping. Lovely. Her firm, dark-tipped breasts pointing directly at the tall, wet, blond guy who had obviously been skinny-dipping

with her, while the blond guy's *schlong* saluted her beauty
with an impressive display of fleshy cantilevering.

The guy had a slight paunch. Nothing big, mind you,
but a paunch all the same. Still, it detracted from the baseball bat he was waggling at Angie.

Michael stopped in his tracks. His face was frozen between a smile and a grimace.

They hadn't seen him yet.

He considered backing into the house, picking up Jenny,
and heading out until the time they were expected to arrive
home tomorrow afternoon. Deal with this when his temper
was less volatile. Deal with it when he was alone with
Angie. Deal with it the way a rational, well-trained psychologist would handle such a situation. Yeah, take care of
it when the situation was less likely to get out of hand,
when the embarrassment could be minimized. There was
no reason to turn this into a nasty scene. Not now. Especially not now, not when he felt so much like crying. He
didn't need to look like a big baby at a time like this.

Right.

He knew he should leave.

"Hi," he said. "We're home early."

He liked the way Angie's eyes and mouth flew open. He
liked that a lot. But not as much as he liked seeing the
Eiffel Tower shrivel back into its blond bush. *Presto
changeo! What goes up must come down!*

He walked out onto the pool deck while Angie made
quick little gestures and tossed spastic glances from him
back to the paunchy blond guy. Michael recognized the guy
now. He was a recently separated neurosurgeon who lived
three houses away. His name was Milo Silklowski, or
something like that. Milo, anyway.

Michael stopped walking and took up a stance directly
across the glimmering pool from Angie and her doctor
friend. He pointed at Milo's crotch. "You should've been a
magician," he said. "You sure made that disappear quick."

Angie found her voice then. "Michael, I'm—"

He raised his eyebrows and grinned at her. He wanted to
hurt her—bad. As badly as he was hurting. The only thing he
wanted to do more at the moment was cry.

Blubber, really. He wanted to blubber. Why be controlled about it? He wanted to blubber and break things.

"I'm so sorry, Michael," Angie said, her voice rich with remorse.

Milo found a towel and wrapped it around himself. He edged self-consciously toward the house. "I think I'd better go," he said.

Angie only nodded.

"Like *that?*" Michael asked, moving to intercept Milo at the French doors. "I couldn't let you leave dressed like that. What kind of a host would I be? I mean, you've enjoyed my wife—at least let me get you a robe or something."

"Michael, don't do anything you'll regret," Angie said. She swept a towel off a nearby patio chair and moved quickly toward the house.

"I'm not about to," Michael said. He put a finger to his lips. "But *shhh,* huh? *Your daughter* is sleeping, and her bedroom door is open."

Milo was busy hesitating, wondering whether he should try to edge his way into the house. Michael bowed and spread wide an arm. "This way, please."

Angie was recovering quickly. "Michael, why don't you go sit down in the living room. I'll—I'll be in to talk in a minute."

"*What?* And send Milo out without clothes?" He held up a hand. "No, please! Let me help the poor man."

Milo's eyes moved restlessly from husband to wife.

Michael headed into the house, down the hallway, and into the master bedroom. "Oh, thank heavens, Milo," he called down the hallway. "You won't have to go home in one of my robes, after all. I've found your clothes." Neatly folded on a chair, they punctuated the sentence spoken by the rumpled bedclothes.

Michael picked up the neurosurgeon's clothes and shoes, and returning to the great room, threw them viciously at the man. "Here are your clothes. Now get the hell out of here." One of the shoes, a loafer with a little leather flower dangling on the top, smacked Milo in the belly and knocked his towel loose. Milo ignored the towel, collected his shoes from the floor, and, his clothes bunched against his belly, hurried toward the front door. Michael wanted to laugh at the silly way Milo's bare cheeks jiggled on their merry way out of the house, but he didn't have quite the energy to cut loose with a guffaw.

Angie, her jaw set, stomped down the hallway to the bedroom.

Michael stopped by Jenny's room on the way to the kitchen and closed the bedroom door. No need for the kid to hear World War Three.

He grabbed an Old Style from the fridge, popped the top, then, on second thought, grabbed another can. He walked back out to the pool and sat down at the patio table. He downed the first can of beer with two healthy glugs and tossed the empty can into the pool. *What the hell?*

He was watching the empty beer can bob on the rippling blue surface of the pool when Angie came out to join him. She'd combed her hair and donned a burgundy-colored robe. She sat down across the table from him and joined him in watching the bobbing beer can.

The can did a full circle of the pool, powered by the filter jets. The night was warm. Gentle waves could be heard lapping against the canal retaining wall only fifteen yards beyond the screen room. The wavering, bluish light from the pool washed the screen room in fantasy lighting.

The beer can was halfway around its second lap, swimming like hell, when Angie decided to break the silence.

"I'm sorry, Mike."

"Hmmm. Me, too."

He sipped at his second beer. He and Angie had not been particularly close for a while, but he hadn't expected something like this. He'd thought they'd be able to work things out. They'd had times like this in the past—a few distant months here and there. But they'd always overcome the distance. Now . . . He took another sip of beer.

"I want to marry him, Mike."

Michael laughed out loud, spraying the air with a fine mist of beer. "Milo? You want to marry Milo the nerd? You used to make jokes about him when he and his wife, what was her name?—Clarice—when they moved into the neighborhood a couple of years ago. Now you want to marry him?"

"He's very sensitive," she said, "and caring."

"I could tell."

She glared at him.

He sipped his beer, said, "Sensitive enough, anyway, to know when the husband was going to be away." He shook his head. "You didn't waste any time. Tonight was the first night I would have been gone in, what, six months?"

"We've been seeing each other for nearly a year."

Her eyes didn't waver when he glanced at her.

"You and Milo?"

"Me and Milo."

"You and Milo?"

She only stared at him this time.

Michael held up his beer can in salute. "Here's to the Eiffel Tower." He took a mouthful of beer.

Angie twisted her face up the way she did when she didn't catch his sense of humor. He ignored the expression.

"Michael, are you going to make this difficult?"

"Me?"

"Yes, you."

"It seems to me that you're the one who's made things a bit difficult. I come waltzing into my happy love nest expecting love and kisses, only to find some guy waving his flagpole at my wife, while she's playing the 'Boogie-Woogie Bugle Girl' and helping him hoist another pair of panties to flutter in the breeze."

"Cute, Mike. Cute."

"You want nasty? I can give you nasty, too. I know how to nasty pretty good."

"I think maybe we shouldn't talk anymore tonight."

"Oh? When should we talk?"

"Soon."

"Good. I'd prefer that it be sooner rather than later."

"At my lawyer's."

Michael glared at his wife. *So this was it.*

He finished off the last of his Old Style; then, feeling powerless, he held the aluminum can before his wife, growled like a caveman, and crushed the can between his fingers.

She shook her head and rose from the table.

Michael set the crushed beer can down and rose alongside her. "I suppose you've already put together a list of what you want, and what I get to keep."

That hit home. Her tight control gave way to a bitter sneer. But she reined in her temper. "As a matter of fact, I have."

No wonder she'd reacted so strongly. He'd hit the nail on the head. He shook his head, felt the tears forming at the corners of his eyes. He looked away. He didn't want to go on with this. He wanted to crawl into bed and have himself a good cry—maybe beat the crap out of a pillow or two.

"You can have the house," she said. "Milo and I will be moving to Clearwater, on the beach. All I want..."

He stood, numb, watching her mouth move, registering her words, without fully comprehending what she was saying. That would come in the morning.

"...that leaves you the Merrill Lynch CMA account, the portfolio Judy Maxwell's been managing for us, your IRA, and the beach house."

He nodded, lost at sea.

"Anyway, we can let the lawyers put the finishing touches on everything. I'd just as soon they did it. I don't want this split to ruin our chances at remaining friends."

Michael studied his wife out of the top half of his eyes. He said nothing for a moment.

"I'll move out in the morning," Angie said then. "If you don't mind, I'll sleep in the guest bedroom tonight."

She started for the doorway.

"Take our room," he said coldly. "I don't think I want to sleep amid the carnage of your and Milo's lovemaking. I think I'd become a mass murderer if I found one of his blond pubic hairs on my pillow."

She stopped at the French doors, eyed him without much emotion.

"Since you're already divvied up the spoils so nicely," he asked, "what did you decide about Jenny?"

"She can stay with you," Angie said.

"Gee, thanks."

"She always liked you better, anyway. I want regular visitation rights, of course. You won't object to that."

He shook his head.

"Good night, then," Angie said.

And she was gone.

A moment later, Michael heard the door to the master bedroom close.

He watched the swimming beer can make several laps of the pool before pulling it out of the drink and tossing it into a wastebasket. He flipped off the pool light and made his way to the kitchen, where he popped the top off another beer. Then he slipped out the front door for a walk.

Beer can in hand, he made his way blindly through the evening, planning the rest of his life, and wondering what the chances were that he could salvage his old life.

Knowing Angie and her once-you-make-your-mind-up-stick-to-itiveness, he spent most of the walk trying to make sense out of his future.

He didn't cry on the walk.

He saved that for the pillows in the guest bedroom.

3

Intuitive.

That was the most common term used to describe Lea Frazzetti.

It was as if she could read desires of women worldwide and transmit those desires immediately into fashion. Some said it was simpler than that. They said she could read the fashion future. She knew what was going to be a hit before it hit, what was going to be in style even before there was such a style. Her bulging bank accounts and investment portfolios were ample proof of one thing at least: She was a very shrewd businesswoman.

She was also bored with it all.

She had been born to money and born with a gift. Success had come with ease. By the time she was twenty-one her name had become an international symbol for style and success. At twenty-two she'd opened Frazzetti Designs, with offices in Paris and New York. She'd started with clothing. The public had gone mad for anything with the name *Frazzetti* on the tag. By now, at age thirty, her Frazzetti Designs not only manufactured one of the world's top lines of clothing, it also was dominant in jewelry, furniture, and accessories. Frazzetti Designs had moved into luxury resort design, had made inroads into automobile design, and was being courted by half a dozen other major industries.

It was all too easy.

"Why?" the blond woman reporter for *People* magazine asked. "Why so easy?"

They were on the broad balcony of Lea's Central Park penthouse. The luxuriant green rectangle sprawled thirty stories below them, looking lush and peaceful under the remarkably clear summer sky. A steady, cool breeze was sweeping the city clean. From this airy vantage point, the walls of concrete and glass surrounding the park resembled the walls of a wealthy prison.

Lea wanted out, wanted something different, wanted adventure, an affair to rip her heart out, someone to disagree with her, someone to agree with her and mean it, wanted to try something totally different—wanted *anything,* just so it would be different.

She'd missed the reporter's question, she realized.

"Pardon me?" she asked, turning from the aerial view of Central Park, and touching bored fingers to her lips.

"Why do you think it's all been so easy for you?"

Lea allowed a little smile to touch her features. *Because I can read minds.* She didn't say that, although she often toyed with the idea of revealing her uncanny gift.

"The Fates," she said with a shrug. It was the kind of

answer the masses loved to read. It made everything, all the riches of the world, all their dreams, seem so close, so within reach. All anyone needed was the right combination of stars, or the right roll of the bones, and—*presto!* Instant success.

"You don't really believe that, do you?" the reporter asked.

Lea reached for the inlaid cigarette case on the coffee table. Beside the cigarette case were the photo proofs for the proposed cover shot. Lea had chosen the top photo for the magazine cover. It caught the golden highlights of her shoulder-length blond hair perfectly, while accentuating her model's figure. The photograph's colors were striking, from the multihued background view of Monte Carlo's waterfront to the contrasting blues of the sky and sea. The picture had been taken on a sailboat anchored in the harbor at Monte Carlo.

From a distance Lea heard the muted, choppy whir of a helicopter carried past on the breeze. Horns honked and a siren wailed, but they were so far away as to be almost subliminal sounds, little more than the pulse of blood at her temples.

"I do," Lea said. She lit her slim cigarette, leaned far out over the chest-high parapet of her balcony, and watched the tiny automobiles and the microscopic pedestrians scurrying hither and thither on their meaningless errands. *What the hell was it all about?* she found herself wondering. Why all the hustle and bustle? For what?

This would be a beautiful place to commit suicide, she thought. Simply spread your wings and fly thirty stories to your grave.

But she wasn't suicidal.

She was, she realized, a woman who had nothing to believe in.

"But how can you?" the reporter went on. "When you've driven yourself to the top of the business world? When you've put so much energy into—"

Lea cut the woman off. "No more," she said. "I don't feel like talking anymore today."

"But your secretary arranged for an hour. We've only had—"

Lea waved her cigarette at the woman and strode into the glass-walled living room. The vast room was filled with light and controlled bold colors. The reporter followed.

"Let me ask you about your reported relationship with Prince—"

Lea raised her voice, aimed it toward the entry foyer. "O'Brian, please show Ms.—whatever-her-name-is—out."

O'Brian was her bodyguard. He'd been a professional football player, a tight end—a phrase that seldom failed to bring a smile to Lea's features—and, for a brief time, a mercenary in the Mideast. He held a master's degree in English literature. He stood six-foot-six. He was a man of strange contrasts. His size, coupled with his smooth grace and soft voice, belied his quickness and his incisive mind. He had proven invaluable on numerous occasions.

This obviously was not one of those occasions, although his presence still had its positive effect.

"Maybe some other time," the reporter said, slipping a bittersweet grin onto her face.

"Yes, we'll finish the interview—soon," Lea said. "Contact my secretary."

While O'Brian showed the woman out, Lea dropped onto a lounge, the reporter quickly forgotten.

She needed to get away for a while.

A trip.

But to where?

Away from the *glitterati*. They made her sick with their public posing, their pettiness, their—

What the hell? Hadn't she used them for her own ends most of the time? And hadn't she done as much posing as anyone?

She was tired of it, tired of it all.

A sudden shiver trembled through her. She felt . . . the way she suspected some highly perceptive people felt when she reached out and read their thoughts . . . slightly different than she had a moment earlier, as if she were being watched, as if—

She turned, glanced toward the foyer.

The reporter was there, standing in the backlighted doorway, a thirty-five-millimeter camera strung around her neck where there hadn't been one a minute earlier.

O'Brian stood beside her, and for an instant Lea thought she saw a tall, graying figure standing behind them.

"What is it?" Lea asked sharply.

"Miss Rawlings doesn't want to leave quite yet," O'Brian said.

Incredulous, Lea said, *"What?"*

O'Brian and the blond reporter crossed into the expanse of the living room. There was no one else with them, Lea noticed. She also sensed something ominous in the deliberate way the two of them were moving.

It was with some surprise that she realized O'Brian and the woman had cut off her routes to the other rooms of the penthouse and cut off any escape via the front door.

Lea stubbed her cigarette out and came to her feet. A cold tension flooded her muscles.

"What's going on, O'Brian?"

O'Brian smiled. "Miss Rawlings wants to get a better story out of you," he said.

Lea's eye bored into those of her bodyguard. He didn't flinch. All she detected there was resolution. He had committed himself to some course of action and was not about to abandon it.

She *reached* into his head to read—

The image stunned her.

She'd seen herself trying to run past him, seen him wraping his arms around her and squeezing, seen him carrying her toward the balcony, toward the vast emptiness of thirty stories of open air. . . . He was preparing himself for whatever options occurred in the situation. Preparing himself coldly, like a football player trying to prepare for whatever play might come his way, preparing himself to react but motivated by an already existing plan fully formed in his mind.

Lea edged away from him, staggered by the unpredictable violence she'd encountered in O'Brian's head. She'd

read him hundreds of times. She'd always found him devoted to her, dependable, trustworthy—

When was the last time she'd read him? Months ago, she
realized. She'd grown accustomed to his devotion, had
been taking him for granted.

Fool!

The woman reporter lifted her camera and clicked a picture. The built-in flash startled Lea, set a hazy sun blazing
in her eyes.

Lea blinked against the fading brightness. Suddenly the
woman's name came clear in her mind. Linda Rawlings.
Lea kicked her mind in gear and reached into the woman's
head and . . . found herself blocked! For the first time in her
life she found herself unable to tap into another's thoughts.

She felt a cold perspiration form on her arms and across
her forehead.

What the hell was going on here?

"A cover story," Linda Rawlings said.

Lea stared at the woman. The reporter had answered the
question, but Lea knew she hadn't asked the question
aloud.

Linda Rawlings moved a step closer.

Lea backed up a step, keeping the same distance between them.

"What do you mean?" Lea asked, searching her mind for
a way past the reporter. "What do you mean, 'a cover
story'?"

O'Brian was moving in on her now, too. Lea shifted
direction, edged toward the nearby sliding glass doors. It
was her only clear way out of the room.

But what good would that do?

All that did was take her out to the balcony.

And open air.

O'Brian's mental images came back to her.

They were herding her toward the balcony.

A mindless panic gripped her for an instant, but she
steeled herself against it and forced it back into its hole.
This was no time for panic. *Talk to them.* That was what
you did with terrorists and hostage-takers. She'd read that
somewhere. Talk to them. Defuse the situation.

"What is this 'cover story' you're after?" she asked. Her voice quavered slightly, but she doubted whether the other two detected it.

"Heiress and talented designer takes dive," Linda Rawlings said.

Lea's brows drew closer together.

"What?"

Linda Rawlings raised her camera again and snapped another picture. This time Lea had time to glance away from the flash.

"Jaded by her riches, strung out on designer drugs, famed socialite commits suicide by splattering herself among the masses on the street."

Lea jabbed her mind at the woman's, trying to find a crack in there to read.

Nothing.

The woman's mind was a stone wall.

The reporter advanced the film in her camera.

O'Brian had moved closer, and Lea had missed the movement while she concentrated on the woman.

"I'll scream."

"Go ahead," Linda Rawlings said. "You remember how much you paid to have this place soundproofed. No one will hear you." She smiled, pulled out a long knife, and added, "Not until you get near street level."

"No!" Lea put a hand out between herself and the woman. "You can't be serious!"

"Oh? Can't I?"

"If you stab me, the police will know it wasn't suicide."

"Smart. You're very smart."

"What do you want? Money? I can give you money. How much do you want? A million? More? How much? Name a figure."

"I want your life."

Lea realized that she had been cornered by the balcony doorway. She didn't want to step outside, didn't want to feel the clean sunshine on her face, didn't want to move voluntarily that much closer to the edge of the balcony.

"Why? Why do you want to kill me? What have I done?"

"Done? Why, nothing except become famous. Which your death can do for me. Think of how well my articles will sell." She raised her camera again and snapped off another shot. The white light seemed not to have disappeared completely when Lea reopened her eyes. Everything was starkly outlined and hyperreal. "With luck I'll get a great shot of your thirty-story swan dive."

"This doesn't make sense."

"It doesn't, does it. But then, who said life was supposed to make sense? Or *death,* for that matter."

O'Brian moved forward.

Lea found herself in the sunshine.

She was sweating and her hands were freezing and her mind felt numb and none of this made sense. Her gaze swept the wide balcony, searching for a weapon. None. The only weapon at hand was O'Brian, her bodyguard, and he was aimed at her.

"You can make this easier," Linda Rawlings said. "Simply move to the parapet, pose for a moment—so I can get a picture—then jump."

O'Brian and the woman were outside now, too. The parapet wall was less than twelve feet away.

"You—is this someone's idea of a cruel joke?"

The reporter's white teeth showed behind her thin smile. "Hardly."

"O'Brian?" Lea pleaded. "You're not going to let her kill me? Not after four years together."

O'Brian lifted a shoulder. "To the highest bidder . . ." he said cryptically.

Lea grasped at the offer. "How much?"

O'Brian perked up.

"How much to stop this?" Lea demanded with a pleading note in her voice.

"I don't know if you can match the offer," he said.

The reporter lifted her camera again and snapped another snapshot.

"Name your price."

"You'd turn me in to the police," O'Brian said. "It's too late now. I'm committed. In for a penny, in for a pound."

"No. I wouldn't."

"How's ten million sound?" he asked, moving a step closer. "Ten million and your word that you won't do anything to try to punish me?"

"It's yours."

O'Brian opened his mouth and laughed softly. "No good, Ms. Frazzetti. It's too late. But I appreciate your interest."

Lea felt her senses swirl, felt her balance affected. O'Brian was within three strides of her, the reporter about an equal distance away. The parapet and thirty stories of empty air were less than two strides away now.

Lea suddenly dove forward, trying to slice between her two antagonists without warning. O'Brian's big arms reached out to block her. The reporter flashed a knife in front of her. Lea lashed out at the woman, caught the blonde on the throat with a vicious backhand swing. The woman stumbled backward.

But O'Brian's hands found her forearms, locked onto her wrists.

Spinning, maddened, a wild animal in designer clothes, she slashed out with her right foot. Her foot connected squarely with the big man's groin. O'Brian moaned. His grip weakened. She grabbed his shirtfront and tried to shove him away. He resisted.

She switched direction abruptly, jerked away from him, popping buttons down the front of his white shirt.

She turned toward the doorway, only to find the reporter back on balance, knife in hand.

Lea hesitated.

The reporter lunged at her, knife flashing in the sun.

Twisting to avoid the long blade, Lea caught hold of the arm of one of the patio chairs. She used it to swing herself aside from the *hissing* arc of the knife.

The blade missed her by inches.

She shoved the chair at the reporter and followed the thrust by driving the chair forward again. Linda Rawlings stumbled backward. Lea slammed the wooden frame of the chair into the woman. The wood cracked on Linda Rawlings's ankles. Lea drove her back against the parapet. Out of the corner of her eye, she saw O'Brian shift over to block her escape through the penthouse doors. He was sucking air in deep, bone-racking gasps.

She desperately willed him to stay where he was.

He appeared to hesitate.

She didn't take time to consider the meaning of his hesitation.

She saw only one alternative now.

The reporter! End it with her, and maybe—just-a-slim-one-chance-in-hell-maybe—she could deal with O'Brian afterward.

Lea yanked the wooden chair back, then smashed it into the reporter's legs again and again. The other woman raked the air with the long knife, but Lea was out of reach. She slammed the reporter with the chair again, driving her off balance. The reporter dropped to one knee.

Lea kicked out with all her might.

She caught the woman full in the face, bowling her backward, slapping her up against the high parapet wall. The knife dropped from the reporter's limp fingers, clattered onto the tile balcony floor. A glassiness hazed the Rawlings woman's eyes.

Lea snatched up the knife.

A glance at O'Brian assured her that he hadn't moved.

He was staring at her, looking puzzled.

She shoved her mind at him, commanding him to stay where he was. She felt herself mingle with his thoughts, made her mind a fist that battered at his very essence.

She'd never done such a thing before, hadn't realized that she could.

O'Brian's face contorted in pain. His hands flew to his head. He dropped to his knees, gasping.

Whirling around, Lea faced the reporter. She was dimly aware of the energy driving her, of the adrenaline-high fueling her self-protective rage, of the flood of oxygen required to keep her at this level, and she realized that she had never felt so alive, so vital, so . . . powerful.

"Up!" she said between ragged breaths.

The reporter glared at her.

"*Up,* I said!"

Linda Rawlings was only beginning to rally her senses.

She shook her head but began to come to her feet. Her camera bounced gently against her breasts.

Lea concentrated, stabbed her mind at the reporter's, and felt herself crash through the strong defenses the woman had raised. Her mind fell into a fog, a nothingness, a strange, bleak landscape without form or recognizable landmarks.

Instinctively, fearfully, Lea pulled her mind back from that of the other. She was trampling in dimensions she'd never known existed before, and she was baffled and alarmed.

"You'll have to kill me," the reporter said, "or I'll kill you."

The knife handle felt slick in Lea's sweaty grasp. *This was insane.*

"I don't want to kill you."

The reporter was grinning now. "You'll have to. Or I'll kill you."

Lea watched in stunned horror as the other woman pushed herself away from the wall and deliberately advanced on her.

"Stay where you are!"

The reporter was silent. Her jaw was set. She moved with a solid sense of destiny.

Lea shook her head, unable to comprehend the woman's behavior. "You don't want to do this," Lea said hoarsely. But the woman obviously did want to do what she was doing. Lea backed off one step...two...wondering if she could kill in cold blood, and almost immediately knowing that she could—and in some odd, macabre way, wondering what the experience would be like.

But before she used the knife, Lea tried an experiment. She jabbed her mind at the reporter's mind and willed the other woman backward. She felt resistance. She thrust harder, thinking very clearly, *Jump, bitch! Jump!* She formed an image in the other woman's mind and pressed it at her. *The top of the balcony wall, the park spread below, a dive into the soaring nothingness over the city streets so far below.*

The reporter halted, stared; then, grinning strangely, she turned, walked to the concrete parapet at the edge of the balcony, climbed on top of it, and disappeared over the edge.

Only the distant sound of traffic and the gentle breeze stirred Lea's senses.

She waited for the scream.

None was forthcoming.

She glanced toward O'Brian. He was gone. Her eyes scanned the balcony.

Empty except for her.

Where was he?

Had he run?

She moved to the parapet, leaned over, looked down, stared.

Traffic moved as usual. Pedestrians scurried like ants. There was no falling body, no broken corpse on the street below, no wild, milling crowd gawking at the carnage.

It was city life as usual.

Lea turned and stumbled back into her living room. She dropped onto a lounge.

Hallucination?

Had someone slipped something into her coffee that morning?

It had all been like a bad LSD trip. But not like it. She had tried LSD while in college and had always known that what she experienced was a hallucination. It had *felt* like a hallucination even as it was occurring.

But not this.

This had been real.

So where had the reporter gone?

And O'Brian?

"O'Brian!" She called him.

Within seconds she heard his soft tread on the carpet. She glanced toward the foyer.

"Yes, Ms. Frazzetti?"

He looked as he always did. Impeccable. Not a button was missing.

"That reporter . . . did she come back here after you showed her out?"

The big, gentle man shook his head. "No, ma'am."

Lea stared at him.

"Is that all?"

She nodded, puzzled.

He turned to return to his office off the foyer.

Lea reached out and touched his mind.

Baseball scores. He was thinking about baseball scores and a sporting article he'd been reading in *Time*. He was totally oblivious to the events of the past few minutes.

She let him go, her confusion mushrooming as she glanced down at the very real butcher knife resting beside her on the couch.

4

All in all, Michael thought Jenny was handling the separation quite well. She'd listened quietly while Michael and Angie explained Angie's decision to move out. Jenny had cried, of course, and asked about four million questions. What could you expect? Then she'd spent most of the day in her room, angry with the world.

But she was in the pool now, playing with two neighbor girls who'd come over without realizing that the end of the world had visited the Jenny Dragon household. Jenny had rallied, and while not exactly a water sprite out there in the pool, she was at least splashing about like a pissed-off little kid.

She was a strong little person. He had faith in her. She'd handled the situation well.

Michael went to the kitchen, poured himself a cup of coffee, and returned to the dining room. He flipped two sections of the Sunday paper to the side and started thumbing through the celebrity section.

The doorbell rang.

On his way to the door, he caught sight of the car out front. He didn't recognize it.

He *did* recognize the woman at the door. "Mrs. Lewis, right?"

"Miss Lewis." She smiled at him but quickly reverted to seriousness. "Carol, actually." Her green eyes seemed too lively to be blind. She wore a summery skirt and blouse combination in bright parrot colors on a deep green background. The open throat revealed the merest curve of her breasts.

Michael glanced past the slim woman in an effort to see how she'd managed to come to the door by herself.

"My friend just went back to the car," she said.

Michael felt self-conscious. "Would you like to come in? I was just having a cup of coffee. Would you like a cup?"

"Please." She held out her left arm. Michael took it as if it were a perfectly natural response he'd done thousands of times before.

"Your friend is welcome to a cup, too."

"Thank you, but she'd feel uncomfortable. I'll only be a few minutes, anyway."

"You're sure?"

She said she was.

Michael led her to the great room, from where he could keep an eye on Jenny and her two friends. The three girls were squealing and chasing each other around the pool decking.

"Oh, you have a pool," Carol Lewis said as she settled onto a couch.

"Yes, it's just outside this room."

"I can smell it."

Michael smiled, wondering exactly what that meant. He sniffed the air discreetly, didn't notice anything out of the ordinary. "I'll be right back," he said. "Would you like cream or sugar?"

"Lots of cream, please. Or milk."

He was back in a minute with both cups of coffee.

"Are the three girls out there all your daughters?" the blind woman asked.

"No. Just one. Jenny. You met her the other day. The other girls are neighbors."

"I remember your daughter."

"Well, what can I do for you?" Michael asked.

"Are we alone?"

"Yes."

"Your wife isn't—"

"She's not here."

Carol Lewis nodded. She lifted her cup of coffee to her mouth, blew on the creamy liquid, sipped gently at it, then returned it to her lap. Her face wore a serious, almost troubled expression. She appeared to be searching for words.

"I . . . I came about what happened yesterday," she said finally.

"I'm sorry about that," Michael said. "I felt, in some way, as if I might be responsible for what happened to Mrs. Danner. I—"

"You were," the woman said.

Michael shut his mouth. The words hadn't been said as an accusation, but still . . .

"Excuse me," he said.

"Oh, I don't know how to say this well," the woman said, "but she—Mrs. Danner—she sensed something about you that frightened her. I'm afraid she'd been having some heart trouble, but it was what she sensed when she touched you that set off her attack."

"That was more than a heart attack she had," Michael said.

"Yes," she said with a nod, "I know. The doctors said she tensed up so hard that she ruptured several blood vessels."

Michael cocked his head at the woman. "Did you have your friend drive you all the way here from Cassadaga just to talk with me?"

"Yes." Carol Lewis nodded, drew her mouth into a tight, straight line.

"Why didn't you call?"

Her mouth twisted, looked worried, then straightened out again. "I—we don't usually tell people negative things when we give them readings," she said. "It doesn't make any sense to frighten people. And since this is something on that order, I felt that I should speak with you in person."

Michael felt his body temperature cool.

"You don't tell people negative things? Does that mean you simply don't give them a reading?"

"If possible."

A picture of Marie Fiero, the first psychic he'd tried to visit, formed in Michael's mind. Had she sensed something she didn't want to get involved with?

"What is this 'something negative' in my future?"

He was beginning to suspect that there was more to this visit than he had thought at first. Money? He hadn't heard of any of the Cassadaga psychics being out-and-out charlatans, but what did he know? Was it possible they wouldn't let you go once you started visiting them? If not *they*, then this one?

That didn't make sense, not in this situation. And not this woman. Michael prided himself on being a good judge of character, and he liked Carol Lewis. He wasn't picking up any of the signals he recognized when he dealt with a smooth sociopath or con artist, and God knew, he'd tested enough of those for the courts.

"You have something very . . . dangerous in your near future," Carol Lewis said.

"What exactly does that mean? And why are you telling this to me if it's your usual policy not to do so?"

Was he being too suspicious?

He watched her features very closely for the smallest telltale nonverbal cues. She struggled with her next words.

"I—I don't know *exactly* what is going to happen to you. I know that Sylvia Danner must have read the same thing I did when she touched you, only . . . maybe more vividly."

"Do you read people the same way as Mrs. Danner?"

"Yes."

"By touching them?"

"Yes. That's the most effective way for me to sense something—though not the only way."

"You took my arm when we came into the living room a moment ago. Did you sense anything then?"

She pursed her lips. "Yes, I did."

"What?"

"The same thing I sensed when I shook your hand yesterday at Sylvia's house."

"Which was?"

She hesitated. "I don't know if it's really that important to get into specifics," she said. "I simply wanted to warn you . . . to ask if you had some plans set for the next week or so that you could change . . . to . . . I don't know exactly." She shook her head, as if feeling her visit had been a mistake. "I know I shouldn't have told you all this. I shouldn't try to intervene. But I . . ." Her voice trailed off. She raised a hand, gestured tensely, then dropped the hand ineffectually.

"You what?"

"I don't want to make this into more than it is, Mr. Dragon. Let's say I simply felt that you should be warned. I wanted to warn you."

She was hiding something.

"Why?"

She flushed slightly, appeared to be weighing her words very carefully.

"Do you know what an aura is?"

"You mean the electrical field that surrounds the body?"

"Basically, yes. Well"—she took a breath—"our auras were very compatible. I . . . sensed something very positive in you. If possible, I wanted to—I want to help you avoid whatever danger it is that's in your immediate future."

"They're not the same things, my aura and this danger?"

"No."

"I see."

They were both silent for a moment. Carol Lewis raised her cup to her mouth. Michael watched her, wondering if there was anything to what she'd said about their auras. He sensed something—an intangible *something*—with this woman in the room. A sense of closeness? He thought they could easily become friends, if the situation allowed it.

More?

There was something about her that he liked, and he

didn't know why. Maybe that was the best and simplest way to put it.

From outside, the muted shouts and laughter of the swimming girls created an odd contrast to the seriousness within the great room.

"This dangerous *something*—could it have been a divorce you were seeing?" he asked.

She shook her head. "No—what I sensed would have completely smothered something as insignificant as—I'm sorry, I didn't realize . . ."

"That's okay. Forget it."

She had, Michael realized, picked up a minute stiffening on his part. It was pretty amazing, but whatever senses she had working for her were doing a damned good job of making up for her lack of vision.

"And you won't tell me what this danger is?"

"I can't. Not specifically. I only touched you for a moment each time."

"You didn't get enough contact, you mean?"

"Enough to sense the danger, to recognize an unmistakable part of it. No more than that."

"What about trying it now?"

She swallowed. Sat silently for a moment. Then, carefully, she reached out and set her coffee saucer and cup on the nearby coffee table. She folded her hands in her lap. "I'm not sure I should."

"Why not? You've made the effort to come this far and warn me in person."

She cocked her head at him in that way she had that made her seem to be studying him. Her emerald eyes glowed.

"I sensed death," she said flatly.

Michael felt his mind and body slow down. "Mine?"

The psychic shrugged. "I didn't have the time to develop the contact."

Michael crossed the living room and sat next to her on the sofa. He sensed her reluctance to continue. In a psychotherapy situation he would cease to push when a client showed this much reluctance to continue with a conversation. But Carol Lewis wasn't a client, this wasn't psychotherapy, and it was his life, *not hers,* they were delving into. Although he had to admit to some hesitancy on his own part, he felt justified in pressing the situation forward.

He took her hands in his. "Let's try."

She trembled at the touch of his fingers. She shifted to face him more directly. She closed her eyes. Her expression was grim.

"What do you sense?"

She shook her head to cut him off. Her soft hands moved gently yet firmly to find their most comfortable—or most powerful?—position of contact. "Don't talk for a while." The husky note in her voice was richer when she talked softly.

Michael studied her face as expressions shifted across her features. She was a very beautiful woman, although not in the way fashion magazines portrayed beauty. Her features weren't so even, so perfectly balanced. High cheekbones. Wide-set eyes. A sensuous mouth with a pronounced Cupid's bow upper lip. Her thick, ginger-blond hair fell to a point halfway down her neck, while a slash of bangs cut sharply across a fourth of her forehead.

She smelled of some very subtle perfume.

She had the kind of face he'd like to kiss.

So had Angie.

A wave of sadness flowed through him for an instant, before breaking and fading away.

Carol Lewis's eyes fluttered open slightly, revealing a brief flash of emerald brilliance, then closed again.

Her brow knit. The corners of her mouth turned down. She appeared to be on the verge of tears. Her fingers were delicately rubbing his hands now, gently massaging his palm, stroking his fingers, caressing, pausing to draw in sensations, moving on. He felt a warmth filling his body. There was something surprisingly sensual in the contact.

Her breathing increased in tempo and depth.

She swallowed.

She took one of his hands now and pressed it between both of hers. She seemed unable to get enough contact. She drew his hand closer and pressed it to the bare flesh just above her breasts. At the moment his fingers touched her skin, she drew in a forceful gasp of air. She held his hand there, trembling, the heel of his hand resting gently on the swell of her breasts. Her lips moved cryptically. Through his fingertips he could feel her heart thundering away within her breast. Her nostrils flared. Beads of perspiration sprung to life on her forehead. Muscles along her jawline tensed. The sinews in her throat stood out in bold relief, quivering with tension. She whimpered, the sound similar to the cries Jenny made when she was having a bad dream. The whimpering mutated to a breathless gasping, to a labored, pained, chest-racking catarrhal wheezing.

Suddenly the psychic's eyelids flew open.

She stared blindly at Michael, her deep green eyes perfectly focused on his.

Gently, then, she eased his hand away from her breast and released it. Her own hands touched briefly at the contact point on her breastbone before dropping to her lap.

Her breathing slowed, evened out, lost its consumptive wheeze.

Michael sat silently, waiting, oddly moved by the experience. His own breath felt trapped in his throat.

Carol Lewis wiped a hand across her lips. She sought her cup and saucer and raised the cup to her lips. "Mmmm, cold," she said.

"Let me freshen it for you." Michael took her cup and his own to the kitchen. He remembered to add extra cream to hers.

He returned to sit beside her on the couch.

"Thank you."

She sipped at her cup, then returned it to the saucer on her lap.

"I sensed more," she said. "I don't know what any of it means, you have to realize that."

"I do. It's like doing dreamwork, I imagine."

"I'm not sure what you mean."

"I'm a psychologist. Occasionally I help clients make sense out of their dreams. The symbolism is as individual as the people I work with. Everyone's different. I'm not about to interpret their dreams for them. I help them sort out the themes and symbols and draw what conclusions they can. That's all I can do. Usually I know less about the meaning of their dreams than they do."

She nodded. "It's very similar."

He waited.

"I sensed more than one death," she said finally, soberly. "A number of them. Very near in time. I don't know whose, or even how many, exactly. All of them were violent." She shuddered, wrapped her arms around her own shoulders, as if to warm herself. "The deaths were filled with fear and agony, even terror. I felt . . . a force . . . more than one . . . life forces, overpoweringly strong-willed life forces . . . unlike anything I've ever experienced before. Some seemed . . . malignant . . . no, that's not strong enough. It was evil I sensed. Pure evil. I felt it, and in feeling it, was certain I was perceived by something in return. It was a horrifying sensation. It was like being stared at by Satan . . . by a very displeased Satan. And there was another force . . ." She shook her head, perplexed, apprehensive. "I couldn't understand it. It wasn't evil, and it wasn't good, it . . . it simply existed. It—I don't understand what I sensed." She shook her head again and fell silent.

Michael was unsure of what to make of her message. His life had been nearly entirely free of violence up to this point. He had a difficult time imagining such a dramatic turnaround in his fortunes.

"This is *my* future you were sensing? Not someone else's?"

"I don't know. You're involved, I'm sure. But I don't know how."

"And you don't know who else is involved?"

"No."

"Are they men? Women?"

She turned her head in thought. "Both."

"Both? You mean both men and women will die? Or the life forces you detected were of both sexes?"

"Both. I sensed both things."

"What about Jenny, my daughter?"

"I sensed a child's life force, but I don't know what happened to it."

The hair along Michael's spine was standing on end. A quick image of the Charlie Manson clan storming his house with flashing knives wafted through his mind. How else could you explain what this woman was predicting?

Unless she was all wrong.

He didn't think he believed in parapsychology, anyway.

God, he hoped to hell she was all wrong.

He was too old and too educated to start believing in all that psychic mumbo jumbo.

Wasn't he?

His dark brooding was interrupted by the sound of the sliding glass door being thrown forcibly open with a loud *bang!*

His wet daughter rushed into the room, followed by her two dripping friends. "Daddy, can we make popcorn? Huh? Say it's okay! I'll promise to clean up the mess if you say yes."

And for a moment at least, faced with Jenny's irrepressible energy and resilience, it was impossible to believe that Carol Lewis's predictions might come true.

The crowd screamed.

Spotlights crisscrossed the swaying throng in the dark arena. Everyone was on their feet, arms waving, cigarette lighters burning, turning the bowl-shaped arena into a pagan religious experience.

The last electronic guitar wails faded away, absorbed by the crowd's fever.

"Thank you! You were a great audience! We had a good time! Good night!"

Drew Garrett and the Hard Rock Experience, faces

painted like dying mimes, abandoned their instruments and disappeared into the swirling, billowing clouds of dry ice that suddenly filled the stage. The ovation was thunderous. A rolling wave of foot-stomping swept grandly through the arena. Diehard fans were shouting, "MORE! MORE! MORE!" while the more reasonable folk were heading for the exits.

"What the hell do they want," Drew asked his drummer, "blood?"

"Forget it," Skinny Winston, the drummer, responded. "We did three encores. That's enough. Hell, I'm fagged."

They made their way through the press of people backstage, heading for their separate dressing rooms.

Drew accepted congratulations from a couple dozen folk who'd managed to force, sneak, or bribe their way backstage. Some graying old dude tossed him a towel. He wiped at the sweat and makeup coating his face and let a couple of loyal roadies elbow a path to his dressing room.

Once in the room, he slammed the door, locked it, leaned back against it, and sighed. The roar from the auditorium still hadn't ceased. The waves of foot-stomping, though, were breaking, dying.

Drew ran the soft towel over his face and let loose with another sigh. Another night. Another town. Another bunch of crazy-assed fans. He shook his head. *The things that turned people on!* Tonight's crowd had gone crazy for profanity. He'd given 'em their fill. Throw around a few *fucks* and a few *cunts* and they went nuts. It was like his music. He always gave the masses of no-taste idiots out there the illusion of what they were looking for. Tales of violence, love, sex, death, and drugs. But never real, always illusion.

Dry ice fogs.

Lewdness that was only an act.

The promise of love where none existed.

All an act.

All illusion.

A means of manipulating their emotions, nothing more.

And he was good at that.

Very good.

He was the master of illusion.

He laughed softly.

The emotions of others were his playthings.

The critics blasted him. Parent groups picketed his performances. But his fans had made him a millionaire because he could read their basest desires and translate them into music. And it wasn't just his lyrics. He had a mad-genius ability to make the band's driving heavy-metal sound mimic the lyrics, emphasize the message, catch the audience with auditory analogies that sprang from their loins, from their anger, from their fears, from their desires, from hidden hellholes within their psyches.

Child of Satan.

He smiled to himself as he finished wiping his face.

Two nationally recognized leaders of the Moral Majority and the Bible Belt Baptists had called him that on a *60 Minutes* segment. They had started a campaign to have his concerts banned across the nation, his music wiped off the airways.

They made him laugh. Their negative publicity had increased the sale of his last two albums by at least a hundred thousand copies apiece. He loved it.

He tossed the dirty towel toward his dressing table.

That was when he saw the girl in the shadows.

Jail bait.

He thought about grabbing her and throwing her out. Then he reconsidered.

Someone knocked at his door.

He debated what he should do.

"I need some time to myself!" he yelled.

"The limo's going to be ten minutes late," one of the roadies called through the door.

"Good!"

The noise from the hallway beyond the door continued unabated. The party was starting. It would go all night, Drew knew. It was the same in every town. It was part of the band's image.

Drew unlocked a travel case on his dressing table. He drew three lines of coke on the tabletop and snorted one.

"Want a hit?" he asked without turning.

A long silence followed.

Drew could already feel the euphoria altering his senses.

"You, in the corner behind my jacket—want a hit?"

After a moment, he heard the clothes rustle.

He turned. "Come on out here where I can see you decently," he said.

She was *maybe* sixteen. But built. And a looker, too. Wild black hair. The color of ravens. With that electric hint of blue in it. And skin the color of milk. Dark, almond-shaped eyes. Almost as dark as her hair. Skimpy little outfit. She had an innie navel, he noted, and one helluva mouth-watering cleavage. Her jewelry looked genuine. She had a lot of gold and glitter around her neck and on her left wrist. She jangled and tinkled softly when she moved.

A Madonna of the streets.

"I didn't think you'd see me," she said. Her voice was soft, scared, vulnerable. Her eyes dropped to the floor.

"What were you going to do?" he asked. "Peep at me while I changed?"

"I—I wanted to meet you," she said. "That's all. I—"

"How old are you?"

"Eighteen."

She didn't bat an eyelash.

"Prove it."

She fumbled in the purse that flopped at her hip, held out a driver's license. Her picture was on it. The birth date made her eighteen. Her name was Rhonda.

Drew looked at her with new interest.

"How'd you get in here?"

He turned and snorted another line.

"I gave the guy at the back door some money?"

Drew faced her again, wiping at his nose. It was numb, felt like it was running. He grinned. Some of these groupies were amazing. They'd go to the most ungodly lengths to touch a *rock star*.

"How much?"

She hesitated.

"How much am I worth to you?"

She gushed. "It's not what you're worth," she said. "but it's all I could afford. I—I'd do anything for you, Drew.

Anything." The languid expression she created with her mouth and eyes told him exactly what that meant.

"How much?"

"All I had. Three hundred dollars."

"You think it'll be worth it?"

She smiled at him. "It already is. I got to talk with you."

He laughed. "Jesus!"

He was feeling grand. He pulled his shirt off and toweled himself some more. "I'm gonna shower," he said. "Don't look."

He stripped.

Out of the corner of his eyes, he saw her staring at him. *Little twat*. He hoped she liked what she saw, imagined she did. He was six-two, weighed one-seventy, and had a three-piece set he'd always been proud of. She wasn't acting any too nervous about his nakedness.

He stepped into the shower, which had been added to the corner of the room sometime after the original construction. The warm water sang on his skin. He lathered heavily, closing his eyes, letting the sharp needles of spray soothe him, letting the performance high drain away from his tense muscles, feeling the languid euphoria of the coke take over his senses.

The shower door opened. He wasn't surprised. He let her slip into the shower in front of him. She was naked. Tentatively, she wrapped her arms around him.

"Well, Rhonda, what's your pleasure?"

He was already growing hard.

She pressed her wet body to his. Her breasts spread out across his chest like great, slick pillows. She nibbled at his neck.

He put a hand up to her hair and pulled her face away from his neck. Water ran in clear rivulets down her even features. "No hickies," he said. "I don't want you leaving any souvenirs behind."

A devilish smile revealed a line of perfectly white teeth. "I promise not to leave any souvenirs behind," she said.

She plunged her face back into his neck, then let her mouth trail down his chest. She chewed on one of his nipples while her hands found his erection. She cupped his balls with one hand and stroked the length of him with the other. She was rough but talented.

He fondled the fullness of her breasts, enjoying the slickness of soap and water on her pliable flesh. It was all a physical thing to him, this instant sex with groupies. He didn't really give a damn about her, he realized. There was even something about this girl that he distrusted, some intangible negative sensation. It was his *gift,* to be able to read people's emotions. It was the root of his success as a songwriter. He had an uncanny ability to *know* what people wanted, what they were feeling in any given situation, to be able to sense what drove them, what made them tick.

His first wife had called him an *emotional chameleon.*

Among other things, his shrink had called him an *empath,* without ever coming close to knowing the real depths of Drew's ability. His shrink had been a climber, a momma-pleasing, ass-kissing, star-struck yuppie who fed his own ego by working with successful entertainers. He had a great reputation. But Drew had been so turned off by the man's all-too-obvious voyeurism that he'd stopped visiting the dude.

Not that he didn't need shrinking.

He did.

He knew it for a dead certainty.

Knew that he was still driven by all the abuse he'd suffered as a child.

Knew that he needed to work that through, to clear it out of his mind, to empty himself of those godawful memories and the emotional residue of his childhood that clung to him like slime.

But now wasn't the time for introspection.

He concentrated on the girl in front of him, closed his eyes, and visualized his mind and hers merging, trying to understand what it was he was sensing from her, seeking a handle on the emotions that drove her to his dressing room. Her emotions were raw, like an open wound. He sensed a need for love, excitement . . . *anger* and *power.*

The sensations of anger and power hunger took him by surprise. He sensed a voraciousness beneath the girl's hunger that was bottomless, a dark pit threatening to engulf him.

The girl slid lower.

He hesitated, wondering whether he should let her take him in her mouth. She bothered him, and he didn't trust her at all—not anymore. Besides, he had this thing about teeth.

She must have caught his indecision. She glanced up at him, squinting against the showering water.

"No," he said. "I'd rather have the real thing."

"You don't know what you're missing."

He felt a strange, foreboding tension around this girl, felt it feeding on some tiny center of fear within him. He should have kicked the little bitch out of his dressing room the instant he saw her. But it was too late now. He had a reputation to think of, and he was losing his hard-on.

He drew her up to him, raised her, and slid himself between her legs. She backed her hips off, smiling at him, teasing him, holding him tightly between her thighs, not giving him maneuvering room to enter her.

"Tease," he said.

She'd made him hard again.

She grinned into his face, and reaching down with one hand, expertly guided him into her. One of her legs was raised high, braced over his hip. She leaned away from him, holding onto his neck with both hands, her large, dark-tipped breasts shuddering luxuriantly with each thrust of her hips.

Drew joined in the movement, dimly aware of a sense of violation. He was being used. But, hell, what did he care? He was using her as much as she was using him.

So enjoy the moment, he told himself. Enjoy it and get it over with. Get her out of here as soon as you can.

There was something malignantly feverish about this girl.

He resisted the temptation to delve into her emotions again, held his senses under control, refused to give in to that nameless fear she engendered in him, that apprehension that reminded him so explicitly of his childhood, of being locked in a dark, stinking basement for hours at a time by a mother diagnosed as a chronic-undifferentiated schizophrenic, a mother driven crazy by...

Stop!

Stop thinking, he ordered himself.

Forget the past.

Just take what's here. Enjoy it.

Then forget it.

Go on with your life.

The girl's flesh was hot where it gripped him. She moved feverishly, grinding her hips against him, snapping back, and jerking him forward with the powerful leg wrapped over his hip. Water cascaded over her breasts, forming tiny falls where it spilled over her nipples.

Drew reached for her breasts again.

She jerked him closer, and suddenly he'd lost it. The orgasm took him by surprise. No buildup. No crescendo of tension. No preparation. Simply an explosion centered in his groin.

She milked him, never ceasing those urgent, driving thrusts of her hips. He felt weak. His legs trembled. He nearly went to his knees.

"Stop, already," he finally said.

She hadn't gotten off, he realized.

But she stopped.

"Did you like it?" she asked.

"What do you think?"

"It was the best, huh?"

He found himself grinning in spite of himself. "What about you?"

"Don't worry about me," she said. "I'm getting what I came for."

He laughed then, softly, morosely. *Groupies.* He didn't feel in such a funk anymore and didn't want to distrust this girl as much as he did. Someday he hoped he'd find *one* person he could trust completely.

He knew it wasn't this girl.

She dropped her leg, slid off him. "I'll let you finish showering," she said.

"But you—"

She was already half out of the shower.

He let her go.

Crazy groupies.

He lathered up again, then rinsed off. He felt drained. Not in the mood to party. He vowed to leave the midnight festivities early.

He stepped from the shower, blinking the last blast of water from his eyes.

He heard a soft *pfffutt*. Something stung him on the shoulder.

"What the—"

The girl stood there, still nude, still grinning that disconcerting grin of hers, her dark hair lying in damp tangles across her shoulders, a small air pistol in her fingers.

"What the hell did you—"

Then he knew what she'd done.

He saw the tiny reddish dart sticking out of the big muscle at the top of his arm. He reached up, pulled it out. His muscles felt . . .

Woozy.

His whole body felt woozy. Dizzy. Limp. Like a column of wet pasta. He staggered toward the couch. The world had hit slow motion with all the speed of a crashing plane. The couch swam in Drew's vision, wavered like something seen in a fun house mirror, drooped like an escapee from a Dali painting. Drew sidled toward it, lost in time, all his senses gone numb. He let himself fall toward the sagging couch-thing, propelled himself through space, and landed, bounced, settled into the cushions, aware of an ungodly, uncomplicated load of helpless terror welling up within his guts, rattling soundlessly within the confines of his skull.

He was on his back.

The girl was above him.

Water still trickled down her whiteness, still dribbled off her taut nipples.

She was laughing.

The sound was lost in a mind-numbing ringing that had taken over Drew's universe.

Her mouth was wide open. Her teeth gleamed white, ringing the shadowy, moist pinkness of her tongue.

Light and colors weren't doing what they normally did. The tones had changed, gone to sleep. Everything was muted. Amber. Shadowy and fire-lit. Nothing seemed substantial. Nothing appeared solid.

Except for the girl.

What was she doing?

Moving now, to his dressing table, turning now, holding a large dressmaker's scissors in one hand, smiling now, letting the sharp blades catch the strange light in the room.

What was she doing?

Crossing the dressing room now.

Drew willed himself to rise off the couch.

He didn't move.

He was bound by invisible ropes.

What was she doing?

Pausing now, bending over him and smiling that smile of hers, showing her teeth, clicking the scissors now, the sound echoing off down the silent corridors of time, talking now, her voice lost in timelessness.

What did she say?

She repeated it, enunciating clearly, the word ringing clear in the thick atmosphere.

"Souvenir."

He followed her eyes.

He screamed, or tried to. Not a sound came out of his mouth. She was going to cut him, to take home a souvenir of their encounter. She was going to . . .

It didn't make sense.

But she was bending over him now, reaching for that helpless bit of flesh at the very center of his being.

What was going on here?

Or coming off . . .

He blinked sweat away from his eyes.

Had to be a dream.

But then, someone had killed Lennon, hadn't he?

So why not *this?*

When an autograph isn't enough . . .

A nightmare.

Had to be.

What was driving her to this?

He tried to concentrate on her, sought desperately to merge with her mind, to read the foulness fueling this insanity. He pressed his eyes closed tightly, forcing his mind to ignore the numbing drug coursing through his veins. Why was this little bitch about to . . .

His eyes popped open.

He blinked again.

The girl wavered but remained in view.

An illusion?

An hallucination?

Could she be an act, like the illusion of violence he and the band concocted onstage? He'd sensed something unreal about her, something—intangible . . . beyond her control . . . something not quite . . . *not quite . . . what?*

He couldn't put a mental finger on it.

But something was rotten in Newark.

It was a good act, if that was what she was doing.

Her fingers found him. He saw her glance at him one last time before she turned her attention back to her task.

This wasn't any act.

Couldn't be.

Drew closed his eyes again and concentrated.

He wasn't picking up any emotions now.

Because of the drug?

Because his mind had been turned to mush?

Or because . . .

None of it was real?

He blinked his eyes open, willed his right hand to come up and grab the girl by the neck. *His arm moved without impediment. He managed to sit up. He shook her, watched the scissors drop from her fingers, watched the metal blades and her body turn to mist, dissolve, fade to nothingness. And like the Cheshire cat, the last part to melt away was her smile. The little bitch had a haunting, sardonic smile.*

Drew trembled, shivered with all the force of a first-rate fever.

He wasn't drugged.

There hadn't been a girl in his room.

It had all been an illusion.

All illusion, except for the fears and insecurities that had welled out of his own mind and almost . . .

Almost what?

Could illusions kill?

And where in hell had the girl come from? His own fears? Or from outside of himself?

Simple hallucination?

Was it a signal that he was going crazy, as his mother had? Was he about to start hearing strange voices delivering even more bizarre messages?

Or was it something else?

He felt cold, and as frightened as he'd ever been. And that meant a lot of frightened, because he'd been frightened by a professional as a kid.

His fright turned to horror when he saw the girl rematerialize in front of him, shears still in hand.

This time his screams did manage to slip from his throat.

His muscles felt rubbery, still drugged. His reactions were spastic, uncoordinated, ineffective.

She was grinning now, moving in on him again, grinning in anger, with a touch of madness thrown in to make it worse.

He raised a hand to ward her off. *Why had his mind played a trick on him, let her disappear? What was happening?*

She slapped his face—hard.

He rocked sideways, fought to retain his balance.

She hit him with a fist this time. He toppled sideways. He floundered helplessly, a paraplegic with minimal control.

"I came for my souvenir," the girl said in a softly threatening voice, "and I intend to leave with it."

Drew concentrated on her again, forced his mind to merge with hers, to read her emotions, and the process worked the way it was supposed to, and, Christ, all he sensed now was that anger and that strange alien presence, and he knew he was about to lose something very important to him unless he managed to find the strength to resist this fucking drug she'd squirted into his veins, unless he managed to get some help, unless . . .

He screamed, "HELP!"

It came out bell clear, ringing bell clear, echoing bell clear.

He screamed it again.

Her face had turned foul. She swung the scissors at him like a knife. He rolled away, felt the scissors gouge flesh at his shoulder, ricochet off bone, and rip free.

But it was bearable.

He was too dopey to feel the full effect. But not too dopey to realize his danger.

Her arm was coming up for another swipe at him with the scissors. . . .

Got to move! he willed himself. *Got to do something!*

The pain of the scissors being driven straight into the muscles at the top of his left arm drove him to his feet. He wavered. His vision swam. He had no strength.

He screamed again.

This time someone responded.

He heard pounding at the door—that goddamn door he'd locked earlier—voices calling his name, asking what was wrong, distant voices, but voices all the same, saviors.

He screamed again.

The girl swung the scissors toward his guts.

Drew sidestepped. It was an ungainly move, he knew, but the blades missed. The girl's momentum dragged her in close. *No strength, use your weight*, Drew commanded himself.

He reached out and hugged the little bitch to him.

She jerked away, twisted in his weak arms.

He held on, screaming, hearing kicks thudding against the locked door. He managed to get one foot into position. He shoved. Together, he and the girl toppled to the carpeted floor. He landed on top, and, except for the one hand struggling to keep those damn scissors away from his body, made himself a dead weight—which was easy to do, as weak as he felt.

She was swearing into his face now, her features twisted into a horrible rictus of raw insanity. Her breath was hot and humid and, crazily, smelled of peppermint. It came out in quick and fevered pants, making the sound of cornered madness. She was still wet from the shower, and slippery, and Drew could feel her struggles slowly gaining freedom for that hand with the scissors in it, and he held on for dear life and screamed for help again, and again, and again, while all the while he could hear those stupid, slow-moving bastards out in the hallway jibber-jabbering at each other pounding on the goddamn door when what they needed to do was break the fucking thing down and pour in here and pull this bitch from hell off him. . . . So what was keeping them?

6

"Daddeeeeeeeeeeeeee!"

Michael jerked awake, the scream still echoing in his ears. His heart was racing. He felt light-headed.

What the . . .

Had he been dreaming?

He reached out for Angie, but stopped his searching before his hands hit the empty sheets beside him. She was gone. God, it felt strange to be sleeping alone after all these years of sharing his life with her.

His blood was still rushing madly through his temples.

He pushed thoughts of Angie out of his head, forced his system to relax—a few deep breaths, a gentle mental nudging, and his sympathetic nervous system faded rapidly toward normal. It was one of the skills he'd learned well during his graduate training, and it served him effectively whenever he needed to control his tension.

He let the last residue of nightmarish fear ebb away while he turned his attention toward the silent house around him.

That scream . . . it had sounded like Jenny . . . but had

seemed more like a nightmare. He listened carefully, probing the night-dark house with all his senses.

The house was silent.

Outside the house, a slight breeze was stirring the
leaves. Gentle waves lapped at the seawall to the rear of
the house.

Michael glanced around the dark, lonely room. The
shapes of the dressers and half-open closet door were familiar yet vaguely unnerving. Night fears. Everyone had
them at times. Dim moonlight caught the blues and reds of
the sun catcher hanging in the back window and glimmered. The face of the digital alarm close by glowed with
a greenish light.

So quiet.

Michael frowned.

He thought he heard a muffled voice.

He listened again.

Nothing now.

Silence.

He crawled out of bed, wondering whether Angie had
come back in the middle of the night to remove some of
her things.

He doubted that she'd do that—not that it was dangerous, or anything. He didn't keep a gun in the house. She
was in no danger from him. But it wasn't her style.

Mmmmpphhhh.

There was that sound again. Subliminal this time. Amost
nonexistent.

His eyes darted toward the hall door.

Maybe Jenny was having a nightmare. Maybe it *had*
been her scream that had awakened him.

He edged around the bed and grabbed a robe. Wiping at
his face, stretching himself awake, he made his way into
the hallway.

He sensed an eerie silence out here. Almost as if the
house were *too* quiet.

He padded softly to his daughter's bedroom door and
touched the knob.

"No!"

He heard Jenny's voice clearly now, muffled but audible.

And again. "NO!" as if she were shouting into her pillow.

He pushed the door open.

There was a tall man kneeling on his daughter's bed, pressing a pillow over Jenny's face. He was straddling her, blocking her struggles by using his body and thighs to hold her in place. Her window was wide open, a gentle breeze stirring the light curtains.

Michael's response was instantaneous.

He drove himself forward and grabbed the unsuspecting man by the shoulders. He whirled the man off Jenny's bed and flung him against a nearby dresser. The man crashed against the wooden dresser, sprawled onto the floor, but swung around almost immediately in a threatening crouch. The figure's features were lost in shadow.

Adrenaline coursed through Michael's veins. Fear made his senses hypersensitive.

He heard Jenny whimper, saw her pillow slide to the side.

"Now's your chance!" he said loudly to the man. "Get out!" He gestured toward the door. His bravado was a bluff, but the maneuver was calculated. Give the guy an out, a means of escape. Don't corner the bastard. That was when crooks were most likely to kill.

There was no hesitation on the intruder's part.

The figure separated itself from the deeper shadows near the wall and launched itself across the foot of the bed—*not in the direction of the door!*

Stunned, Michael tried to comprehend what the guy was—

Then he saw it!

A dark blob on Jenny's nightstand. A black stain against the dark wood. A pistol?

The man was scrabbling across the bedding, arm outstretched.

Jenny screamed again as the man rattled her bed.

Michael dived over the footboard, caught the intruder by the belt, and dug into the bedclothes with his knees.

Couldn't let the bastard reach the pistol.

The man fell flat on the covers, lying across Jenny's legs. He reached around and clawed at Michael's face. Michael twisted away, twisted with all his might, twisted the man's belt and body away from the nightstand, twisted the outstretched arm away from its target.

Jenny was moving now, scrabbling out of bed.

The man jerked around, trying to get better leverage.

Michael threw his own weight forward suddenly, taking advantage of the man's momentum, driving them both off the bed onto the narrow floor between bed and wall, just below the nightstand. Michael landed on top of the struggling figure. He lay sprawled, prone on top of the sweating, bucking intruder. He could smell the man's sweat, could taste the man's fear and hatred.

"Jenny . . ." he gasped out. "Cops . . . call cops . . ."

He heard her feet pad out of the room.

An elbow cracked into his ribs from below. Again. Again.

Michael shifted.

The elbow missed, but the move gave the intruder room to maneuver. The man used his free arm and right leg to roll onto his side, grunting, panting, working to get to his back, where he could get at Michael with his hands.

Michael wrenched the man's working arm from the floor, tried to twist it up behind his back. The man pressed it to his side, clawed his fingers around his belt, held on, his arm now immobile, able to resist Michael's efforts with ease.

Michael raised his head, craned his neck, tried to see what it was the man was after on the nightstand.

It was a pistol. An automatic with a long, bulbous barrel. A silencer?

Michael reached for it.

The man beneath, sensing Michael's intention, went wild. A mad, growling scream escaped the man's throat. He bucked insanely, clawed at Michael's arm with his one free hand. Words crawled out of the man's mouth with a guttural, breathless intensity. "I'll kill you . . . kill you, scumbag . . . kill you . . ."

Michael held on, rode out the man's struggles as best as he could.

After a moment, the struggles eased off.

That was how violent psychiatric patients responded. An instant of violence followed by a few seconds of relative stillness in order to build their energy level back up, then another fit of violence until . . . until they were subdued, or until they wore themselves out . . . or until they won their objective.

The man snapped again, this time managing to get both of his feet into position to give himself leverage against the wall and one of the bedposts. His breath reeked of sour, cheap wine. Michael strained to hold the man in place again but felt the body beneath him turning this time despite his efforts to stop the movement.

The man was on his back now . . . both hands free.

One hand reached for Michael's eyes.

Michael swung his arms over the other man's, blocked the gouging fingers, fell forward, hugging the stinking figure, face pressed against the other's cheek in an insane embrace.

How long could he hold the man?

How long could he keep this up?

How long—

The man had Michael by the hair. The pain at the base of Michael's skull jerked his head backward. He saw the man's moist teeth gleaming in the dimness, the lips pulled back from them in a vicious sneer. The man was gaining the inches of freedom he needed.

Have to stop him . . . no matter what . . .

Michael shifted, thrust his right hand toward the man's throat, grabbed it, clawed the sweaty flesh between his fingers, tried to squeeze the very life out of the man, to press the big artery in the bastard's throat closed, to shut off the blood to his brain, to bring this insanity to an end. The man jerked his head back and forth, back and forth. He let go of Michael's hair. But now the man had gained another few inches in his struggle to get free. Michael felt himself slipping down beside the man, his own back pressing against the side rails of the bed now, no longer fully on

top of the struggle. In another few inches, the man on the
floor would have the advantage, Michael realized in horror. In another inch ... maybe two ... three ... four ... the
man would be able to raise a knee into position ... a move
the guy was already trying to manage ... to raise a knee up
and cram Michael under the bed—cram him helplessly
under the bed.

Michael conserved energy, held on until muscle fatigue
made the man ease off again for an instant. The man's
groaning grunts signaled the moment as they faded, as his
foul breath escaped his throat.

Michael screamed madly in the man's ear.

Frighten him, the way they did in karate.

Unleash the energy for attack and fear in that same split
second.

Michael screamed insanely and convulsed upward with
all his strength. The man's finger ripped at Michael's pa-
jama sleeve. The sleeve tore, ripped away.

On his knees now, with some room to move, Michael
lashed out with a hard punch to the man's face. He connected with bone, heard something crackle under his
knuckles. He swung again, furious, driven by a fear and
anger unlike anything he had ever experienced.

The man's hands dropped away to block his face.

That was what Michael was looking for.

He drove himself off the man, grabbed the man's pistol
from the nightstand, and threw himself backward onto the
bedclothes. Using his momentum, he continued his roll toward the far side of the bed. Twisting to the side as he
rolled, Michael landed on one knee on the far side of the
bed. He swung around, slapped his arms forward onto the
mattress, shoving the long, fat-barreled, heavy automatic
out in front of him, aimed at the empty wall at the far side
of the bed, aimed at the spot the guy's head would have to
show if the bastard wanted to keep coming. His hands were
shaking.

"Don't fucking move!" he yelled firmly. "I've got your
gun! You're a dead man if you move so much as a goddamn inch!"

Dead man.

Christ, who did he think he was, talking like that? Dirty Harry Callahan?

Besides . . . how did he know if this gun was loaded?

Or if it was on safety?

Or where the goddamn safety was, if it was on?

The guy moved, still out of sight.

Michael, hoping to scare the bugger, pulled the trigger.

The trigger didn't move.

It was locked solid.

Oh, God.

He felt the side of the pistol.

Left side first.

Then the right.

He didn't know what he was feeling for, just knew the goddamn thing had to have a little flick switch that put it on and took it off safety. Why the hell hadn't his father taught him how to shoot these things? A man should know how to kill with every weapon in the book, for Christ's sake!

The man moved again, rustled in the darkness, shifted against the bed. Michael felt the bed shift.

Oh, God.

He put his left hand up the left side of the gun again, felt at the cold metal with his fingertips.

Probably near the trigger guard, or the handle, or . . . the top—*real technical stuff, these guns*. They had tops and bottoms and backs and fronts. You held the back—what experts called the handle, no doubt—and you shot at people with the front part . . . if you could find out how to take the goddamn thing off safety.

His fingers felt all sorts of odd-shaped bumps and ridges on the side of the pistol. He started shoving and twisting at everything his fingers touched.

Meanwhile, the man was moving again.

His head was visible now, and he was standing up now, leaning across the bed, reaching out, deliberately, not hurrying, because he knew the dumb-ass psychologist didn't know the first thing about guns and because he knew he had all the time in the world to wring the dumb-ass psychologist's neck now, and—

Click!

The man paused in midreach. His head cocked to the side.

Michael felt sweat trickling down his face, running in his eyes. But it didn't matter because he'd found the goddamn safety catch.

"Back," he said, hoping the intruder hadn't caught the catch in his voice.

Was the bastard smiling at him?

The guy eased back. Silhouetted against the wall, he looked as if he stood—good Christ!—six and a half feet tall! He was a goodamn tree.

"Down on your knees!" Michael commanded. "Down and don't move until the police get here. Otherwise I'll shoot you."

"You won't shoot me," the mountain said. He had a nondescript voice, the voice of a male telephone operator. "I'll walk right out of here, and you won't shoot me. And you won't ever be sure when I'll be coming back."

The guy moved.

But he'd said the wrong thing.

There was no way that son of a bitch was coming back in this house!

Michael pulled the trigger.

Coughffftt.

The bullet smacked the bedroom wall.

Silence.

The silenced weapon hardly had the *booming* effect Michael had hoped for. Still, it had captured the creep's attention.

"I *will* shoot you."

The guy smiled again. His teeth shimmered in the darkness.

He took a step.

Michael brandished the pistol. "I mean it."

The guy took another step.

And another.

He was free of the bed now, less than four steps from the doorway.

"Daddy?"

Jenny, calling from the hallway.

The guy started to move fast.

Michael saw only a flash of the man straddling his daughter in her own bed, imagined the bastard grabbing her in the hallway and holding her hostage.

He pointed low, pulled the trigger again.

Two times.

The intruder spun off balance as he hit the open doorway. His heavy shoulder slammed the doorjamb, peeling off a strip of doorframe. It made a soft, crackling sound. The man hit the floor in the hallway, swearing.

"Run, Jenny!" Michael shouted. *"Get away from the hallway. Go outside and hide."*

He heard her running footsteps disappear down the hallway.

The man was coming to his knees.

"You! Stay on the goddamn floor! I don't want to shoot you again!"

The guy wouldn't listen.

He was getting up, bracing himself against the wall, but not moving away as he had been. He limped a step forward, was blocking the doorway now, coming back into the bedroom.

"You shouldn't've done that, Mr. Dragon. I'm injured now, and I gotta go to a doctor, and that means I'm caught. You shouldn't've shot me."

Michael shook his head, uncomprehending. What the hell was happening to his life? First that psychic does a flopper on him, then his wife runs off on him, then this crazy bastard breaks in and—

—comes for him.

"Get down on the floor!" Michael said, taking a step backward. He only had one more backward step to take before he came up against the wall. He pointed the pistol. The barrel wavered.

The guy had him cornered.

"Get down on the floor until the cops come." *If* those bastards were *ever* going to come.

The guy wasn't a good listener.

He limped okay, though.

"I'm going to shoot you again if you come any closer."

The guy came closer.

Only three steps away now.

Close enough to dive in and start the fight all over again.

But Michael wasn't having any of that.

He shot again.

It made the guy limp worse, was all.

So he had to do it one more time, aiming low and hoping that big damn tree of a man would topple over without crushing him in the process, because he didn't want to have to grapple with that big, stinking bastard again, didn't want to have to shoot him again. . . .

7

Lea picked up the telephone. "Yes?"

It was O'Brian, calling from his office off the foyer. A tall, redheaded woman was there, he said. Could she have a few moments of Lea's time?

"No," Lea said. "I told you I wanted to be left alone today."

"Her name is Helen Locklear," O'Brian said.

"What's that to me? I don't want to see anyone."

"She's coming in anyway."

"O'Brian, I—"

The line had gone dead.

Lea felt a numbness touch her limbs. She returned the telephone receiver to its hook. The scene from the day before came vividly back to mind. It, too, had started with O'Brian ushering a woman into the living room.

Lea came off the couch.

She faced the entry foyer, reached out, and sought O'Brian's mind. He was at the front door. His mind was peaceful. He was admitting a woman without the slightest sense that he was violating Lea's orders. His mind was at peace with itself. It almost seemed . . . in a trance.

Lea stiffened. She glanced around, moved into position to flee for the kitchen hallway and the rear entrance. She didn't want to find herself cornered the way she had been the day before . . . even though she wasn't sure anymore whether the incident had really happened.

I should fire O'Brian, she thought. His presence, alone, was enough to remind her of the terror she'd faced the day before, of that reporter diving off the parapet and vanishing . . . into thin air—not that the air of New York was all that thin. It was probably richer with minerals than air anywhere else in the world. It was filthy air.

"Miss Frazzetti?" the woman asked, glancing around the huge living room. Lea noted the English accent.

The redhead was attractive. Her clothes were originals. She wore them well. Her milky complexion was perfect. Her long red hair, rich and luxuriant. She was probably older than she looked.

"How did you manage to convince O'Brian to let you in?" Lea asked.

The redhead moved into the room without missing a beat. "I suggested it to him," she said, a thin smile touching her even features. She moved, uninvited, to a section of the sofa and sat down.

Lea let her mind reach out to the redhead's. It was the quickest way to get to the bottom of—

Hello, Lea.

Lea gaped at the woman.

Helen Locklear hadn't spoken, yet her message had come across loud and clear the instant Lea's mind had touched hers.

"You . . . ?"

"Yes. I also read minds," Helen Locklear said. "I do a great many other things, as well." She gestured Lea toward the couch. "We have many things to discuss," she said. "Why don't you make yourself comfortable."

Lea hesitated.

Was this another hallucination? Like yesterday?

She pressed her mind at the redhead's again. She sensed the boundaries of Helen Locklear's being but was unable to enter.

"You're really quite good for not having been trained," Helen said.

"What?"

"Your mind reading. I barely sense your presence when you approach."

Lea felt an uneasy smile forming behind her lips. She controlled it, kept it hidden.

"It's fine with me if you want to smile," Helen Locklear said. "I meant what I said as a compliment. You are very good. Which, basically, is why I'm here."

Lea let the smile form. It faded almost immediately. She moved toward a chair near the windows, across the conversation area from this Helen Locklear, whoever she was. "What do you mean?"

"I've come to offer you a chance at learning a great deal more about how to use your abilities."

"How did you know I could read minds?"

"I know your father."

"*What?* My father hasn't the slightest idea that I know how to read minds."

"You mean Carlo Frazzetti, of course."

"He *is* my father."

"Yes, the dear man, in a way he is."

Lea let herself settle deeper into the cushions of the chair. She sensed that this woman was about to tell her something about herself that she had suspected most of her life, suspected since her mother's untimely death in an auto accident. Lea had been four years old at that time.

"What do you mean, 'in a way'?"

"He thought he was your father. He treated you as a favorite daughter. As he should have, since, to him, you were his only child."

"He's not my father?" Lea's voice was flat, toneless. She was trying to absorb this conversation, to make sense of it. At the moment she didn't believe it nor disbelieve it.

Helen Locklear shook her head.

"Who was my father?"

"You'll learn that soon enough," Helen said. "If, of course, you choose to do so."

Lea was silent for a moment. She was aware of a strange tension humming through her body. She studied Helen Locklear's flawless features.

"What is this you were saying about, 'my powers' and about 'learning how to use them'?"

A subtle smile touched the other woman's features. Her eyes sparkled. "Shall we say, your father has need of your powers—or, rather, of one of his children's powers."

Lea frowned.

"Call it a test, if you like," Helen Locklear said. That smile formed again. It was an irritating smile. Not condescending, but . . . irritating, as if the woman had such a deep knowledge about life that she could afford to ignore the feelings of others. "It would really be your second test."

Lea's eyelids dropped slightly. "Second test?"

Helen Locklear nodded. "You *do* remember yesterday?"

Lea felt a stillness move through her body.

"Ah, I see that you do." Again that smile. "Frightening, wasn't it?"

"What do you know about yesterday?"

"Everything," Helen Locklear said. "I was here for the show."

Lea shook her head.

"Yes, I was. So was your father."

Lea's brows knit in thought. She remembered . . . now . . . she'd sensed the presence of someone else when that reporter returned. A tall, gray-haired figure . . . standing in the entry foyer. And she remembered that strange sensation she'd experienced for an instant before the reporter returned . . . as if someone were watching her.

Her gaze moved back to Helen Locklear's face.

The other woman nodded.

"That's the memory," she said.

"You can read my mind that easily?"

The other woman nodded yes.

"I didn't even sense your presence."

"It's part of the training. And if your father is right—

which he usually is—you should be much better at it than I."

Lea crossed her arms, shook her head incredulously. "I don't believe this."

"You *believed* yesterday. You thought that reporter had returned to kill you. You not only *believed*, you were *terrified*."

This woman did know what she was talking about. If she hadn't been in the apartment, how would she have known—

"That was a *test*?"

"You impressed your father."

"What was all *that*? Hallucinations?"

"You could call it that. He suggested that you see what you did . . . and you did. He created the scenario."

"So it was all a charade, a—"

"Hardly a *charade*, I assure you. It was very real."

"What would have happened if I'd done nothing?"

That smile again.

"More than likely, you would have died."

Lea's mind registered the whiteness of the woman's teeth, the silence of the broad living room, and the incongruous tranquillity of her home and the woman's words.

"How?"

"She would have stabbed you."

"But she wasn't . . . *real*."

"She was to you. Besides, she could have been real. You had to defend yourself to find out."

"Wait a minute. You're going too fast for this poor little rich girl." Lea came to her feet, gesturing, trying to make sense of what this woman was telling her. "She wasn't real . . . but I would have died anyway if she'd stabbed me."

"Correct. Give the poor little rich girl an A."

"How?"

"You would have believed you were bleeding to death, and you would have done just that."

Lea chewed a lip. "That's hard to swallow."

"Is it? Think of all the stories you've heard about voodoo. People believe they've had a spell cast over them, and they whither and die. Think about women swelling up with hysterical pregnancies. Think—"

Lea held up a hand. "Those are gradual things. Those people don't simply think they have a hole in them, then immediately bleed to death."

"Don't people die of fright?" Helen Locklear asked. "And what do you make of the hysterical believers who show the stigmata and whose palms bleed on Good Friday? All hallucination?" She shook her head. "No. The line between reality and fantasy is much broader than you want to believe. In fact, it's not a line at all. It's more of a gray area, a shadowy borderland ... maybe it's what Rod Serling called the Twilight Zone. If you had let that reporter stab you, you would have died. You would have bled to death."

"Because she was real to me."

"Exactly."

Lea let that sink in. It made an awful sort of sense. It fit with her view of reality, with what she knew of hysterical reactions. The mind had strange and wondrous powers over the body. Science was proving that more and more every day.

Lea moved to the bar, thinking. She poured herself a glass of sparkling cider. Helen Locklear accepted a stemmed glass of the same.

Lea moved to the sliding glass doors, stared out at the hazy skyline of the city, at the majestic cloud formations in the distance.

"All right. The reporter was an hallucination, but she was real to me. You also said that she could have been real and not an hallucination."

"It gets interesting, doesn't it."

"Explain what you mean."

Despite herself, despite the remembered fear from the day before, Lea was finding herself drawn to this woman and to her premise. She wasn't convinced yet that Helen Locklear was all that she claimed to be, but Lea wasn't ready to discount the woman's story either—not just yet, not after the convincing demonstration of mind reading the woman had delivered. If there was the slightest grain of truth in what the woman was saying, Lea wanted to have a further taste of its *reality*. This could be her way out of the boredom that had gripped her for so many months now.

"The hallucination could have been hers," Helen Locklear said, "not yours."

Lea considered the other woman's words. They made sense to her. She knew she had a slight ability to press her thoughts onto others, to manipulate them into doing what she wanted. That was why, yesterday, she'd used her mind to try to force the reporter over the parapet. It had been an experiment forced by the necessity of survival. But was it possible to control others in the scope this woman was talking about?

"She could have been flesh and blood, could have come back here to kill me because she believed she had to—for whatever reason."

Helen Locklear nodded. "Good. Very good."

Lea felt as if she were being treated like a schoolchild, which, in a way, she was, she realized. A pupil, at least. She decided to ignore the other woman's slightly condescending attitude.

"Someone could make her believe that she had to kill me."

"Exactly."

"And, therefore, she would try to kill me."

Helen Locklear was silent.

"And she would be real."

She stopped her audible thinking and tried to digest what it meant. "So, if she'd stabbed me, I would have died, because it would have been real. I would have had a real knife hole in me."

"And because you would have believed it."

Lea's brow scrunched down on itself.

"It's all a matter of belief," Helen Locklear said. "It's how yogis stop themselves from bleeding. The same thing can be accomplished through self-hypnosis. The techniques are basically the same. It's mind over body, that's all." She shook her head. "Yet hypnosis and Yoga are in no way comparable to the skills that can be yours if you choose to seek them."

"You mean, if I were stabbed, I wouldn't have to bleed to death."

"I mean that and a great deal more. It's not only what you believe that is important. It's what you can make others believe. If they believe in what you want them to believe, you control them. It's what all religious gurus do. Yet it's deeper, like Chinese boxes, level upon level of intricate control. If you control the controller's dreams or beliefs, you're in control."

"Unless someone else controls me."

Helen Locklear laughed softly. "You learn fast." She sipped at the golden cider in her stemmed glass.

"And you're saying I can learn how to control others' thoughts like that? To make them see what I want them to see, to taste, hear, feel, and smell what I want them to, to believe what I want them to believe?"

Helen Locklear nodded, that smile back in place. "I sense your doubt."

Lea moved away from the windows and the hazy blue skyline. "You hardly have to be psychic to read that."

"You want proof."

It wasn't a question.

The telephone rang again, interrupting Lea's thoughts. When Lea answered it, O'Brian said, "Your sister is here."

Puzzled, Lea told O'Brian to send her in. She hung up and turned to Helen Locklear. "My sister Deanna is dropping by for something. I'm sure it won't take long. Will you excuse me?"

"Of course," Helen Locklear said.

Lea strode toward the foyer.

Deanna swept into the room, all bubbly, the way she always made her entrance. Grand, elegant, devil-may-care. Lea hugged her, exchanged kisses, greeted her, asked what she'd come for.

Deanna grinned, said, "This," and her face began to melt.

Lea started to scream but caught it in midinhale. She held her hand to her mouth as she watched *her sister* Deanna's soft, creamy skin burn to a deep red, a scorched red, and start to peel, then bubble, then ooze downward, drawn by the inexorable force of gravity. Deanna's eyes, first one, then the other, popped softly with an audible *plup* and drained down the thick and discolored, molasseslike flesh drooping from her cheekbones. Her thick, dark hair dried, frizzed, trailed limply into the oozing stench that had become her flesh. The figure's mouth fell open. Its tongue lolled out, turned to a pink taffy, and drooled in a long, stringy line of glistening, rubbery flesh to the floor.

Lea gaped as the figure's flesh slowly drained off its skeleton and formed a hideously undulant, flesh-and-blood–colored puddle of gel at the feet of the gaunt, flesh-less effigy who, strangely, still retained its clothes. The moving puddle on the carpet made *squelching* sounds.

Then the skeletal figure sagged, rattled softly like a muffled bamboo wind chime, and crumpled into the gel.

Lea felt sick.

Still, she started to laugh softly, not believing her eyes, yet totally convinced by what she'd witnessed.

As she laughed, the damp, shuddering vile gel on the floor slowly seeped through the carpet and drained away without leaving the slightest stain.

Lea shook her head.

"That was child's play," Helen Locklear said, "a creation straight out of the horror comics. Just an example."

"I don't have a sister," Lea said incredulously, "but for a moment there, I thought I did."

"Do you believe now?"

"Not in my sister, but in what you say, yes," Lea said, aware of a deep sense of awe permeating her body, filling her mind with mad fantasies. The power of the images she'd experienced was beyond her comprehension. She had to have it, had to know how to control it. She knew, now, the rapture and awe of conversion. She would never scoff at believers again.

"And you want to learn the skills?"

"Yes."

Lea faced the woman, caught the glint of red off Helen Locklear's amazing red hair.

"It will be dangerous. You may not survive."

Lea considered her options. She could go on as she had been for the first thirty years of her life, or . . .

"I'll take the chance."

Helen Locklear's strange smile touched her features again.

"It will not be easy," she said, "and from now on, you will never know what is real and what is not unless you have the strength to fathom the difference."

Lea felt alive with energy. She wanted to know more, wanted to know it all, wanted it *now!*

"What do I have to do?"

"First, you meet your father."

"Where?"

"London. Tomorrow." And, as if by magic, the redhead produced an airline ticket from the purse at her side. "It's all been arranged. You leave at seven A.M."

8

Michael rose from his desk and crossed his office. He met the tall redhead as his secretary ushered the woman through the door. One of his long-term clients had canceled their session at the last minute. Coincidentally, this woman had walked into the office, seeking an appointment at the earliest moment.

Good timing, Michael thought.

Sometimes the Fates worked that way.

"This is Miss Locklear," Michael's secretary said before leaving.

Michael took the woman's hand. "Nice to meet you."

She responded in kind with a pleasant English accent. He gestured for her to take a seat on his office couch. She complied. He took a seat opposite her, in a stuffed chair.

She glanced around the office, her eyes appearing to take in everything, from the relaxing oil paintings to the harbor view beyond the window. While she appraised his office, he studied her.

She was an attractive woman. Fortyish, but looking much younger. Blue eyes that glinted like faceted turquoise. She looked very composed, even self-assured.

This was always an awkward moment, the first meeting between therapist and client. At that instant Michael was still having difficulty sorting out his own experience from the night before, and he wondered if he didn't need a psychologist as much as or more than this woman needed him. He'd never shot anyone before. He'd never shot anything living in his entire life, except for a sparrow he'd killed with a slingshot as a child. He'd felt horrible about that for weeks afterward, remembering that cooling, fragile body resting in the palm of his hand and knowing that he'd been the one to end its life, senselessly. Thank God Angie had not been in her bedroom to witness the carnage.

"What brings you here?" he asked. He usually found the most direct route the simplest one.

"You," the woman said.

Michael smiled. "I'm not sure I understand what you mean."

"You had a rather horrifying experience last night, I believe."

Michael stared at her. The incident hadn't hit the morning papers. "How did you—ah, *the radio*?"

She shook her head. "I helped send the man to visit you."

Michael felt the muscles of his face go slack. He detected no sign of humor in the woman's voice, no physical sign that she didn't mean what she'd said in exactly the way she'd said it. His clinical training took over. *Schizophrenic,* he thought. Possibly a character disorder. But he couldn't imagine what she expected to gain by this beginning. No. Paranoid-schiz was his guess. Maybe manic, but she wasn't showing any of the nonverbal signs he'd come to expect from a manic. No, he discounted the manic diagnosis. Hell. Had to be schizophrenic. He didn't see many

of them in his private practice, and he didn't relish the idea
of working with one—not now, not today, not after last
night, especially not when the first words out of her mouth
were designed to ensnare him in her delusional system.

"Oh, how did you do that?"

"Telepathic commands," the woman said. She was as
serious as the pope.

Yup, schizophrenic.

God, schizophrenics, the things they came up with.
He'd done his share of hours on an inpatient unit during his
internship. He'd seen enough psychopathology on parade
to last him a lifetime. He'd also learned that you didn't
usually get anywhere with a schizophrenic in midhallucin-
ation or delusion unless you bought into their craziness, at
least for a little while. It was the only way to build the
relationship with them to the point where they felt they
could trust you.

"Telepathic commands," Michael said, nodding empath-
ically. "That's interesting. How, exactly, are you able to do
that?" He didn't know when or how he'd learned to respond straight-faced in situations like this, but he thanked
God that he'd somehow managed to learn the trick. He
knew several clinicians who would have laughed in the
woman's face.

The woman smiled.

She sure as hell didn't look schizophrenic, but then the
paranoid ones often didn't.

Michael felt his head suddenly invaded by an alien presence.

Like this.

Michael stared at her. It felt as if his head were swelling,
stretching to the bursting point.

Those amazing blue eyes of hers bored into his very
psyche.

Now do you believe me?

She wasn't talking. She was communicating directly
with his brain.

"I . . . I don't know what to say."

He'd started to perspire. He felt clammy. He shivered.
He'd never sensed anything like this before.

The sense of pressure eased. He blinked.

The sound of the woman's voice brought him back to reality. "I take it you no longer think I'm schizophrenic."

He didn't know what to think. He ran a hand over his face, shook his head to clear it. A high level of adrenaline was still flooding his veins. He could feel the arousal, the desire to act. But how?

"You say you sent the man to my house last night," he said, groping for a direction.

"I helped," the woman said, her English voice soft and even. It was the kind of voice a man would like to wake up to.

"Why?"

"Let's say it was done to assess your reactions. As a psychologist, I'm sure you understand what I mean."

"But why?"

"We had to know your abilities, your strengths, to probe the depths of your capabilities."

He swallowed, uncomprehending. His nervous laugh was short and abrupt. It was followed by a welling anger, an anger bordering on rage.

"Someone could have been killed," he said hotly.

"Several have been."

She'd stunned him again.

Nothing he said had the slightest impact on this woman.

"What do you mean?" he asked.

"You were not the only one to be tested. There were others. Two, besides yourself, survived their tests. Three did not."

Michael didn't know what to say. He wanted to say she was crazy and dismiss her words, but . . . that mental presence in the midst of his mind—it changed everything.

"What are these *tests* for?"

"To determine who shall follow in your father's footsteps."

Michael was completely lost now. Lost and angry. "I haven't the slightest idea what you're talking about."

"I know, but it is not my place to explain fully. That is your father's task."

"My father is dead. He died of a heart attack while I was in college, over fifteen years ago."

"You were adopted."

"Are you saying—no, no!" He stood up and walked behind his desk. "My natural father is dead, too. I went through the court bit and got access to my birth and adoption records. My natural mother died in childbirth, carrying me. When I looked further, I found that my natural father was killed in the Korean War. He was a pilot, shot down over the North."

"He wasn't your natural father."

"His name was Keller. Ira Keller."

"He wasn't your natural father."

"I don't believe you."

"Your natural father is someone quite different, I assure you. Quite unique. He has powers beyond anything you've ever imagined. He fathered you, and the others, as safeguards against a time like the present."

Michael stared. He had an overwhelming desire to move around, to wave his arms and expend energy. He didn't believe this. Worse, he didn't believe his half acceptance of this woman's story.

"We could go for a walk," the woman suggested as if she were reading his mind, knew of his need for physical activity.

Michael took the offer. He led the way out. In the lobby, he told Linda, his secretary, that he'd be back in thirty minutes, in plenty of time for his next appointment.

The Florida heat hit him as soon as he stepped from the building. It was like a living presence, something huge, soft, yielding, yet smothering. It was 3:30 P.M., on the down side of the hottest time of day. Michael took off his suit coat and draped it over his arm. He headed toward a nearby botanical park. The redheaded woman matched his stride. She was tall, athletic, with a striking figure.

"All right," Michael said, "go on with your story."

Half a block ahead of them, the green foliage of the botanical gardens beckoned, offering green-dappled shade and coolness.

"I've told most of it," the woman said. "You passed the

test. You proved yourself, and now your father wants you to come to him so that he can train you for a greater existence. He wants you by his side."

"Who is *my father*?"

"I'm not at liberty to tell you. He will do that when the time comes."

Michael was silent for a moment.

They crossed the quiet residential street and entered the shaded foliage of the botanical garden. Three winding pathways led deeper into the tropical wonderland. All three were canopied by a wild tangle of planned vegetation. Here and there along the paths were tranquil rest areas—wooden benches and gurgling, man-made streams. It was one of Michael's favorite spots for a brown-bag lunch, a place for clearing his mind and simply experiencing the wonder of being. He took the right fork and let his body enjoy the coolness beneath the greenery.

The gardens were nearly deserted at this time of day.

"Then, who are you? How do you fit into"—he waved a hand—"all this?"

"I'm a friend of your father's."

Michael waited for more. When nothing else was forthcoming, he paused, turned to face the woman. The last few days were taking their toll on him. His anger was burning again, being stoked by this insane conversation. He was becoming as crazy as this woman most likely was. And if she'd had anything to do with exposing Jenny to that bastard who'd broken into the house last night, she deserved to have him unload on her.

But he controlled himself. He still wasn't totally convinced she hadn't come to him for help, that she wasn't schizophrenic—wasn't totally convinced that she'd made him experience that little telepathic jolt he thought he'd felt earlier, in his office.

"Why are you here?" he asked.

"To give you this."

She handed him an airline ticket envelope. He looked at it dumbly, then opened the flap.

Tampa to London. One way. Leaving the next morning.

"I don't understand."

"He wants you to join him. He needs you. He can teach you things you've never imagined. You have the abilities. He's certain of it."

"What abilities?"

"He'll tell you."

"No, dammit! You played a parlor trick on me back there in my office, and you said you had something to do with putting my daughter in danger, so *you explain*! You're the one who's here, who's come to feed me some cock-and-bull story about telepathy and mind control. I'm not going anywhere just because some woman hands me a ticket to London and some cockamamy story about telepathy and a mystery 'father figure' with 'powers.' I hear these kinds of stories pretty damned often, and usually there's a very simple explanation for them: pathology; pure and simple craziness. If this *father* of mine is so *powerful*, why didn't he come to see me in person? And why has he waited until this moment to do so?"

"He's nearby."

"Then have him show himself."

"It wouldn't be safe. He's nearby, take my word for it. He is the source of what little powers I have, and I must be close to him in order to use them."

"It seems I'm to take your word for a great deal. More than I care to take your word for."

A strange smile tugged the woman's lips away from her teeth. "You are very disbelieving."

"I'm a scientist. I was trained to disbelieve. I listen, I watch, I hear and file things away, but I very seldom believe until I've seen enough proof to convince me that what I'm seeing or hearing cannot possibly be other than what it purports to be. Even then, I'm likely to doubt what I believe in."

"It is not safe for your father to be in your presence here."

"Why?"

She shook her head. "There are those who would cherish the chance of finding him with one of his untrained offspring outside the sanctuary of his caverns."

Michael only glared at the woman now. He'd had about

enough of her double-talk. He handed the airline ticket back to her.

She refused to take it.

"Take it," he said. "As much as I'd like to go to London, I have to turn it down. I have other plans for the next few days."

The hint of a smile left her face.

He shoved the ticket at her again.

She wouldn't take it.

Michael set it down on a nearby shaded bench. He straightened, opened his hands, backed away. "I didn't ask for it. I don't want it. I'm not telepathic. I'm not anything except a reasonably competent psychologist and a fair father. I'm not in the market for learning new 'powers,' thank you."

"You are a good psychologist *because* of your powers," the woman said. "You read more than behaviors and words. You do more than empathize. You sense more than your science taught you to sense. You are successful because your deeper powers allow you to gain more treatment compliance than you could without them. You seed suggestions that people cannot ignore. Yet you are trained to see it only as science. You are training-blind. You cannot see your success for what it is: You are telepathic . . . and more."

Michael edged away a few steps. "I'm not listening to you anymore," he said. "I'm returning to my office now, and I'm going to forget that we met." He nodded, touched the brim of his nonexistent hat by way of good-bye, and turned.

And, abruptly, turned again.

To face the woman.

He couldn't pull away, and his mind had that pregnant, swelling sensation again.

She was staring at him.

He felt locked in the focus of her eyes.

Everything around him seemed to shimmer.

Something rustled in the nearby bushes, and for an instant Michael sensed the presence of another person. Then the rustling stopped. Someone was retreating. He caught a glimpse of gray hair.

I can make you do what I want.

Not a voice.

Again that instantaneous, alien thought in his head.

Let me show you some of the powers I've only hinted at so far.

Michael stood frozen, like a statue. His eyes could track. That was about all. He watched the woman point at a nearby bench. The wooden bench crackled, splintered, and collapsed in on itself. She glanced back in his direction, and he felt himself pressed toward the earth, crammed down, as if he were being trod upon by some huge, unseen force. He found himself on his stomach, on the rich, loamy path. The smell of vegetation and dampness was full, over-powering, spicy. He tried to speak. No words formed. He felt powerless to control his own muscles. He concen-trated, focused his energy, willing himself to speak in spite of the irresistible force holding him in its grip. He broke out in a sweat. His head began to ache. He—

A snake slithered out of the nearby brush.

It was a cobra.

It wound its way forward, moving in an agonizingly slow motion. It shimmered, reared up, opened its flared hood, and exposed its long, dripping fangs, its pink mouth and elastic jaw.

Michael tried to cry out.

Nothing.

The snake slithered closer, paused inches form his face, met his gaze, eye to eye. The forked tongue slithered in and out of the serpent's mouth, in and out, in and out, moving with a sinuous, hypnotic regularity. The snake tensed, pulled back, appeared ready to strike, then moved off, angled to the side, slithered in closer, and disappeared from Michael's view.

He couldn't see it anymore, but his other senses seemed suddenly magnified. He heard the gentle, soft slithering of the snake's scaly belly sliding across damp, packed earth, heard the serpent's approach, then felt the slick, scaly skin and the strong muscular contractions as the creature slithered across his neck and onto his back. The snake paused. Michael's breathing stopped. In terror, he imagined the cobra's beady eyes focusing on the pulsing veins in his neck.

He tried to speak again.

Again, nothing came out of his mouth.

He concentrated, bore down on his thoughts, fought the force controlling him, sensed unknown, previously undiscovered barricades in his mind that he threw up against the external power dominating his will, drove the ungodly power back, away from him, and, painfully, agonizingly, forced his own thoughts to form clearly in his mind, coughed words out.

"No. It's not real. I don't believe it."

The snake evaporated.

Michael felt the cloying, controlling power fade. His eyes adjusted, and he saw the bench behind the woman. It was unharmed; the airline ticket still rested on the seat.

He was sweating from the exertion, but he was pleased to be free of the woman's mental hold. He had no idea why she'd released him, or whether his effort to deny what he'd seen had anything to do with his regained freedom.

He didn't care at the moment.

But he did know one thing for certain.

She was not schizophrenic, that was for damn sure.

"You can create images of whatever you'd like," the woman's soft voice said. "You can have whatever riches of the world you choose. All you have to do is accept your father's offer—and survive."

Michael glared at her.

He was angry, but his anger was tempered by a strange, nearly irresistible curiosity. This woman was capable of behaviors and mental processes no human could perform. He wanted to study her, to learn her secrets. At the same time he felt a revulsion toward her and what she'd done to him—what she'd done here, in the botanical gardens, and what she'd participated in the night before.

Michael had not wanted to shoot that man.

But the guy was in the hospital right now, the victim of three very real and painful bullet wounds to his legs, apparently because of some deadly game this woman was playing, a game for which she was passing the responsibility off onto—

—*my father?*

It didn't make sense.

He didn't want it to make sense.

He wanted to forget what he'd been through, what he'd experienced.

But he couldn't.

The woman handed him the airline ticket. "Take this. Think it over. I'm sure you'll do the right thing."

Michael took the ticket. He looked at it again, torn by the ambiguous emotions warring within his head.

What did this ticket mean?

It frightened him.

It felt evil.

And he knew he wouldn't use it.

He raised his head to give it back, but the woman was gone. He was alone in the sun-dappled coolness of the botanical gardens. Alone with an airline ticket and his tormented thoughts.

His glance caught the scribbled words on the front of the envelope.

One way.

To London.

9

Drew tossed the anchor off the sailboat's bow and stripped his clothes off. It was early evening in the Florida Keys. The low sun still cast its luxuriant glow across the calm, blue-green water.

At a distance of fifty yards, a scimitar of white sand

beach nearly encircled the small, protected harbor into which Drew had pulled his thirty-foot, obsidian-black sailboat, the *Midnight Reefer*. He'd named the boat after his first gold single. Beyond the narrow beach, low scrub brush rose to a flat, sandy peak less than fifteen feet above high tide. This was one of Drew's favorite getaways between gigs. This was his island. He owned it. And there wasn't a damn thing on it except solitude, birds, and a few mice.

In several dozen overnight trips to the island, where he intended someday to build a retreat, he'd seen only one other boat enter the bay, and that had belonged to a friend who'd followed him out here.

Naked, Drew dropped down into the cabin.

The girl he'd brought with him, a brunette by the name of Julie, hadn't budged from the forward cabin in over an hour. He stuck his head through the entry.

"Hey, Jules, how you doin'?"

She'd been sleeping. She turned her pasty face toward him. Pressure lines from where she'd slept on the bundled sheets crossed her cheek diagonally. Her eyes were hooded, unhealthy-looking. She held the back of an arm over her forehead, either shading her eyes or relieving pressure.

"Oh, Drew, honey, I'm sorry. I didn't think I'd get so sick." She sounded slightly drunk and a lot ill. "All that bouncing...those waves." They'd been sipping homemade sangria all afternoon. A little over an hour earlier the juice, the sun, and the waves had conspired to make her toss her cookies into the sea.

Drew sat on the side of the mattress. The forecabin was cramped, with a low ceiling. It was little more than a triangular-shaped bed with a small area near the door in which to stand up. This close to the brunette, Drew could smell her sour breath. "You going to be okay?"

She nodded with obvious effort, her forehead still protected by her forearm. "But I gotta have some more sleep. The world keeps spinning."

Drew gently slapped the sheet-shrouded curve of her hip. "I'll let you get some sleep. When you wake up, I'll be topside. If you're hungry then, I'll cook us up some steaks."

"Yuck. I'm not going to eat for a month."

Drew kissed her forehead.

She rolled away, pulled the sheet over her head.

Drew closed the door behind him, crossed the main cabin, and climbed the steep steps topside.

A warm breeze was blowing out of the west. Drew dived into the bay and let the cool water soothe his tired muscles. They'd sailed for over five hours today. He was bushed.

After a leisurely splash about, he climbed back aboard the *Midnight Reefer,* spread a towel on the teak decking, and sprawled out to dry off in the still, warm rays from the sun. The boat bobbed gently on the smooth water of the bay. It rocked him like a baby. The rhythmic, soft slapping of the waves was hypnotic.

He was dozing within a matter of minutes.

Dreaming within a few more.

There was a woman in the dream, tall, redheaded, beckoning him with languid gestures, moving away from him through the streets of a strange city. He ran to catch her, found himself gaining when he could keep her in sight, but each time she rounded a corner and disappeared, she managed, somehow, to regain the same lead she'd had since the start.

The city was dark.

It was night.

The streets were narrow, lined with old, leaning buildings, aswirl with fog and indistinct light.

Through street after street he ran, following the woman. She was dressed in a hooded robe. After the first few corners, she drew her hood about her face and became even more of a mystery.

Why was he chasing her?

He couldn't answer. He simply had to.

She led him into seedier and more decrepit neighborhoods. Alleyways lined with garbage cans and spilled refuse soon became littered with humanity itself. Human forms lay tossed this way and that among the garbage and the puddled stench of the back ways. Forms dressed in tatters, smelling as bad as the alley itself, male and female forms, the derelicts, the lost, the . . . they reminded Drew of his mother, of the last time he'd seen her alive.

Insane and drunk.

The woman led him to an alley door. He followed her through the doorway. Uneven steps led down into the musty depths of a cellar. Smoke and the smell of stale beer and sweat greeted him at the bottom. It was the entrance to a low-ceilinged bar. A small stage dominated one end of the room. A long bar lined the far wall, booths hugged this side. Crowded tables filled in the remainder of the floor space. Voices murmured. The room was alive with nondescript humanity, faceless, nameless bodies moving without meaning.

Drew's eyes searched the smoke-hazed room. The woman, her cowl still covering her head, shadowing her face, beckoned him to a vacant table near the silent stage. He joined her there. Chairs scraped on the dirty floor, creaked as he sat down. A whiskey bottle appeared. Neat whiskey disappeared through the open front of the woman's dark cowl.

Drew slugged down a shot glass of the fiery liquid. He wiped his lips with his fingers and waited for the woman to speak.

Her white face was barely visible within the cowl.

Her voice was English.

"You want immortality, don't you."

Drew laughed.

"Doesn't everyone?"

"It doesn't exist."

Drew was silent. He knew this was a dream. Immortality should exist, at least in his dreams.

"My music is a form of immortality," he said.

"Your music is your redemption." The voice was soft, enticing.

He said nothing.

The voice from the cowl went on. "Your music is an escape from your past, a means of denying the stark reality of your childhood. It is your way of repressing the memories of your insane mother and all the horrendous acts she perpetrated on you."

Drew felt the smoky bar closing in on him. He swallowed, glanced around, had the mad sensation that everyone in the murmuring room was surreptitiously watching him.

This woman was accurate, he realized. All his life he'd been fleeing from those godawful childhood memories. No father. A crazy mother who trailed an endless chain of abusive, stinking, drunken males in and out of her bedroom. A mother who'd sell herself for a bottle of wine; who wasn't above renting her only-begotten child to some pervert for an evening; a mother who locked him in closets and basements and abandoned cars when she needed a few hours to herself; a mother who couldn't care for herself, let alone the impressionable mind of a growing child; a mother just smart enough to avoid the social workers but too out of touch with reality to avoid her own living hell.

"Why did you lead me here?" he asked.

A sparkle of white teeth reflected from the depths of the cowl. "For the play, of course."

The woman's long, thin, marble-white fingers extended beyond the full folds of the robe and gestured grandly toward the nearby stage.

On cue, dim stage lights flickered on, and an uneven drumroll, muffled by the heavy curtains, echoed from backstage. The houselights dimmed, the murmur of the patrons faded to a background sound.

The curtains opened.

Drew stiffened.

His mother stood there, in a dark alley, smiling her crazy smile. She had a purple shawl thrown over her shoulders and wore a sequined, form-fitting gown. The makeup on her face resembled something pasted on to the face of a corpse, or the face of an eighty-year-old whore. Too much red, too much black, too much powder. She was as gaunt as death.

She started to dance.

Tears formed in Drew's eyes.

His mother danced to silence.

The voices in the bar murmured like the uncaring voice of distant traffic. Glasses tinkled. Someone cleared his throat.

There was a strained poignancy to his mother's dance. She picked a flower from a broken flowerpot, hugged the flower to her breast. She fluttered her eyelids. She moved with a fragile grace, like a piece of living porcelain waiting for life to smash her to the dirty, cobbled alleyway.

Drew wanted to touch her, to carry her from that filthy alley. He found himself reaching out toward his mother.

Long, white fingers closed on his arm. The cowled woman gestured him back into his chair.

The dance continued.

Only the sound of the muted, scuffling, dancing shoes disturbed the eerie scene.

But the background was changing. Shifting shades of light were washing the alleyway, brightening it before his eyes, putting a fresh coat of paint and polish on every available bit of metal and wood. The facades of the buildings shimmered, grew colorful awnings, sprouted flower boxes, glimmered with warm, interior lights and gay, stained glass windows. It became a daytime scene, a street scene in a cafe district of some colorful city. Sidewalk cafes sprung to life, chairs and tables sprouted people, laughter, tinkling glasses of wine, and sunshine. Waiters bustled about.

And his mother's dance continued in silence.

Her hideous makeup had vanished.

She was younger. Her skin, milky-white and smooth, unlined, perfect. Her eyes gleaming with hope.

"What could have been," the soft voice within the cowl said.

"No," Drew said softly. "Impossible."

"You can change your past," the woman whispered.

"How?"

"Ask your father."

"I never knew my father."

"He's here."

Drew stared into the shadowy interior of the cowl,

catching the barest glimpse of the woman's ethereal face. His question was written on his face.

The woman pointed. "Up there."

A man joined the dance onstage. The lighting focused on him, dimmed around the edges of the stage, sent the street scene into a frozen limbo of shadow. The man was tall, gray-haired, with a distinctive, lined face.

Drew gaped. The man . . .

"He was backstage at the arena the other day. He gave me a towel."

The woman touched Drew's arm again. He fell silent.

The man onstage swept forward, took Drew's mother in his arms, and together the couple whirled across the stage. Lighting hit with a blinding flash, the stage was an open amphitheater now, where tall, marble columns soared to the heavens . . . and there was music, the glorious, wafting, mind-filling wonder of a full orchestra. The couple floated majestically across the shining silver stage, more graceful than Astaire and Rogers. The man swept Drew's startlingly beautiful mother across the stage in grand twirls and smooth, never-ending spins.

Tears blurred Drew's vision.

"I wish . . ." was all he could say. "I wish."

"You have the ability to change your past," the woman said. "You are your father's son."

"And my mother's."

There was a surprising bite of bitterness in his voice.

"Genius . . . madness . . ." the woman's soothing voice said, mysteriously wending its way between the swelling orchestral music, "they are very close. You have your father's powers within you, and perhaps a touch of genius from your mother."

Drew couldn't pull his eyes from the wondrous dance onstage.

"If only . . ."

"You can have it all, Drew. It's yours for the taking."

"How?"

"Come to your father's house. Join him in London. Come learn what powers lie within your genes."

"I don't understand."

"You will."

"When?"

"When you awake."

"How?"

"By accepting this . . ." The woman's fingers stroked the nape of Drew's neck. He felt a subtle tingle of energy flood upward from her fingers, surge through his brain. His senses grew suddenly acute.

"What is . . ." He turned to face the woman across the dimly lit bar table.

"A taste of what you may become," she said. "Try it when you awake. Create anything you like."

"I don't understa——"

Darkness engulfed him.

And silence.

He jerked his head around.

The dim bar was empty.

Chairs were stacked upside down on tables.

The stage was silent, its fading, mildewed curtains closed and unmoving.

The beautiful fantasy of his mother was gone.

And a nameless fear had taken her place.

It jogged him out of his dream . . . out of his sleep.

He awoke, sweating, sat up.

His senses resisted the readjustment to reality.

He felt the sailboat bobbing beneath him, sensed the still, warm rays of the sun at his back. His heart was racing, throbbing heavily at his temples with the insistence of a bass drum. Fifty yards away, his Florida Keys island lay beautiful and silent.

He raised a hand to wipe at his face, thinking, *crazy dream*, when he paused, his hand held at an odd angle before his face. A colored envelope fluttered between his fingers. He frowned. He looked closely at the envelope, aware immediately of what it was but equally confused as to where it had come from.

He opened the envelope.

An airline ticket.

One way.

Miami to London.

Dated for tomorrow.

He stared at it.

He felt numb.

One hand strayed to the base of his skull, to the nape of his neck, and he remembered the dream.

He rose to his feet. He felt unsteady, drunk on something more potent than wine.

"Create anything you like." The words came back to him clearly, as a perfect echo. Even the soft timbre of the woman's voice sounded in his ears.

What the hell had she meant?

He stared at his island, then, chuckling to himself, he imagined a dinosaur on the beach. A tyrannosaur.

The air shimmered, then coalesced immediately.

A *Tyrannosaurus rex* stood on the beach, fifty yards away, its great, carnivorous head cocked at an angle, its beady eyes blinking out across the water.

Drew shook his head.

Jesus.

It was like drugs, only controllable.

Better.

Much better.

He laughed softly, then had another idea.

He willed the thunder lizard on the beach to gambol about like a puppy.

The dinosaur gamboled.

The earth shook.

Drew laughed until tears formed in his eyes and ran down his cheeks. He knew he wasn't high, knew he wasn't . . . *crazy?*

The thought stopped him dead.

His mother had seen things all her life. At various times, the visions had been different.

She'd talked with God.

Walked with Jesus and Satan.

Seen little pink men with purple hair who'd come from Venus.

Believed that aliens from Saturn were monitoring her on a special frequency sent out through her intergalactic IUD.

She'd had absolutely no control over her visions.

Drew watched the playful dinosaur splashing along the shallow waters of the sandy beach.

He willed the beast to be gone.

The dinosaur disappeared, leaving only ripples behind.

He willed it back.

It returned, cocked its head, and stared mindlessly at him across the now still water.

He willed the beast to turn pink.

A pink *Tyrannosaurus rex* danced in the gentle waves.

Be gone.

The beach was silent.

Come back.

A thunder lizard rolled on the beach, kicking sprays of sand and water high into the air, where the sun caught the droplets and turned them into prisms and cast a faint rainbow over the beach.

Drew roared with laughter, with the wondrous power he sensed within his mind, with the sheer joy of living, and when Julie poked her sleep-tousled head out of the cabin, he laughed even more and grabbed her and kissed her and slowly, so gently, so perfectly, made love first to her; next, to Cleopatra; and finally, to Marie Antoinette.

That was when the power turned ugly.

He'd always heard Marie Antoinette was beautiful, stacked like Jayne Mansfield, but he'd never seen her picture. What he conjured up was exactly what he remembered . . . another similarity with Mansfield . . .

Marie without a head . . .

Marie with a flowing, dark emptiness between her shoulders.

Marie with a wound so gaping that he thought he would drown in it.

His scream echoed across the still evening waters of his sanctuary. Like everything in his life, there were treacherous shoals beneath the surface beauty.

10

Michael left the police station a little after 9:00 P.M. He was exhausted, emotionally drained. The police detectives had questioned him for the past forty-five minutes without a break.

The man he'd shot had died.

Trauma, the physicians were saying.

A freak death.

The bullet wounds weren't that serious. Three wounds to the legs. No major artery had been hit.

But somehow the man had died.

Michael felt numb.

He made his way to his Buick, barely noticing the evening traffic cruising past on the nearby street, the taxi setting silently on the street near the parking lot. He drove through the sultry evening with his windows open, oblivious to the flow of cars, the jungle of neon lights, the freeway entrance and exit.

He'd never felt so . . . empty.

On a whim, as he swung into Ivy Lane, he continued on past his house. Three houses farther along the street sat Milo Silklowski's low ranch house. Michael slowed the car, pulled to the curb, flicked his lights off, and for a moment stared at the draperied windows. Lights burned inside the house. Palm trees lined the drive like silent sentinels.

Angie was in there.

He couldn't see her car, but he knew she was in there.

Jenny was with her for the night. When he'd learned he'd be home late, he'd called Angie and asked her if she'd take Jenny until the next morning. She'd agreed.

Tears welled up in his eyes as he thought about the two of them, Angie and Jenny.

. . . too much!

He cleared his throat, sniffed, blinked away the blur of sadness. Things were building up within him, getting to be *too much*. He didn't know how much more he could take. He'd received a phone call from Angie's lawyer about five that afternoon. Angie and her attorney wanted to meet with Michael and his attorney to discuss the split.

So, as far as Angie was concerned, it was over.

Without so much as a good argument.

His eyes blurred again.

This is stupid, he thought. *You're just making yourself suffer. Go home.*

He took one last glance at Silklowski's house, then glanced over his shoulder to see if it was safe to pull out into the street. A taxicab was sitting half a block back, in front of his own house.

Curious, Michael turned his headlights back on and made a quick U-turn. As he drew next to the taxi, he slowed. His lights barely illuminated the lone figure sitting in the backseat.

He recognized her.

Carol Lewis, the blind psychic.

The cab suddenly flashed its lights on and pulled away.

Michael pulled into his driveway, considering what to do. It was his guess that the woman had been following him. He remembered the taxi he'd seen outside the police station, guessed that it had been hers.

The question was *why?*

He parked and walked back to the street. The taxi had been going toward the dead end of the street. It had to come back this way, unless it could float on the bay.

He was right.

The taxi was coming back this way.

He stepped into the street, making sure to be picked up in the taxi's headlights.

The taxi slowed. Michael waved it to a stop. He walked over and opened the rear door.

"You were following me," he said.

The blonde fidgeted on the rear seat. "I . . . I was, I guess, yes. I wanted to talk with you. I . . ." Her head turned toward the taxi driver, as if she were weighing her words, considering what could be said in the man's presence and what could not.

"It's late," Michael said. "Are you staying in town?"

"Yes," she said, "near the airport."

"If you'd like to talk, I'll give you a ride home later."

She hesitated, then quickly made up her mind and reached toward the front seat with several bills in her fingers. "Keep it," she said to the driver. "You've been very patient."

Michael heard the cab driver mumble his thanks and reached to help the blind woman out of the taxi.

At the touch of his fingers on her bare arm, she went suddenly rigid.

"What is it?" he asked.

She shook her head and climbed from the car. The cabbie pulled the door closed and drove off.

The blind psychic was wearing a frozen, worried expression.

"What is it?" Michael insisted. "You sensed something when I touched you."

She nodded. "Please, let's go into your house."

He led the way.

Once inside, he flipped on several lights and guided her to the great room. "Can I get you something?"

Her head shake was tense, overcontrolled.

Michael sat next to her.

Tears spilled down the woman's cheeks. Her green eyes glimmered.

"What is it?"

"I'm too late," she said.

"Too late for what?"

"I wanted to warn you. I felt something this afternoon. I—I didn't go back to Cassadaga today. After what I told you yesterday I felt that I owed you . . . I don't know what. I shouldn't have told you those things, and after I did, I felt that I should stay near, in case there was something I could do. But now . . ."

Michael waited.

"I feel like a failure."

The tears were flowing full force now. From her purse the woman pulled a tissue and held it to her eyes.

After a moment, she gained control of her emotions again. "They have your daughter," she said.

Michael came reflexively to his feet. "What are you saying?"

The tears flowed without letup. "I sensed the danger a little while ago, and I wanted to warn you, but before I could—I knew they'd gotten to her already."

"Who? Who are you talking about?"

"I don't know." She wiped at her eyes, then steeled herself and cut the crying. When she spoke again, it was a stronger woman, a woman in control of her emotions, herself, her life. "There was a woman and a man. That's all I know. Not American, I don't think, but . . . I'm not sure."

Michael eyed the woman sideways. "Jenny was with Angie and—*her friend.*"

The psychic nodded. "She's not with them now."

Michael started for the phone, then stopped. "Stay here," he said. He bolted for the front door.

Milo Silklowski's house was less than a hundred yards away. Michael made the distance in less than half a minute. He pounded at the door. No one answered. He pounded again. He was about to try the door handle when the door swung open.

It was Angie, wearing a bathrobe. Her hair was wet.

"Hello, Mike."

"Where's Jenny?"

"Why, with you, of course."

Michael saw Angie's newfound love leave the living room for the depths of the house, as if Milo were uncomfortable with Michael's presence . . . or as if he had something to hide.

"But I called you earlier, asked you to take her for the night."

"I know. But you also called back an hour ago and told me it was okay to send her home. Which I did. Don't you remember?" There was a biting snap to her voice.

"No. I don't. Because I didn't."

"You most certainly did! I know your voice, Michael!"

Michael pushed his way past his wife and into Milo's living room. It had a vaguely African flavor to it, with tribal masks on the walls, a lion skin rug on the floor.

Jesus. A lion skin. The psychologist in him couldn't resist the implications.

"I want to look in the bedrooms."

Angie was becoming agitated now, too. "You're serious? You didn't call?"

"I didn't." He left the living room, scanned the nearby kitchen and family room, then ran for a hallway that he assumed led to the bedrooms.

Angie grabbed his arm and stopped him. "Well then who the hell called for me to send her home?"

Michael shook his head. "I don't know." He pulled away and shoved a door open. It was a utility room. Jenny wasn't in it.

"She's not at home?"

"No."

Michael moved to the next room, swung the door wide. Bedroom.

His daughter wasn't there.

On a mad urge, he swung open the double closet doors.

"I told you, Michael, she isn't here. I sent her home an hour ago."

"How the hell could you do that?"

"It was—I thought it was your voice, you bastard. It was broad daylight out. She only had to cross three front lawns to get home!"

Michael jerked open two more doors. At the master bedroom, he flung back the bathroom door. Milo was standing there, urinating. "Scared the piss out of you, hey, Milo."

He closed the door on the blushing neurosurgeon before the man could think of a rejoinder.

"Leave him alone, Mike. He's not going to fight you, you know. He doesn't have the sarcastic streak you do."

"Call her friends and see if she's at anybody's house," Michael said, ignoring Angie's admonitions.

"She's always home by now, Mike."

"There's always a first time for kids to stay out late."

Angie bit off a reply, headed for the telephone in the kitchen. Michael paced the hallway while Angie called Jenny's friends. He checked the garage, the pool area, the backyards.

No luck.

No daughter.

He strode into the kitchen as Angie hung up from her last call. Milo was standing beside her.

"She's not at any of her friends' houses."

"Then call the police. Tell them she's been grabbed. And tell them to come see me at the house."

"You don't think the police have released that man who broke in last—"

"He died," Michael said flatly.

Angie's face turned sour. She stared at him with a strange mixture of confusion and disbelief on her features.

Michael left her that way.

He ran toward home.

He'd crossed two lawns when he saw the solitary woman standing on the sidewalk.

"You!"

The redhead—Helen Locklear. She smiled at him.

He ran to her, reached to grab her, almost fell on his face. His hands had floated straight through the apparition. He stumbled back around to face the form. The woman looked solid enough. He grabbed at her again, came up with night air.

"Your daughter is safe," the apparition said.

"Where?"

"On her way to London."

"Why, for Christ's sake? Why grab my little girl?"

"Your father wants to make sure you arrive in London tomorrow night. He sensed that you wouldn't make it without a little encouragement."

"Who—"

But the bitch was gone.

Blink.

Out like a light.

He must look like a fool, standing there talking to a light pole. He scanned the neighborhood. No one was in sight.

He ran for his house.

It took the police nearly ten minutes to arrive at the house. Two uniformed officers arrived in a squad car. Their names were Linholm and Burns. Linholm was short and burly, built like a blond bowling ball. Burns was as black as coffee and looked as if he should be a pro basketball player.

Michael met them in his driveway, in the wash of the front yard's floodlights. Angie joined them within a minute of the squad car's arrival. She was very worried, as upset as Michael ever remembered seeing her. But there were no tears. They weren't her style. Not in front of others.

He tried to comfort her, but she pulled away from him.

"Leave me alone."

Michael left her alone.

He gave the police all the information he could, but he was feeling the futility of the situation. He told the police about the incident the night before and suggested that the dead man might have had an accomplice. He gave them the description of the redheaded woman he'd spent an hour with that afternoon, on the outside chance that they would find her. He scrupulously avoided any reference to the telepathic commands, the hallucinations, and the ghostly figure he'd seen on the sidewalk ten minutes earlier.

He knew what it took to get locked up, and he wasn't about to cross that line.

The police were not going to do him any good. He knew that for a certainty, and he silently wished for them to be gone as soon as possible. As crazy as the idea sounded to him, he knew he was going to catch that flight to London in the morning. He'd seen enough to convince himself that he was dealing with something far beyond ordinary.

Either that, or he was slipping into psychosis.

And he'd seen enough psychosis to realize that people didn't usually know what they were getting into when, in fact, that was *exactly* what they were getting into. Psychotic or not, he knew he'd be on that plane in the morning.

While Linholm returned to the squad car to radio Jenny's description to his dispatcher, Burns followed Michael into the house. Burns had to stoop to keep from hitting his head on the top of the doorjamb. Milo had finally arrived. He and Angie brought up the rear.

Angie stumbled onto Carol Lewis in the living room while Burns gave the house a quick once-over. Michael introduced the two women and Milo, then followed Burns on his appointed rounds.

Ten minutes later, Michael and Angie waved good-bye to the police from the front steps.

As the squad car backed out of the drive, Angie said, "It sure didn't take you long to adjust to my leaving."

Michael glanced at her blankly.

She was holding back tears. A trick she'd often used to control her real emotions was to get mad. She was acting mad now.

She tilted her head toward the interior of the house. "She's nice-looking. Are the blind easier to hustle?"

Michael rolled his eyes, stepped past his wife into the house.

She followed him.

"Get Milo and go home," he said, pausing in the foyer.

"You don't seem very upset about Jenny," Angie accused.

"I *am* upset. What do you want me to do, scream and wail and flail myself with hot wires?"

She paused, shook her head, then averted her face. A few of those well-controlled tears stole into her eyes.

Michael pulled her close. She formed herself to his body, let him hold her while she sobbed silently against his chest. It felt like old times, only sadder.

When she'd cried herself through the first bout of tears, Angie pushed herself away from him. "What do you think's happened to her?" She wiped at her nose with a tissue.

Michael shrugged. "Are you going to be okay?"

Angie nodded stiffly. Her shield was back up. She took a

deep, fortifying breath. "I'll be okay." She blew her nose. "Call me if you hear anything."

Michael nodded.

Angie went to the living room and retrieved her potbellied paramour.

Michael watched them walk across the lawns until they were out of sight. The sense of sadness and regret was so deep within his breast that he couldn't have spoken to save his life. He closed and locked the front door and returned to the living room. He sat across the room from Carol Lewis.

A long silence filled the nothingness.

"I'm sorry."

Her voice brought Michael out of his stupor.

"There's nothing you could do," he said. "You've tried your best to warn me since we first met."

Nothingness filled the silence.

Michael began to cry.

He was frightened for Jenny, angry with the forces at work around him, furious at the redhead who was playing such godawful fucking games with his mind. Worst of all was the helplessness.

All his life he'd fought to be in control, to be in charge of his life, to know who he was, where he was going, why he was going there, and how he was going to get there. And here he was, cut off from all that was ordinary, cut off from the base he'd spent so much energy building. His daughter was gone—kidnapped. His marriage was *kaput!* His wife was down the block in the arms of some sluggish physician who had the personality of a trained orangutan. He'd shot a man, who'd died soon after. Whether the bastard deserved to be dead or not wasn't the point. *He*—Michael Dragon—had pulled the trigger that had injured another human being. All his life he'd done his damndest to help put maimed and destroyed people back together, and here he was, a killer—in his own mind, at least.

A killer who gave every indication that he was losing his gourd.

Seeing snakes.

Apparitions in the night.

Talking to light poles.

Jesus.

He wiped at his damp face.

He heard the couch shift, and looked up as Carol Lewis crossed to his side. She sat down next to him on the love seat. Without talking, she felt for his hand. He let her hold it. Out of the corner of his eyes he noticed the moisture in her eyes. He reached out and wrapped his arms around her.

She let him hold her close, hugged him even tighter, and for a long time neither of them let go.

She felt good to hold.

And it felt good to be held.

Michael gave himself over to the comforting sensations that, for a little while, overrode the cyclone of anguish, fear, and rage that was threatening to tear him apart.

11

Lea Frazzetti escaped the huge customs shed at Heathrow and wound her way toward the reception area. A dutiful skycap followed, limping on a left leg that appeared to have been deformed by polio, rolling her baggage along on a four-wheeled cart. One of the wheels was off-true, and it *squeak-squeak-squeaked* unmercifully. It grated on her nerves. Crowds of people waited behind a metal gate, necks craning for their first glimpses of long-unseen friends and relatives, or for family returning from business abroad.

Beyond the smiling faces and jostling bodies, Lea could make out the first of the automobile rental desks off to the right. The atmosphere was gay, happy, expectant.

Yet the setting left something to be desired.

Lea regretted the demise of the great European train sta-

tions and transatlantic docks, with their elegant and sometimes overdone architecture, their chandeliers and restau-
rants and bustle of servants. She'd never lived in their era,
she'd only read about them, but they suited her tempera-
ment and style better than this stockyard of industrial transportation. She felt a little like a heifer being moved from
one pen to the next at the whim of some unseen, capricious
civil servant. The place smelled like a warehouse.

Lea's eyes scanned the crowd, searching for
Helen Locklear's rich, long red hair and for the tall,
gray-haired man she'd seen for such a brief instant in her
foyer.

It was Helen's controlled hand wave that caught Lea's
attention. Helen pointed to a spot just beyond the throng of
waiting people, then disappeared into the crush.

Lea turned to her rented servant with his *screeching* cart
and said, "This way."

Dutifully, the thin skycap limped after her to the accom-
paniment of his *squeak-squeak-squeaking* cart. They separated from the main crowd in a matter of yards. Here there
was room to move without fighting elbows, carry-on luggage, and big feet.

"Welcome to London," Helen Locklear said. "I hope you
had a good flight."

"I did. And short, thank God. I love the Concorde. How
was yours?"

Helen Locklear's expression hinted at relief. "Unevent-
ful," was all she said.

Helen handed the limping skycap a rolled bill. "Wait a
moment." She then signaled to two men in smart, dark
blue uniforms and caps who had been standing at a respect-
ful distance. The two men strode quickly forward. "Take
Miss Frazzetti's luggage to the car."

"Yes, ma'am."

The two burly men loaded themselves with her luggage
and moved toward a nearby door. Lea and Helen Locklear
followed.

"I thought *my father* would be here to greet me," Lea
said.

She caught the thin expression of concern that crossed Helen Locklear's features before it faded quickly.

"It is no longer safe for him to be out and about in London," she said. "Especially not in the company of his children."

Lea had been given some sense of the danger Helen Locklear was referring to. Lea knew that she would be meeting two half brothers and that they would be her most immediate danger. But beyond the peril presented by them, she knew absolutely nothing of the larger danger.

"What, exactly, is the danger?"

The two women followed the uniformed men out into the cool, midafternoon sunshine. Twin Rolls-Royce Silver shadows stood at the crub. They were old, impressive, immaculately kept automobiles from a different era. They gleamed in the sunshine and reminded Lea of Jay Gatsby and Daisy and the decadence of days long lost. They suited Lea's taste just fine.

The men loaded Lea's bags into the trunk of the rear Rolls. The trunk lid slammed closed with a substantial *whumpf,* and the two men aligned themselves beside the rear fender, awaiting their next instructions.

"Just as we'd planned," Helen Locklear said then, with a brief wave of her hand.

Twin "Yes, ma'am's" followed immediately. The men split. One climbed into the driver's right-side door of the rear Rolls, while the other opened a rear door of the Rolls in front.

"After you," Helen Locklear said.

Lea slipped into the sumptuous rear seat. The soft, supple upholstery was of the finest grade Scandinavian leather. Opulent walnut inlay decorated the doors, while thick gray carpet blanketed the floor. It was like slipping into a rolling den.

"Would you like some lunch?" Helen Locklear asked.

"Yes, a bite would be nice. I didn't eat on the plane."

"We'd like to go to Tiddy Dol's, Lawrence," Helen Locklear said as the driver climbed into the right front seat.

"Right away, ma'am."

The big car purred to life and majestically floated into

the airport traffic, more like a small ship than an automobile.

"You asked about the danger," Helen Locklear said, settling back into the soft cushions for the half-hour ride into the city. She arranged her shoulders, crossed her legs, gazed absently out the window.

Lea waited.

"Aaron will explain everything later this evening, around ten o'clock. The others will be here by then."

It was the first time Lea had heard her mysterious *father*'s name.

"Aaron," she said, tasting the word. "What's his last name?"

"Caine."

Lea had never heard the name before, which surprised her. A man as rich as this Caine appeared to be—she should have run across his name or face somewhere before.

"I've never heard that name before," she said.

"No, I don't s'pose you have. He's quite a private man." Helen Locklear smiled. "He has to be."

"Because of the danger you mentioned?"

"Yes."

Lea saw a slight frown thicken the other woman's brow.

"And you don't want to tell me about that yet?"

"It's not that—it's that I would be unable to communicate it fully to you. I'm really only Aaron's familiar—do you know what I mean by that?"

"I think I do."

"My abilities are very, shall we say, *mundane* compared to his. I act as a conduit for his powers at times, but that's all. I am his friend and companion. I take care of the details of his life."

"I understand. And you'd rather let him explain the situation."

"Yes." The redhead was silent for a moment. "Although I will say that the danger is quite real, as I'm sure you will learn if you survive the next few days."

Lea felt her pulse slow. She glanced at Helen Locklear in an attempt to decipher the last comment more fully. The other woman was giving away nothing by her expression.

"What is Aaron Caine?" Lea asked.

That smile Lea had come to know so well formed on Helen Locklear's face. "Why, haven't I told you?"

"No."

"He's a sorcerer."

Lea stared thoughtfully at the other woman, her mind turning thoughts over slowly, trying to make sense of everything.

"And, I take it, he's not the only one around."

Helen Locklear's smile died.

"*That* has become a problem."

Drew Garrett watched the London streets roll past the window of the Rolls. Every once in a while, when they passed a dark building or drove through a tree-shaded park, the window darkened, and he caught a reflection of the tall redhead seated on the far side of the gray leather seat.

It had been an odd sensation to meet this woman in the flesh. She was the same woman he'd encountered in his dream. The same smooth skin; same long, lush hair; same gestures and carriage; same soft, inviting English voice. She was *the same woman*, and that was what amazed him.

And bothered him.

Truthfully, it frightened him.

The sheer, unimaginable power this woman and this *Aaron Caine* must have—it boggled his mind. To be able to play with someone's dreams, to be able to create a living, breathing girl whom you could touch and who could touch you, who was capable of taking a dressmaker's shears and whacking off your wang—Jesus!

He wasn't sure what he was getting into, or if he wanted to continue with this apparently very real, very serious game.

He had a good life.

He lived as he pleased.

In his own realm, he was a king, and he lived like one. So why was he here, allowing himself to be drawn into the web of a spider he as yet was unable to comprehend?

Something about the whole thing made his flesh crawl beneath his skin.

Premonition?

Or nerves?

Or lack of confidence in his own ability to play the cards dealt by this dealer, this—he laughed abruptly, softly—this *joker*?

To hell with the worry, he told himself. Forget it. You've walked away from a past that would have swamped 99 percent of the human race, and you're still going. Screw the self-doubts. You're well past that stage.

But he knew he wasn't.

That was the thing that nagged at his mind, nipped at his heels every step of his career.

Self-doubts. Lack of confidence. Fear of failure. And, as his shrink had pointed out, fear of success. He didn't think he was worth the clothes on his back, and all his posturing and partying and throwing money around did was reinforce that shit picture of himself. Even with the phenomenal success of his records, the mad, screaming reception given to the Hard Rock Experience, he still felt less deserving, less intelligent, less attractive, less *everything* than half the people he met.

He owed it all to his mother.

The crazy bitch.

She hadn't always been that way. She'd been beautiful once, a talented pianist. He'd seen pictures of her, read yellowed newspaper articles about the beauty of her music, about her exquisite interpretations of the classics.

But it didn't last.

Two failed marriages by the time she was twenty-seven.

A succession of men and booze bottles.

Somewhere along the way, her mind snapped.

He hadn't even gone to her funeral.

She'd been dead five months before he heard about it. He'd been living in a foster home at the time. He'd run away, one of a dozen or so such attempts at escaping his past. But it hadn't done him any good. The army of social workers out there had tracked him down, hauled his ass off to a residential treatment center, and locked him up for three months. He was fifteen at the time. He ran again, stealing a car to get out of the state, stealing gas on his way to California. This time the cops nabbed his behind and the social workers shoved him into a training school—a nice name for a reform school, a kiddie prison.

That was where he'd learned to play the guitar.

He'd seen enough fucked-up kids in that place to realize that they were all birds of a feather, all condemned, all headed to hell in a handbasket on the fastest rocket available. Each one had become a mirror, pointing their fingers and failures back at him and saying, *"you—you—you, too!"*

He'd rejected them, barricaded himself behind a wall of moody silence and behind the closed door of his room. He poured his anger into the strings of a cracked, worn, scarred-up, old, out-of-tune guitar. If he'd inherited one positive trait from his mother, it was her musical ability. And the guitar had been invented for him. He picked it up fast. His roommate was a wimp who'd been arrested once too often for stealing women's panties off clotheslines. He was no problem. He kept his mouth shut when Drew told him to, straightened up the room when Drew wanted it straightened, and performed the duties of an all-around, obedient housemaid. The fact that he was the "girlfriend" of one of the training school guards didn't faze Drew in the least.

He'd seen everything.

And there wasn't anything that was going to beat him again.

Strange thoughts, he realized.

Was all that part of why he was here?

One more way of proving that he wasn't his mother's son?

"We're almost there," the woman's voice said, pulling Drew out of his inner sanctum.

The heavy car slowed.

Drew peered out the windows at rows of high Georgian houses, some with ornate ironwork decorating the balconies and windows, others with intricate scrollwork around the windows and eaves. Here and there, tall trees managed to survive. They lent the neighborhood a distinct grandeur.

"Where are we?"

"Mayfair," Helen Locklear said. "Near Grosvenor Square. The American embassy is near here."

"Impressive."

She said nothing.

The Rolls approached an ancient stone wall that stretched around a single, huge Georgian mansion set in the middle of the city block. The story and a half-high wall cut off the view of the bottom two stories of the building, but there were still three stories in clear view. Ornate iron-work decorated the windows, while providing, no doubt, very effective burglarproofing. Not that it was likely any burglar would ever reach the house. Pointed iron spikes set into a rounded cylinder lined the top of the fence. The place resembled a minicastle, set in the middle of one of the most peaceful neighborhoods in London.

Two gigantic iron gates swung silently inward. The Rolls edged its way past the gates and followed a narrow brick drive across the small, green courtyard to a covered entrance at the side of the tall house. From here it appeared that the fence surrounded the house like the walls of a fort, while a sixty- to seventy-five-foot strip of garden and lawn separated the walls from the house itself. The roofs of other tall houses could be seen beyond the high fence.

"I take it Mr. Caine likes his privacy," Drew said as the chauffeur opened his door.

"You would, too, in his position," Helen Locklear said.

Drew strode to the rear of the Rolls and looked up at the front of the house. It was in perfect repair. Leaded lattice windows peeked out of what must have been at least twelve to fifteen rooms on this side alone. Massive trees, resembling sycamores, towered above the perfectly mani-cured front lawn. A set of chromium boccie balls lay on a neatly trimmed grass court. Nearby stood a small gazebo and several groupings of white, cast-iron lawn furniture. At the far corner of the house Drew noticed the striped post and twin wire hoops of a croquet court. Colorful flower beds lined the high stone wall and circled the bases of the huge trees.

"Very nice," he said.

"There's a small rose garden at the rear of the house,"

Helen Locklear said. "It's a nice place for sorting out one's thoughts."

Drew thought she gave him a rather pointed glance, but he ignored it. He knew she could read his mind to some extent. He'd asked that of her before he climbed into the Rolls at the airport. She hadn't lied. She could read his mind and, with help, insinuate herself into his dreams. He honestly didn't care, didn't even care if she'd been following his thoughts on the way into London from Heathrow. He was here because he had something Caine wanted, something stronger than this redhead possessed, and because, he'd been told, he was Caine's son. And he was here because of the sheer power that had fueled the illusion and dream he'd experienced, and because of the promise that he might be able to develop that same power.

"I might find a use for it later," Drew said.

Helen Locklear started toward the door off the carport. "This way," she said.

He followed. "When do I meet Caine?"

"Later," the woman said.

"And the competition?"

"You'll meet them all at the same time." She paused at the top of the low stoop, faced him, looking down on him from that angle. He didn't like the sensation. That playful smile of hers displayed the whiteness of her teeth between her red lips. In a way, Drew decided, it was more of a leer, and he wasn't sure he liked the woman. "You sound eager to do battle."

She had told him that he should be prepared for anything, that as long as his half siblings lived he was in danger.

So be it.

He'd made his choice.

He was here.

And once he committed himself to something, he went all out for it. That was why he was where he was in life.

"I'm eager for anything, honey. Haven't you read the fanzines?"

"The what?"

"The fan magazines. They'll tell you what I'm made of."

It was all bravado and sword-rattling. But it helped. And for a little while, at least, his memories didn't bother him.

12

The plane eased into a steeper glide path, seemed to hit heavier air. It slowed.

Michael glanced out the nearby window. There was still a vast stretch of ocean far below, but the shoreline of Ireland was just breaking into view. London was less than half an hour away.

Michael eyed the sleeping woman next to him and considered not waking her. She was really quite beautiful, refined—even in sleep. The only detraction sleep brought to her was that it hid those startling emerald eyes.

He still couldn't believe he'd gone along with her insistence that she accompany him to England.

Still, he had assented.

And he wasn't displeased with the thought, although he was still somewhat hesitant about getting her involved in his mess.

He gently nudged her shoulder.

Carol Lewis roused, turned his way, then reached out and touched his arm.

"Are we"—she broke off to cover a yawn—"are we almost there?"

"We'll be landing in about twenty minutes," he said. "Ireland's just coming into view."

"I've heard it's a beautiful country."

"Green," he said, aware that he was staring at her eyes. *Christ!* It was inconceivable that she couldn't see out of those strikingly perfect eyes. She'd lost her sight at age seven, falling off a bicycle, she'd told him. Three operations, two of which were experimental, had failed to bring it back. She was resigned to darkness. The accident had also marked the onset of her psychic experiences, and she expressed mixed emotions about the switch in abilities. He wanted to talk with her about how she'd adjusted to the change but felt hesitant to pry into her life.

Maybe, if he got to know her better...

Instead he said, "I want to try this one more time. I—"

"No." She said it firmly while she reached into her purse to draw out a wide-toothed comb. She started to fluff her hair with it.

"I have no idea what's in store for me over here," Michael went on, missing barely a beat. He dropped his voice to a near whisper. "These people have kidnapped my daughter. Who in hell knows what they might be capable of?"

"We know what they're capable of," she said, whispering also. "Kidnapping, at least. Not to mention *attempted murder*—even the real thing, if your friend Ms. Locklear is to be believed." She smiled, turned her face his way. "How do I look?"

Michael chuckled. "You look great."

"Are you talking about my hair?"

"I was talking about you, actually," Michael said, somewhat surprised that he'd said that.

"Thank you. But what about my hair?"

"It looks fine." He reached out and flipped an errant curl into place. "Perfect."

"Thank you." She returned her comb to her purse. "I can't wait to take a shower."

"Listen," Michael said, returning to his main point. "So we know they're capable of almost anything. There's no reason for you to put yourself in danger over—"

"No, Michael. No. N-O."

He stared at her.

It was too damn bad she couldn't read his expression, he thought. The majority of human communication occurred visually, and she had this beautiful defense of blindness.

She couldn't see his anger, so he had to try to communicate it verbally. Somehow he felt as if she had him at a disadvantage.

"At least listen to me."

"I already have. We've been through all your arguments three times already on this flight. If you absolutely insist, I'll stay somewhere else. But I'm staying in London as long as you do."

He shook his head, defeated. "Why?" he asked in futility.

Carol's face softened. She pursed her lips. She glanced away from him. "Because . . . because I care," she said softly. "I care what happens to you."

Michael felt the emotion behind her words, was aware that she was taking a chance by saying that. There was a strong woman under that beautiful exterior, he realized, but also a woman who wasn't used to sharing her own deep emotions with others. She hadn't used that argument in her earlier attempts to sway him. Then she'd been all rational, arguing that she might be able to help him because of her sixth sense, because she could sometimes read the immediate future.

He reached out and took her hand.

She kept her face averted.

He raised her hand to his lips and kissed it, once.

She turned her head his way. A single tear glistened in the corner of one eye.

"I'll shut up," Michael said.

She smiled weakly. "Thank you."

"You're welcome to come along."

She dabbed at her eyes with a tissue. "I knew you couldn't withstand the tears."

He studied her face.

She elbowed him in the ribs. "That was a joke, son."

He laughed softly. "I don't know you well enough yet to know when you're joking or being serious."

She didn't reply, simply found his hand again and gave it a squeeze.

"I think it might be fun to get to know you better."

"It could be a pain in the keester, too," she said. "Don't forget: I have a bit of a handicap."

Michael tried to judge the meaning in her words. He wasn't sure if there was anything more than a simple small caution.

"I think I can deal with that."

He felt her squeeze his hand again, but this time she felt the need to avert her face, to hide her expression from him.

It was then that Michael realized he could fall in love with this woman. She cared more than she was letting on to him, but she wasn't going to be the one to push it. If he wanted a relationship with this blind woman, he was going to have to be the one to push it.

A smile touched his features.

Then a frown.

He thought of Angie, and of Milo, and of how quickly life changed the cards in your hand.

What could he do but play the cards it dealt him?

It wasn't a pleasant greeting at the airport. Michael was not in the mood for Helen Locklear's easy friendliness toward him, nor for her coolness toward Carol. His first abrupt question concerned Jenny.

"I assure you that she's all right," the tall redhead said. "By way of proof..." She held out an envelope.

Michael took it, recognized Jenny's childish scrawl on the front.

Daddy

He ripped it open.

The front of the card showed a picture of Dracula with his gleaming white teeth about to munch down onto the creamy white neck of a beautiful peasant girl. Inside, the card said, *Having a good time. Nobody's bitten me yet.* The *yet* was underlined.

It was Jenny's signature, all right. Along with the words *Really, Dad, I'm okay, and nobody's done anything bad to me*.

"I want to see her."

"You will."

"Now."

Helen Locklear smiled. "We rather expected you to respond that way. We can meet her for dinner, if you'd like."

"I'd like. Where?"

"You've been to London before, I believe. Where would you like to meet her?"

Michael considered. "Where does Mr. Caine live?"

"In Mayfair."

"Then let's make it Harrods. It's not that far from Mayfair, if I remember right."

"Harrods it is. Let me make a phone call." Before the redhead moved off to a telephone, she directed two uniformed men to take the luggage.

Carol had stood silently beside Michael during the brief conversation. Now she spoke. "I don't think Ms. Locklear wants me around."

"I didn't want you around either," Michael said, patting her hand on his arm.

"I think her objections are a bit more sinister," Carol said.

"Second thoughts?"

She shook her head. "No. If I have any, I'll tell you."

They waited in the lobby for less than five minutes.

Helen Locklear came striding back. She beamed. "All arranged. We meet in three quarters of an hour." She barely broke stride as she held an arm out, ushering them toward the nearby exit doors. "This way," she said. "The car is waiting."

Michael followed the woman.

She was tall and regal-looking and, in her high heels, walked with the rolling smoothness of a fashion model. Her hips moved with a gentle, snappy sway.

For an instant Michael wondered what Carol looked like from behind as she walked. He couldn't recall having had more than a passing chance to watch her walk.

"Harrods, ma'am."

The voice of the chauffeur pulled Michael back to reality. He'd been watching the city float past beyond the windows of the majestic Rolls-Royce while softly describing landmarks and sights to Carol as they rode past.

The heavy car slowed to a stop.

Michael stepped out and helped Carol join him on the sidewalk beside Helen Locklear.

Harrods towered above them. Evening was approaching fast, and the seven-story, seven-acre emporium of capitalist wonders was aglow with lights. Strings of white bulbs outlined the building's main and top floors and formed columns of light in between. The dome atop the building, also outlined in lights, resembled a fairy-tale castle, something you'd see in Disneyland rather in downtown London. A row of cloudlike awnings above the walkway sheltered the passersby and provided an elegant view of the riches beyond the windows.

"What does it look like?" Carol asked.

"Magnificent," Michael said. "I'll tell you about it later. But rumor has it that there isn't anything under the sun you can't buy here, or can't arrange to buy through one of their departments."

Harrods was a mecca of money, worldwide. Throngs of people passed by, dressed in half a dozen national styles and speaking twice as many languages.

"It sounds like a fair."

"It is. Believe me. Maybe even more of a circus."

Helen Locklear interrupted them. She gestured toward a nearby doorway. "This way. Your daughter is waiting."

Michael followed the woman into the building. Carol's hand rested lightly on his arm. She moved through the crowded main floor as if directed by radar. Never once did she bump into one of the shoppers.

They caught the elevator and emerged on the top shopping floor. The dining room was huge. Chandeliers dangling from the soaring heights of the ceiling lighted the vast room.

"Daddy!"

Michael whirled in time to catch Jenny as she leaped into his arms. They hugged for a long moment. Beyond them stood two large men wearing the same uniform the chauffeur had worn, and a woman dressed as a nanny. They were here with Jenny, but Michael also sensed that they had come along to watch him. He was acutely aware of their unflinching attention. Michael tried to ignore them. He snuggled his face into Jenny's hair and smelled that wonderful freshness that she seemed to carry with her wherever she went. He kissed her on the cheek and knelt down beside her.

"You're okay?" he asked, holding her out at arm's length and giving her a quick once-over.

"I'm fine, Daddy. Really."

"Nobody's hurt you?"

She shook her head no, growing serious for the first time. "They said you wanted me to go with them. They were at our house." She cocked her head sideways, eyeing him quizzically. "You act worried. What's the matter, Dad?"

Michael felt a hand on his shoulder. Glancing up, he noticed that it belonged to Helen Locklear, not Carol, as he'd expected.

"Our table's over here," Helen Locklear said.

Michael rose, holding his daughter's hand.

"Dad?"

"Nothing's wrong Jenny. I'm just glad to see you." He drew Carol toward him and took her hand. "You remember Miss Lewis, don't you, pumpkin."

Jenny nodded. "Yup. Hi! You were at our house the other day." Jenny turned her attention back toward Michael. "Is Mom coming, too?"

Michael shook his head. "No. Mom's not."

Jenny scrunched her features and looked from Carol back to Michael. In nearly a whisper, she asked, "Is she your girlfriend, Dad?"

Michael laughed softly. He glanced back at Carol's softly smiling face, then back to his daughter. "She might be," he said.

"That's okay by me," Jenny said. "She's a lot nicer than that Milo guy Mom's living with. He's a nerd. I mean, he's nice and all, but he's . . . you know . . . he's too sweetsie. If you and Mom don't get back together, I hope she finds someone better than him."

"I do, too, honey. I do, too."

Michael turned his daughter and led the three of them

through the dining room to a corner table, where Helen
Locklear was waiting. The two uniformed men and the
nanny stood at a discreet distance. Michael helped Carol
and Jenny into their chairs.

"I'm hungry," Jenny said.

For a little while it seemed almost like old times.

"It's time to go," Helen Locklear said.

Michael had been expecting the meal to end for the past
ten minutes. They'd nursed coffee and sweets longer than
he'd thought they would. He'd been contemplating how to
handle it when it came.

"We're not leaving," he said.

He felt Carol tense beside him.

"I'm afraid we are," Helen Locklear said. She made a
gesture with one hand.

Out of the corner of his eye, Michael saw the two uniformed men and the nanny moving toward the table. He
pushed his chair away and came to his feet.

"I wouldn't make a scene, Mr. Dragon," Helen Locklear
said. "It won't do you any good. Not yet. You don't know
what you're up against."

"I'm not letting you take my daughter again."

"You have no choice. Not now."

Michael reached for Jenny's hand.

He stopped suddenly. Frozen. His mind reeled. Before
his eyes, he watched Jenny dissolve, turn to mist. He tried
to grab for her. His hands didn't move. He felt mired in
molasses. He knew it was another of the mind games this
woman was capable of playing. He had to stop it, had to
find some way of overcoming this strange power she had
over him, over . . .

He concentrated—hard.

She'd said he had more powers than he knew of, that he
could learn to create images the way she did, that his abilities were stronger than hers, that all he had to do was learn
how to tap them.

Well, dammit, now was the time to start!

He forced his mind to bear down on the power gripping

him. He felt hot, as if his body were in the grip of a fever. He pressed his mind outward against the power holding him, closed his eyes, and tried his damndest to find a means of combating the unseen control, and, surprisingly, he felt a strange shift take place somewhere directly behind his eyes, straight back from the bridge of his nose.

The powers gripping him in molasses broke.

He grabbed for his daughter.

But she was gone.

Michael spun around.

Jenny was disappearing through the main salon doors under the protection of the two uniformed men and the nanny.

He started after her.

The floor turned to rubber, the room to elastic.

He tried to cry out.

His words were little more than a whisper.

He reached around for balance.

His fingers encountered a fabric-backed chair. He held on as the room heaved, as his vision swam.

All an hallucination!

Stop it!

He concentrated, pressed his mind against the numbing force that made him feel so helpless, felt that odd *click* occur in the depths of his mind.

Bingo!

The dining room returned with the clarity it had held during the meal.

Michael felt a hand on his arm.

He was about to pull away when he realized it was Carol.

Her voice was anguished.

"She's gone, Mike. Gone. Let her go. They're not going to let you take her from them until they want you to have her, if . . ."

She didn't have to finish her thought. . . . *if they want you to have her*.

He felt a strained tenseness drain from his muscles. He glanced around. The dining room was nearly empty. It was nearing closing time. No one in the room appeared to have noticed his private agony—no one except for Carol and Helen Locklear.

The tall redhead joined them.

"For a man who didn't know he had the power until a day ago, you do quite well, Mr. Dragon. Quite well, indeed. If you'll only let yourself believe in your abilities, you might surprise yourself."

Michael straightened, stared hotly at the woman.

He *believed,* all right.

He didn't know how much he believed, or how far he thought his abilities could be developed, but dammit, yes, now he believed. And he was going to do everything in his power to learn how to get the hell out from under the control that was being thrust upon him against his will. He didn't like feeling helpless, feeling that he was simply a pawn to be shoved about at someone else's whim.

He didn't like it at all.

And he especially didn't like the fact that his daughter had been made a pawn in this game.

That was where this woman and Mr. Caine had made a mistake.

They'd overstepped their boundaries.

And before this was over, they'd know it.

If I have anything to say about it, Michael thought. *If . . .*

"Shall we go," Helen Locklear suggested, arm extended. "I believe you have some other people to meet."

13

The house was impressive even in darkness.

Michael stepped from the Rolls beneath the covered portico. He watched the massive iron gates swing closed with a dull *clung* at the front of the house, effectively sealing the grounds off from the surrounding city. It was like entering a walled kingdom, set off by itself in a corner of the world. From beyond the high stone walls, the sounds of the city were muted. Overhead, the sky glowed with the reflected lights of the metropolis that surrounded them.

It was a quiet evening.

Michael offered Carol a hand. Her shoes crunched a stray bit of stone on the brick driveway.

Michael led her through the open doorway at the top of a low flight of stairs. A doorman stood silently to the side as they passed. He, like the other servants Michael had seen so far, was uniformed and silent.

The entry foyer was grand. A sweep of dark mahogany staircase with blaze-white stairs wound three fourths of the way around the large, three-story-high room and disappeared into a hallway barely visible from this angle. Parquet marble flooring gleamed beneath the sparkling crystal chandelier that provided the main lighting. The ceiling was beamed, with ornate paintings done directly on the ceiling in the spaces between the beams. Small wall lamps and table lamps were spaced perfectly around the dark-paneled walls, providing puddles of amber light here and there to brighten the dark corners.

Helen Locklear paused at the base of the stairs. A maid,

uniformed in black and white, stood nearby, on the first
step of the wide staircase.

"Ellen will show you to your rooms," she said. "Your
things are already up there." She smiled then, and added,
"Mr. Caine would like to meet at precisely ten o'clock. If
you'll be ready at quarter of the hour, Mr. Dragon, someone will come for you."

"What about Carol?"

"I'm afraid she's not invited. But I assure you, she'll be
safe. We've given you adjoining rooms. She'll be there
when you return."

Michael studied the woman's face, unwilling to take
anything she told him at face value. But, for now, he didn't
see that he had much choice. He had to accept what he
said, had to accept her conditions.

The broad staircase, enclosed by a heavy mahogany
banister, swept them onto the second floor. A long hallway
stretched to a latticed window at the far end. Half a dozen
rooms opened off each side of the hallway. Ornately carved
and heavily oiled beams decorated the ceiling and ran
down the walls in several places. Michael guessed that they
were more than ornamental, that they were part of the original house and designed to provide additional support for
the floors above ground level.

The maid moved silently along the carpeted hall and
opened a heavy wooden door. She stood aside as Michael
and Carol entered.

"This is the gentleman's room," the maid said softly.
She crossed the large, airy room. "And my lady's room
is through this doorway. Each room has its own bath." A
fire crackled pleasantly in the fireplace about ten feet
from the adjoining door. Twin, life-size statues carved in
swirling chocolate and vanilla marble supported a huge
and ornate mantel above the fireplace. The maid paused
in the middle of the room. A high, canopy bed of rich
cherry wood stood behind her, its four posts soaring
fourteen feet into the air. The finely embroidered spread
covering the high mattress matched the canopy billowing
overhead. "If you need anything, simply pull on the rope

beside the bed. Someone will attend you in a minute or two, at most. Is there anything I can get you now?"

Michael shook his head no.

Carol said, "No."

Smiling, the maid strode to the hallway door. "I hope you enjoy your stay." With that, she departed, closing the huge mahogany door behind her.

"What's the room like?" Carol asked. "It feels huge. The way the maid's voice was absorbed, it must be very high."

"It is," Michael said. He described it for her as he walked toward two carved cherry wardrobes. Persian carpets created small islands within the room, one around the bed, another near the fireplace, where two plush couches faced each other across a carved coffee table. A tray of crystal glasses and three decanters sparkled in the reflected light from the fireplace. Another Persian created a separate dressing area near what proved to be the bathroom. Still another Persian set off a small reading area near one of the room's two high leaded-glass windows. A small writing desk sat against the sidewall near the window, while two wing-backed leather chairs flanked a small end table in front of the window.

Michael opened the nearest wardrobe. His clothes had been neatly hung on the right side, or folded and set into drawers on the left side. The interior of the high chest smelled like cedar, or some other aromatic wood.

The other wardrobe contained extra robes, sweaters, slippers, raincoats, umbrellas, and new, unused personal bath items.

"They've certainly thought of everything," Carol said.

"I'm afraid it looks as if they're expecting this to be a long stay," Michael said.

He peeked his head in the bathroom and let out a whistle.

"What is it?"

"The bathroom—marble sink and tub. Marble floor and walls. Halfway up, the walls are papered in an old-ish Cotswold print with soft pastel colors. The spigots in the sink and bathtub are brass—I don't think it's gold

—no, it's not. Just brass. They look like spitting dragons."

"Show me."

Not quite understanding, Michael stepped aside.

Carol eased her way past him.

Catching her intention, he guided her to the sink, first, then the tub, where she explored the dragon spigots with her fingers. She ran her hands over the wall, along the gentle arch of the tub.

Even the commode looked to be made from a single piece of marble.

"Incredible place," Michael said.

"Let's go see my room," Carol urged.

He led her across the large bedroom toward the adjoining doorway.

Carol paused near the sofas in front of the fireplace.

"I love the smell of the fireplace," she said.

"After we see your room, we can come sit in front of it."

"I'd like that."

Michael lifted the top off each of the three decanters. "We can have a drink, too. My guess is we've got red wine, a cream sherry, and some brandy." He sniffed the last decanter a second time. "Correction: I think the brandy is a cognac."

"What about my room?"

Michael felt an odd hesitancy to show her the second room, but he shrugged it off.

Her room turned out to be much the same, although the furnishings were more feminine in taste, and the colors lighter.

Returning to his room, Michael guided Carol to one of the couches in front of the fire.

"What would you like to drink?"

"I'll try the sherry."

He poured two glasses, handed her one, and replaced the decanter on the tray. The crystal *clinked* softly. He joined her on the sofa.

She hadn't touched her wine yet. She held it up to him, her green eyes twinkling in the firelight. They were focused nearly perfectly on his face. "Here's to you, Michael Dragon. You're in it now."

Michael clinked glasses with her, tasted the rich sweetness of the cream sherry. It was very good. Smooth. It warmed him on its way to his stomach.

"I wish I knew what *it* was," he said.

"You'll find out soon enough. What time is it?"

He glanced at his watch. "Ten after nine."

"In fifty minutes you should hear some answers," Carol said. "I'll be interested in hearing what you learn."

"What makes you think I'll tell you?" Michael teased.

"What makes you think I'll sleep with you?"

Michael was silent.

He'd been wondering about that.

At precisely 9:45 P.M., a knock sounded at the door.

Michael answered it.

Helen Locklear greeted him pleasantly. She pointed toward the balcony at the head of the main staircase. "We'll be meeting there in a minute or two, Mr. Dragon."

She moved off down the hallway.

As Michael closed the door, he heard her rap on another door nearby.

Michael crossed the room. Carol had come to her feet. She had her arms crossed in front of her. Michael took her by the arms, just above her elbows. "Will you be okay?"

She nodded, reached out to touch him with one hand.

The move was transparent.

"What do you sense?"

Her brows knit. She shook her head. "Nothing to do with your meeting."

His eyes hooded slightly. "What then?"

She tossed her head a little and smiled. "A girl doesn't give away all her secrets. Neither should a guy."

Michael felt himself begin to blush, but turned it into a light laugh. "I'll be back as soon as I can."

He started to turn away, to leave. She didn't let him go. Gently, she touched one hand up to his cheek. Finding it, she raised herself on tiptoes and kissed him once on the mouth, lightly.

"I'll wait up for you," she said.

Michael touched a finger to her lips, then left the room.

In the hallway, he nearly bumped into a tall blonde who was making her way toward the top of the staircase.

"Excuse me," he apologized.

He was aware of her quick scrutiny. She smiled, and he felt an odd sensation invade his mind. It was subtle, but not unlike the presence he'd experienced in Harrods when Helen Locklear had blocked him from going after Jenny.

Instinctively, he clamped his mind shut against the intrusion.

He saw the attractive blonde flinch.

If his action had bothered her, she hid it well. She extended a long, thin hand decorated with several large gemstones. "I'm Lea Frazzetti," she said. She had a good voice, slightly husky, but clear as a bell. "And you're Michael Dragon."

He took her hand, shook it gently.

"Right you are."

There was, he realized with a mild start, a distinct resemblance between them. Mainly he picked up the genetic similarity across the brows, eyes, and cheekbones, although there was some similarity at the corner of the jaw as well.

"I'm beginning to believe this man might be my father after all," he said.

She was appraising him with, if anything, more intense interest. "I see the resemblance," she said. "Amazing. I don't know what to say."

"Hi, sis."

Her brows rose, and she laughed softly.

They moved toward the staircase. "Yes, I suppose that's appropriate. Hello, brother."

Before they reached the head of the staircase, they heard another door open. Curiosity pulled them both around.

They watched the third member of their trio join them, followed closely by Helen Locklear.

Locklear made the introductions. "Lea Frazzetti," she said, gesturing toward Lea, "and Michael Dragon. This is Drew Garrett."

Michael recognized Garrett. He was a rock star whose videos had been hitting TV lately. He'd seen photos of Garrett without the satanic makeup he wore onstage. Garrett looked taller and thinner than he appeared in his photos. Michael shook Garrett's hand. Their resemblance was less easy to pick out than it had been with Lea Frazzetti, but again, it showed up across the eyes, the bridge of the nose, and the forehead. Somewhere, not too far back in time, it was a pretty good bet they'd shared a common ancestor.

"Now," Helen Locklear said, "it's time to meet your father."

She led them down the sweeping staircase.

Michael took up the rear, preferring to observe the other two without having to make it obvious that was what he was doing. On the main floor of the foyer, Helen Locklear touched a button on the wall. A section of paneling slid out of the way, revealing another staircase leading farther down—into a basement, perhaps.

"Watch your step in here," she cautioned. "The steps are old and worn."

Again, Michael took the rear.

The worn brick steps in the narrow passageway soon left the modern world behind.

As they dropped lower, Michael realized that the stone in the walls had grown older. It was worn smooth in many places from the rubbing of numerous arms and hands as people passed by. Michael added his own touch to the timeworn stone.

"Is this Roman?" Lea Frazzetti asked.

"Yes," Helen Locklear's voice echoed back. "It's part of an old Roman fortification. The house is built on top of it."

Forty feet below the main floor of the house, the stairs ended. The small group of people stepped through a low doorway, into the broad expanse of an underground Roman bath. Modern lighting cast a strangely harsh, although still somber, light about the high-ceilinged room. Stone columns enclosed the rectangular bath itself, while narrow seating areas formed a larger rectangle beyond the columns. While obviously ancient, the bath appeared to be in remarkable condition. The shimmering surface of the ancient pool played havoc with the eerie underwater lights, casting flickering shadows about the entire room, all the way to the top of the low dome covering the pool area.

Seated on a raised platform on the far side of the water, Michael recognized the figure of a tall, gray-haired man. The figure resembled something carved out of alabaster. A soft overhead light cast dramatic shadows over the man's face and over the small grouping of comfortable chairs facing him.

"Welcome to Roman London." The man's voice boomed and echoed deeper into the unseen depths of the ancient baths. Other chambers led off the main bath area.

Michael followed the others around the bath.

The old man came to his feet. Up close he looked quite old, although Michael found himself unable to guess at the number of decades the man had lived.

"It's nice to meet you all," the old man said. "My name is Aaron Caine. And, as I gather, you have all recently learned that I am your father."

It was his eyes and the strength of his brow that he had passed on to the three of them, Michael noticed. Caine's brow was prominent, and there was a remarkable depth to the man's eyes.

Caine stepped forward and shook each of their hands in turn. Then he gestured toward the comfortable chairs spaced evenly around the raised areas overlooking the shimmering bath. "Please, be seated." Helen Locklear took the chair to Caine's right. Her attention to the three newcomers was ceaseless. She reminded Michael of an attentive watchdog—which, in a way, he supposed she was.

Caine moved a hand to encompass his surroundings.

"Roman ruins," he said. "A fitting place for this meeting." A wry smile distorted his lips, then faded. "But you did not come here for small talk, heh? Each of you knows some of the story. None of you knows all of it. So let me begin."

14

Caine told them about their conceptions, of how, in his travels, he made a point of seeking out women with qualities compatible to his, qualities he wanted to see in his children. He sought genius and beauty, any special talent or hint of magic— At which point he laughed softly.

"Not *magic* as you see onstage or on television. No, not even the magic of the sorcerer, although that would certainly qualify. No. I refer instead to a state of being, an excitement with life. Magic. Love of life."

But he wanted someone with a gift.

Every few years he found such a woman.

A number of them bore him children.

Children were a precaution, he said. A precaution against the inevitable day when he could no longer fulfill his responsibilities. Everyone needs to plan for that day.

"Even a sorcerer," he added. "And, for me, that day is near."

He fell silent for a moment.

"What exactly do you mean by *sorcerer*?" Lea Frazzetti asked. "I know the meaning of the word, but—"

Caine waved her to silence, that thin smile back on his face. "By sorcerer I mean this . . ."

A young boy appeared in the midst of the ring formed by the chairs. The boy smiled, held his hands out, cupped together. Opening them, he released an expanding globe of star-flecked night. The ball of night floated above the heads of the group, fluttered outward to encompass the entire domed ceiling of the bath. There it stopped, forming a flawless night sky. Even a breeze had been struck. Crickets sang in invisible bushes. And the young boy was gone.

"What is *this*?" Michael asked.

Caine nodded. "A good question. It's an illusion. That, sadly, is all we can do, we sorcerers. Most of us, anyway. We are grand illusionists. We create beliefs in the minds of others, both man and animal. We don't create a night sky. We create the belief in the night sky. Belief is much easier to create. Take any of the great religious figures of history—Jesus, Buddha, Muhammad —they had some of the powers." He raised a cautionary finger. "But only some. The brotherhood of sorcery stretches much farther back into history than the chants and rituals of even the oldest religions. We are a very ancient breed."

Michael asked, "What did you mean when you said, 'most of us . . .'?"

Caine opened his hands, then cast one to the side, as if wishing he could toss the question away as easily. A small smile touched his features. "In my lifetime, I have known a number such as myself. All were as I am. Nothing more, nor, perhaps, less. But there have been two of our number who were as none other."

"Who?"

Caine eyed Michael carefully, as if reminding himself to beware of this one. Michael couldn't say why that thought formed in his mind, but it did—clearly.

"One's name you have heard spoken of as Merlin. He—"

Lea Frazzetti interjected, "You're not serious?"

Caine nodded. "I am as serious as death, Miss Frazzetti. There is evidence to suggest that he was more than others of our breed, that perhaps—and I must emphasize the *perhaps*—he was *perhaps* capable of creating more than hallucinations in the minds of man and animal."

"Why put it so . . . tentatively?" Lea asked.

Caine stared at the night sky spread above him for several moments. "Let me put it this way," Caine said, choosing his words carefully. "There is evidence that Merlin did, in fact, tamper with reality, that he was capable of calling upon greater powers than simply the minds of sentient animals . . ." Caine paused, then scanned the faces before him. "But there is no proof." He shook his head. "Merlin was something of a chimera; he still is. He was a very private, even reclusive man. All of our calling are, more or less, but he more than most . . . so the legends tell us. If he had greater secrets and powers, he did not pass them on with his passing. If he had the powers legend says he did, they disappeared with him."

"Then he's dead?" Michael asked. "Legends say he was entombed in a cave or in a crystalline rock, don't they?"

"The legends say many things of Merlin," Caine said. "What is true and what is fabrication?" He shrugged. "Of one thing I am certain: Merlin was mortal, as are all of us." He let his eyes pass over the small circle again. His perfect white teeth showed behind his small smile. "Although mortal life comes in many lengths, especially to those of our calling, and it is impossible to know the length of your candle." He shrugged his shoulders again, opened his palms. "Who knows? It is possible that Merlin still lives, buried in some long-forgotten cave. But I doubt it. I was born in 1189, the year of Richard Lionheart's first crusade. I have lived through nearly eight full centuries and have never once sensed a glimmer of Merlin, the man—or of the reality behind the legend. But, as I say, who knows? Merlin was, and remains, a fifth-century enigma."

"You said there was another," Lea Frazzetti pressed.

Caine nodded. "Of whom even less is known," he said. "Even her name is lost in the mists of prehistory. Her deeds are spoken of in Egypt, over six thousand years ago, before the building of the great pyramids." He shook his head. "She is legend. Nothing more." A trace of a smile again pulled his lips. "Eleanor has devoted herself to unearthing the secrets of this *missing one*."

He fell silent again, his eyes focused on events from a distant past.

"So you're telling us that we three—that we're all sorcerers?" Drew Garrett asked.

Caine's gray head shook slightly, side to side. "No. You are the offspring of one. There are many in the history of the world who have had such parentage. There are many who have shown the powers you have without having such parentage." He shook his head. "No. You are not sorcerers, though, with luck, one of you may prove worthy."

The room was silent except for the gentle slap of water in the huge pool-size bath.

"Then why—"

Caine cut Garrett off. "There are three sorcerers in the world," he said. "Three for balance. There must always be three, for if there are not, the world as men know it shakes to its very core. Only when Merlin and *the missing one* reigned was the world safe with only one. Each of the three acts as a counterweight to the others, keeping the system finely balanced. If one becomes ruled by a lust for power, the other two compensate. The world stays in balance. If one becomes the embodiment of—as men call it—*evil,* then the other two must replace him . . . or her . . . with another more suited to the tasks and responsibilities. If one should die unexpectedly, as occurred in 1915, then a successor must be found and groomed. If there are not three in place, then the world becomes unstable. Havoc reigns."

"Such as when?" Drew Garrett asked.

Caine focused on Garrett for a long moment. "Many times. The last major unbalancing occurred in the earlier part of this century. For thirty years the world trembled, from roughly 1915 to 1945."

"The period of the world wars," Drew said.

"Exactly. One of us was killed by accident. It was thirty years before the storm subsided, before a worthy third was found. Meanwhile, the world stumbled to its knees and nearly slid back into a second dark age. The world was at war, and the two were at war. It was not a healthy time to be alive."

"What do you mean, 'the two were at war'?" Michael asked.

"The remaining two sorcerers," Caine said. "We were at odds."

"You were one of them?"

"Yes."

"And the other?"

Caine's mouth pulled tight. "Eleanor is her name. She still lives. We battled while the world tore itself to shreds. She is a strong woman, Eleanor is. And very skilled. She wanted to control the destiny of mankind, of this world. She tried. And for thirty years we struggled until a third cornerstone emerged to put us back in balance."

"There are three now?"

Caine nodded. "Mahafed is the third." If it was possible, Caine appeared to grow more serious. "But he is young, and he has come under the sway of Eleanor's influence. They are out there, now, beyond the walls of this house, waiting like vultures to devour whoever survives the next few days. They are in my territory, but they know that I am still quite capable of fending them off or wreaking havoc on them and their portions of the world should they attempt something premature. I doubt that they will attack or interfere with us. They tried recently, when I was in an unsafe, even foolhardy position. But they failed, and they received fitting retributions for their attempt." He shook his head. "No. It is much smarter for them to wait for my death now, to bide their time that they might test the untried strength of my successor. They have sensed that I am dying, which is why they are behaving like such vultures. And, like vultures, they will wait until I am carrion before they come to feed."

"What prevents them from coming after us here?" Michael asked.

"As long as they know I am alive and safe, you are in no danger. As long as I am outside their power, you can come and go with impunity. After their recent failed attempt on my life, they have agreed to leave you three alone until they sense I am dead. Were they to interfere in the choice of a successor, they know my wrath, and the damage I can wreak to their worlds." A smug expression pulled at his mouth, twinkled in his eyes. "But the moment they sense I am dead, or am perceived by them as being unable to resist their power, you are safe nowhere—not even here, within this compound. At that moment, you will be alone, whichever of you are still alive. Eleanor and Mahafed will be certain to come for you—especially if there is more than one of you remaining alive, for that will mean that a successor has not been found and trained. It is my hope that one of you will be selected soon, that I might pass what knowledge I can to you before my passing. For when I am gone and only one of you is left, it will be solely up to you to establish your right to this Western third of the world."

"And if we fail?" Drew Garrett asked.

"You die," Caine said simply. "And the world is thrown into chaos until a suitable third is found, or declares himself or herself. If Eleanor and Mahafed have their way, the third will become their minion, *if* a third is chosen at all during their lifetimes."

"I don't see how we can defend ourselves against the two of them," Lea Frazzetti said. "Not with you gone."

Caine nodded with understanding. "If a successor has not been trained, there would be no defense. With a single successor, given time and training, the odds that the balance will not be shaken are very high. *If there is time for training*. If not . . ." He opened his arms to the obvious.

Michael started to ask another question, but Caine blocked him by raising a hand, palm outward.

"Which brings me to why you three are here," Caine said then, his voice losing its earlier expressiveness. "I am old, and I am dying." He looked each of them in the eyes. "And I do not want the world to fall into the hands of those two alone. It is time I found a successor and passed my knowledge on to that chosen one. On to one of you. You hold the best hopes of being able to combat Eleanor and

Mahafed, of being able to keep the balance that will be lost with my death."

Michael leaned back, absorbing the information. His eyes caught the glimmer of the overhead stars that had been created by Caine. Michael closed his eyes and willed the illusion away. When his mind shifted in that strange little way he had learned, he opened his eyes again. The ancient Roman dome was back, the stars but a memory.

"Only one of us will make it?" Lea Frazzetti asked.

Caine nodded soberly. "That is correct. You three are the strongest. Three have already died. They were unable to respond effectively to their trials. The three of you will be pitted against each other. The strongest will survive to learn my secrets. It must be this way. It has been thus since the dawn of time. Just as a strong and true sword must survive the crucible, so must a strong and true sorcerer."

"And the others?" Drew Garrett asked. "What happens to them?"

"They will die. There is no other way. This is a trial to the death."

"And if we don't want any part of this?"

Caine turned his attention on Michael. "I was aware of your hesitancy," he said. "That is why I took your daughter."

Michael stared at the old man's lined features.

"You are a man of science. You disdain much of this as trickery and magic. You hesitate to give up your *scientific beliefs* because they are rational, because thousands of idiotic studies by unimaginative, narrow-minded scientists say this is so and that is such, and because you have been brainwashed by twentieth-century thinking." Caine shook his head disdainfully. "Twentieth-century knowledge is but a whisper in the cacophony of history. There is only one way for you again to see your daughter alive."

"I'm not so sure that Eleanor and Mahafed are the evil ones."

Caine's thin smile didn't leave his face. "Evil," he said with a gentle laugh. "Evil is in the eye of the beholder. There *is* only what there *is* in the world. Man is the one who labels, who says, 'This is evil, this is good.' But that is not reality. That is man's label. And every man has a different set of labels for the same events. Maybe I am evil. Aren't we all, to some extent?" He nodded. "Yes, if I accept your labels, it is *evil,* as you put it, to take your daughter captive. But it is reality. It is a behavior that is as old as man. Older, even. It is a behavior that gains compliance with one's wishes. And in this instance, I must decide which is more important. Do I allow you and your daughter to leave, preventing the small *evil* of keeping her hostage, and perhaps creating the larger *evil* of, possibly, choosing less than the strongest as my successor? Or do I commit the small *evil* in hopes of preventing the larger *evil* of choosing a successor who is less capable of coping with Eleanor and Mahafed?" He opened his hands before him. "That was my choice. I have chosen. If you want to see your daughter alive again, you will do your best to become my successor. If not, you will both die."

Michael felt the anger bubbling in his veins, but there was nothing he could do with it for the moment except control it. When he spoke, the control was evident in his tone and along his tense jawline. "I have no choice."

Caine nodded, smiled smugly. "Good. I am glad you are a man of reason, rather than some zealot filled with blind *conviction.*" Caine turned to the others. "I trust neither of you needs further convincing."

Both Lea Frazzetti and Drew Garrett shook their heads.

"Good," Caine said. To them all, he said, "You will learn more when the time is right. As for now, simply realize that you all have approximately the same abilities. You have each developed them differently, and each of you, because of lack of training, is blind to much of what you are capable of doing. You have not begun to tap the resources buried within your brain. To help each of you realize that potential, I offer this . . ."

Abruptly, the world changed.

Michael felt a piercing pain shoot up his spine and embed itself in the base of his brain. Sparks of lightning sizzled along his nerves, crackled across tortured synapses, energized dormant areas in all parts of his brain. He felt his head swell, experienced sensations he'd never known existed, tasted colors, smelled visions, saw the embodiment of sounds waver in the air, felt the very essence of life. A dizziness swept over him, overloaded all his senses, and . . . he felt . . . *different* . . . somehow, very different.

He knew he would never be the same again.

The very structure of his brain felt altered—or maybe, for the first time, it was truly *alive*.

The sensations ebbed.

Michael glanced quickly around and realized that the other two had experienced something similar.

"Go now," Caine said. "Sleep tonight. Tomorrow at sunrise the challenge begins. The world is your battleground. When there is only one of you left, return to this house. I will be waiting—if I am still alive."

Drew Garrett came to his feet. "How does it begin? What are you expecting us to—"

Caine's smile was barely perceptible. "From now on you must find your own answers." His even white teeth showed now. "Or make them."

And with that, Caine vanished.

Michael blinked, and for a moment he wondered whether Caine had really been in their presence at all.

For some reason, the answer seemed important.

15

Drew let the others precede him up the stairs. He had to step aside and make a fairly dramatic gesture to encourage *the Dragon* to get ahead of him on the stairs.

He'd quickly come up with names for the troops. It made everything seem more like a game, less like a threat.

The dragon was, of course, Michael Dragon.

The Lear was the Locklear woman.

Frizzy was the name he'd given Lea Frazzetti. He had met her several years earlier at a party in Cannes, at the film festival. He doubted whether she remembered him. But he remembered her. She was a cool piece of merchandise.

The others ahead of him were silent.

His mind was racing.

No doubt, so were theirs.

The trick was to make his mind work faster and harder than theirs, to grab a head start in this race and never look back.

The question was *how?*

He had to grab some hours tonight to figure out what the hell kind of changes had occurred in his head down there. Caine had done *something* to his brain. Already Drew was aware that he could hear things a hell of a lot better than he ever had before. He could smell more. His normal senses had been rearranged. But what he really needed to play with were his abnormal senses . . . his ability to sense others' emotions and thoughts, his ability to create an illusion for someone else the way Caine and the Lear were able to do it for him—and for countless others, no doubt. He had to learn what he was capable of before the others learned, and then . . . then what?

Death was the end product for them, right? So why not just kill them tonight and get it over with?

Drew followed the others into the main foyer. He watched while the Lear closed the hidden doorway in the paneling.

"Good night," the Lear said.

Everyone moved off. No one seemed in the mood for chitchat. He couldn't blame them. They were probably already thinking along the same track he was.

Drew wondered whether it mattered how the others died.

Hell, he could walk into their rooms tonight and stab them with a kitchen knife, if he wanted. Why wait for sunrise tomorrow morning?

He wondered what his chances of succeeding at that would be.

It would hardly be a majestic beginning for the next great sorcerer of the Western world. Still . . .

Could he create an illusion that could kill them? Had Caine rearranged his brain enough to allow him to do that? And how would he know if he could do that? Would he see the same illusion as the person he was creating it for?

He doubted it.

He started up the wide staircase that led to his room. The Dragon and Frizzy were ahead of him, both nearing the top of the stairs, talking with each other.

What about an experiment? Why not try to unleash a few of the newly discovered parts of his brain in a dry run?

The idea struck Drew as funny.

Why the hell not?

But what should he try?

And on whom?

He reached the top of the stairs. Small, shaded wall lamps created pools of soft, amber light in the bedroom hallway. The Dragon was heading for his room, Frizzy for hers. Could he con Frizzy into the sack? Create a

smash fantasy for her, and... No. Too dangerous. It
was dog eat dog now. He couldn't afford to fraternize
with the enemy. He smiled. He liked that word. Fraternize. He couldn't afford to get that close to Frizzy, but
what if he . . .

He watched the Dragon slip into the first room on the
left, sensed the presence of another, a woman, but put
that thought out of mind. As soon as the Dragon's door
closed, Drew paused, his attention on Frizzy. He
watched Frizzy's luscious body moving away from him,
heading toward her room, and concentrated on her.

He had an idea.

He stepped behind one of the thick beams supporting the
upper stories of the house. He wasn't completely hidden,
but he doubted whether it would matter. He didn't expect
Frizzy to look his way.

He formed as vivid a picture in his mind as he could and
then mentally shot it at her.

As he peered around the carved beam, Frizzy staggered.
She reached out to the wall for support. She was two yards
shy of her bedroom. She turned her head his way slightly,
mouth slack with passion.

Drew beared down on the illusion he was creating.

Frizzy was leaning against the wall now, breathing heavily.

Drew smiled, tried his damndest to make the illusion
real for her.

Lea felt the first waves of the orgasm sweep outward
from the very center of her being.

She held on to the wall, astounded by the unbelievable
force of the contractions. Her vision blurred.

Christ! It felt almost as she imagined a seizure must feel.
The closest thing to oblivion you could imagine.

Her body rocked, taken by the rolling spasms.

What the hell was causing—

She blocked the sensations, forced her body not to respond, straightened, turned to stare down the hallway
she'd just traversed. Her breathing was still ragged, but
she'd wiped out the cause of her surprise gift. She thought

she could make out the outline of someone's shoulder, someone hiding behind one of the huge beams that supported the old house.

"Bastard," she muttered. "I know you're behind that beam."

She sensed a hesitation from whoever it was, then heard the hesitation break into a brittle, self-conscious laugh.

Drew Garrett stepped from behind the beam.

"You should've seen the look on your face," he said, sidling toward her, hands tucked into his belt.

He was tall and thin and good-looking, the perfect rock 'n' roller. Too cocksure and too full of himself, but with an unsinkable air about him. Lea recognized the air. It was a cover-up for a weak ego, a facade erected by someone frightened by his own shadow.

She decided to play it cool with him.

She'd met him once before, she recalled, but she wasn't about to admit to that. She closed her mind down, blocked it against any intrusion. She had no idea what abilities this creep had, but she knew he had to be good in order to be here.

"That was very nice," she said. "Thank you. It was nicely done."

Her tact surprised him, she realized. He'd expected anger.

Good.

Keep the bastard off balance.

"If that was your first salvo in the war, it didn't seem very dangerous."

He smirked. "I was just testing the equipment."

He moved his hips when he said that. Just enough to hint at his thoughts, not enough to be obvious. She wasn't even sure whether he was conscious of what he'd done.

"You seem pretty confident of yourself," she said.

He grinned. "Hey, why not?"

He might be dangerous, she thought, but she would lay odds that the one to worry about was the other guy,

Michael Dragon. A follow-up thought stumbled right into that one.

"You interested in forming a team?"

Garrett eyed her sideways. "What do you mean?"

She considered how to propose the idea that had hit her. She tossed her head toward her room. "We can talk in there, if you'd like. It's a bit more private. We could have a drink."

He considered it a moment before nodding. "Okay."

She led him into the room she'd been provided by Caine. A high, carved screen divided the room in two, blocking the sleeping area from the rest of the room. She gestured Garrett toward the chairs and sofa arranged in front of the fireplace.

Before he took a seat on one of the single chairs, he stirred the embers in the fireplace and dropped several more logs in place. The dried bark caught fire almost immediately. It crackled softly.

"Drink?" she asked.

He lifted one of the carafes and poured himself half a tumbler of cognac. She poured herself a glass of burgundy.

"You made a proposal," Garrett said carefully.

Lea noted the close attention he was paying to her face. She let her mind reach gently out toward his, felt his presence, and felt his mind draw back from hers.

He held up a finger. "Ungh-ungh-ungh-ungh," he said, waggling the finger. "You stay out of my head for now, and I stay out of yours." He grinned, and made a slight slurping sound when he sucked at his cognac. "Call it a truce, huh? For now?"

"Okay," Lea said. "A truce it is."

"Let's hear your proposal."

"You heard it in the hallway."

"You want to team up with me."

"It's an idea."

Garrett studied her face.

Yellowish light flickered from the fireplace. One of the logs hissed like a serpent.

"What's the advantage?"

"You and me against the competition."

Garrett twisted his lips. "You mean, you and I team up to dump the Dragon into his grave."

She nodded.

"Then what?"

"Then the alliance ends."

Garrett chuckled.

"You're a hard-boiled egg . . . that you are."

She sipped at her wine. It was full-bodied and rich, with an earthy aftertaste. She could almost taste the soil that had fed the grapes.

"I'm not sure I see the advantage," Garrett said.

"It's simple. We don't get blindsided by a third force while we're paying attention to someone else. And we reduce the odds against each of us."

Garrett was wound very tightly, she sensed. He was smart and driven, but fueled by forces that seemed somewhat wild. She wondered what made him tick, what kind of childhood he'd had. There was something brittle about his personality, as if he could be pushed to violence easily, or over the edge. The more she thought about it, the more her offer to him made sense to her. With Dragon out of the picture, she was certain she could handle Garrett's fragile psyche.

"But in the end, it still comes down to you and me."

She nodded. "One against one."

Garrett's brow knit in thought. When the skin over his eyes relaxed, he said, "How about I give you my answer in the morning?"

She studied him with care. Was he playing it straight with her, or biding his time, waiting to play another angle? She decided to give him the benefit of the doubt.

Still, she intended to be on her guard.

"Fair enough," she said. "Is it a truce until then?"

Garrett beamed cockily. "Okay by me—unless you'd like another cheap thrill in the meantime."

"Thanks. I think I'll pass."

She couldn't believe it, but the ass actually winked at her.

* * *

"You're so tense," Carol said. She was lying on her side, propped on an elbow, running the fingers of one hand lightly over Michael's chest.

They were in Michael's room, in the huge canopied bed. Michael was lying on his back, staring blankly at the pattern in the canopy. He'd just finished telling her everything that had occurred in the presence of Aaron Caine.

"I don't want to be here," he said.

Carol's hand stopped its movement.

"*Here*, I mean," Michael said. "In London. In this house. It has nothing to do with you." He glanced at her. In the subdued glow from the fireplace, her skin resembled spun gold. "I like being here, in bed, with you."

Carol's fingers tentatively started to move again, tracing the muscles of his chest. He watched her left breast move with each shift of her arm. It was a pleasing sight. He liked the shape of her breasts. They were a handful, no more, with slightly upturned nipples. They brought out something protective within him. They reminded him of small white doves that needed to be handled oh, so delicately.

But at the moment he was not in total control of his mind or body, and sex was not the topmost thing on his mind.

"You're wondering about your daughter, aren't you," Carol said.

"Mmm-mm."

"She's safe."

Michael twisted his head about to watch her face.

"You sense that?"

"Mmm-mm."

"Where is she?"

"Not close."

"Do you sense anything more . . . more specific?"

"Water."

"Water?"

"I get a picture of hills and water. A lake, I think. Not the ocean—though it could be an inlet or sheltered bay, I suppose."

"The lake district?"

"I don't know what that is."

"It's a hilly area in the very northwestern part of England, just south of Scotland."

"I don't know if that's the area or not. It could be." She looked puzzled, shifted position slightly, her head cocked at an inquisitive angle. Then she extended a tentative finger and pointed. "I sense her in that direction. Is that north?"

"No. It's almost due west."

"She's somewhere over there, I think."

Due west, Michael thought. The stomping grounds of Merlin lay in that direction. "We could take a drive out that way. Maybe leave before dawn and . . . whatever that might bring. Would that help you locate her, if you were closer?"

Carol nodded. "Usually that helps. But what good would that do you? From what Caine said, if I got it right, the only way you're going to see Jenny again is if you become his successor." She laughed self-consciously then, and Michael picked up a whiff of fear. "God, listen to me! Talking about sorcery as if it were a common coffee-klatch topic." She shook her head. "Do you believe this?"

Michael was silent.

He didn't want to, but, yes, he believed it.

His altered senses told him that Caine was deadly serious, that this whole business of Caine seeking a successor was as real as anything ever was in this world. He also realized that soon his life and Jenny's—and probably Carol's—were going to ride directly on his ability to use whatever powers his mind had hidden away within it.

That was the problem.

He had no idea what his mind was capable of doing. Could he create the same kinds of hallucinations he'd witnessed in Helen Locklear's presence? Read minds? More?

"Michael?"

He pulled himself away from his thoughts. "Mmm?"

"Kiss me."

He drew her close to him and kissed her. At first their lips barely touched. He kissed her again, deeper this time, sensing a raw need within Carol and within himself, aware of the warmth she stirred within him. Her eyes were open. The emerald flecks in them sparkled in the firelight.

At first they were awkward together, unsure of where the other liked to be touched, unsure of how to move when the other shifted position. Making love was an event that needed to be choreographed and practiced, that needed to have the bugs worked out before it became the smooth performance people dreamed of. The first time at anything with a new partner could be hell.

At one point, while shifting her weight to let Michael explore her breasts with his lips, Carol whacked him in the ear with an elbow. There was no embarrassment, only laughter, and a comment about "Laurel and Hardy in bed together." Then, gently, she guided his mouth to where she wanted it.

It was a tentative lovemaking, a careful, controlled process without hurry. It was gentle and intense, a slow dance to a rapidly improving orchestra. It built gradually to a sharp crescendo, then faded slowly, its notes lingering pleasantly for long moments in the air.

Carol lay with her head on Michael's chest. He could feel her breath on his skin. And he sensed something new in her. It was as if a weight had been lifted from her shoulders.

He wanted to know what she was thinking.

Experimentally, he jogged his mind, let it reach out and spread open like a flower opening to the sun. This was a new experience to him. Tentatively, he tried to read Carol's thoughts.

Nothing came to him.

He concentrated, pressing his mind at her. He felt even clumsier than he had during their first moments of making love.

His mind touched something. He felt a slight resistance. Then, in the next instant, the resistance was gone.

He sensed her being in a way he'd never experienced another before. He sensed a tranquil, languid state, a—

He felt her tense on his breast.

She raised her head. "What are you doing?"

Immediately he pulled his mind back within his skull.

She sat up straighter. She was looking down at him with her blind eyes flashing in the firelight. "Michael, what were you doing?"

"I was trying to read your mind."

The muscles along her jaw tightened.

"Did you?"

"No. Not really. I sensed a relaxation, a peacefulness. But I didn't read any thoughts."

"I should be mad at you."

"Why?"

"I don't want you to read my mind without knowing you're going to do it."

"I should have asked. Sorry."

The tension lines along her jaw relaxed.

"It's okay." She put her head back on his chest. "It's not that I would have minded you reading what I was thinking then, it's just . . . I don't know. An invasion of privacy."

"How did you know I was doing something?"

"I . . . I felt your mind touching mine. You forget, I'm psychic."

They were silent for a moment.

"I almost didn't notice it," Carol said. "I think you could learn to do it without my knowing you were doing it."

"I don't want to do that to you."

"I know. I trust you. But it could come in handy with others."

Michael let that thought rattle around his head for a moment.

"Want to try again?" Carol asked. "You can, if you'd like. It's a good idea for you to learn what you're capable of doing."

"You won't mind?"

He felt her shake her head against his chest. Her hair tickled along his neck.

"Okay."

He relaxed, let his mind expand outward again. This time, when he encountered Carol's mind, he felt no resistance. The tranquillity had changed, yet there was still a sense of peace.

And love.

It surprised him.

Love was the word and sensation he'd encountered. And now he read more. *So now you know.* And he sensed a concern, a tiny thread of fear, a doubt that she should have let him know her feelings for him.

He folded an arm across her back, pressed her to him.

"I'm glad you let me know."

She didn't say anything, but he felt a tear slide across his chest. For a long moment they lay without moving. She let him explore other parts of her mind, and Michael couldn't help but feel the swelling emotions within his own breast. This was a woman he could love, he realized. And with that realization, he eased his mind back, away from her private thoughts.

He thought she'd sensed his emotions, but he didn't ask.

A few minutes later, she said, "You should see what else you can do."

"What do you mean?"

"Maybe you could locate Jenny."

Michael tossed the idea around in his head. He tried to create a vision of his daughter, to get in touch with her.

Nothing.

He shifted his mind this way and that.

Still nothing.

He shook his head, helpless. "Nothing comes to me."

"Try something else. Can you create visions, the way Helen Locklear and Caine do?"

Michael considered the problem. It seemed to him that some of the newly accessed areas in his right brain ought to be the ones to tap for visions. He tried to form an image at the foot of the bed.

Carol sat up. "I felt something." She pointed.

Michael concentrated, formed as full an image of Carol as he could. When he thought he had it, he let his mind reach out to Carol's mind, and he tried to form the image for her to see, inside her brain.

Her eyes gaped.

"Michael, I see it."

"It's in your brain."

"I know. I see it. I *see* it. I see it the way I used to see before I lost my vision." A brilliant smile brightened her face. A tear formed and rolled down alongside her nose. "My God, Michael, you don't know what it's like to be able to see after so many years of darkness." She shook her head. "That's me," she said with a note of wonder in her voice. "I don't think I'm as attractive as that."

Michael let the image walk around the room, let it model for her.

"Is that really how I look?"

He laughed, pulled her close. "Yes." He let the image evaporate.

Carol relaxed against him. She hugged him tightly, slid higher, and buried her face in his neck. She was crying softly, tears of happiness. "I never thought I'd see again, not even a glimpse of light."

"How old were you when you lost your sight?"

He felt her grow cooler. "Thirteen."

"You don't want to talk about it now, do you?"

She shook her head. "I don't want to ruin the mood. Tomorrow, okay. I'll tell you about it tomorrow."

He wrapped his arms tightly around her. "Whenever you want."

"Right now I want you to try some other things."

"Such as?"

"See if you can create an illusion that you see."

"Such as?"

"I don't know. Make me at the foot of the bed again."

"Okay."

And he did, almost without effort.

"Am I there?"

"Uh-huh. You're going to move around the bed and touch yourself."

Carol stiffened as the solid-looking vision of her

walked around the room and gently touched Carol on the shoulder.

Carol shivered. "Is that me touching me?"

"Both my hands are on you," Michael said, patting her with his hands. "That other hand is yours."

He let the image fade away.

"Do something else?"

"Like what?"

"Make Dracula. I want to hear him talk to me."

Michael concentrated. It got easier with each attempt.

Dracula strode majestically around the bed, touched Carol on the shoulder. "Vould you like a kissss?"

Carol laughed and gagged at the same time. She sat up again. "Oh, God, Michael. I felt his nails."

"Feel my teeth," Dracula said.

Carol recoiled from the hands that took her shoulders, tried to stretch away from the cold mouth pressed ever so gently to her throat. Her smile froze, looking strained.

"Stop it, Michael. Please."

Michael let Dracula vanish. Carol shifted position, as if released from the hands and mouth of a flesh-and-blood vampire. She put a hand on his chest. He noticed that her breath had caught in her throat.

"It felt so real," she said. "He was clammy. For a minute I thought . . ."

"Thought what?"

"Thought you were going to let him bite me for real."

Michael pulled her down to him and held her close. He was only beginning to realize the potential of the powers within his mind. It was a frightening prospect.

"I won't scare you again," he said.

"Okay, but let's not stop seeing what you can do."

Michael laughed.

Carol slapped his bare chest. "It's not funny," she said. "This is a matter of life and death."

Michael sobered.

She was right, he realized. At sunrise tomorrow, all the rules he'd lived his life by would be altered; he realized, then, that they might have changed already.

And for the next several hours he practiced using his

mind to create illusions that couldn't be distinguished from reality. He practiced hard, as if his life depended on it—because it did.

Carol acted as his coach—or tried to.

16

Naked, Lea opened the drapes of her east-facing bedroom. It was dark out yet, though less dense at the horizon. Dawn was not far off. Barely visible beyond the window was the imposing high wall of Caine's compound, with its rolling drum of knives on top. Beyond the wall stretched the shadowy, predawn rooftops of London, like a painting done in muted grays, browns, and dirty reds. She stretched like a cat, elongating and accentuating the curves of her body. Then she returned to her bed, pulled the rope for the servants, and crawled back between the covers.

She was propped demurely against the fluffy pillows and headboard when the servant knocked a moment later.

"Come in."

It was one of the maids, a pretty, petite young woman with the dark eyes of a Gypsy and the smile of a street urchin. Her black uniform and white apron were impeccable.

"I'd like some breakfast, please."

"It's not yet dawn, ma'am."

Lea smiled. "I know." She intended to get a very early start today.

"Yes, ma'am. Anything in particular?"

"Eggs Benedict and a split of champagne would be nice."

"Yes, ma'am. Will that be all?"

"And coffee. Strong. With a pot of hot milk."

The maid bowed herself out of the room.

Lea stretched again and yawned. She would have to be careful as dawn approached. She wanted to be awake fully by then. She expected one of the other two, Dragon or Garrett, to try something the instant the sun peeked over the horizon. If they didn't, she would. Lea glanced at the grandfather clock that ticked and swayed its pendulum on the far side of the ornately decorated room. It was only 4:45 A.M. She had over an hour and a half to . . . *kill*.

The word brought a concerned yet confident expression to her face.

An hour and a half to kill. That was exactly right.

Provided that no snag came along to break her plans, Michael Dragon should be the first.

As soon after sunrise as possible.

It would be foolish to waste any time, she thought. The sooner she eliminated the competition, the sooner she could get on with the business of learning sorcery.

She'd given Dragon a great deal of thought during the evening—even, vaguely, recalled dreaming about the man. She'd considered trying to draw him to her bed but had discovered he'd come to London with some woman. Dragon and the woman had slept together the night before, Lea knew. She'd tried to read Dragon's mind sometime around midnight. She'd failed to do so. Dragon had sensed her presence and jarred her with the frightening image of herself as an old, withered woman, and the sound of her own crying.

That keening lament of her own aged image crying for herself still sent gooseflesh up her back.

Drew Garrett, on the other hand . . . that was an entirely different story. The man was a social cretin. Attractive, with a sort of animal magnetism, but an arrogant ass grasping for gratification with every move he made. Drawing him to bed would be an easy feat, and it could prove to be a convenient distraction for killing him. The thought brought a smile to her face. It was not unlike a sport. She could feint with her body and kill him while his mind was on his pleasure.

But, hopefully, not until he'd helped her get rid of Dragon.

She wondered whether Garrett would accept her offer to team up. She hoped so.

Dragon was the one to worry about.

She was sure Caine knew that as well. Why else had Caine kidnapped the man's daughter? *. . . to make sure that the best is chosen . . .* Hadn't Caine said something like that? And the old man had been talking to Dragon at the time.

Little did Caine know. . .

From outside her window, Lea heard the soft, throaty rumble of a well-tuned car. Tires crunched on the drive. Out of curiosity, Lea let her mind drift in that direction, to sense who was . . .

She threw the heavy down covers back and took three quick strides to the latticed window. Three stories below she saw the lights of a dark Jaguar sedan pull out of sight under the side portico.

Damn!

She stood there, fuming, while below her in the darkness she heard the scuffle and thump of someone loading the car.

Dragon!

Goddamn the man!

It was too late to do anything, now. And too early . . . The challenge began at sunrise, Caine had instructed.

What if she tried to stop Dragon now?

She'd practiced a few rather ingenious gimmicks in the night.

She concentrated on Dragon's brain waves, three stories below her, considering her options. What would Caine do if she tried to stop Dragon now? Did the man give a damn? And hadn't he said something about them making their own rules from now on, answering their own questions?

Lea closed her eyes, rubbed her temples, stoked the

emotional fires beneath her desires, and then sharply fired
a stunning image at Dragon's mind.

She heard a dull thud three stories below.

She beared down on her thoughts, sending agonies of
pain coursing through Dragon's chest. Give the man a heart
attack. Make him think it's the real thing. Make him believe it, and it will become his reality.

She heard feet thrashing, hitting metal and rubber.

The muted sound of a woman's voice fluttered across the
lawn. "Michael? What is it?"

Lea sensed Dragon now. His defenses were down.

He was on the brick drive, on his back, thrashing about
beside the Jaguar, clutching his chest.

Lea's eyes opened, though they still focused on the
mental image of what was occurring beneath her on the
portico. She was sweating from the mental exertion.

Try to sneak out on me before dawn, you bastard!

She willed the muscles of Dragon's chest to constrict, to
crush the frightened bloody bird that thudded away within
his ribs.

"*Michael!*" That same frightened female voice.

And another mind was in the melee now.

Whose, goddammit? Whose?

A mind searching, sensing, prying at the edges of Lea's
control.

Dragon's lady?

Was she psychic?

It didn't matter!

Lea bore down even harder on the muscles in Dragon's
chest.

She heard Dragon's gasping, felt a weakening of his resistance to the pressure in his chest.

Lea felt an exhilaration flood through her.

Was he passing out?

Ah, Christ, this could be so easy!

She rubbed at her temples furiously, stoking the fiery
strength of her powers.

He'd be defenseless if he passed out.

A voice murmured down below.

She sensed the deeper, gasped rumblings of Dragon's reply.

A headache was building in the center of her forehead, fueled by the exhausting pressure she was building within her own skull. Her breathing came in deep drafts now; she was panting like a wild animal, working her mind for all it was worth, gloating over the fact that she was able to get rid of Dragon so easily, simply by surprising the bastard. That was what he got for trying to sneak away from her at dawn.

Bastard!

Die, Dragon! Die!

Your heart is already dead. It's only flopping about like that because of the short circuits of death.

"Die, Dragon," she said in a strained whisper.

"Die."

At what felt like the lowest ebb of his strength, Lea felt something else occur. There was a slight hesitation, a moment snatched out of time. In the next instant, a raging, tumultuous force slammed her between the eyes—from inside her skull.

Her hands flew to cover her eyes.

She reeled.

Stumbled backward.

Twisting sideways, she threw herself toward the soft cushion of the bed. Her head felt as if it would explode. She hit the high mattress, slid down beside the bed, dragging bedding and pillows down with her. She heard a small whimper, a groan...realized it was she making the sounds.

She held on to her head. Tears ran down her cheeks.

She couldn't take this any longer.

Every blood vessel in her brain felt as if it were rupturing.

Then she realized what it was.

All illusion.

Like Dragon's heart attack.

She willed the pain away.

It ebbed.

She gathered her strength, and she closed her mind to outside forces.

The pain was gone, leaving only a tingling, numbing aura behind.

The bitter taste of metal coated her tongue.

She clutched at the bedding, dragged her body onto the bed, and swung her legs around after her, breathing in shallow gulps.

From below her window, she heard the Jaguar growl away from the house and disappear beyond the high wall.

A knock sounded at her door.

"Just a minute," she said weakly.

She shifted toward the headboard. Her head had begun to throb again. This time it was only a headache—dull and heavy.

"Come in."

The maid entered, carrying a tray. "Would you like this in bed?" she asked.

Lea shook her head yes and regretted it immediately. With an effort, she indicated the low coffee table near the window.

"Yes, ma'am."

The maid set the tray on the coffee table. It contained a silver plate with cover, two silver serving pots, a champagne glass, and a small, towel-draped bucket of ice from which the neck of a champagne split peered.

"Shall I open this?" the maid asked brightly.

"No. I'll do it."

"Will there be anything else?"

"No."

"Thank you, ma'am. Have a nice day."

The maid slipped out of the room.

Silence prevailed, and for a long time Lea lay in bed. She was more convinced than ever that she needed to pair up with Drew Garrett to get Dragon out of the picture. She didn't much care for the thought of what she might have to stoop to in order to convince Garrett to join her, but she could see no other way out of it.

Some things just had to be done.

* * *

Michael pulled into a vacant parking spot across the street from the entrance to the grounds of Glastonbury's most famous tourist attraction, Glastonbury Abbey. It could hardly be called an abbey anymore. Tall columns of cut stone soared upward to a nonexistent arch supporting a nonexistent roof, while once majestic, now rubbled walls stretched away from them to end in open air. The window arches were vacant, staring blankly at the future, while revealing a tiny glimpse of the glory that once was. Long gone was the multicolored glass of the windows. Long gone was the abbey's glory. The entire abbey was open to the sky. Flowers and weeds poked from the broken walls. Broad green lawns surrounded the ruins, carpeted what had once been a glorious nave.

"Welcome to Glastonbury," Michael said. Almost casually he tossed a visual image of the ruined abbey into Carol's mind.

She smiled, set a hand on his left thigh. "It's beautiful."

"Hungry?"

She nodded. "Starving." She touched her Braille watch. "It's been nearly five hours since breakfast, if you can call two pieces of toast *breakfast*."

Michael glanced along the street in front of him and spotted a pub less than a block distant. Its gaily painted sign and front door beckoned him.

"How's pub food sound?"

"I don't know. I've never had any."

Michael stepped from the Jaguar and circled to Carol's curbside door. She was already out, standing on the narrow sidewalk. She took his arm as smoothly as if she'd been doing so for years.

The pub's stone walls were uneven. Bubbled glass alternated with clear panes in the front windows. Inside, the pub was comprised of one long, low-ceilinged room, with a bar running half the length of one side, while the floor space was cluttered with a mishmash of old, uncoordinated tables and chairs. Dark-stained oak beams crossed the ceiling, supported by two huge, handhewn, floor-to-ceiling timbers.

Michael guided Carol to a low table near the deep brick fireplace. Ancient lances decorated the whitewashed walls. Most of the wooden furniture looked as though it might have come from the same era—sixteenth century, possibly. But the red and gold carpet was brand new.

It absorbed the murmur of conversation from the busy patrons.

Michael glanced at a menu that had been left on the table.

"What'll you be havin'?" a short, chubby girl with rosy cheeks asked. She'd appeared from nowhere.

Michael ordered a pint of Stone's for himself and a slice of meat pie. Carol asked for a dry sparkling cider and a plowman's lunch.

Michael created an image of the pub for Carol while they waited. The waitress returned to them before Carol had finished absorbing the pub's atmosphere.

As Carol tore apart a thick piece of dark bread, she said, "You don't seem to be carrying around any of the ill effects of Miss Frazzetti's handiwork."

Without thinking, Michael put a hand to his chest. He'd felt minor cramps a few times during the drive from London, but felt nothing out of the ordinary now. For a while he'd been concerned that Lea Frazzetti's premature attempt to kill him had left some permanent damage. He doubted that now. The fear, he realized, had come as much from the memory of his own father's death from a heart attack as from the agony Lea Frazzetti had inflicted that morning.

"I'm not."

"I don't think she followed us," Carol said.

Michael was pleased that he'd thought to leave London before dawn. By leaving, rather than attacking one of the other two, he was sure he'd upset their plans. His best guess had been that both Lea Frazzetti and Drew Garrett had planned to go after him with the first rays of dawn. Lea Frazzetti's predawn strike had taken him by surprise, but it confirmed the wisdom of his decision to get away from the house before dawn.

He felt safer with a few miles between himself and the other two.

"No, I haven't sensed her or Drew for the past hour or two." His sentence ended slightly high in tone, almost as if it were a question.

Carol picked up on it.

"You sound hesitant." She popped a thick chunk of dark-yellow cheese into her mouth and chewed on it.

Michael didn't want to bother her with the other nagging sensations he'd been feeling since leaving Caine's compound in London. Before he could think of a smooth way to avoid the topic, Carol's hand snaked out and caught his. She held it for a moment, blind eyes staring into the distance over his shoulder.

"So who do you think you've been sensing?" she said then.

"That wasn't nice."

She smiled, sipped at her cider. "I know, but I could tell you were getting ready to bullshit me."

He chuckled. "I was."

"So—who?"

Michael took a swallow of the rich ale, savored the aftertaste a moment, then said softly, "Caine's friends."

"Who—you mean those other two... what were their names? Eleanor and..."

"Mahafed."

"They're following us?"

"I don't think so."

"Then what?"

"They're keeping tabs on us."

"Oh."

"The... whatever it is I pick up from them is a lot more powerful than the sensations I read from Lea Frazzetti and Drew Garrett." What he'd said didn't really capture what he sensed. "More powerful," he added, "and a lot more subtle at the same time. Nearly subliminal." He'd been sensing something else, too, another presence, but he said nothing about that one. It was too indistinct, too ethereal.

"It's only natural that they'll keep tabs on you and the other two," Carol said. "I would if I were in their place."

"So would I."

"But you still don't sense Jenny?"

"No." He felt like shaking his head but didn't. It was odd, but he was getting used to communicating with Carol in the same sensory modes she used. "Do you?"

"Yes. But there's something else here that's confusing to me."

"Something else?"

"Yes." She wiped at her lips with a napkin, her brow knit in thought.

Michael took a forkful of his cold meat pie. It was delicious. He didn't understand why English cooking was maligned by so many people he knew.

"It's like interference," she said then. "Like static on a radio. It's not coming from you ... but it blocks out everything except you when I touch you. It's as if it's coming *through* you, as if you were the transmitter, the ... conduit, or whatever you'd call it."

Experimentally, she reached out and touched Michael's hand again. "There's some force near here that's mucking up my senses."

Michael knew what she was referring to. It was the same presence he'd been feeling.

"You sense it, too," Carol said with some surprise.

This time he nodded. She was holding his hand, and he knew she could feel his response.

"Wha—— no, who do you think it is?"

Michael lifted a shoulder, dropped it. "He feels old."

"He?"

"Yeah, he."

Carol paused with a piece of cold cut just below her lips. "Merlin?"

Michael laughed, as if to brush the name aside. The laugh was brittle and accomplished the exact opposite of what he'd intended.

"You've been wondering about him, too, haven't you?"

"Yes."

"Do you think he's still alive? Buried somewhere? I mean, what the hell, Caine told you he was born in the twelfth century, didn't he? Why couldn't Merlin still be alive?"

"I don't think he is. What I'm reading is too weak. It's more like a residue, an . . . an afterimage."

"A ghost?"

"No. Not a ghost. Just a remnant of what once was, like the fading light you see for a minute after you look directly at the sun."

They ate in silence for a few minutes. When Carol spoke again, it was with a deeper, more serious tone to her already deep voice.

"Do you think you can kill them?" she asked.

It was odd, but Michael had been wondering the same thing.

Odder still that both of them could contemplate the idea so coolly.

"I don't know."

Was there still too much of the psychologist in him? Too much of the civilized man, the scientist, as Caine had said? Too much of the rational, law-abiding, sworn-to-help-humanity liberal?

"You did okay with Lea Frazzetti this morning."

"I didn't try to kill her."

"You probably could have."

"I know."

He nibbled quietly at the crust of his pie, sipped at the last of his ale.

"She doesn't have the same concern for you," Carol said, reaching out to find his hand again.

Michael knew that was true. He was the odd man out of the trio, the only one who apparently had any qualms about using the strange and awful powers to which Caine had opened their eyes.

"I suppose I don't have any choice. I'll have to fight them. And kill them, if the chance presents itself." He swallowed, let his eyes wander over the lunchtime patrons in the pub. What a strange conversation to be having in such a peaceful setting, he thought. "I'm in this whether I want to be or not. Caine has Jenny."

That seemed to say it all.

As he was about to change the topic, he felt a swirling sensation overtake him. He grabbed the edge of the table and held on. *What now?* Lea Frazzetti again? Or Drew?

Images formed unbidden in his mind and swam dizzyingly around and around in his head. He closed his eyes.

"Michael, what is it?" He heard the desperation in Carol's voice. She grabbed his hands.

Did she sense it, too?

"Michael . . . ?"

Not Frazzetti.

Not Drew.

Someone else was sending this message.

----------- *17* -----------

Drew awoke sweating.

His mind reeled.

He'd dozed off beside Frizzy in her bed after having a bout of the quick-and-dirty. She'd been good. So had he. But now his head was spinning and he was sure she'd taken him for a ride—the bitch.

He sat up and slapped his hands to his head to try to recapture some balance.

What the hell was going on?

The room spun around him, whirled as if being drawn into a whirlpool. He grabbed the side of the mattress and held on.

Beside him, he became dimly aware of Frizzy.

She was doing this to him! Goddamn her!

He willed the cyclone to end.

It didn't. If anything, it intensified.

Desperately, he swung around in the bed and grabbed at Frizzy.

She was oblivious to him. Her eyes were rolled up into her head. She appeared to be in the grip of some kind of seizure.

Drew released her. His own muscles were losing their receptivity to his commands.

The world was growing dark.

Images slammed into his mind, sent him reeling. Images of power. Images of fire and blood and waving swords. Images of storm-tossed seas and broken bodies. Images of horror and war and pestilence, of starvation and death, in all its guises.

Drew collapsed back into the enfolding softness of the mattress, his hands pressed to his ears.

Voices cried out in the swirling mists of vague visions.

Babies cried.

Women wailed.

Flames crackled.

Wind howled.

Horses whinnied and squealed in terror.

And then, abruptly, the sun shone clear in the vision. Clouds parted, turned fleecy white, and gently faded away.

Waves stroked a peaceful shore.

Birds sang.

People, wearing clothing from a different era, frolicked on grassy fields.

Other people laughed and squealed in delight at a turn-of-the-century baseball game.

Children danced and sang, their voices sweet and timeless.

The maelstrom slowed, settled into one coherent image.

It was the image of a book. An old book, bound in worn leather. Oversized. Clutched between two gnarled and veined hands. Held up to the night sky, wavering in uneven, yellowish light from an open fire. A pale, sallow, indistinct face was barely visible in the darkness behind the book, a gaunt, hollow-eyed face outlined by firelit silver hair—glowing, ghostly hair that trailed down the old man's back until it evaporated into the darkness.

This can be yours.

The message formed in his head. His guts twisted. The message hadn't come in verbal form, not in words, not in a language Drew understood. There was something visceral about the message, something digested, sensed within the body, known, absorbed, taken in without knowing exactly how it came to be. It was as if he had always known the message.

This can be yours.

And the book—Drew knew what that was, too. Had always known it, as if the knowledge of it had been passed to him through Caine's genes, from father to son.

This can be yours.

The repetition of the message was almost hypnotic.

Yours for the taking.

He realized that the book contained the secrets he sought.

Yours for the taking.

But where was it?

Yours for the taking.

It belonged to Caine. The knowledge of it came from Drew's flesh, seeped into the base of his brain. It contained the secrets of Caine's forebears.

Kill him for it.

Kill him? Him was Caine. Why Caine? He was dying. Why not kill the other two, Frizzy and the Dragon?

Kill him and it is yours.

What was this? A revelation? Kill Caine. Forget about the other two. Make a direct assault on the master without bothering to worry about fighting the others. Could it be done?

At what cost?

Kill Caine and the book is yours.

What would it take to kill Caine? Would he be expecting an attack?

Knowledge is yours for the taking.

The book. It filled Drew's mind. Pages flipped open, flipped past, flipped fast, revealing ancient calligraphy and scribblings, detailed drawings, sketches, phrases, tidbits of information on this plant and that mineral, page after page of knowledge, forbidden knowledge, hidden, secretive knowledge. . . .

Yours for the taking.

Drew felt a fever inside. He was burning.

He wanted that book.

He had to have it.

To hell with the cost.

Yours for the—

Drew tensed. His breath caught in his throat.

A worm of doubt burrowed into his gray matter.

Paranoia.

Strikes deep.

Into your life it will creep.

The words of the old Buffalo Springfield song caromed through his mind.

Who was playing with his mind? Where was this daymare coming from?

Dragon?

Frizzy?

He stretched his mind out, absorbing every bit of information he could sense, as far as his senses could reach.

Nothing came to him.

Not from the comatose form of Frizzy next to him and not from any other source he could identify.

It wasn't the Dragon or Frizzy, he was certain.

He willed the vision to cease.

It didn't go away.

No need to play by his constraining rules.

The image of the book, its pages fluttering in some unholy wind, filled Drew's inner vision. The image altered, shifted. He saw stairs leading down, down, down, deep into the earth. He recognized the simple Doric columns, the glimmering waters of the subterranean Roman bath. The vision wavered. Another stairwell appeared, taking him deeper into the earth. Taking him into a near-complete darkness. Down...down...down, darker and dimmer and more shadowy.

Into another room.

With a vaulted ceiling and a worn, stone floor. Walls of crumbling stone. Candles on a raised dais. Not an altar. A table. Like the table of an ancient library, or the table of a medieval scribe.

There, fluttering in the dim light, lay the book.

Kill him and the prize is yours.

Knowledge is yours.

Victory is yours.

The vision altered again, blurred, shimmered into a vapor, and evaporated.

The world had gone still. It was an unreal, surrealistic stillness, a silence that rang, like the silence following a shotgun blast in a closed, stone room.

He glanced quickly about himself.

Little had changed.

Frizzy lay beside him, blinking, stunned, bathed in perspiration. The bedclothes felt damp. The grandfather clock tocked softly to itself in the corner. The subdued Victorian clutter and colors of the room belied the heated emotions flowing through Drew's veins, the chilly sweat clinging to his body.

It was barely noon.

He felt the bed shift as Frizzy pulled herself up against the headboard. Her full breasts peeked over the top of the bedclothes.

Softly, she said, "Jesus."

Drew nodded. "You had the dream, too?"

She looked at him, the angles of her face gone dead serious. "The book?"

He nodded again. "And the message to kill Caine."

It was her turn to nod. "The same."

"Where do you think it came from?"

"You mean, 'from whom?' My guess is it was Caine's fearsome duo."

"Eleanor and Mahafed?"

"Mmmm."

Drew snorted a bitter laugh. The vision had seemed

too good to be true. And what good could it do him with Frizzy privy to the same info? "Trying to set us up to kill Caine so they can move in and pick our bones."

Frizzy was quiet, thinking.

Drew opened his mind a tiny crack, searched gingerly for the fringe of Frizzy's thoughts. He wanted to know what was going on in that pretty little head of hers.

"Don't," she said coldly.

Drew pressed a little harder.

A sharp pain knifed into his skull, just above his left ear.

He flinched, stopped his probing.

"That was part of the agreement," Frizzy said. "You stay out of my head, I stay out of yours. We have a truce until Dragon is out of the way. Don't mess it up."

Drew tossed a gentle, disarming chuckle her way. "Hey, it was no big deal."

"Listen, Drew. I'm not one of your dumb groupies who's so enamored of your fame and wealth that I'm going to kiss your fanny simply because you flash it at me. So cut with the cutesy, I-was-only-being-a-bad-little-boy routine. It won't work with me. And I don't think it's cute. You agreed to stay out of my head, so do it, or the deal's off."

Drew felt his face freeze.

This was one hell of a tough bitch.

Cold.

As cold as a polar bear's butt.

"Okay," he said. "Okay. Sorry. I was only trying to figure out what you had in mind about Caine."

Half of her mouth twitched into a smile. "You mean, 'Should we kill him?'"

Her eyes locked on his. "He said Eleanor and Mahafed would eat us alive if he were dead."

"Does he have to die in order for us to get ahold of that book?"

Drew grinned. "I like the way you think."

Frizzy glanced away, her mouth held in an unreadable straight line. "If we have the book, we have an obvious advantage over Dragon."

"Who is far, far away at the moment," Drew said, gloating. He'd sensed the Dragon's fading emanations before dawn, after being awakened by the ungodly psychic din coming from Frizzy's room.

"If we act fast . . ."

She didn't have to finish the sentence.

Drew could tell that her mind was racing, searching for a solution, a rational, workable way to snatch that book without bringing on their own deaths.

His own mind was racing, too.

He wanted that book.

For himself.

Screw the Frizz.

If he played his cards right, if he and Frizzy came up with a way to nab the book from Caine, the trick would be to turn on her before she knew what hit her. With the book he doubted whether he'd need her help anymore. For him the process was simple: Neutralize Caine—for a while. Cop the book. Fry the Frizz. And Zap the Dragon. One . . . two . . . three. Simple as a recipe.

With Frizzy and the Dragon gone, Caine wouldn't be in any position to bitch. There would be only one successor around.

Me.

Drew Garrett, sorcerer *extraordinaire*!

He smiled smugly, quite pleased with himself.

"The difficult part," Frizzy said thoughtfully, "is figuring out a way to convince Caine to part with the book—or putting him in such a position that he can't stop us from grabbing it."

"How do we know he's protecting the book?" Drew asked.

Frizzy considered his question. For a moment, the focus of her eyes drifted. A second later, she was back. "He's here," she said. "Somewhere in the ruins below the house." She touched a finger to her lip. "I'm sure he's not going to want to part with that book—not yet, anyway."

They were driving in a high-walled, leafy canyon created by massive hedgerows crowding both sides of the narrow road. Michael swerved to his left to avoid an oncoming delivery van, which had wobbled around a sharp turn fifty yards in front of the Jaguar. The passenger side of the dark green Jaguar slashed at the foliage growing on the dangerously solid stone wall of the hedgerow. The foliage made sharp slapping sounds against the car body.

The delivery truck, still swerving, slithered past to Michael's right, with scant inches to spare.

God, the way the English drove on these treacherous, winding roads!

For an odd moment, he was glad Carol hadn't been able to see how close they'd come to smashing up.

"How fast are we going?" Carol asked.

"Too fast," Michael replied, easing his foot slightly off the accelerator. "Another ten minutes isn't going to mean anything."

He concentrated on his driving, keeping the perfectly responsive car at the edge of the safety limit. It wouldn't be long before he left the narrow country roads and hit M3, the main freeway that would carry them straight back to London. He could really make time then, until he hit the snags and snarls of London.

He flashed past the sparse outlying buildings of a small village whose name he didn't catch, and swung a sharp left into a traffic circle. He missed his exit the first time around, and had to make another full circle before slicing off again in the direction of London.

"Feels like a horizontal roller coaster," Carol said.

"It was one of those traffic circles I showed you on the way out here this morning. It's nice you don't have to stop at them, but Jesus, they can sure be confusing if you don't know the road well."

Once again he settled back for a long run through the rolling countryside.

"Have you made any more sense of the vision?" Carol asked.

He'd been pondering it since leaving the pub and Glastonbury. People in the pub had thought he was sick, at first. Thank God, he'd been able to bring himself under control within a few seconds. He knew he'd acted dazed

for a while, but he'd managed to ride out the confusing
images without looking too bad. He hated making a public
fool of himself, could imagine how godawful his father
must have felt having suffered more than a dozen severe
heart attacks in public before finally buying the farm at a
Cubs game.

The goddamn Cubs had even lost that one.

"It had to be Mahafed and Eleanor constructing it," he
said. He hit the steering wheel. "Dammit, I shouldn't have
left that house this morning." He shook his head. "I
thought I was being so damn smart, clearing out of there
before dawn and leaving the other two to go after each
other. And now this has to happen."

"You don't know that they received the same vision."

"I don't *know* it, but I'm pretty damn sure."

"And you think they might be stupid enough to kill
Caine?"

"Or try to. Especially that character-disordered rock 'n'
roller."

Michael touched the brakes, then pressed them harder,
downshifting as he did to take some of the strain off the
brakes. He stopped in the middle of nowhere, on an
open plain, and let a flock of sheep *ba* and *bleet* and
jiggle their fluffy bodies across the road. A black and
white farm dog nipped at their heels, keeping them moving and in a solid formation. The wrinkled and muddy
farm boy bringing up the rear was giving the Jaguar a
darn good look-over.

Once the woolly beasts were off the road, Michael
moved off again, rapidly regaining his former speed.

"Do you think there's really such a book hidden in those
ruins below Caine's house?" Carol asked.

"I have no way of knowing." Michael frowned. "That
was part of what was so confusing..." His mind vividly
re-created that part of the vision. *The book.* Held in
those ancient, liver-spotted hands. Fluttering. Lit by the
uneven, guttering candlelight. But superimposed over
that image had been another...fainter, indistinct, like a
double-exposed photograph...even less clear than that
...subliminal, like mild interference on a television

screen . . . something long and cylindrical . . . with knobs
on the end . . . about the size of a short baseball bat and
built like a rolling pin—straight, like that, only less
solid. The color of aged paper, brown and yellowed,
with patches of stain creating uneven patterns on the barrel of whatever it was. Seen in shadow. Against an uneven, coarsely cut rock wall and a jumble of white
sticks . . . or bones, maybe.

The only thing the image suggested was an ancient
scroll.

But the image hadn't felt like it was part of the main
vision. There was a different quality to the image of the
scroll, and it had faded rapidly, appearing for less than two
or three heartbeats.

"What do you mean, 'confusing'?" Carol asked.

"Why would Eleanor and Mahafed give that book to
Garrett and Frazzetti, or to me?"

"If it results in Caine's death, it's to their advantage."

"I know. But that's too simplistic. Even with the book
in their hands, they wouldn't be able to absorb its secrets
in time to use them to defend against Mahafed and
Eleanor."

"I don't think it's so simplistic. You yourself said you
thought Drew Garrett was a fairly disturbed individual,
and capable of most anything that fed his distorted ego.
He might think he could pull it off successfully."

Michael nodded. It was true. He did think Garrett was
a marginal person, capable of almost any kind of behavior.

"But I think he's smart enough to realize that killing
Caine at this point won't be to his advantage."

Beside him, in her comfortable leather bucket seat, he
caught Carol's unconvinced shrug. "But you're not sure."

"No, I'm not. Which is why I want to get back to London before Garrett or Lea Frazzetti pull some bonehead
act."

"You're sure they didn't send the vision as a means of
luring you back?"

"I don't think so. I . . . don't know for sure, but somehow, I'd expect a different kind of ploy from them. This

one is too subtle for either of them. I think it was Eleanor and
Mahafed. And *that's* why I have to get back there. According
to Caine, Eleanor and Mahafed can't—or won't—directly
enter Caine's property with Caine alive. But what's to stop
them from playing mind games with Caine's guests? I think
they're forcing this whole thing to a showdown as fast as they
can, and trying to get rid of Caine in the process." He bit down
on his lip for a second. "I can't let that happen. Without Caine
to protect us, I think Garrett, Frazzetti, and myself are
goners."

Carol was quiet for several miles.

In the distance Michael saw the entrance to M3, the
freeway aimed like an arrow at the heart of London. Without conscious thought, he pressed harder on the accelerator.

"What about the other vision you mentioned?"

"The scroll thing?"

"Yes. Where do you think that came from, or what it
meant?"

Michael had racked his brain trying to make sense of
that. He had ideas, but they seemed farfetched.

"I don't know."

And it was true.

But somewhere deep within his brain, a niggling little
question was beginning to gnaw at his already overloaded
nervous system.

18

Drew listened to the subterranean sounds of the Roman
ruins. It was the sound of the grave.

Absolute stillness.

Beside him he saw Frizzy extend an arm and point to

a narrow, dark stone archway to one side of the rectangular pool. Tucked away in a corner behind two double stone columns, it was nearly invisible from most of the bath.

Frizzy moved off that way, stepping silently.

Drew waited a moment before following her. He held a chair leg in one hand. It would be so easy to conk her here and be done with her, he thought, but he realized that he needed her for a few minutes longer. Once they subdued Caine, he'd deal with her.

He fell into stride behind her, careful to make no sound on the coarse rock floor.

They'd decided on a very simple plan.

The two of them would control Caine's powers, helping the other as much as possible. They had no idea how powerful Caine was, or what kind of defense he would throw at them, but together they thought they had a chance of keeping the man busy and off guard for a brief moment. A few seconds would be all they would need to subdue Caine.

The entire plan rested on one simple idea.

Back to basics.

They didn't know how well they could do battle with Caine using their newly acquired skills. Not well, they feared, especially not if Caine were warned of their intentions in time to plan a defense.

Even then, their plan had a good chance of succeeding.

Its success rested in its simplicity.

Surprise.

Speed.

And basic human strength rather than reliance on their unproven new skills, although, hopefully, those would come in handy as well.

If Drew could get close enough to Caine, he could knock the old man unconscious. Unconscious meant no mind games from the master.

An unconscious Caine also meant a quick turn on Frizzy. Only Drew didn't intend to give her the light tap he planned for Caine.

He was going to smash her fucking skull to pieces.

One down ... then two ... and three in the wings, as soon as he could locate the Dragon.

Lea lead the way through the narrow, hidden archway. Beyond it was a comfortable room decorated in much the same Victorian fashion as the Georgian house built on top of the ruins. A large fire crackled in a giant fireplace dominating the far wall of the stone-walled room. The room had high ceilings. The walls were draped with tapestries, the floor, as upstairs, covered with the rich colors of Persian rugs.

Caine was there, standing near the fireplace. Beside him, seated in a comfortable leather chair, perched on the edge of the seat, was his redheaded familiar, the Lear.

Drew kept the chair leg to his side, hidden behind his leg, kept his mind steeled for any kind of assault that Caine might try.

"Stop right there," Caine said.

Drew hesitated. He stopped only when Frizzy pulled up short.

"I don't like the sensations I feel," Caine said.

"We haven't come to hurt you," Frizzy said.

She moved a step closer, Drew realized. He followed her example.

"I'm not so sure of that," Caine said.

Drew felt a jarring jolt hit his mind. He concentrated and fended it off. He saw Frizzy doing the same.

Frizzy kept moving.

Once we start, she had said, *it has to be fast. There'll be no turning back.*

And she wasn't turning back, that was for certain.

"Stop," Caine said, "or I will be forced to—"

Rushing, stomping feet sounded behind Drew. He turned, astounded to see a dozen huge men rushing into the room. He blinked.

Illusion.

Be ready for anything!

He and Frizzy had warned each other a hundred times.

He blinked the illusion away.

It faded but didn't die.

The men rushed at him. He sidestepped, moving into a defensive stance he'd learned in a self-defense class.

But he didn't have to use his paltry karate.

The men rushed past him, rushed toward Caine.

Frizzy was throwing this hallucination at Caine.

Drew turned, followed the rush of men. He had seconds to do what was necessary.

Flames *whooshed* up in front of him and soared to the ceiling, creating a curtain of roaring fire.

Men screamed. Burst afire. Twisted to the side, off target, helpless against the flames. They vanished.

Illusion! Drew reminded himself. All illusion.

The flames wavered.

He rushed forward.

Ignore the flames.

"Block his mind!" Drew yelled to Frizzy. "Block his goddamn mind!"

He felt the pressure in the room as Frizzy bore down on Caine's mind with all her powers. He tried to add his own powers to the psychic melee, tried to draw a black curtain down over Caine's eyes.

He saw the Lear moving.

He ignored her.

She wasn't the primary danger.

Caine was.

They had to subdue him, *NOW!*

Drew stormed through the flames.

They didn't hurt.

They didn't exist except in his mind.

He focused his entire being on Caine.

Caine lowered a shotgun.

The shotgun belched flame.

Drew, stunned, felt the shot slam into his chest. He was lifted from the floor, spun lazily around like a top, knew he was dying, when all of a sudden he heard Frizzy yelling . . .

"Don't believe it!"

Drew blinked. He was stumbling to the floor but unharmed.

His eyes swept to Caine.

The old fart didn't have any goddamn shotgun in his paws.

Drew jumped up, dived toward Caine. Caine was moving away now, shimmering into invisibility.

Drew concentrated, blocked the ploy.

Caine solidified again.

Drew closed in.

Caine took him by surprise, turned on the attack, and dived at Drew.

Drew brought the chair leg up, swung it at the old man, hit nothing but air.

The diving Caine disappeared.

The real Caine had managed to get to the other side of the huge room, was fleeing toward the exit to the bath area.

Drew swung around. He had the angle on Caine.

Ignore whatever comes at you! he commanded himself.

Ignore it.

Just hit the bastard!

He charged Caine.

Razor-sharp spikes sprouted from the floor.

Not real.

Ignoring them, Drew trampled through the brittle steel blades, heard them breaking underfoot, but refused to believe the pain with which Caine was trying to control him.

He was on Caine now.

He swung the chair leg.

Caine ducked.

The leg grazed the man's scalp.

The razor-edge spikes disappeared.

The unreal pain in Drew's feet ceased.

Caine was stumbling.

Drew brought the leg up again and, very controlled, very deliberately, *whacked* it down onto the right side of Caine's gray head.

Caine sagged, sprawled to the carpeted stone floor.

Drew, fueled by the rush of adrenaline flooding his body, shouted and jumped in the air, twisting around as he did so, intent on locating Frizzy before she had ab-

sorbed the fact that Caine was out for the count. "We did
i——"

His landing was not so comfortable.

His arms suddenly felt like rubber.

His knees buckled.

His face froze in a rictus of pain.

Illusion, he told himself. *Illusion. Not real. Seal it off.
All in your head.*

But he knew it wasn't an illusion.

Some things you just know.

Lea let Garrett's weight do the work for her. She stood
with her feet spread wide, her arms locked in front of her.
Garrett was as stupid as she had thought he was—jumping
for joy! God, what an emotional cretin!

It had given her a better angle than she could have hoped
for.

He'd come down in perfect position, spread-eagled, unprotected. The long, slim butcher knife gripped in her fists
had slid into his belly as easily as the proverbial hot knife
into butter.

It was encountering something tougher than mere flesh
now, something that crackled and popped softly near the
base of his breastbone. Gristle?

His face had gone pale.

It hung in the air immediately in front of her.

He was getting heavy, sagging against her, letting her
take all the weight now.

She stepped back a bit and let go of the long-bladed
knife.

Drew Garrett slid down her arms, his eyes seeking hers.
He was muttering something to himself, something that
sounded like, "Illusion, not real, don't believe it." She
couldn't understand it all that well. Garrett landed on his
knees, erect, swaying. His chair leg *clunked* to the floor. A
foul smell filled the air.

Quickly, Lea checked on the whereabouts of Helen
Locklear.

Caine's familiar was on her knees beside Caine's prone
body.

Lea forgot about the woman.

Her attention returned to Garrett.

His eyes were already filming over, even as he tried to focus on her face.

"You weren't quick enough," she said.

Slurred, he said, "Illusion."

Lea shook her head. "Reality."

She put her hand on his head and gently pushed him to the side. "Night-night," she said.

He toppled without a word, with barely a sound.

Lea turned her attention back to Helen Locklear. The redhead held up a hand. "I won't fight you. Aaron instructed me not to."

"Is he alive?"

Locklear nodded yes.

"Good. Do you know where the book is?"

Locklear stared at her, dumbfounded. "How did you know about—"

"Never mind that. Get it for me. I'll stay with Mr. Caine. I don't want him reviving until I've had a chance to look at that book."

The Locklear woman rose to her feet and started away.

"And don't try anything foolish with the book," Lea called after her. "You and I both know that you're not a match for me anymore."

The redhead's nod was barely perceptible, but she'd acknowledged Lea's words. Lea cast a quick look at the redhead's thoughts. All she read was compliance.

She smiled.

One to go.

Michael knew something was wrong as soon as he neared the front gate of Caine's estate. He could feel it.

He pulled the Jaguar to the curb half a block from the gate leading into the estate.

"What is it?" Carol asked.

He told her of his uneasiness. He let his mind drift out of himself, let it permeate the grounds of Caine's estate. He felt Caine's presence, and the presence of Helen

Locklear. He also sensed Lea Frazzetti. And a number of servants.

But no rock 'n' roller.

Michael guessed that Lea Frazzetti had taken care of Garrett.

He had to admit that he felt little remorse.

He let his mind touch at Caine's, found the man unresisting. He pushed his way into Caine's existence and sensed only darkness and blurred, distorted images lacking meaning. Caine was alive, but unconscious.

Michael shifted his attention back toward Lea Frazzetti, but paused.

He sensed the presence of others nearby.

Powerful others.

Eleanor and Mahafed.

The vultures were sniffing the carrion.

He was sure they would move quickly with Caine unable to defend himself.

He had no time to waste.

"I'm going in," he said to Carol. He opened his car door.

"I'm coming with you."

He rounded the car and rested a restraining hand on her shoulder. "No. You won't be able to help. Not this time."

Carol gripped his hand.

"What do you see?"

She shook her head. "Nothing. I can't get a reading. There are forces around here interfering with me." Her eyes looked tense.

"If I don't come for you in half an hour," Michael said, "find someone to take you to the American embassy. Get away from here, and don't tell anyone any of what's happened. They won't believe you, anyway. They'll stick you in an inpatient unit for observation if you start babbling about sorcerers and hallucinations. Just tell them you got separated from your friends and need help returning to the States."

Her blind eyes focused directly on his face. It gave Michael an eerie sensation, as if she could see.

"And if I don't come back, do what you can to find Jenny. Promise?"

"Promise."

Michael bent and kissed her. His lips lingered on hers. He wondered if he would ever kiss that mouth again.

"Do as I said, okay?"

She nodded, her lower lip gripped tightly against her teeth.

Michael jogged to the iron gate in Caine's massive stone wall. Cut into the base of the left gate was a man-size door. It was opened by a servant. Michael followed the drive to the portico.

Once in the house, he stopped to catch his breath.

Caine, Locklear, and Lea Frazzetti were in the ruins below the house, he realized.

Caine was still out cold, although Michael thought he detected a slight easing of the darkness within the man's mind.

He debated what he should do.

He had no idea of how best to fight Lea Frazzetti, but he was certain that that was exactly what he would have to do within the next few minutes.

He touched her mind with his, caught a strong surge of power and confidence, then felt a blinding pain sear through the frontal lobe of his brain.

Damn! He'd given his presence away.

What now?

He knew he didn't have much time.

He really had no choice.

He had to go after Lea Frazzetti before Eleanor and Mahafed took advantage of Caine's disability.

He had to go after her in the ruins.

He moved to the wall panel and the stairwell. There had to be some strategy he could use to stop Lea Frazzetti.

But what was it?

Lea pointed toward the fireplace. "Drag Caine over there," she ordered the Locklear woman. "And you, sit in that chair and don't move."

The goddamn book in her hands wasn't going to do her a bit of good right now, Lea realized. She'd had it in her possession for less than twenty minutes. She'd scanned its drawings without understanding. She'd started reading at the beginning, and half of what she read was gobbledygook. She'd have to study this damn thing word by word to make sense of it.

And she didn't have time because that goddamn Dragon was on his way downstairs.

She closed the book and dropped it onto a small table in the grouping around the fireplace. She glanced past Garrett's body toward the entrance to the vast room.

So be it.

Me and Dragon.

May the best *woman* win.

A cold, intense expression not unlike a smile locked onto her jaw.

She'd subdued Caine and killed Drew Garrett. She should be able to deal with Dragon.

But how?

Directly, as she'd dealt with Garrett.

Or with hallucinations.

She had no idea what would be most effective.

She moved to Garrett's body, rolled it on its back, and tugged the knife out of Garrett's breastbone. She had to step on his chest and yank hard in order to free the weapon. She wiped its deadly nine-inch blade on Garrett's shirt, then rolled the pale face back to the floor.

A lot of fans would mourn his disappearance, she realized.

Perversely, it also occurred to her that his disappearance would probably ensure the immortality of his name. His disappearance too closely mimicked the insanity of his records.

She hid the knife under her blouse, as she'd done with Garrett, slipped it under her belt.

When the time was ripe . . .

"Lea."

She swung around to face the wide doorway into Caine's subterranean retreat. Dragon stood there, his feet set firmly beneath him, as if expecting the wrath of God to visit him.

Hallucination or guile?

She caught Dragon's glance toward Garrett's body and the rich redness surrounding it.

"Congratulations," Dragon said.

Lea waited, expecting any instant to have to react to and fend off some horror of Dragon's creation.

Dragon moved easily into the room.

His footsteps echoed off the high ceiling until he stepped onto a carpet.

"Now, I imagine, it's my turn," he said.

Lea considered the man's calmness.

It was unnerving.

Why didn't the bastard try something?

He studied Caine and Helen Locklear without batting an eyelash. Then his gaze fell to the book on the low table.

"I see you've found the book."

Lea nodded.

Without changing expression, she fired a sharp thought between Dragon's eyes.

Dragon staggered.

She took a step forward but stopped.

Dragon recovered quickly.

"That was good," he said. "It hurt. It nearly blinded me."

He was good, she realized. *Very good.* It was very possible she would not win in a battle of minds with him.

But a battle of wits was another thing entirely.

"What did you find in the book?" Dragon asked.

He was standing casually now, as if the pressure was off him, as if he now knew that he was stronger than she.

Goddamn the man! Why didn't he try something?

"It needs to be studied," she said. Dragon was moving toward the book now. She felt the tension rising in her breast. She didn't want him to put his hands on it.

"You realize, of course," Dragon was saying, "that Eleanor and Mahafed are likely to show up any moment with Caine in that condition." He nodded in Caine's direction.

Lea didn't bother looking.

"Stop," she said.

Dragon paused. "Why?"

She was thinking fast. What if the bastard was right about Eleanor and Mahafed? Damn! "We could share the book," she said.

Dragon studied her for a long moment. She felt like some kind of slimy thing under a microscope. Why was he taking so long to answer, for Christ's sake?

When he responded, all he said was, "Go on."

Lea edged toward the table where the oversized book rested. She didn't know why, she just didn't want him close to the book.

"We could keep Caine in a groggy state," she said, "with drugs or something. We could keep him alive long enough to learn what's in the book. Why can't there be four sorcerers? Who says you and I can't fight Eleanor and Mahafed together? Or kill one of them and share the spoils?"

Dragon pursed his lips, considering her words. He moved beside the table holding the book.

"Are you suggesting a truce?"

A weak smile formed on her lips. "Exactly."

"Did you have one with him?" Dragon pointed toward Garrett's body.

"Yes, and I lived up to it. But he tried to kill me as soon as Caine was unconscious. I beat him to it."

"So how long do we set our truce for?"

"As long as you like," she said. "We could both live here. It's a big enough place."

She realized Dragon was smiling a little now. "I'm sure we could trust each other."

"We could," she said.

He picked up the book, thumbed several pages, eyes intent on what he saw.

"How about it?" she asked. She moved to a position across the table from him.

He edged a half step farther away.

If she could just get close to him—

"This looks like complicated stuff," he said.

"We could learn it together. There's no reason we can't trust each other."

Dragon studied her again, his eyes hooded slightly. He said, "Me think you speak with forked tongue, paleface."

"What?"

He laughed out loud then, and she felt herself flushing because he was laughing at her, and she didn't quite understand why, and beyond that, she didn't like to be laughed at.

Suddenly she felt frightfully out of her league.

What was this bastard up to?

Psyching her out?

Of course! He was a shrink, wasn't he?

She knew she would have to make her move soon.

If only that bastard would let her get a little closer.

She tried to buy some time. "What do you mean, I speak with a forked tongue?"

He laughed again, softer this time.

She used his laugh to move closer to him.

He smiled at her then and turned his face directly toward her. "Let me show you a forked tongue," he said.

Lea gaped as Dragon opened his mouth and a long, muscular, forked tongue the color of snakeskin writhed out and wrapped itself around her throat.

She gagged, startled into immobility.

Fold upon greenish fold of stringy-wet tongue slithered out of Dragon's open mouth. Fold upon fold wrapped itself about her and drew her closer to him.

She wanted to scream, but the tight, contracting, snake-like flesh about her throat wouldn't let the sound out.

Then she wanted to laugh.

The joke's on you, you bastard, she thought. *On you!*

The hallucination he'd created was going to be the death of him.

She did nothing to dispel the illusion Dragon was creating.

She told herself to breathe easily, and she did.

But she didn't destroy his hallucination.

Let him believe in it until the very last moment.

She relaxed her terrified body and let the foul, writhing tongue drag her forward. She reached to embrace Dragon, the knife slipping easily from beneath her blouse. She encircled him with her arms, looked into his eyes.

She wanted to see the look in them when she plunged the knife into his back.

The foul fiend pressed her to his chest, searching her eyes for the first sign of death.

Lea joined her hands behind Dragon's back and entwined the fingers of both hands over the hilt of her knife. She had to do this right. She would get only one chance. If she hit bone, and the knife stopped, it was doubtful she'd get a second chance. The knife had to go all the way through the man, had to slice that bastard's heart in two. She had to give it every ounce of strength she had. She tensed, and with a delicious, forceful jerk —strong enough to pierce through bone—she pulled the knife forward, driving it deep into the unresisting flesh of Dragon's back, driving it through the bastard's flesh, through—

There was no change in his eyes.

But there was a pain in her chest.

She coughed.

Blood burbled out of her lips.

And slowly, ever so agonizingly slowly, Dragon and his tongue turned to mist.

Lea stared down at the knife struck to the hilt in her own breast, at the sticky redness pumping out beneath her blouse.

She didn't feel any pain.

She coughed again.

Now she felt pain, pain as she'd never experienced it before, deep in the very core of her being.

She pulled the knife out of her breast. It clattered onto the nearby low table. She sat down on the table, stunned. She'd stabbed herself.

The blood bubbled from her breast in gentle little spurts.

She watched the stain trickle down to her belt and spread out there.

How had he—

She heard a sound, glanced toward the one doorway into the room.

Her vision wavered. She felt weak. She blinked.

Dragon stood there, in the doorway.

Unharmed.

He'd confronted her with an illusion.

She'd stabbed empty air.

Empty air and—

Stop the bleeding.

The thought hit her like a hammer.

The room swam about her.

If you believed you were dying, you were going to die.

She concentrated.

The bubbling in her breast slowed.

She smiled, shook her head weakly to clear it.

She was doing it.

Stopping the bleeding.

She was doing it!

Dizzy, but in control . . .

She was . . .

. . . too late.

In the next moment, she toppled forward.

Her head made a dull *thunk* when it hit the floor.

She didn't hear the awful sound.

She didn't hear anything anymore.

19

"Very good, Mr. Dragon. Very good. I am proud to call you my son."

Michael's eyes left the still-quivering body of Lea Frazzetti and focused on the old man propped against the stone of the fireplace. Caine's lined features looked drawn and weak. The firelight threw bizarre shadows across his face. Beside Caine knelt his trusty friend, Helen Locklear.

Michael moved into the vast room.

He was not proud of what he'd done, but he knew he'd had no choice. His only real consolation was the fact that Lea Frazzetti had died by her own hand. In a way, he hadn't killed her. She'd killed herself.

Michael stepped into the center of the small grouping of furniture facing the blazing fire.

"I must teach you your first lesson," Caine said. His voice was weak and wavering.

"What's that?"

"The taking of a life force."

"What?"

"You heard me."

Michael said nothing.

Caine motioned for Helen Locklear to help him to his feet. She was strong, but the old man came off the floor with great difficulty. Michael moved to his side to help him stand.

The muscles of Caine's left side felt like rubber. There was no muscle tone there. His arm dropped uselessly when Michael let go of it. Caine leaned against his longtime friend and faced Michael.

"Yes, you're right," Caine said. "I have been hurt."

"How?"

Caine nodded toward the two bodies on the floor. "Those two, with a little help from Eleanor and Mahafed, I'm afraid."

"What happened?"

"Mr. Garrett hit me with a chair leg," Caine said.

Michael spotted the swelling and trace of blood high on top of Caine's scalp. That explained the left-side paralysis. The blow had damaged the motor strip in the right hemisphere of Caine's brain.

"Let's put him on the sofa," Michael said to Helen Locklear.

"No," Caine said. Michael was surprised at the force behind the man's words. Caine gestured toward Lea Frazzetti's body. "Helen."

"Help us," Helen Locklear said.

"Not understanding exactly what Caine was up to, Michael did as he was asked.

At Lea Frazzetti's body, Helen Locklear stopped. "Help me lower him to the floor."

Michael assisted.

Once on the floor, Caine crawled closer to Lea Frazzetti's body. "Turn her," he instructed.

He moved sideways, like a crab. Only his right side provided him with motility. There was something obscene in the movement, something not quite human.

Helen Locklear turned Lea Frazzetti's body on its back. Lea's pale face with its open, staring eyes was only inches from Caine's face. "Listen carefully, Mr. Dragon. This is how you take another's life force. It is very simple for ones such as we. You simply place your mouth over the dead person's mouth and, while willing the energy free of the body, you inhale with as much strength as you can."

Michael stared.

"It is how we stay alive so long," Caine said. "As long as the person has been dead for less than five minutes or so, you are safe. Longer than that after death, and you risk being sucked down into death with them."

"No. I don't believe this."

Caine's bloodshot eyes focused on Michael's face. His thin, wrinkled, blue-tinged lips formed into a sneer. "You still insist on being the man of science?"

"What was all that noble crap you fed us the other night? You're nothing better than a vampire."

"I assure you we have nothing in common with those vile creatures," Caine said. "We do not indiscriminately choose whose life force to take. Nor do we take it from the innocent." His eyes shifted to Lea Frazzetti's body and back. "Miss Frazzetti could hardly be considered an innocent. Watch closely, Mr. Dragon."

Michael couldn't believe his eyes.

Dragon placed his mouth over Lea Frazzetti's and with barely a hesitation sucked backward with as much force as his frail body could muster. Lea Frazzetti's body trembled ever so slightly, head to toes. Her eyes rolled even farther back into her head. Then she went slack.

And it was over.

The body, if that was possible, appeared even more dead than it had a moment before. More pathetic, certainly.

Caine rolled to the side and stared at the distant vaulted ceiling. A deep sigh escaped his lips. His ancient, bony chest heaved up and down with a renewed strength.

"Help me up," he said to Helen Locklear. His voice was much stronger.

She moved to his side, stooped, lifted his useless left arm over her head, and stood up. Caine came to his feet easily this time, providing himself adequate assistance with his still-intact right side. Caine's eyes went to the still form that had once been Drew Garrett. "Pity," Caine said, "but Mr. Garrett's been dead a bit too long to chance the process on him."

Caine signaled for Helen Locklear to help him to a chair near the fire.

"How often do you do that?" Michael asked. "How often do you have to take a life force?"

"Not often when you are young, as you are," Caine said.

"But as you grow older, you need your"—he paused to smile wryly—"you need your *fix* more often. Only you will know what is necessary to maintain your own powers."

Michael paced, still not believing this madness.

"So what do you do then? Just go out and find someone to kill?"

Caine adjusted himself as comfortably as possible in his chair. "Someone deserving of it, of course."

"Of course," Michael said sarcastically.

Caine fixed him with eyes suddenly much clearer, the whites startlingly whiter than they'd been minutes earlier. "Have you never thought someone deserved to die?" Caine asked.

Michael said nothing.

"Even you have," Caine said. "Even the rational scientist, the altruistic psychologist out to save the world! We all have," Caine went on. "And despite the zeitgeist, the spirit of the times, no matter how liberal and enlightened some societies become, there are always those who deserve to die."

"No."

"Yes," Caine said emphatically. "The mass murderer, the serial killer, the commandant at an extermination camp, the terrorist who blows up a busload of children —they all deserve to die. It is an insane society that is unable to face that, that places such blind trust in rehabilitation. The people who perform the acts I mentioned are incapable of rehabilitation, Mr. Dragon. And even if they were able to be rehabilitated, who would want them around? Retribution is good for the heart of man, Mr. Dragon. The death of one such as I've described serves a very real and healthy purpose for the society exacting their vengeance."

"What purpose?"

"Revenge. And a resolution to the ache brought on by that person's crime. Their rightful death puts a great many minds to rest, Mr. Dragon. Do not underestimate the power of vengeance."

"So you kill these people?"

"Exactly," Caine said. "If possible, before they commit their crimes. Take the man who attacked you and your daughter as an example."

Michael stared at Caine. "You had something to do with that."

"He was used to test you because he had performed a number of similar crimes. Crimes, I might add, for which he was never caught. But this time, I'm afraid he ran up against someone stronger than he was: *you*. Rather than let him continue his life of crime, I chose to end it while he was in the hospital. As far as the physicians are concerned, the man died of natural causes. Drawing the life force from a living person simply causes their death. It doesn't leave any suggestion as to how the person passed on. It's quite clean."

Michael could think of nothing to say for a moment. In a crazy sort of way Caine's explanation made sense.

Except for one part.

"If you kill them before they commit their crimes," he asked, "why couldn't you simply stop them from doing whatever it was they were intent on, and let them go?"

"I think you know the answer to that as well as I, Mr. Dragon."

Michael considered his own question. Caine was right. A mass murderer was probably going to murder, no matter what. So was a serial killer. So was a terrorist. Even beneath all his scientific training, he believed that. Once people had sunk that low, nothing was going to bring them back.

"I need my rest, Mr. Dragon. And you, if I am not mistaken, have a lady friend waiting for you outside."

Michael sensed the old man's weariness.

"What about my daughter?"

"I will arrange for her return," Caine said. "You will see her this evening."

"Where is she?"

"In Wales. Near Cardiff."

Michael nodded. He and Carol had been on the right track. Cardiff lay just to the northwest of Glastonbury. He was quiet, still numbed by the past fifteen minutes.

"Take the book, Mr. Dragon. Read it. We will talk later this evening."

Michael rubbed his eyes and let the book rest in his lap. He was sitting in one of the wing-backed chairs near the fireplace. Carol lay on the bed, dozing. A languid fire *snapped* and *whuffed* in the firebox. Idly, lost in thought, Michael ran his fingertips over the dry, yellowing parchment pages of the ancient book. The gentle pressure made the paper crackle softly.

The book was an amalgam of writings spanning three millennia. Every page was handwritten. No more than a dozen or so pages in succession were written in the same handwriting. Sorcerer after sorcerer had added something to the book. The last seven pages to have been added to the expandable leather volume were notes scribbled in Caine's pinched style and bearing his name.

Earlier pages, written in languages Michael had never seen before, strangely, made sense to him. Earlier notes described chants and rituals that were later described as unnecessary. Later sorcerers had discovered that the chants and rituals simply opened up access to various brain centers that could be reached more easily and quickly through trained concentration. Later writing made mention that once the brain was opened and made perfectly receptive, learning became a thing of ease, and even indecipherable ancient languages posed no problem.

This explained why the earlier passages made any sense at all to Michael.

A number of times Michael practiced the mental processes mentioned in the book.

He may have been awkward at times, but he never failed to replicate the technique or skill he attempted.

The book was a primer on the use of what Michael had taken to calling the *sixth senses*, because, he discovered, there were hundreds beyond the five considered normal.

Outside, it was beginning to blow toward a storm. It was dark already, nearing 11:00 P.M. Michael wondered when Caine would call him. He had expected it to be earlier.

And he wanted to see Jenny. Wanted to hold her, to feel her wiry strength, to smell the summer straw scent of her hair.

Wanted to be certain she was unharmed.

"Michael?"

He glanced around.

Carol was propped on an elbow, her face turned his way.

"Right here."

"Do you feel what I feel?"

He knew immediately what she was talking about.

He'd sensed it earlier. There was an oppressive psychic stillness around them. But it was a strange calm, as if the eye of a hurricane had formed around the house, insulating them in quietude while a screaming, earth-shattering storm raged just beyond the confines of Caine's estate.

"I feel it."

"What is it?"

"I think Caine may be dying."

Carol let her legs swing off the bed. She walked carefully in his direction. Mentally, he tossed her a visual image of the room.

"Thank you." She smiled. She liked to be able to see, even if only for brief flashes.

She kissed him tenderly on the lips, then tucked her legs under her and sat on the rug. She leaned back against Michael's legs. She held one hand out toward the warmth of the fire. Golden, honey-rich highlights glinted in her hair, reflecting the play of firelight.

"I don't sense his death," she said.

"No?"

She shook her head.

"What then?"

He saw her eyes narrow.

"Others, I guess." Her lips were drawn tightly over her teeth.

"Their deaths?"

"No. Just their presence."

"Eleanor and Mahafed."

She nodded, said nothing.

"They're waiting for Caine to give up the ghost."

"Oh, God; Michael, what a horrible phrase!"

He laughed softly. He'd told her about Caine taking away Lea Frazzetti's life force. He understood her reservation about his choice of words.

"Sorry."

She hugged his legs. "I'm frightened for you," she said. "I wish there was a way—"

A knock at the door cut off her wishes.

It was Helen Locklear.

"He needs you now," was all she said, speaking directly to Michael.

Michael kissed Carol, told her he'd be back in a few minutes, then joined Caine's familiar for the trek to the ruins.

While Michael and Helen Locklear were descending the staircase into the foyer, the storm broke outside. Rain lashed at the windows. Wind buffeted the rock-solid house and wailed through the eaves. Thunder rumbled long and low and ominously, vibrating the chandelier enough to make it *tinkle*.

In Caine's deep cellar room, the bodies of Lea Frazzetti and Drew Garrett had been removed. Not a stain remained of their lives.

Caine, covered by an afghan quilt, lay on the long leather sofa. The sofa had been turned toward the fire. Caine's head was propped up on a pillow. Weakly, Caine gestured for Michael to sit near him.

Michael slid a chair near the head of the sofa, sat down with his elbows resting expectantly on his knees. Helen Locklear touched Caine's cheek, then withdrew from the room.

The old man's face was drawn and ivory-hued. Blue veins snaked here and there across his temples and forehead. Liver spots were displayed vividly against such a pale background. The blue of Caine's eyes looked washed out and timeworn.

"My time is nearer than I thought," he said.

His voice was weak, yet controlled.

"I had hoped to have time to apprentice you properly,"

he said. He reached out a frail hand and clasped Michael's right hand in his cold, bony claw. "I had hoped for months more, even years. But it is not to be."

Michael waited.

"Mr. Garrett's blow to my head has done more damage than I thought at first," he said. "The paralysis is spreading."

"Have you tried to stop it?"

The old man's teeth showed in a weak smile. "Reality sometimes defies our best efforts, Michael Dragon. In the end, it is always reality that wins out, sad to say. Yes, I've tried. But I am too old, and the damage is too serious. It will not be long before I step down to mingle my bones with the dust of the past."

"Is there anything I can do?"

Caine shook his head gently. "It is my time. I have lived long enough. It is time for you to step into my shoes. This"—he gestured slowly—"is all yours now." He coughed softly. "When I am gone, see that I am burned. Helen will help you. She has instructed that a pyre be built behind the house."

"I will."

"Rely on her to help you," he said. "Helen has been by my side for over twenty years." His voice took on a deep tenderness. "And take care of her."

Michael nodded.

"I am sorry I cannot better prepare you to deal with Eleanor and Mahafed. They are waiting. Can you sense their presence?"

"I know they're near."

Caine studied him.

"I have read the book," Michael said.

"And experimented, I hope."

"With everything."

"You found most of it within your abilities?"

"I could do it all. Some, not so easy, but I managed."

"Even travel out of your body?"

"Yes."

The old man's eyebrows raised, and Michael realized

that Caine was surprised. "You are the one," Caine said. "For most of us, it took years to master that art."

"I wouldn't say that I had it mastered."

"To be able to do it so soon—it will not be difficult for you to master it." That tight scrutiny formed on Caine's face again. "And what has happened to the man of science?" Caine asked.

Michael shrugged. "He's still inside me. But I'm different. *How different,* I can't say."

"Time will show you how best to use your abilities."

"If I survive Eleanor and Mahafed."

"Yes," the old man said with a nod. *"if . . ."*

"I have a question for you."

"Of course," Caine said. "You must have many. Ask. Ask quickly. I want to tell you what I can while I still have a voice to speak with."

"When I learned of the book—"

"In that vision from Eleanor and Mahafed?"

"Yes. When I learned of it, I experienced another vision at the same time."

Caine's eyes focused cleanly on Michael's face. "Go on."

"Are there scrolls of some sort? Like the book?"

Michael saw a frozen expression sweep over Caine's features. It thawed as quickly as it had formed.

"You saw scrolls?"

Michael dropped his head slightly, in answer.

Caine's eyes focused far beyond the vaulted ceiling overhead.

His voice was soft. "There have always been rumors," he said. "But none who has lived in my lifetime ever saw the scrolls—not even in a vision, which is how our kind experiences much of this world, especially that which is not easily explained." He shifted his head back and forth. "You saw the scrolls?"

"I'm not sure what I saw."

Caine's attention came fully back to Michael now. "Tell me about the scrolls."

Michael told of his vision.

"Where were you when this occurred?"

"In Glastonbury."

Caine's eyes did that focusing again.

"Merlin's country," he said.

"And Merlin's scrolls?" Michael asked.

Caine did not reply for a long moment. Then he coughed and said, "Maybe there is more to the legend than mere rumor. But, sadly, I shall never know." He drew Michael's hand to his ancient, lined lips and kissed the back of the hand. The old man's lips felt cold, lifeless. "Think well of me, Michael Dragon. Do not be taken in by Eleanor and Mahafed. They are full of tricks, are those two."

"I'll do my best," Michael said.

"You have no other choice," Caine said, his voice sounding weaker. "At this point, you are too much of a danger to Eleanor and Mahafed. They will try to destroy you. If they cannot, they will strike a bargain with you, and the balance will be restored. But you can be certain they will not leave you alive if it is within their powers to do otherwise."

Michael felt cold. He understood. His nod communicated his understanding to the old man, to Caine, his father.

Caine pointed past Michael's shoulder. "My promise is fulfilled."

Michael turned his head.

Jenny stood in the doorway.

"Daddy!"

For a while Michael forgot all about being his father's son and thought only of being his daughter's father.

20

Michael lay in bed listening to the wailing of the storm beyond the windows. Rain whipped at the swirling glass in gusty sheets.

The room was lighted eerily by the fading embers from the fireplace. It was only a little after 4:00 A.M.

He and Jenny and Carol had talked for hours, talked and hugged and talked some more. Here and there a few tears had been shed.

Now Jenny was asleep in the next room, the room that had been set aside for Carol.

She'd been well cared for, had, in fact, not been frightened because she'd been convinced by Helen Locklear that her father wanted her to go on the trip. She'd gone voluntarily, expecting to meet Michael within a day or two.

Michael was thankful for the power of Helen Locklear's persuasive abilities and for her obvious ability to sense Jenny's fears and to quell them before they got out of control.

Though Helen Locklear wasn't as strong as one of Caine's children, she was a damn talented woman in her own right.

A cymbal crash of thunder rattled the windows. In the same instant, the bedroom was lit with a flash of blazing white light.

Carol rolled over beside Michael, mumbled sleepily, then fell silent again. She was sound asleep.

Michael found himself growing more and more frightened for her and Jenny by the minute.

Jenny had been used as a pawn once, already. What

was to prevent Eleanor and Mahafed from trying to use her?

Michael couldn't decide on the safest course to take.

If he kept Jenny here, in the house, she would be at the center of whatever occurred once Caine died.

If he sent her away, she would be unprotected, and at Eleanor and Mahafed's mercy as if she were found.

Which was better?

He could not decide.

But he had an idea, now, that he liked.

He concentrated on blocking the thoughts and images of all those in the house, on sealing off the compound from any and all peering inner eyes.

Only then did he turn to Carol. Gently, he nudged her shoulder.

She stirred. He nudged her again and quietly told her his idea. She liked it and quickly dressed.

While she was readying herself, Michael rang for a servant. When the bleary-eyed maid arrived at the door, Michael asked for one of the chauffeurs to be awakened.

The maid nodded and put a hand up to stifle a yawn. A wisp of unruly hair furled out the side of her cap. She'd obviously been sleeping.

"Yes, sir. Right away, sir."

Michael dressed in slacks and a shirt, then carried his sleeping daughter into the room he'd been sharing with Carol and laid her on the bed. Jenny didn't stir. She was dead to the world.

Michael helped Carol pack several bags. Then, with a bag in one hand and Jenny held to his chest with the other arm, he guided Carol to the main floor and out the portico door. The chauffeur was waiting for them just inside the doorway. He was dressed in yellow raingear. His face was flecked with beads of rainwater. Beyond the frosted glass window set in the door, Michael could see the illumination of the stark headlight beams meekly trying to peer through the stormy night.

Outside, the storm howled and threw pebbles of rain against the house. A dribble of water had trickled beneath the exterior door and puddled on the parquet flooring. The chauffeur was adding his own drippings to the growing stain.

"It's a nasty night, sir," the chauffeur said.

"It sounds like it."

"Not a night for safe driving, sir. There'll be few people out on the roads with the weather like this."

The man did not want to go out in the storm, Michael realized. It was bad enough that he'd been hauled out of bed at this ungodly hour, but to have to face the slicing rain and uncertain wind was more than the man had bargained for when he'd signed on as chauffeur.

"I know," Michael said. "I'm relying on that."

"Sir?"

Michael didn't bother to explain. "I wouldn't have asked for you if it wasn't absolutely necessary," was all he said.

The chauffeur took the bags and gingerly stepped into the screaming storm. Michael followed on the man's heels, Jenny supported against his chest, still sleeping. The rain slashed in at about a thirty-degree angle to the ground. Even the broad, covered portico did little to shield them from the storm's fury. Michael backed out to the car, shielding Jenny from the fury of the wind and water. Within seconds, his back was soaked through to the skin.

The chauffeur was driving the same dark green Jaguar sedan Michael had taken in the predawn hours less than a full day earlier.

It was amazing to him that less than twenty-four hours had passed since then.

Twenty-four hours and two lives.

Soon to be three.

Michael laid Jenny in the backseat of the Jaguar and tossed a blanket over her. He tucked the blanket neatly around Jenny's form and folded it down beneath her chin. Her cheeks were pink and warm. He kissed his daughter on one and closed the car door.

The limbs of the great trees in the yard whipped back and forth with a loud rustling of leaves that could be heard even above the howling of the wind.

The chauffeur helped stow the few cases in the Jaguar's trunk. "Where will we be going, sir?" he asked loudly, to be heard above the wind.

"I won't be going along," Michael said. "Just the two ladies."

"Yes, sir."

The chauffeur closed the trunk lid. It closed with a soft click.

Michael went back into the house for Carol.

She took his hand and, shielding her face from the driven rain, let him guide her quickly into the front passenger seat.

The chauffeur stood obediently by, awaiting his orders.

"You can hop in," Michael told the man. "Miss Lewis will tell you where to take her when you're well away from here."

"Yes, sir." There was a relieved tone in the man's voice. He hustled around to the right side of the car and slid behind the wheel. The solid car rocked slightly when the chauffeur closed the door.

Michael leaned in the passenger side and kissed Carol good-bye.

"You're sure you want me to do this?" she asked.

He nodded grimly.

"I don't want to know where you are. I don't want anyone reading it and being able to find you and Jenny. Wait until you're well out of London before you select a place to go. We want to give Eleanor and Mahafed as little chance as possible of knowing where you're staying."

"I promise," she said.

Michael glanced across the front seat and made eye contact with the chauffeur. "You're to stay with them until they're ready to return. There will be a substantial bonus if everything goes well."

"Yes, sir."

Turning his attention back to Carol, he said, "And don't call here, whatever you do. I simply want you and Jenny to disappear."

"I understand."

"When everything is settled here, I'll find you."

She nodded, tried to smile encouragingly. Michael kissed her again, then stepped back. "Good-bye," he said.

He closed the door.

He stood in the slicing rain and watched the car until its red taillights disappeared beyond the high iron gate. He didn't move even when he heard the reassuring *clung* of the gate locking itself. He stood for a long time, sensing the departing emanations from Carol and Jenny and doing his best to protect them, to shield them, and to block anyone from sensing their presence.

His temples throbbed from the effort.

The nagging apprehension that had been bothering him for the past few hours was still there. But he'd committed himself now, and committed Jenny and Carol to the consequences of his judgment.

God help me.

And them.

When he felt he'd given them as much protection as they needed to escape the city, he returned to his room, toweled off, hung his clothes up to dry, then crawled into bed. Gingerly, he touched his temples and concentrated. While it was still somewhat taxing to use his powers, it was taking him less and less effort to create what he wanted. The ease with which he created a second Jenny surprised him.

She stood at the foot of the bed, smiling and wide awake.

"Come give me a kiss," he said, "then go crawl into bed."

"'Night, Daddy," she said, after she kissed him on the cheek. Then, obediently, she hurried into the other room and crawled into bed.

Michael willed the illusion to send out vibrant sensations of life, willed it to toss and turn in the bed in the other room, willed it to talk in its sleep and go to the bathroom and ask for water, to do all those things a flesh-and-blood nine-year-old girl did in the middle of the night, and he created as full an aura around her as he was yet able to create.

Then he turned his attention to creating a beautiful blind woman to share his bed.

She was real enough to snuggle with.

She smelled good enough to fool his nose.

He hoped she was real enough to fool Eleanor and Mahafed.

Only then did he let go of the massive dome of psychic silence he'd settled over Caine's estate.

Only then did he take a chance on sleep.

He dozed.

And dreamed.

And felt frightened.

He dreamed of his boyhood. Of his father, whom he now knew wasn't his father, and of his mother and sister.

His mother was a beauty. In the dream he saw her much as he remembered her during his early childhood. She wore her hair straight, with a tight curl at the ends, near her neck, like an attractive, different version of one of the Andrews sisters.

He saw her in the arms of a tall man, a gray-haired man. They were dancing. She had a sensual expression on her mouth he'd never seen in all his days as her son. The expression surprised him. He'd never imagined her as a sexual being, and here she was, obviously aroused.

Michael recognized the gray-haired man.

Caine.

A picture of his father came to mind, in a distant motel room, samples cases spread out on a bed. His father had been a salesman at the time of Michael's birth. He'd traveled a lot. There'd been a lot of fights about that. Michael even remembered some of them. They hadn't ceased until his father had gone into business for himself.

Michael had been six years old then.

He saw his father's storefront, the opening day banners fluttering colorfully in the breeze.

The hardware store had done well.

A sister was born.

Michael saw himself ride his bicycle off a low bridge into a river on a dare. He had to be pulled off a sandbar by a couple of firemen. He'd been seven years old at the time. And he remembered it, because it was the last time he did anything anyone else told him to do without making up his own mind about the decision.

He saw his sixth-grade girlfriend.

And his pubescent buddies, two of whom had been killed in Nam.

He saw his first date, relived his junior prom when he'd spilled chocolate ice cream on his date's chiffon gown, bawled his fanny off at his father's funeral, crashed up in his only automobile accident at age seventeen, got drunk for the first time that same year, and stoned for the first time while traveling through San Francisco in the late sixties, got screwed the first time—which was exactly what had happened, because it hadn't been his idea, but he hadn't turned the offer down, either. He stumbled through college, bumped into Angie all over again in the student union, and wound up married before he knew what had hit him, and Jenny came along and he finished school and people were calling him Doctor for the first time, and before he knew what was happening, he was snarling at Milo Silklowski and chuckling at the man's nakedness and crying at his own emptiness, and then he stumbled onto Carol and someone had Jenny, someone who wasn't going to give her back and—

He awoke to the sound of blood rushing through his temples, to the incessant, frightened pounding of his heart, to the jittery tenseness he experienced with lack of sleep and too much coffee.

Had he heard something?

He listened, his heart still racing.

He remembered the dream.

The dream wasn't comforting.

Not at all.

He heard the sound again. Someone was knocking softly at his bedroom door.

You weren't supposed to have your life flash before your eyes like that.

Not unless you were about to die.

Michael checked to make sure that Carol and Jenny were in bed, as he'd created them, threw on a robe, then went to the door.

It was Helen Locklear.

"What time is it?"

"Nearly six A.M.," she said.

"What's up?"

Michael realized that he must look like hell.

"Aaron is gone."

Michael felt a sinking sensation in his chest, a churning in his guts.

"Dead, you mean?"

The redhead inclined her head. The answer was obvious. Tears stood in her eyes. "I'm having his body taken to the back of the house."

"I'll be right there."

"He asked that you light the fire."

"I will."

He swung around and dressed quickly in a dry pair of slacks and a shirt. He slipped on his loafers without socks, then decided he should wear some socks after all, since this was a funeral he was going to—a funeral of sorts.

He listened for a moment.

There was still a wind outside, but not a stiff one. The rain had ceased. He could hear no thunder.

Within minutes he was out back of the house.

A thin spray of pink and purple watercolor stained the sky to the east. Dawn was only a short way off.

In the darkness, the trees in the backyard appeared to loom over the scene.

Helen Locklear and two of the male servants were busy near the rear wall of the estate. In the distance, beyond the three-story-high wall, Michael could make out the indistinct, oddly angled roofs of nearby houses. Michael crossed the wet grass to the three busy shadows.

They were stacking branches and broken bits of lumber in a neat pile. The pile looked about four times the size of a coffin.

"Do you think that will be big enough to burn him?" Michael asked.

"We've placed charcoal on the bottom," Helen Locklear said.

Michael helped stack several heavy lengths of four-by-four lumber on the growing pyre. He said nothing. He understood the necessity for burning Caine's body. He'd read about it in the book. Sorcerers' bones were more valuable than the bones of saints—to the wrong sorts of people.

Michael was sweating by the time the pyre was head high.

"That's enough," Helen Locklear said.

"Yes, ma'am," one of the male servants said. Without further word, the two servants disappeared into the house.

Michael wiped his hands on his slacks.

His feet felt cold and clammy from the wet grass.

While he waited beside the tall, reserved redhead, he let his mind drift about the immediate area. He sensed no one. It was that same godawful stillness he'd sensed hours earlier with Carol. The lull before the storm.

It made the hair on the back of his neck stand up.

The sky to the east was aflame now. Full dawn was only a few minutes away.

"We'll wait until the sun's up," Helen Locklear said. "We don't want anyone to see the flames and report a fire."

Michael nodded.

A moment later, the two servants left the shadows at the rear of the huge Georgian house and crossed the lawn. Between them they carried a stretcher. They set the stretcher on the pyre they'd helped build.

"That will be all for now," Helen Locklear said.

The two men left.

Michael looked down at the upturned face of the man

who was his father, at the liver-spotted, colorless, lifeless
face of the man about whom he knew so little. He knew
Caine's birth date: 1189. And the year of his passing:
1988. He knew of the man's abilities. But he hadn't known
the man beneath the facade.

They hadn't had time to get to know each other.

Father and son.

Strangers.

Death had shriveled the man, slid his soft flesh back
against his skull, deepened the sockets of his eyes.

Death was not a very flattering artist.

"It's time."

Michael nodded.

Without ceremony, he used a match to light a torch
held out to him by Helen Locklear. Then, patiently, he
moved about the tumbled stack of wood branches, pausing long enough here and there to let the flames catch.

There was little smoke.

The wood was very dry.

The sun came out. It was brilliant, as brilliant as it is
only after a violent storm. The flames burned a bright orange, yellow, and blue. It was a very hot fire.

Michael stood in a reverent, awed, and somewhat
stunned stupor while the flames licked their way upward
and engulfed the frail, still figure lying atop the pyre. The
dead sorcerer's body wavered in the heat waves, then
began to blister. His gray hair frizzed, poofed, then disappeared behind a wall of fire.

Michael stepped back from the heat.

He stood there a long time.

Until the flames died down and until the pile of wood
collapsed in on itself, spewing a shower of sparks and fluttering black ash into the air.

Until the remaining bones of the sorcerer were unrecog-
nizable lumps among the coals.

Until Helen Locklear began raking through the cooling
ash to scatter the remains of the once-proud man into oblivion.

When Michael finally turned back toward the house, it was with a rising level of tension.

His protector was gone.

He was on his own now.

----------------- *21* -----------------

Despite his growing apprehension, Michael spent the early morning exploring the mansion that had been bequeathed to him. He had no idea of where or when Eleanor and Mahafed would come for him, and he sensed that it made sense for him to know the ins and outs of Caine's—of *his* home territory. Helen Locklear acted as his tour guide, pointing out architectural oddities and historical artifacts.

The building's five stories were jam-packed with history.

The entire fifth floor had been converted to a private museum and art gallery. Large, gabled windows bathed the open room in subdued light. Low room dividers, done in white fabric, matched the modernistic white of the walls. Original oil paintings decorated the walls, while original sculpture, highlighted by strategically placed lighting, created subtle fantasies in the various nooks and crannies designed for each individual piece.

The Flemish artists were represented, as was Rubens. Several Picassos adorned one nook, while the next harbored a gigantic Dali. One very unprepossessing grouping of charcoal and chalk drawings turned out to be the preliminary sketchings, from different perspectives, of the same uncompleted work by Da Vinci.

Interspersed in open areas stood majestic glass cases and glass display bells. Here was a golden statue of an

Egyptian jackal-headed god, there a life-size porcelain palace guard from ancient China, and there a small grouping of Fabergé eggs. And over in another corner a samurai's suit of armor, looking like something out of a science fiction movie, stared across the room at a shining silver suit of Italian armor. A handprinted, ornately bordered Bible rested under glass in a softly lit alcove.

Each piece was meticulously labeled with a discreetly framed calligraphic note etched in brass.

The Bible, Michael noted, had been completed in 1066, the year of the Norman invasion of England, and given to William the Conqueror by the monks of a seclusive monastery shortly after his triumph at Hastings.

Michael followed Helen Locklear to the nearest staircase. They descended.

Michael was acutely aware of the tension in his guts. It was difficult taking this tour when he found his mind continually scanning the area beyond the estate, searching for the first sign of an approach by Eleanor and Mahafed. The effort of keeping his ersatz daughter and lover alive in the rooms below only added to the burden.

He realized how immobilizing it was to live this way, and he felt a stronger degree of empathy for the paranoid-schizophrenics he'd worked with so often. Many of them lived under this tension and in this state of constant suspicion many days of their lives.

No wonder so many of them died young, or died by their own hands.

Another thought was bothering him, too.

The vision he'd had of the scrolls.

Caine's book referred to them several times without ever describing their contents.

Merlin's scrolls, they were called.

Or the lost scrolls of the missing one.

A sorcerer from the third century B.C. claimed to have seen them, to have unrolled one of them.

But he couldn't read it.

The lessons in the scrolls had been beyond his powers.

But not beyond Merlin's abilities.

Merlin, it was said, read them with ease.

Michael wanted those scrolls.

He did his damndest to sense their presence but came away with nothing.

He'd sensed them in Glastonbury.

Maybe he would have to return there to find them.

The fourth floor was given over to one spacious apartment. It was here that Caine had spent most of his time while in London. It, like the three floors below, was decorated in tasteful antiques. The clutter of Caine's Victorian period dominated the bedrooms and living area, while his taste for history and art was again displayed on the walls and in the dozens of tiny, unobtrusive alcoves and spotlighted corners.

One room contained a darkly paneled office equipped with a modern computer system.

Another room was obviously set aside for Helen Locklear. It was the one room in the apartment that displayed the obvious hand of a woman in the decorating scheme. Still, there was not a bed in the room. It was apparent that Helen Locklear had shared more than Caine's house.

The third floor was arranged much like the second, but rather than contain a smattering of guest rooms, its small rooms contained a library; card room; a weight and exercise room; and a game room replete with two pool tables, several dart boards, and a number of gaming tables, one of which displayed a chess game broken in midcontest.

"I was winning," Helen Locklear said, nodding at the chess table.

The room was comfortable, open, and masculine. From the carved marble fireplace to the leather chairs, from the tall potted plants to the soaring, ornately inlaid ceiling, the room reminded Michael of the man who had been his father.

The second floor's guest bedrooms were arranged in suites that could be closed off or spread wide open, depending on the whims of the guests or the size of their parties. The rooms were much the same as the one Michael currently occupied.

Michael stopped in his rooms and said hello to Jenny and Carol. He gave them each a hug and a kiss, and he talked softly to them for a moment, out of Helen Lock-lear's earshot.

Outwardly, the two visions perfectly matched the fe-males they were created to supplant. Inwardly, they seethed with the same emotions. They even sent off the same psychic auras.

Yet inside of Michael there was an emptiness that was hard to conceal.

These weren't the two females he cared so much about, no matter how much they looked and felt and smelled and sounded like them. He found it difficult to stay with them.

But he had to keep his interaction with them looking natural, he told himself. He couldn't afford to let the slightest flaw show in his relationship with his bogus daughter and lover.

Cautiously, he let his senses roam the English country-side, probing gently for some sign of where his daughter was, or where Carol was. This was a new skill for him, and he did not feel competent with it.

At the first tentative contact, he dropped the exercise.

They were somewhere to the north of London. North-northwest.

But he didn't want to know where, not exactly. He didn't want to have that knowledge in his head should someone else gain access to it.

He blocked the thoughts about Carol and Jenny and paid attention to the two figures living in his apartment.

He stayed as long as he thought necessary to commu-nicate the message he wanted Helen Locklear to read. Then he rejoined Helen in the second-floor hallway.

"Will you be moving upstairs?" Helen Locklear asked.

Michael shrugged, then nodded, somewhat noncommit-tally, he realized. He hadn't given the idea any thought yet. "I imagine," he said.

It still didn't feel right to him, moving in here, abandon-ing the life he'd built for himself in the States—even if his marriage had crumbled.

"I'll see that my things are moved out," Helen said.

"There's no hurry," Michael said. He stopped on the

staircase to the main floor and met the woman's eyes. "I would appreciate your staying for a while. I know you have a lot to help me with."

The tall redhead nodded her head, once. "I could take one of the second-floor suites, if you'd like."

"That would be fine."

The prospect of living in this walled estate in the heart of London set off mixed, even warring emotions in Michael's heart.

But, more importantly, at the moment, the reality of it seemed doubtful. There was something unreal to the possibility—unreal because of the brooding sensation that held his mind in its grip.

It was that eye-of-the-hurricane feeling again.

He had no idea what the next hours or days would hold for him.

He knew Eleanor and Mahafed would move soon. It would not be to their advantage to delay. The longer they waited, the stronger he would get, the more experienced he would become with the tools of his new trade as described in the book.

No.

They would act soon.

He tried to sense them, to locate the two who threatened his very existence.

But they were like a fog.

They were there, all around him, somewhere in the city, but untouchable.

He wondered when the fog would close in on him.

And wondered whether he should try to find the scrolls before that happened.

Helen was leading him through the grand dining room on the main floor of the house, completing his tour. There was a reception room beyond the dining room, and behind the dining room, a large, well-equipped modern kitchen with walk-in pantries and a walk-in freezer. Several rooms off the kitchen were devoted to a comfortable rest and relaxation area for the servants. This room, designed much like a great room, was as sumptuous as the rest of the house. The servants did not suffer.

And below the main floor were the servants' rooms. High, half-length windows caught soft light from window wells set around the base of the house and illuminated the pleasant rooms. There were seven rooms set aside for servants, each with its own bathroom.

A subbasement contained the central heating and a small workshop. A wide staircase and an open cage elevator ascended to a small, exterior loading and service area at the side of the house.

Michael followed Helen into the sunshine and took a quick tour of the grounds and the five-stall garage. The garage contained the two Rolls-Royces Michael remembered from the airport. An empty stall reminded him of the Jaguar that had carried off Jenny and Carol during the night. The other two stalls contained a small pickup truck and a perfectly maintained, burgundy-colored XKE convertible. Its long, phallic hood glinted in the light from a nearby window.

"That concludes the ha'penny tour," Helen Locklear said, then, "Any questions?"

Yes. What the hell are Mahafed and Eleanor waiting for?

For noon.

The butler, McCauliff, waited patiently while Michael, Carol, and Jenny spooned out the last of their fresh cream of mushroom soup, then silently disappeared into the kitchen with the empty bowls.

"That was good soup," Jenny said.

Michael smiled at her.

Carol smiled back at him.

Michael felt lonely as hell.

He felt an odd sensation tickle his mind and glanced toward the swinging mahogany doors through which McCauliff had disappeared.

There was a woman standing near the doors, Michael realized with a start. She was dressed stylishly, with her long, dark brown hair pulled up and tied loosely near the top of her head. The style left a lot of her long white neck showing.

In her youth she must have been very attractive.

She was still striking, with astoundingly high cheek-bones and deep, wide-set eyes that looked as dark as her hair.

Michael's eyes narrowed. His mind went out to the woman, touched her. He sensed her mind reaching for his.

Eleanor?

The woman nodded.

There was something stiff about this woman, something incomplete.

Michael thought he knew the explanation.

"Michael, who is that?" Carol asked with some apprehension.

Michael rose from the table. He gestured to the nearby double doors into the reception room. "We can talk in here."

To Jenny and Carol he said, "I won't be long. Finish your lunch. I'll find you later."

Once Eleanor followed him into the reception room, Michael closed the high sliding doors. Though heavy, they rolled on perfectly oiled overhead casters that took little effort to maneuver.

Eleanor declined to be seated. "I've come to offer you a way out of this confrontation," she said. She had a mild Mediterranean accent—Greek, Michael guessed, but an accent decayed by years of speaking other languages and living in foreign places.

"Go on."

"You were never apprenticed properly," she said. "Without that, and without Caine's protection, you do not stand a chance of surviving a battle against Mahafed and myself."

Michael waited.

His paranoia was in high gear.

He half expected to sense Mahafed tiptoeing up behind him with a raised scimitar in his hands.

But the room was empty except for this woman and himself.

"Leave here," the woman said, "return to your home in the United States, resume your practice of psychology. Forget about what you have learned here."

Michael had considered that option earlier, but he knew he could never return to that life.

It was too late.

"You would simply bide your time and kill me when I was off guard," he said.

"I see Caine has poisoned your mind against us."

"It's you and Mahafed who are here, well within the boundaries of Caine's—of my—lands. I am not in your territory."

Eleanor laughed softly. "True. And Caine explained that we were out to destroy him, is that it? To split the world in half rather than thirds?"

"And you're going to tell me that isn't so."

"Exactly."

"Then why are you concerned with me? Why not return to your sanctuary—" A sudden image popped into Michael's mind. He'd read something beneath the surface of the woman's mind. "Why not return to Madagascar and leave me in peace?"

The woman's face tightened, but she did her best to hide her surprise. "So you know where I live? That proves nothing."

"I can come after you, as you come after me," he said. "I might suggest that you and Mahafed be the ones to return to your homelands and that you make the choice to live in peace with *me*."

"We have to know your intentions," she said. "You must let us into your mind so that we may know your intentions."

"Why?"

"Because it was not Mahafed and myself who were out to control the world. It was Caine. He started the confrontation. We only fear that you are another of his weapons, that you intend to continue what he began."

"I am not Caine's weapon. Caine is dead, and I'm his successor. I am willing to live in peace with you," Michael said. "I have no desire to upset the balance."

"Then let us into your mind."

Michael smiled. "The book says that for one sorcerer to allow another access to his most inner thoughts is to court death. You would know my defenses. What secrets would I have to protect myself with? How would I protect my loved ones?"

"So you have read the book."

"You doubted that?"

She said nothing.

"Would you let me enter your mind and read your innermost thoughts? Would you allow me to trample around in your fears and insecurities with my muddy boots? Would you want me to know your weaknesses and your defenses, the faces behind your masks, your terrors?" He shook his head. "No. I rather doubt it."

She stared at him without comment.

"You have a choice, Eleanor. Return to Madagascar and urge Mahafed to return to his island in the Pacific. Or come for me—here, or wherever I am. If you choose the latter, I will be waiting for you." He opened his hands. "It is your choice."

"Caine has caused us grievous harm," she said. "He has defiled my lands and tried to kill me at every turn since 1915. He has dealt the same way with Mahafed since 1945. We do not trust him, nor his offspring. But maybe you are right. Maybe we should return to our lands and live in peace. I don't sense Caine's wantonness in you, nor do I sense Caine's presence about you. Yet I sense something I do not trust. Your refusal to cooperate surprises me in one so inexperienced."

"It's your choice," Michael repeated.

"Yes," she said. "It is *our* choice."

A thin, self-satisfied smile brightened her attractive features.

"We'll let you know what we decide."

"I'm sure you will."

Michael was not surprised when Eleanor vanished from where she'd been standing. He'd suspected from her first appearance that she was a vision created for his benefit.

It bothered him that he'd been able to sense that so easily, and his mind went quickly to Jenny and Carol. Was his handiwork as transparent?

If it was, they were in grave danger.

Because he didn't think Eleanor and Mahafed had any decision to make other than when and where and how . . . to kill him.

And he realized that he had a few other preparations to make before he would be ready to deal with Eleanor and Mahafed. A few other preparations and a trip to make.

For Merlin's scrolls.

The big question was: Would he be able to find them?

Did they exist in anything other than legend and in his own fevered visions?

Were they, possibly, a tantalizing creation sent his way by Mahafed and Eleanor?

Then he realized that there was an even bigger question.

What if he did find them? Would he be able to read them?

That niggling worm of doubt gnawed deeper into his brain and left him feeling just a little less confident.

It was just what he neded.

About as much as he needed . . . a hole in his head.

For some reason that image refused to let go of his mind. Him with a hole in his head. Dead on a funeral pyre. He watched his own body consumed by fire, felt the blistering heat, and, paradoxically, shivered. The vision was as vivid as Caine's cremation had been. It frightened Michael and wouldn't go away.

It could become reality all too easily.

All too soon.

22

The regal Rolls rumbled along in placid, well-tuned silence. Carol's visage sat in the passenger seat, to Michael's left, quietly enjoying the hills, hedgerows, and green fields gliding past the car. His surrogate daughter sat stoically in the broad rear seat. Both of the females were silent.

Michael left them that way.

He needed time to think.

Besides, it was simply the presence of Carol and Jenny he wanted Eleanor and Mahafed to sense, if the sorcerers cast about for their whereabouts. It would be natural for him to keep Carol and Jenny with him, where he could protect them. It didn't take much effort to maintain the auras of the two females, and Michael thought the possible results worth the effort.

He hoped the illusions would do the trick. To him, their images and the *reality* of their presence seemed stronger than the vision Eleanor had sent into the estate.

That was all he could do.

That, and hope.

Michael touched the brakes and slowed for a tractor crossing the road. In a moment, he resumed speed, the powerful car responding like a thoroughbred.

He had needed to get back to Glastonbury, needed to hunt for those scrolls, needed to make certain he could defend himself against Eleanor and Mahafed.

And he'd grown sick and tired of waiting around for Eleanor and Mahafed to attack him.

They hadn't returned to their lands.

They wouldn't.

He was sure of it.

Caine had said they would not stop until they had killed him, or until he had proven himself.

So be it.

But he could fight them in his own way. He didn't have to sit around like a cornered rat in a trap, waiting for them to squash him underfoot.

Michael swung the magnificent car around a sharp curve. Ahead, in the distance, he spotted the graceful spire of a cathedral. He realized that he was over halfway to Glastonbury. The spire, no doubt, belonged to Salisbury Cathedral.

Within minutes, he swirled through a series of traffic circles that took him around the city.

Ten minutes later, the visions started.

Ahead of him, while traveling at over sixty miles an hour, he saw a large Mercedes truck swerve into his lane.

Instinctively, he hit the brakes. The Rolls went into a tight, angling slide aimed at a nearby stone fence. Michael fought the wheel and braced himself for a collision. Beside him, he saw the illusory Carol Lewis blink out of existence. His mind lost the concentration necessary to keep her alive.

The truck plowed into the Rolls-Royce.

Michael blinked.

The truck was gone.

The Rolls's steering wheel bucked in Michael's hands as the heavy car caught the shoulder, rocked violently, and slewed gravel and clods of dirt into the air. Spattering stones rattled off the undercarriage with the *rat-a-tat* of a machine gun. Within seconds, the car lurched to rest.

Luckily, Michael had managed to keep the car from slamming into the nearby stone fence. He took a quick gulp of air and glanced around.

There was no traffic behind or ahead of him.

His heart hammered away at his ribs.

He nodded to himself.

He should have expected something like that.

Eleanor and Mahafed had made their choice.

He would have to be more careful.

Still trembling slightly, Michael backed the Rolls onto the pavement, pulled the front end around to the west, and stepped on the gas. The car accelerated smoothly, purring contentedly, as if happy to be rolling.

Except for himself, the car was empty.

It was a strange sensation, seeing Carol and Jenny blink in and out of existence. He wasn't quite used to the schizophrenic nature of the self-created hallucinations.

They blinked back into existence.

Carol smiled delightfully.

"Where'd you go?" Michael asked.

"Away," Carol said. She pointed through the windshield. "Keep your mind on your driving."

"Welcome back," he said.

He returned his attention to the road.

Eleanor and Mahafed would try for him again, he knew. But where, when, and how was anybody's guess.

At the mouth to a narrow farm lane outlined in stone, a blond, toddling child in a diaper suddenly stumbled into the road.

Michael concentrated.

Carol's shriek filled the interior of the car. *"Michael!"*

Without slowing, the front bumper of the car hit the tiny child with a godawful sound. The *whump* was followed immediately by a soft thudding beneath the tires.

Michael never slowed down.

A glance in the mirror confirmed his suspicions.

"Michael?" It was Carol, casting his own thoughts back at him. He was a ventriloquist—in a very bizarre sense.

"It wasn't real?" he said.

He was sweating. His hands were slippery on the leather steering wheel.

"What do you mean, 'It wasn't real?'? Didn't you feel the impact?"

"It wasn't real."

"Michael, this is getting crazy."

"I know. Getting crazy and more and more unreal."

"How do you know it wasn't real?"

"I blinked."

"What do you mean, you 'blinked'?"

"I concentrated and blinked. The kid wasn't there. It was an illusion. There was nobody on the road when I looked in the mirror. No . . . body."

"Eleanor and Mahafed?"

He nodded.

"But how can you be sure?"

"I just am."

"But didn't you feel the—"

"Shut up."

Carol's image closed its mouth.

Michael was shaking.

He knew what it meant to be psychotic.

It had been *too* real. Even though he'd concentrated, even though he'd managed to block the visual image, Eleanor and Mahafed had managed to get through to him on other sensory channels.

Jesus, they were good.

He wondered what his chances of making it to Glastonbury were.

He hadn't realized the extent of their abilities, the imminent danger he placed himself in by driving while they were intent on killing him.

No wonder a balance was so important.

Without it, without some semblance of normalcy, without some guarantee of personal safety, without a truce, a cooperation, a division of the world, there was no way to live a reasonable life.

Anything could become a danger.

Everything could kill.

What if the child had been real, and Eleanor and Mahafed had willed him not to see it?

He swallowed.

He didn't want this burden.

Why the hell had this happened to him?

Why the hell had his marriage disintegrated?

Why the hell couldn't he step back a week in time and

take a different fork in life? Just a week. Maybe he
could have saved his marriage. Maybe he'd be sitting
over breakfast with Angie right now, making plans
for...

Stupid thoughts.

That was all over. Angie and he had been growing apart
for years. He'd been too proud and too wrapped up in his
own life to admit it or do anything about it.

Angie and he were a thing of the past.

He was here, now.

Angie was there...with her lover, the limp Eiffel
Tower.

And Eleanor and Mahafed were waiting.

On the road ahead.

Michael touched the brakes.

There was a bus ahead of him, three hundred yards
off, coming his way, thundering along the narrow lane,
funneled in his direction by two long, chest-high stone
walls.

He blinked.

It was a real bus.

It was hogging the middle of the narrow, two-lane road.

Michael felt the cold, drying sweat on his forehead.

Anything and everything can kill.

There was no boundary between fantasy and reality anymore, he realized.

He stomped the brakes, eased off as the Rolls went into
a mild slide, stomped them again and again.

He pushed his consciousness at the mind of the woman
driver in the bus.

The woman was nearly comatose. She was a marionette.
Her strings were being pulled from somewhere outside her
own being. She was no illusion. She was a real, flesh-and-
blood human being who knew only that she had to drive
the way she was driving because something was telling her
she had to drive that way, something very real to her,
something menacing in the road ahead of her, something
that might make her do something drastic in order to avoid
the worst.

Michael shoved his willpower at her.

Hit your brakes!

The bus continued to chew up the distance between them.

Michael jerked the Rolls off to the left side of the road, bounced to a stop.

Hit your brakes!

He could see her now, through the wide glass windshield of the lumbering, straining bus, less than fifty yards ahead of him, slewing into his lane, heading straight for him, spewing rocks and turf now from the shoulder as she edged farther off the road to avoid the illusion of something in her way.

Michael shoved open the right-side door and dived across the road.

The bus driver reacted to some inner vision with a meaning sent for only her to read.

The behemoth of metal and rubber and glass roared and spit rocks as it dug in to the shoulder and tarmac to change course.

Michael stumbled.

The bus was thirty yards away, tires beginning to squeal in agony as it twisted sideways in the narrow, stone-hemmed lane. Pale, gaping-mouthed faces stared in horror from the row of huge windows along the side of the bus.

Michael regained his balance.

The bus started to topple—at over fifty miles an hour it tilted, bounced, and started to roll in his direction.

Michael hit the stone wall. Cold, coarse, mossy stones slipped in his grip.

Metal screamed behind him.

He stuck a foot into the uneven slippery spaces at the base of the fence and catapulted himself up and over the wall. Off balance, he stumbled as far away from the impact sight as he could before spread-eagling himself in a grain-field.

The bus screeched onto its side, bounced, spun, crashed into the Rolls, and jammed itself between the two stone walls on either side of the narrow lane. Heavy rocks thumped to the ground nearby, barely missing Mi-

chael's legs. The noise was tremendous. Metal shrieked
and ground over stones. Muffled screams echoed from
within the bus's interior. A low, heavy *whump* exploded,
and a ball of flame and black smoke belched skyward at
the rear of the bus, from the crumpled wreckage of the
Rolls.

Michael stood.

He concentrated on the bus, on the screaming people
inside.

They were real.

Many were hurt.

He clambered back over the fence.

The bus had come to rest on its side. Michael jumped
onto the side of it, now the top, and kicked in a window.
About half a dozen people were moving about. Another
five or six were too stunned to move. A few were clearly
unconscious—or dead.

"This way!" Michael screamed. *"Out! Out, now!"*

He helped the first several people out through the window he'd kicked in. Behind the bus, the remains of the
Rolls crackled and writhed in vivid flames.

Michael dropped into the bus. The bus driver was crumpled against a door, unmoving. He sensed that she was
alive. He stepped over her and kicked out the giant windshield. Two men helped him lift the driver out through the
gaping front of the bus.

Within minutes, with the help of the first two motorists
to hit the scene, they'd removed all the people.

Only two were unconscious now.

None dead.

One middle-aged farmer was bleeding badly from a
deep cut in his left thigh, but Michael bore down on the
man's mind and felt the man's nerves contract around the
severed artery. He applied a tourniquet, and he instructed
a teenage girl in how to keep it tight and how often to
release it.

Then, when he was certain that everyone was well away
from the burning car and the possibly explosive carcass of
the bus, he slipped back over the stone wall and trotted
away across the small grainfield.

His departure had gone unnoticed, he was certain. Everyone was too intent on their own misfortunes to bother with him.

They would be in greater danger with him near than with him gone.

So he made himself gone.

He felt alone.

He was alone.

He'd given up trying to keep Carol and Jenny at his side. What did it matter, now?

Eleanor and Mahafed were after him, and they were nearby, on his heels, closing in for the kill. He needed to use his energies to keep himself alive now. There was no time to be fancy.

He stopped near a rocky stream and splashed clean, sparkling water on his face. For a moment, he rested on a rock.

The stream burbled softly at his feet.

There was a mild scent of manure in the air. It was a sweet smell, mingled with the smell of flowers and the cool, damp scent of the wet streambanks.

He sensed the presence of the others near him—Eleanor and Mahafed.

He was unsure of how well they could read the emanations from his mind. But they knew where he was; he sensed that.

Was there a way to block himself from them? To shut down completely the meager signals they must be reading in order to follow him?

He tried to think of a way to make himself unreadable. If possible, something even more powerful than he'd tried in the early morning hours to shelter Jenny and Carol.

He imagined himself surrounded by a darkness, by an enclosed, circumscribed bubble of energy. He concentrated on locking his energies inside that space, on preventing even the slightest sense of his essence from escaping.

For a long time he sat without moving, thinking of nothing else.

When he broke his concentration, it was to let his mind reach out around him.

He still sensed Eleanor and Mahafed.

But they were not as close now.

He enclosed his energies again, and, still concentrating, rose from the side of the stream and moved off across the walled fields.

He had things to do.

His mind raced as he walked.

He still wanted to get to Glastonbury, still hoped to recapture a shred of that vision he'd experienced in the pub, still felt that what he was looking for would be found in those scrolls—if they could be located.

They had to be real.

Why else had they formed in his vision?

It took him less than ten minutes to stumble onto another country lane. It was even narrower than the one he was fleeing from. He walked the side of the road, moving west, toward Glastonbury. He stuck his thumb out at three cars and a rickety pickup. They ignored him, swung past without a second glance, except for one driver, who tossed a cigarette butt at him.

He needed to warn Carol to keep on the move, he thought. Needed to come up with a better way to protect them.

He needed to find another car.

Maybe a place to stay.

He needed . . .

He needed to stop simply *reacting* to Eleanor and Mahafed.

He needed to make them react to him.

He needed, he realized, to go on the offensive.

If he continued to run, to try to dodge them, to stay one step ahead of them while he searched for something that could turn out to be a figment of his imagination, it would be only a matter of time before they found him and eliminated him.

In less than an hour now, they'd tried for him three times.

Twice, they'd damn near been successful.

He was out of his league, he realized. But what choice did he have?

None.

He was in it.

So he might as well act like it, instead of running his ass off trying to buy time.

If the worm turned, maybe he could catch the birds of prey by surprise.

The trick was in knowing how to fight them.

He saw a yellow Renault coming his way. He stuck his thumb out. The woman driving it didn't slow. She pulled to the right to slip around him.

Michael concentrated, sent her the image of an old woman standing beside a disabled car.

The yellow Renault slowed.

Michael bore down.

The car pulled to the side of the road.

Michael hurried along the shoulder, but not too fast to ruin the image of an elderly woman in distress.

He opened the passenger-side door of the Renault.

"Car troubles?" the middle-aged woman asked.

There were a number of packages on the rear seat.

"Yes," Michael said, willing the words to sound feminine. "Can you take me to the nearest town?"

"Of course," the driver said, beaming. "This is no place for a lady to be stranded by herself, is it?"

Michael settled in beside the woman.

"Pull your skirt in," the driver said. "You wouldn't want to get it caught in the door."

Michael complied.

The little car moved off.

23

The grease-stained garage owner was glad to accept Michael's credit card as payment for the rental car. After taking the impression, the heavyset man pushed his cap back on his balding head and squinted at a line of four nondescript cars lining the side of his small station's parking area.

"Take your pick, Guv. The red Cortina is probably the best of the lot."

"I'll take that one, then."

"Right you are."

The man lumbered to a keyboard near the door to his workbay, selected a key, and lumbered back. His greasy coveralls were stretched taut over his roundness. He passed the key over. "She's full of petrol and ready to roll," he said with a smile. "Bring her back with a full tank and you'll save yourself a quid or two."

"Will do," Michael said.

The man jotted a final bit of information on a sheaf of papers, ripped a copy off for Michael, then waved Michael on his way. "If you need her for another day, just give a ring," he said. "The number's on the paperwork."

The red Cortina sounded like a big sewing machine, but it ran cleanly. Michael hit the road and turned west, heading for A361 and Glastonbury.

It would be near evening by the time he reached Glastonbury. He would undoubtedly have to spend the night there.

He didn't like that, didn't like the idea of having to spend any amount of time in one place. And if he was

asleep, what defense did he have against Eleanor and Mahafed?

Did he need to sleep?

As if in answer, he reached a hand up to stifle a yawn.

But first things first.

He stopped just outside a little village named Evercreech
and shut the car off. With as much power as he could
muster, he spread a sensory net toward the north. He
wanted to find Carol and Jenny.

It took him several minutes of trial-and-error mental
processes before he sensed Carol's presence.

She sensed him immediately and let him into her mind.

He saw through her eyes. She was standing on a shoreline, looking out over a peaceful lake. Rolling hills bordered the picturesque lake. A number of small sailboats
bobbed at anchor just beyond the shore.

It reminded Michael of scenes he'd seen in a book about
the Lake District.

Move on, Michael thought forcefully. *Don't stay. Keep
moving*.

He felt Carol's mind respond.

He repeated the message.

Again.

And again.

He sensed a tenderness in Carol's thoughts, and a deep
concern. He was unsure of how to communicate effectively
with her at this distance, was simply pleased that she'd
been able to receive his message.

He caught a glimpse of Jenny through Carol's eyes.

Then the tenuous connection was broken.

He tried to reopen the connection, but stopped when he
sensed another presence nearby.

Stupid.

Stupid.

Stupid.

Eleanor and Mahafed had zeroed in on him again.

He started the car and eased through the streets of Evercreech. He didn't have far to go. Glastonbury was just
ahead.

Michael closed off his energies again, concentrated on

thwarting Eleanor and Mahafed's attempts to locate him
with any precision.

It was a good bet they knew he was heading for Glastonbury.

There was nothing he could do about that except prepare
a warm reception for them if they decided to follow him
there.

It was growing dark when he reached the city limits of
Glastonbury. He drove the city streets, concentrating,
trying to catch a glimpse of the same vision that had
come to him the day before. In a field on the outskirts of
town, he saw a small traveling carnival setting up its
tents. Its colorful banners, limp and unlighted, looked
forlorn in the fading daylight. One wasn't meant to see
behind the facade, Michael reflected. It ruined the fantasy. He drove on, unable to recapture the sensations of
yesterday. The back streets were quiet. Most of the
townsfolk were already home, settled into their favorite
chairs, staring at their tellys. Michael spotted a high
church tower, and beyond it an even higher hill with an
eerie stone tower at its very peak. He pulled off to the
side of the street and closed his eyes. He formed an
image of the scrolls he'd seen in his vision, and held it
for a long while.

The image held, became as real to him as the car in
which he sat.

But nothing else happened.

He tried to shift his mind this way and that, jogging the
image, trying to sense something more than he'd felt in the
pub.

Nothing came to him.

He tried to sense the subtle power he'd felt the day before—the unreadable interference that had caused Carol
concern.

That he sensed.

But it was directionless, pervasive, endemic to the site,
as if it had always been there.

It felt like a life force, yet unlike one. More like the
decayed remains of something very powerful, like the rem-

nants of some radioactive element whose half-lives have nearly faded beyond recognition.

Michael climbed from the car, concentrated on the vague energy source. He turned slightly, aware suddenly that what little energy he sensed was coming from the direction of the nearby hill.

Two teenage boys were approaching on foot. He held out a hand to stop them.

"What is that?" he asked.

The boys looked at each other, as if thinking he was daft.

"It's the church," one of the boys said. "St. John's."

"I mean the hill."

"Why, the Tor, of course," the same boy said.

The other asked, "You a Yank?"

Michael nodded yes.

"That's a church tower on top," the boy said. "The only people who go up there much are tourists. Lots of legends about that hill, there is."

"Such as?"

The boy lifted a shoulder, glanced at his friend, as if sorry he'd brought up the subject. "Some say the Holy Grail's buried under that hill. Some say it's religious grounds that was used by the Druids. Some say 'bout anything the tourists want them to say." He moved a few steps away. "It's a strange-looking hill, anyway, with peculiar kinds of ramp things and all." He touched a hand to his imaginary cap. "I gotta be going."

Before they got too far away, Michael called after them, asking where there might be a place to spend the night.

The boy who'd done most of the talking pointed up a nearby road. "Follow that. You'll run into a curve before long, and a sign right there for Tor House. It's an old manor house what's been made into a B and B."

Michael drove the red Cortina in the direction indicated.

He found Tor House within a few minutes. It was set atop a low hill. A broad expanse of open, green lawn sloped down to the main road.

Michael drove up the long, straight, unpaved drive. He parked in a narrow parking lot on the south side of the house. Ten other cars were already parked there.

The big house was three stories high and made of Cotswold stone. Its roof looked to be covered with shale. There was a washed-out appearance to the plaee, as if time had taken its toll on the buildings. Woodwork near the gabled third story was obviously in need of painting. One of the high, multipaned windows on the second floor was covered with plywood.

As Michael made his way to the front door, he found himself wondering what fate had befallen the once-proud owners of the estate. The heavy, sturdy construction had obviously been the work of master craftsmen, centuries earlier. The house looked as if it could stand, untouched, for at least a few more. It was nearly impossible to detect the seams between the stones.

Michael rapped the brass door-knocker.

The landlady's name was Carruthers. She was a fifty-year-old gossip with the easy smile and manner of a barmaid. Slightly orangish hair framed a ruddy complexion and twinkling blue eyes. She was buxom and constantly in motion.

"Your room'll be on the top floor," she said, handing him a key. "You're lucky we've a room at all, this season. But we had a cancellation not ten minutes ago." The woman bustled up a nearby stairs. "Follow me. I'll show you the room."

Michael followed.

The woman never stopped talking.

The house had been in her family for four centuries. She and her husband ran it as a guest house to make ends meet. Most of the lands that had once belonged to the estate had long since been sold off. It had a great view of the Tor. Did he know that the house had been built in the fifteenth century? No? And that the National Trust was interested in the house, but hadn't made up their minds whether to help preserve it or not, and wouldn't it be a shame if the house had to be sold and not kept for the public to see, and her son, who was a

SORCERER 243

physician living in Canada, was hoping to make enough money to keep it in the family if the National Trust didn't manage to make a decision soon, and . . .

Michael missed half of what the woman said.

He was preoccupied with his own thoughts and barely noticed the narrow stairwells, the creaking floors, and the uneven walls.

His room had a grand view of the Tor and of the church tower on top. A large, four-poster bed, a small bureau, and two chairs comprised the furnishings. The walls were painted a light blue. The floor was worn and stained hardwood.

"The loo's the door we passed on the first landing below us," the woman said. "Towels and the like are in the bureau. Breakfast's served half past six to half past eight. If you want to watch the telly, you're welcome to use the lounge, just down the hallway. There's about a dozen Germans in the house at the moment, only one of whom speaks English, so's you'd recognize it wasn't Polish, so don't expect to strike up a conversation with them, though they're nice folks, and all. Still, my one brother did lose his life in the war—he was a bombardier, you know—and I can't hardly not think of that sometimes. They're traveling in a sort of caravan, the Germans are, and . . ."

Then, mercifully, she left him in peace.

He locked the door, settled onto the bed, and closed his eyes.

He yawned.

He was tired.

Just a little rest, then he'd get up and decide what to do next.

He wanted to climb the Tor.

And he needed to think of how to deal with Eleanor and Mahafed.

He didn't feel them at the moment.

He . . .

. . . dozed off.

He woke up to the sound of muted voices in the hallway beyond his room.

For an instant, he was disoriented.

Strange room. Odd, nearly complete darkness. A bed that creaked, and the alien sensation of a coarse bedspread beneath his fingers.

Then he remembered where he was.

And he realized that he'd been asleep.

Damn.

He listened.

There were people in the hallway, people trying to be quiet.

He opened his senses and was overwhelmed by the confused rush of hostility and fear that tore at his mind. He couldn't count the number of people beyond the door. They were a mob, their minds thinking as one, driven by a maddened fear.

Michael sensed the driving forces.

His friends.

He came out of bed, and for a moment he hesitated.

The cluster of people beyond the door were waiting for someone. He concentrated, picked up an image of a man carrying an old, double-barreled shotgun. The man was rangy. He was talking to his wife—the woman's orange hair caught Michael's attention.

This was Carruthers, the landlord.

Michael felt the man slide two shells into the broken breech of the weapon, felt the metallic jarring snap as the man snapped the heavy weapon closed. Carruthers left the room he was in and started up a narrow staircase.

He's coming for me, Michael realized.

Beneath the seething, raw aggression he sensed beyond the door of his room, Michael felt the unmerciful energy of two powerful minds.

The crowd sensed the presence of a fiend in this room; they were ready to kill. Michael sensed the bloodlust seated deep in the brains of the people beyond his door. Their minds were working as one. They were driven as one.

Michael heard footsteps on the staircase.

He had to do something.

He concentrated hard, sending as much power as he could muster out to encircle the small mob preparing to storm his door. He wanted to seal them off from the control of Mahafed and Eleanor. But it was no good.

As soon as his mind touched the minds of the crowd, another force clawed its way into Michael's senses.

Michael reeled away from the door.

They were out there.

Mahafed and Eleanor were in the house.

They were directing the attack from scant feet behind the crowd.

Their psyches dominated the hallway.

Michael realized that he had no choice but to flee.

The doorknob jiggled slightly.

The movement caught his eye.

It turned again, ever so slightly.

He heard keys rattle.

He turned toward the nearby window.

It was the old-fashioned kind that swung open like shutters. He opened both the windows.

It was three stories to the ground. The soft light from a partly cloudy and starlit sky barely illuminated the drive leading to the house, and the lawns stretching to the nearby main road.

He was too high up to jump.

But he had to get out.

He heard a key turn in the lock.

Facing the door, he created the image of a huge, misshapen man with a halo of wild hair. He put a club in the figure's bearlike fists. Then, holding the image, Michael crawled over the lip of the windowsill. He was hanging by his elbows, easing himself down as far as he could before he was forced to drop.

The door opened.

The landlord stood there, his double-barreled shotgun at his shoulder. Pale faces and gleaming eyes peered past the landlord's shoulder. A dozen people stood there, looking like zombies, their fists clutching makeshift weapons. Broken bottles held by their necks, a rake, an ax handle . . .

Michael didn't wait for the people to attack. He sent his creation into action.

The huge, hulking figure shouted, raised its weapon, and charged the clutch of bodies blocking the doorway.

The landlord's shotgun flashed, boomed, shook the house. Its blast ripped into the nearby wall.

The blast's target did not react.

Michael sent his creation, swinging its club, into the crowd.

Women screamed.

The shotgun's muzzle exploded again, and the bed jumped as it absorbed the second shot.

Michael didn't stay around to watch the melee.

He stretched himself downward and dangled by his hands. There was nothing nearby to shift his grip to, no way to ease himself to the ground. He would have to make a full two-story drop to a hard courtyard.

He concentrated, ignoring the cries and scuffles from above, and told himself he could make the drop without hurting himself.

Land and roll backward.

Touch and roll.

Someone's fingers grabbed at his on the windowsill, scrabbled for a grip on his wrist.

He released his grip.

The fall felt as if it were occurring in slow motion. He looked down, saw the ground coming up at him. He started to buckle in preparation for the jarring landing. He hit.

But not as hard as he'd expected to.

He rolled.

And came up limping.

Damn! Something wasn't right with his left ankle.

Damn!

He limped toward the side of the house, toward the parking lot and the red Cortina.

Behind him, from within the house, he heard a stammering pounding that didn't make any sense at first.

At second, it did make sense.

Footsteps pounding down stairs.

Ignore the pain. No pain. No ankle problem.

He felt the pain go away. He ran.

The Cortina stood there, silent and locked. He fumbled the keys out of his pocket and jabbed them at the door.

He heard the thick wooden front door of the old house rattle open, heard screaming voices and running feet. Three men rounded the corner of the house, the vanguard of those after him.

Michael glared at them, commanded them to stop.

He sensed their hesitation.

He slammed his mind at them. If he couldn't stop them now, he was lost. He shot agonizing pains at them, watched the three men grab at their heads and cry out.

He didn't want to hurt them, but he had no choice.

He knocked the men to the ground.

He jabbed his key into the door lock. This time it slid home. He jerked the door open and piled in. He stuck the key into the ignition and turned it.

Nothing happened.

He twisted it back and forth.

Nothing.

Damn!

The hood, he noticed, was not fully closed. Someone had been under the hood.

Ah, God!

He bailed out of the car, eyes searching for the best direction to run.

Not toward the front of the house.

Four or five people were there now, running. Shouting.

He shoved pains at their eyes, drove ice picks into their brains, dropped them to their knees.

How long could he keep this up?

Not long.

Not once Eleanor and Mahafed moved to block him.

He was cornered. His only option was to flee on foot.

Unless another car was unlocked.

He tried one.

No dice.

Grabbed the door handle of another.

Locked.

He smashed his elbow through the side window of the second car, then realized it would do him no good, since he didn't have a key for the ignition.

People were screaming and coming to their feet.

Michael swung around and started toward the rear of the house, toward the sheltering darkness of the nearby woods.

Someone stepped from beyond the house, blocking his route, and strode into the parking lot.

Michael caught the glint of light along the double barrels.

Carruthers.

The gun swung in Michael's direction.

If only that car could . . .

Michael concentrated. A dark Volvo parked against the fence line suddenly broke loose and rolled at Carruthers. The shotgun in Carruthers's hands spit fire and roared. Pellets skipped and whined off the gravel. Carruthers stumbled, and he screamed in pain as the rolling Volvo clipped him and pinned him against another parked car.

Michael ran.

Off balance, Carruthers' final blast roared ineffectually, followed by the tinkling of glass.

Running feet pounded behind Michael.

He stopped once, at the edge of the wooded shadows. Mentally he set a massive string of fireworks in the way of the charging half dozen or so figures still chasing him. Rockets *boomed* and *hissed* and *screeched* across the parking lot, sending the vanguard of the mob into a wild, diving scramble for safety. Brilliant, multihued explosions of light flashed, turned beautiful and deadly among the fleeing, frightened figures. Screeching demons of burning light writhed terrifying trails across the dark ground, slashing their fiery tails this way and that as they shot off into the dark oblivion of the nearby woods, or burst into a cascade of sparks at the base of the house's stone wall. Screaming people caught fire and ran, human

torches lighting the tall side of the house with eerily
dancing light. Fluttering balls of light flowered near the
ground, fluttered skyward. Streamers of glittering color
snaked up the side of the majestic old house, burst low
in the sky overhead, *boom, whump, wham, caboom,*
scattering bits and pieces of daylight in all directions.
People stumbled, cried out, grabbed their heads in agony.

Michael paused for a moment to watch before he disappeared into the darkness beneath the trees.

No one was seriously hurt.

Except for Carruthers.

It was nearly all illusion.

Nearly.

But not quite.

24

Michael wrapped himself with a cloak of darkness and silence. Dimly, just beyond the essence of his being, he
sensed the furious forces of Mahafed and Eleanor scouring
the night-shrouded English countryside. He cowered within
his self-made cocoon of stillness and waited. Overhead,
the towering trees pointed their gnarled fingers toward the
misty night sky.

Michael sat on the earth, his back against a tree. He had
not moved for several hours. Any movement, he feared,
would draw the senses of the other two.

His ankle throbbed dully, but he'd concentrated on it
and prevented it from swelling. Nothing was broken. He
had sustained a bad sprain but was aware that he'd been
able to minimize its effects through concentrating on the
damage and willing it to restore itself.

It was a bit insane, this sorcery.

But it worked.

Better than Caine had intimated.

Michael flexed his ankle. Even the throbbing was fading now.

He massaged the ankle again with kneading fingers, willing power to the bruised joint. It felt as if he were infusing his flesh with electricity. He felt the bone beneath his fingers vibrate gently, felt the flesh relax.

He was learning the tricks of the trade quite fast, he realized.

He had to.

His survival depended on it.

He rotated his ankle again.

He felt the bones rub over each other.

But no pain.

He smiled gently to himself.

No more sprain.

Mind over body.

It was no more than what Caine had said he would be able to do.

But *the Volvo* . . . the Volvo had been something entirely different.

A crystalline image of the parking lot at Tor House formed in Michael's mind. He saw Carruthers raising his shotgun again, heard the blast, felt the concussion flutter the night air, turned from the spurt of flame at the muzzle, and watched in fascination as the dark Volvo rolled so purposively into Carruthers and pinned him against the other car. The image in Michael's head faded as the last shotgun blast sounded, faded with the dying notes of Carruthers's cry of pain and surprise.

Leaves rustled. Branches clicked softly in the surrounding darkness.

Michael sensed a weakening in the psychic forces about him. Mahafed and Eleanor were moving on, expanding their search for his scent.

He felt confident that they'd lost him for the moment.

His mind returned to the Volvo.

I moved the Volvo.

I moved it.

Simply by concentrating.

It had not been an illusion.

Not like the imagery of the fireworks—frightening but harmless, or nearly so.

Cold, lifeless metal and rubber had responded to his commands.

And Caine had said that couldn't be done.

It was not just an example of mind over mind . . .

Not mere mind over body. . . .

But mind over matter.

The implications made Michael cold.

Merlin had made real that which could not be real. Only Merlin and the *missing one* had been able to escape the bounds of imagery, trickery, and illusion. Only they had been able to manipulate the very fabric of existence, to move the inanimate, to make the dead walk again. . . .

They and, perhaps . . . Christ?

. . . who gave sight to the blind.

Easy, when you were dealing with hysterical blindness.

Nothing special in that, nothing a regular, run-of-the-mill sorcerer couldn't do. Even a shrink could do that at times.

But what about real, nerve-dead blindness?

Could that be reversed?

Could the person be made to see again, on their own, without needing someone to insert visions into their cortex continually?

Michael's mind formed an image of Carol . . . a Carol with sparkling emerald eyes that flashed in the sunlight, followed birds soaring on the wind, read picture books to tiny children—a Carol with eyes that could *see*.

If only . . .

He became aware of a dull ache in his chest.

He was more attached to this woman than he'd been admitting to himself. He wanted her safe.

More.

He wanted *her*.

More than he'd ever consciously wanted Angie.

Almost more than he wanted life.

He needed to protect her, now, more than ever.

But how?

Michael racked his brain.

How, indeed, at this distance?

It was a problem that tormented him. No solution was foolproof.

But if he was good enough . . . if he *was* the heir to Merlin's skills . . . *if* all that . . . then *maybe* his original plan *was* best. Just maybe . . . maybe he could pull it off.

In the next instant, Michael froze.

He sensed the intense presence of Eleanor and Mahafed. It vibrated deep in his brain, like some unheard sound just below the threshold of human ears. They were nearby, their minds scanning the dark forest for him. He closed himself down, drew his aura inward, created an impenetrable shell around himself, and waited. He felt vulnerable, unprotected, like a child lying in short weeds while trying to elude some horrible predator. He kept his thoughts at a minimum. He didn't want the slightest hint of his existence to reach the other two. Together, they were too powerful for him. Together, he knew he didn't stand a chance against them.

Eleanor was angry.

He sensed the heat of her thoughts. They burned through the woods like a scorching wind. She was intemperate in her rage and did not let her mind linger as it passed. Michael filed that away in the depths of his mind. Angered, Eleanor would miss things.

He can't have escaped! she was thinking.

He is not here. He has moved on, to somewhere else.

Michael recognized the low psychic rumble and Middle Eastern flavor of Mahafed's thought pattern. There was less fury in Mahafed's thoughts. He was a man of control, a man who used his emotions rather than letting them make a slave of him.

I sense him. Mahafed to Eleanor.

Where?

Michael defeated himself. He'd grown too complacent, too sure of himself and his powers. Reading another was communication. To a sorcerer, communication was contact.

I cannot find him now.

Where was he?

I do not know. Near. But it was not clear what I felt. He is very good, is our Mr. Dragon.

I sense him.

Michael blocked his mind entirely.

He lost all contact with the others.

He waited.

A bead of perspiration trailed from his temple, past his ear, down his shoulder to pool and cool in the small depression near his shoulder blade. He imagined the silent well of terror a hunted submariner must feel in war, sitting on the bottom of the ocean, hiding, waiting expectantly, apprehensively for the sound that you *knew* must come, for that final explosion, the sound of tearing metal and the feared *whooshing* inrush of chill water, then panic and death.

Time moved through deep water.

Through water deeper than man had ever experienced.

Through water the density of honey.

Still, Michael waited.

Minutes turned to a quarter hour . . . to half an hour . . . while Michael blocked as much of the functions of his mind as possible. He was as near to death as a living, healthy mind could be without crossing that line.

Minutes slid by . . .

. . . like sand through an hourglass . . .

Soap opera stuff. It brought a smile to Michael's features.

Over an hour had passed.

A false dawn washed subtly across the horizon. It was still an hour or more to sunrise.

Michael let his defenses relax. Tentatively, he let his mind search the nearby woods. He smelled the damp foliage, the subtle spice scent of decaying leaves. A small nocturnal animal rustled nearby, then went to ground. The air was chilly. Michael felt damp, chilled.

He willed himself warm.

His body responded like a finely tuned furnace.

He cast his mind out in a broader net.

The psychic winds were silent.

Mahafed and Eleanor were gone.

Michael rose stiffly to his feet. He stretched and rubbed tired, cramped muscles.

Eleanor and Mahafed were no longer in the forest. They'd missed him. The question now was *where are they?*

Michael put a hand out to the cool, night-damp roughness of a nearby tree and scanned the area beyond the forest. Glastonbury . . . that was where the two had gone. He sensed the emanations from that direction.

He stood silently then, for a long moment. He had two immediate goals in mind. First, to ensure Carol and Jenny's safety. Second, to find a way to separate Eleanor and Mahafed.

He'd had plenty of time to think in that last hour.

Time enough to realize that he had no choice *but* to go on the offensive. To survive, the prey had to turn on the hunters. That meant finding a way to split Mahafed and Eleanor. He didn't think he could fight them together.

He moved off through the dark forest. Night was no obstacle to him. His eyes were the eyes of a nighttime predator. Leaves and dried foliage crackled softly underfoot. Michael thought of the Volvo, wondered about the extent of his powers, then willed the leaves to silence beneath his feet.

He couldn't explain the process, even to himself, but the crackling ceased. He moved in total silence, more silently than even the small mice and moles that rustled around him in the last minutes before dawn.

Breaking through a tangle of brush, he nearly stumbled onto a road.

He started along it. Glastonbury was less than three miles away. He approached the lights of the city as dawn began to throw wild, blood-hued swaths of paint across the eastern horizon, a paint watered and thinned by a rapidly thickening fog.

On the fringe of the town, now bound in fog, a friendly rectangle of light and the smell of frying bacon drew him to a small restaurant. The Pretty Wench, it was called. From the outside, it looked as if it had served as a wayfarers' stop for centuries. Its uneven stone walls and narrow carriage-entrance looked tired.

The restaurant was low-ceilinged, with sagging walls. The rich aroma of coffee filled the small room. Tables and chairs cluttered the dining area, covered in soft blue and white tablecloths. It was early yet, not yet 5:30 A.M., and fewer than a dozen people were clustered at the tables. A small black-and-white television murmured behind the cash register near the entrance.

"Sit anywhere," one of the two waitresses said.

The conversation among the patrons was friendly, bantering. It was a workday, and these were working people catching their last free moments before starting the day's tasks. From the easy joking between customers and waitresses, it was obvious that most of the clients were regulars.

Michael tapped a chair. "Coffee," he said, "black. Which way to your rest rooms?"

The waitress tossed him a puzzled look. Her eyes scanned his rumpled clothes. "Are you tired?"

It was Michael's turn to pass her a quizzical frown.

Then the woman brightened. "You're American." She laughed softly. "The toilet is back that way." She laughed softly again. "Sometimes I don't think we speak the same language."

As Michael made his way toward a side hallway door, he heard the waitress chuckling with the other waitress about *Americans and their rest rooms*. "I thought the bloke was looking for a place to lay down." The closing hallway door cut off the sound of the other waitress's laughter.

It felt good to splash cold water on his face.

He combed his hair, then brushed his teeth with a finger rubbed on soap. *God,* it tasted awful. Then it dawned on him that he didn't need to brush his teeth. If he could will the Volvo to roll, couldn't he simply will the plaque away?

He was about to try it, when he remembered Eleanor and Mahafed.

They would be sure to feel his presence if he tried something so stupid this near to them.

He ignored the soapy taste as well as he could.

His coffee was steaming on the table when he returned to the dining room. He ordered fried tomatoes, eggs, toast, and a rasher of bacon. While he waited, he sipped his coffee and warmed his fingers on the heavy, hot mug.

He realized then that something had changed.

The restaurant was quiet, where minutes earlier it had been buzzing with conversation.

He sipped his coffee again, thoughtfully, scanning the curiously averted faces of the . . .

Suddenly, hot coffee sloshed his face, searing his cheek. Rough hands grabbed his arms from behind and jerked him backward. His wooden chair clattered on the hardwood floor. Two strong sets of shoulders twisted his arms up toward the back of his neck. Craning around, Michael saw two large and weatherbeaten men in coveralls, their faces straining and red. He tried to pull away, but they held him tightly.

"They're on they're way!" Michael heard one of the waitresses call breathlessly from the counter near the entrance. She was hanging up the telephone as she spoke.

Another large man, ruddy-faced, balding, with the belly of a beer drinker, rose from his table and placed himself self-importantly in front of Michael.

"You might as well calm down, Mr. Dragon," the man said. "Those two who've got you in their glaums ain't about to let you go, and you ain't about to fight your way free of Ian and Jimmy Coker."

Michael ceased his struggles. The sound of his own name brought a chill over him. His arms felt as if they were being torn from his shoulders. His feet barely touched the floor.

"What the hell's going on?" he asked, with as much indignation as he could muster.

Everyone in the place was staring at him with either cold, unfeeling eyes, or with barely concealed disgust.

The beer belly jerked a thumb at the nearby television.

"You're right famous, you are, Mr. Dragon. *The rapist*, they've been callin' you on the telly. We've been talking about you and the doings up at the Carruthers place since The Wench opened for business this morning. And such a nice-looking man, too, Janey over here's been saying about you. Why would such a nice-looking young man as yourself want to rape and stab a young girl the way you did?"

"I don't know what you're talking about."

"Give him one in the snot locker," a voice from the corner said. "Tell the coppers he was giving us a nasty fight."

"I didn't rape anyone."

"You can tell that to the police," Beer Belly said. He looked as if he was toying with the idea tossed from the peanut gallery. "You Yanks, you come over here and act as if you own the world. Well, let me show you what it's like to have a little withdrawn from your account."

Michael felt the strong arms behind him raise him off the floor, tilt him into position for the coming blow from Beer Belly's big fist.

Michael concentrated on Beer Belly's balding head.

Beer Belly pulled his arm back, moved in close, and when he uncoiled, smashed one of the Coker boys clean in the chops.

Michael twisted around suddenly, stared cleanly into the eyes of the other Coker brother, and willed the man to feel his head exploding.

The second Coker boy let go of Michael and reeled away, hands clasped to his head, wailing. Michael backed away from the confused, stricken people at the tables, vividly creating the table-smashing, chair-flinging image of himself, Beer Belly, and the Cokers locked in a vicious brawl in the middle of the restaurant. While the patrons stared on in fascination, Michael slipped out the door.

In the distance, he heard ululating sirens—several of them—screaming their way toward The Pretty Wench.

Michael slipped through the carriage gate, around the

restaurant, and onto a two-rut, weed-infested alley leading into the city.

He let his mind open out to the city as he ran.

As he feared, he sensed Mahafed and Eleanor.

And they sensed him.

They knew where he was.

Even the morning fog couldn't hide him from them.

25

Life had become a nightmare.

No matter where he turned, he was hunted.

It was time to put an end to that.

Michael stopped running. He put a hand out to the rough stone and mortar of an ancient backyard fence. His breathing faded from ragged to heavy. His mind spread out beyond himself, searching the fogbound city.

So be it, he thought.

Let this be the battlefield.

His senses located his two enemies. They were near each other, but not together. The three of them formed a geographic triangle in the city. Mahafed and Eleanor were homing in on him. He didn't have much time.

And still he didn't know how best to fight them.

Fool! Use your mind! Think!

The thought hit him with a palpable, painful impact, as if it were a weapon thrown at him by another—a hidden enemy. He couldn't tell if it had been his own thought process or that of another.

So what? *Think*. What did that mean?

Michael twisted at the frayed edges of his mind. What could he do?

Stay the hell away from people, for one thing. They

were too easily influenced by Mahafed and Eleanor—by any sorcerer. He had to separate Mahafed and Eleanor from the crowds, had to split the two of them if possible, split . . .

Split . . .

Something rang a bell.

Split?

What?

Give them an army to fight.

It didn't make sense. What the hell kind of thought was that?

It could work.

What could work? It still didn't make sense to him yet.

Then die.

I can't.

Oh, yes, you can.

I have to protect Carol and Jenny.

Then be creative.

It was that insane schizophrenic thought process again. One side tugging against the other. Crazy-making.

"Who are you?" Michael asked in a torn whisper.

Only the silent, mist-shrouded emptiness replied. Michael felt a presence beyond that of himself and his enemy, that same endemic presence he'd sensed the— *God, was it only the day before?* But it wasn't talking to him. It simply existed. It was his own thoughts that were driving him crazy.

Michael knelt and pressed the palms of both hands to the chilly, damp dirt of the rutted lane. He felt the dim life force emanating from the depths of the earth. "Who are you?"

Silence.

Deep silence.

Silence reverberating with the dying half-lives of power long forgotten.

Silence so profound that it had the effect of screaming multitudes.

Merlin's land.

He was here. Somewhere nearby. Locked in a cavern. Buried. Waiting. Shrouded in a cloak of darkness and stillness so impenetrable that Michael knew it had been centuries since anyone had read the signs. Long dead, yet still communicating with his kind.

His kind . . .

Michael hesitated to number himself on the same list.

Yet he was aware that it might be true.

Was he heir to Merlin's legacy?

Heir to the scrolls?

If he could survive this morning.

It was a big *if*.

So . . . think.

Think or die.

Michael considered the absurd thoughts that had hit him moments earlier. Create an army?

Surely Mahafed and Eleanor would see through that.

But hadn't they done essentially that? Hadn't they brought an army to bear on him at Tor House?

Michael hesitated. He resisted the thought of using innocent others for his own ends. It was foolish, he knew, but it was how he was made. He knew that Mahafed and Eleanor would laugh at him. So would Caine, if he were alive.

So what choices does that leave you, Mr. Straight?

Few.

But an idea was forming now.

Simple.

If he could manage it.

Too simple?

He wouldn't know unless he tried.

It certainly had to be more convincing than mere illusion.

He concentrated—on the whereabouts of Mahafed and Eleanor.

Eleanor was downtown, in the center of the city.

Mahafed was on the move, heading in a diagonal direction toward the outskirts of the city.

To flank me, Michael realized.

The two of them were choreographing their moves, based on their knowledge of where Michael was.

So let's give you two of us.

Michael, still kneeling in the hard-packed ruts of the alleyway, closed his eyes and concentrated. Bits of the lyrics of an old Beatles song formed in his mind: "... the two of us ...." He willed himself to separate, felt a strange sensation as part of his mind began to coalesce outside his body. He opened his eyes and watched the transition take place, watched in fascination as his body did as he willed it. At first his body shimmered insubstantially; then it began to stretch sideways in two directions at once, elongating, stretching painfully, giving his vision strange double images. Michael willed the images to clear. There was a strange scent in the chilly, foggy air, the smell of sweat and blood and ... he couldn't place the other scent ... the smell of tilled fields and time, like the smell of a long-unopened pyramid ... and the stench of something else. ... He heard the subdued crackle of static, as if the fabric of the world were being softly torn apart. He felt a deep, gut-wrenching pain as cell for cell his body came apart at the seams, as it tore flesh from living flesh—accompanied by the flesh-wet sounds of birth.

He moaned in agony as he felt his flesh tearing.

And then it was finished.

Michael found himself gasping and weak, barely able to keep his balance, even on his hands and knees as he was.

And, on *his* knees, next to him, Michael saw the other *him*.

Identical.

Naked.

With the remnants of his clothes hanging limply from its body.

Michael switched perspective.

Now he saw the world from the other's eyes.

Which was he? Which a creation?

Even Michael was unsure.

This was a very different process than he'd used in duplicating Jenny and Carol. He had brought forth living flesh from his own body this time, created another being —played God and conjured another life from nothing more than a rib and air.

He sensed the world from both bodies, was aware of two similar existences at once. He was in two places at once, or so it seemed.

A wisp of acrid smoke wafted past Michael's noses, and he recognized the smell he'd been wondering about. Something burned.

Two sets of eyes dropped toward the smoldering earth beneath and between the two kneeling forms. Raw dirt had melted between them, forming a murky, glimmering brown glass in the alleyway, as if some awesome electrical power had been concentrated on that spot. It was the stench of sulfur he'd sensed, the stink of creation.

His eyes met the eyes of the other Michael.

He reached out and touched the other's shoulder.

The other was as tangible as he was.

Solid.

A being drawn from the mud of existence.

There was no need for talk. They understood each other perfectly. They were in perfect synch. One was to be a decoy, the other the hunter.

Michael rose unsteadily to his feet. His vision wavered. He felt dizzy, drained of energy. He'd created another version of himself, but at what cost? He felt weak, only half as strong as before.

His twin rose from the steaming alleyway. Brittle brown glass crackled underfoot.

Of course!

There were two of him now. He couldn't possibly expect both, individually, to have the same energy as one.

Michael sucked in deep drafts of the chilly, moisture-laden air and forced his muscles to steady themselves. For an instant he let his consciousness settle into the mind of his counterpart, Dragon II. It was an uncanny sensation, seeing yourself through another's eyes. And he was aware of something else.

There were two of him now, two bodies to inhabit, yet the core of his consciousness, the essence of his being, *his soul?*—was that what he sensed?—was still singular. It was as if he'd created a zombie, a soulless clone of himself that existed in it own right, that contained all the necessary cells and synpases for life, yet that lacked the magical spark of true existence. This second version of himself was physically identical to the original, yet they had but one true consciousness to share between them. If he were to die, if his *soul* were to be extinguished, this other body would live on in his image—in his image, yet lacking his vitality.

Yet *he* could exist in whichever body he chose.

It was simply a matter of shifting perspective. While he lived in one, the other functioned without a soul.

He didn't fully comprehend the process, yet he vaguely realized that the core of his being could exist in only one place at a time. There was only one *him*, only one Michael Dragon, though he now had the use of two bodies.

So use them.

He kneeled, grabbed a handful of coarse brown glass and dirt from the alleyway. He clenched it in his fist, willed it to change, squeezed it tightly, breathed a different shape into it. The raw material in his hand smoldered. Smoke drifted from it. He dropped the shifting shapes to the ground, smoothed them out, watched them unfold into steaming, newly formed cloth. In a moment the process stopped.

Michael dressed in the newly formed clothes. They were rough but real—serviceable. Not bad for a first try. Michael's alter ego followed his lead, stooped to pluck the clothes from the alley and quickly donned them.

Michael shifted his will, and the two Dragons moved off through the fog in different directions. In a moment they faded from each other's view, yet their movements were known intimately by the other.

Michael shifted his consciousness between bodies.

Now he was in Dragon II, moving toward the main business area.

Now he was in Dragon I again, hurrying toward the outskirts.

Now Dragon II, concentrating, sending signals to that ancient bitch who was hunting him.

Eleanor sensed him near the business district.

Dragon II shifted direction, headed toward the abbey ruins.

Once he was certain that Eleanor was on his trail, Michael left his psychic clone and returned to the body he considered his original, the one in whom his consciousness had remained during the creation.

His hands were cold. His breathing came in shallow, nervous whispers. He sensed Mahafed nearby, on the outskirts of the city.

Michael paused. He was on a narrow, hilly street. Large stone houses with thatched or tile roofs were set at odd angles behind dreamlike hedges. Hedges cut in the shape of clouds. Hedges made indistinct by the fog and by the dissipated brightness of the hidden morning sun. Lights illuminated several hazy windows. The city was coming to life.

And Mahafed . . .

. . . was very close.

Closer than Michael had earlier thought.

Michael risked exposure by letting his mind spread a net through the neighborhood.

The net evaporated on contact with the other sorcerer.

Welcome, Dragon.

It was a deceiving message. Its source was indistinct, seemed to come from several locations at once.

And why not? Michael thought.

If I can split, I should expect something similar from the others. After all, they've been at this longer than I have.

Michael moved into the shadow of one of the giant hedges. Gnarled branches and coarse foliage scraped soft music on his jacket. Beyond the thick growth, he could barely make out the lighted windows of a large Cotswold stone house. A Mercedes sat in the driveway. Tentatively, Michael let his senses enter the house. There were five people inside. A family. Three teenagers and their parents.

Anyone else?

Not that he could sense.

I could be anywhere, Dragon.

Mahafed was playing with him, Michael realized. He was tempted to reply but thought better of it.

For a moment he let his mind float to Dragon II. It was getting easier to do. One instant, he was staring at the house beyond the hedge, and in the next split second he was peering through other eyes, around smooth stone ruins nearly a mile away. He sensed Eleanor nearby. She'd taken the bait, was tracking Dragon II through the ruins of the ancient abbey. The towering ruins disappeared into the misty sky above Dragon II. Michael sensed the wet grass beneath II's feet, felt the chill air, smelled the dampness of wet stone. Thick fog softened the edges of everything that came into sight, turned the world into a cotton-shrouded, near-silent fantasy world in which vision was almost a useless sense. It confused and distorted more than it clarified. Shadows appeared where there was none. Solid walls looked insubstantial, appeared to shift and move like mist.

If only the fog was as confusing for Eleanor, he hoped.

If only he could keep Mahafed and Eleanor separated . . .

If only he could live through this day.

He returned to Dragon I, to the thick hedge beyond the stone and thatched-roof house.

I have him cornered, Michael heard inside his head. It was Eleanor, calling for Mahafed to join her in the abbey ruins.

No, I've found him, Mahafed responded. *Here. On the edge of the city.*

Silence.

Michael shifted slightly, felt the rough foliage of the hedge brush his cheek.

The quiet lengthened.

You are good, Michael Dragon. Very good.

It was Mahafed.

But not good enough.

The sheltering wall of hedge into which Michael was pressed suddenly *whoofed* into flame.

Michael jerked away from the billowing wall of flame.

He heard a laugh rumble through the fog.

The fire died. The hedge was untouched.

Illusion, Michael realized.

I know where you are, Dragon.

Michael scanned the immediate area, searching with all the senses he could muster. He felt Mahafed's presence but could not locate the source.

Must we continue this game of cat and mouse? Mahafed asked. *You cannot stand against us, Dragon.*

Michael tried to locate Eleanor.

He sensed nothing.

He fluttered his mind into that of Dragon II, within the abbey ruins.

Still nothing.

Eleanor had disappeared.

Were she and Mahafed still in communication with each other? Or was she moving on her own?

And where the hell was she?

Michael leaped back across the mist-shrouded city, brought his consciousness home to Dragon I.

He felt suddenly cornered.

He needed space to think, to make sense of what was happening. He felt as if he were at the center of a vortex, spinning, spinning, spinning at an ever-accelerating pace, blown off course and balance by hurricane-force winds generated by powers beyond his control.

He closed himself off, shutting down as much of his existence as he could. He needed to escape again. Needed to hide. He'd misjudged his skills, misjudged the abilities of Mahafed and Eleanor, maybe made a fatal mistake.

That won't help you now. Mahafed thought again, gloating. *I am too close for you to evade me that way.*

Michael felt his muscles tense expectantly. He felt as if he were under a microscope, as if his every move were known, as if his life were about to be snuffed out—and he didn't know where the danger was. He couldn't read Mahafed clearly. The other sorcerer was doing something to distort his aura, and Michael couldn't decipher what it was, couldn't tell where the other was, couldn't sense what Mahafed was doing.

Another goddamned mistake?

By splitting in two, Michael realized, he'd dissipated his energies, spread himself too thin.

He wondered if it hadn't been Mahafed and Eleanor who'd suggested that he split, in the first place.

That subliminal psychic voice . . . not Merlin at all . . . but those two . . .

But how could they have known he was capable of splitting?

They were sorcerers, of course.

They sensed such things. And, like Caine, Michael realized that they knew his abilities better than he knew them himself . . .

. . . *at this point in time.*

Then he knew for a certainty what had happened.

They'd used his own needs to manipulate him, to fool him. They'd simply tapped into his own projective desires and let him produce his own Waterloo. He wanted to believe in Merlin so badly that he'd fallen for their very simple suggestion.

Divide and conquer?

That had been his aim—to split the other two, and fight them one at a time.

But now it was he—himself—who was split in two! Divided, weakened, and waiting to be conquered.

Damn! Damn! Damn!

Michael realized then that he could no longer rely on any of his old senses and beliefs. The rules of his existence had been changed, and he hadn't been given a copy of the new ones. The game had been changed, and no one had bothered to tell him how the new one worked.

He was on his own.

Playing by Eleanor and Mahafed's rules.

Unless . . .

He didn't know what to do. Didn't know where to turn. Didn't know what his best strategy was.

He considered entering the house beyond the hedge, considered using the family within as a buffer against Mahafed and Eleanor, then decided against it. Enough innocents had been harmed already.

He turned and ran.

He needed space . . . needed time . . . needed . . .

Soft, muffled laughter rolled after him through the fog.

There's no place to hide, Mr. Dragon.

Mahafed's psychic voice echoed insanely in the mist-shrouded silence.

Michael felt the chill air filling his chest as he leaped a small fence and cut across several large backyards. He realized now that he had no idea what weapons Mahafed and Eleanor could bring to bear on him. He was a neophyte at this—maybe he *did* have more ability than Lea Frazzetti or Drew Garrett, but he wasn't up against beginners any longer.

A high stone wall blocked his path. He skirted the thick masonry until he found a gate. He grabbed it.

Locked.

Mahafed's laughter rolled through the fog again. Directionless. Near, yet untouchable. Mocking and distant.

You cannot escape us, Dragon. There is no place to hide. The other sorcerer's thoughts reverberated in Michael's head.

Michael rattled the locked gate.

It was solid, unmoving.

He ran on—then kicked himself. *Stupid!* He could have broken that lock simply by concentrating on it.

He was about to return to the gate, when a cat cried and jerked into motion at his feet, scampered up the wall, and disappeared. Michael took its lead. This would be faster. He jumped for the wall, scraped a shoulder on the rough stone, began climbing, painstakingly pulling himself up the vertical surface. His fingernails ached from trying to hold his weight, from trying to gain a secure grip on the damp stone. His breath rasped in his throat.

If only I were a cat, he thought.

And he wondered why he couldn't be.

He concentrated, dug his claws into the stone, felt powerful muscles pull him effortlessly upward now. His vision swam with the imperfect transformation, but he saw a dark furred foreleg stretch above him and pull him over the top of the wall—*his foreleg.*

The change didn't surprise him. It was something new, something unexpected, but he was losing all sense of surprise.

He was a cat—at least very close to being a complete cat.

The hues of the fog had changed, metamorphosed, taken on deeper, friendlier tones. He felt suddenly more at home in the mist, a hunter moving through its natural environment, pleased with the protective cover provided by the mist. He paused atop the wall, listening to the silence of the fog. His long tongue darted out and preened his shoulder where it had scraped the wall. It was a very human shoulder, caressed by a very inhuman tongue. His dark, slitted pupils surveyed the ghostly shapes looming nearby in the fog. His ears rotated, independent of each other. He heard the sounds of arrogant laughter dying in someone's throat, smelled the peculiar, mingled scent of prey and hunter inseparably linked, both together in a paradoxical, mind-numbing combination. He turned his head with infinite smoothness, with a timeless feline gesture as old as the species, and surveyed the field beyond the fence.

Vague, elephantine forms loomed through the heavy murkiness. Strange forms. Large forms. Insubstantial forms. Forms dangling limp banners. Forms stretched taut by spidering legs of rope.

The carnival.

Silent in its fogbound morning slumber.

Michael recalled having driven past it the evening before, while it was being raised on the outskirts of town.

Here it was, now. Silent. Veiled in a shroud as thick as that covering the River Styx. A small, ratty, traveling carnival barely capable of preserving its facade of fantasy for even the youngest of children.

Michael crouched lower atop the stone fence, suddenly alert to the presence of others nearby. There was no laughter now. But he recognized the emanations he sensed.

Eleanor.

Mahafed.

Together again.

And he was still divided.

But learning.

Let them come, he thought.

With a flick of his long, sinuous panther tail, Michael bounded effortlessly from the high wall and loped across the tall grass of the field. The fog parted as he passed, then swirled closed behind him, like ephemeral curtains stirred by the passing of a breeze. He disappeared around one of the softly fluttering tents, then sat on his haunches and faced the direction from which he had come.

He left his newfound feline body and fluttered across the cloudbound city into Dragon II's consciousness. The lines from another old song floated through his mind, words from a Disney movie, Hayley Mills singing, "Let's get together, yeah, yeah, yeah..." And Dragon II reacted. He came to his feet, began running.

Michael felt the soft, perfectly mown turf beneath his feet, beneath the feet of Dragon II, as he pounded his way across the lawns of the ancient abbey ruins, pounded his way through mists as thick as time itself, pounded a course toward the fields at the edge of the town.

And that refrain never ceased:

"Let's get together, yeah, yeah, yeah..." Subliminal yet insistent.

He needed to reunite with himself, needed to bring his strength back to one core.

Dragon II ran, his breath tearing at his lungs, ripping through his throat. He had to find Dragon I, had to "...get together..."

Then he laughed, a breathless laugh, and spread his arms wide, willing them to become wings—and he sailed into the air, breast muscles straining effortlessly, wings beating strongly at the mist, parting it, lifting him into a soupy fog that reminded Michael of what the beginning of time must have been like. He'd become a falcon, a merlin, and the earth no longer bound him to its surface. The wind had become his brother.

The rules *had* changed.

It was time he started writing his own.

Find the carnival, he willed the merlin.

Find yourself.

And he left the swift-flying hawk, dropped with near-instantaneous speed back into the feline mind he'd left only seconds before.

Peacefulness settled around him. The rush of wind faded from his ears. Stiff canvas rustled beside him again as he rested back on his feline haunches. Other tents whispered in the early-morning mist, their shapes looming nearby. Michael turned feline eyes toward the wall from which he'd recently leaped.

They were there—his enemies—just beyond the stone, speaking in soft voices to each other. Aware that something had changed in their world, that a new force was on the loose, that maybe it was they who had miscalculated, who had misjudged the skills of their quarry.

Michael let go of the feline shape he had created for himself. He felt his body shift, felt thick fur draw back into his flesh, sucked gently in through tingling pores, felt his skin stretch like stiff rubber, felt his muscles knot and flex and writhe and finally felt himself settle awkwardly onto the wet, flattened grass beneath him. A quick glance confirmed that he no longer had a furred foreleg. He rose from his haunches, from the uncomfortable position in which he found himself, and stood to his full height as a man.

He had so much to learn, he realized.

And such little time to learn it all.

He knew, now, that he could shift his shape at will—into anything.

It was not just illusion, as the others used.

It was reality.

He could become anything he wished.

He had already changed himself into two beings, *had* made himself into a hawk and a great cat—almost a cat.

The imperfection in that transformation was almost humorous. One shoulder and most of that arm had failed to shift shape. Why?

He had no idea why. The skill was too new for him to comprehend fully. He had willed the transformation while dangling by that human arm. It hadn't changed completely. That was all he knew.

He needed time to understand more.

And time was a commodity he did not have in abundance.

Glancing down, he realized that he was naked again. He'd lost his clothes with his transformation into the cat. He knelt, dug his fingers into the soil beneath the grass, spread it across his chest and downward, willing the damp earth to change, to mutate, to become soft wool.

A swipe of dark wool formed over his flesh. He passed his hand over his body, and that quickly painted a new set of clothes.

Something drew his attention.

Something distant, but approaching fast.

He picked a sound out of the mist—high, overhead— the rhythmic beating of powerful wings—the wings of a merlin.

Coming home.

26

Michael held out an arm. He felt the concussion of the beating wings before he saw the falcon emerge from the mist. The majestic bird swooped in from behind him, its wings ruffling the air with powerful strokes, and settled gently onto his forearm.

Intelligent falcon eyes blinked once, met his.

Michael felt a surge of energy flow through him.

He shifted focus, stared into his human face through the painfully sharp eyes of the small hawk. From this vantage, too, he felt the reuniting surge of power.

Did he need to merge again with this other part of himself? Or was proximity enough to reunite their energies?

He had so much to learn about this business of sorcery. Too much?

He sensed a concussion of raw energy nearby and whirled away from the sheltering wall of the tent only an instant before something hard and fast slapped the stiff canvas. His wings *thrummed* the air, carrying him aloft. A sharp, crackling explosion rippled through the chill dawn air, muffled by the fog.

Michael fluttered there, sharp falcon eyes watching his human body rolling away from the tent, rolling and coming to his feet and scrabbling away, as another harsh *braak* broke the stillness. A spray of dirt kicked up inches from the earthbound Michael's outstretched fingers.

Michael shifted focus, dropped his awareness into the human body on the ground, commanded it to spin around and make a diving retreat in the opposite direction.

Once more the stillness reverberated with an angry *craack!*

This time the bullet ricocheted off a metal tent stake a good five feet off target.

Michael rolled behind the cover of a large wooden freight box. He pulled himself into a crouching position and waited for the next shot.

Nothing happened.

He cast his senses about him in a broad net.

Mahafed had taken position on the fence near the spot Michael had clambered over. Michael concentrated on the spot. His senses clearly picked out the cold steel sensation of the other sorcerer's rifle.

The realization that Mahafed had chosen such a mundane weapon with which to hunt him brought a thin smile to Michael's face. *In a country of illusion, the man with reality is king,* Michael thought. Mahafed had failed to bring Michael to his knees using his psychic powers, so now he'd decided to—

Michael paused, puzzled.

He closed his eyes, focused on Mahafed's energies, and bore down on the image.

Something was wrong.

Michael felt a cold trickle of sweat roll down his spine.

He furrowed his brows in concentration.

He didn't like what he felt, but he couldn't read it accurately—couldn't read it at all. Eleanor was there, too, nearby, but . . . unreadable . . . fumbling with something on the ground. . . .

Michael shifted perspective, slipped upward, lost himself in the oblivion of the soupy sky until he merged into the still-hovering form of the merlin.

Below, all was silent, shrouded in the downy fog.

Michael tipped a wingtip, sailed yards closer to the fence, invisible below. The world was a timeless morass of dense mist. Even the soft whisper of wind through his feathers sounded distant, unreal. His sharp eyes were useless, his ears nearly so.

Someone was moving around near the fence.

Michael dropped lower, searching the gray nothingness for the first sign of earthly existence.

Spurting fire was the first sign.

It erupted upward—directly at him.

Instinctively, Michael reeled over sideways, his wings digging into the heavy air like oars, pulling him aside with all the effort he could muster.

He wasn't fast enough.

Something slammed him, ripped through the soft flesh near his neck, spit feathers into the air, sent him spinning through the dizzying fogbank, one wing flapping helplessly while the other dangled loose, like something dead. He sensed a burning pain.

Illusion, Michael told himself. *Illusion. The wing is okay. The pain will go away.*

But it didn't go away.

The wing couldn't catch the breeze, couldn't move at all.

His plunge earthward was quick.

At a sharp angle, Michael hit the packed and matted grass of the carnival field with a soft *whupp* and thumped roughly to a stop. Stunned, he tried to rise erect on his talons. His neck burned. He fluttered sideways, off balance, too unstable to stand erect. He let himself collapse into the grass, blinking, trying to make sense of what had happened to him. He was in a state near shock. He felt the tiny heart within his ribs beating erratically. A tremor fluttered through his body.

Eleanor and Mahafed had trapped him.

With real guns.

And curiosity.

His own curiosity.

The world felt spongy. Reality was a shifting, unsteady, swaying deck. Michael tried to rise again, unsure of why he was attempting the feat. He snapped his hooked beak to the side . . . once, twice . . . and again to clear the numbness from his mind.

His head snapped around, radared to a stop facing the nearby fence lost somewhere in the fog. Brilliant eyes blinked, blinked, blinked, trying to see through the mist.

No vision came to him.

Eleanor and Mahafed had shrouded themselves in a psychic fog as thick as the real fog that swathed the world in silence.

But they were moving out there . . . approaching him warily.

He was sure of it.

He tried to rise again.

And toppled to his side once more.

He lay with his beak open, panting. He could see a wet redness speckled across his feathers. He'd taken a good portion of the shotgun blast, he realized. His left wing was nearly useless.

He was a fool.

He should have reunited with himself when he was sitting on the other Dragon's arm, should have merged back together and . . .

Something rustled in the grass just beyond his vision.

He cocked his head, grew still, listening, waiting.

If Mahafed and Eleanor found him like this, he would be at their mercy. If he left the merlin's body, and it was killed, he would be giving up a great share of his power.

He couldn't do that—couldn't abandon such an important part of himself. To do so would be to put himself clearly at their mercy.

You're a goddamn fool, Dragon, he told himself.

But fool or not, he had to do something.

It was either *something* or forfeit that part of his strength he'd invested in Dragon II.

He concentrated on the raw, oozing wound at the base of his left wing. *Heal! Heal, dammit!* he willed. He pictured torn flesh closing, sealing itself off, felt the hawk's body beginning to respond, when he heard a soft footfall within yards of him.

His concentration was broken.

"It's over, Dragon."

Eleanor, this time, speaking in a very real voice, her words emerging from the thick fog as if from darkness. No psychic games for her. She enjoyed the tête-à-tête of death too much to miss out on the personal touch.

"We've come for you, Dragon. We know you're hurt. You might as well let us end this quickly."

She had a soft voice, an enticing voice, the voice of an angel.

The angel of death.

Michael's rattled senses searched the jackstraw grasses around him. He sensed the two sorcerers within yards, could even see the dim outline of one of them . . . a billowing scarf fluttering in the light breeze, blending with the mist, giving the figure a ghostly appearance.

Eleanor . . .

He willed pain at the figure.

It took a great deal out of him.

He felt weak, sick to his stomach. He'd lost a lot of blood.

The ghost paused, then disdainfully drew closer.

"You are weak, Dragon. It's over for you."

Another life force was circling behind him, Michael realized. He scrabbled around on the uneven, matted grass, his one unharmed wing flopping absurdly for balance, his eyes searching the mist for the figure, for Mahafed, wondering from which direction death would come—in which guise.

Did they see him?

He thought not.

Though he was certain they sensed his whereabouts. It was only seconds before they would use their very real weapons.

He concentrated and flung a searing bolt of crackling blue lightning at the one shimmering figure he saw through the wisps of fog. The crooked bolt spat, sizzled, and flickered off Eleanor's aura, outlining her in vibrant neon color and sound before dying in a fading hiss.

A fold of mist wafted across the spot, hiding Eleanor's vague form from view.

"You have more talent than most," Eleanor said. "It's too bad you wouldn't listen to reason."

"Say your prayers, Dragon."

Mahafed, now, his mocking voice coming out of nowhere, being absorbed within scant feet of its utterance by the cotton-shrouded world around them.

Michael fluttered his uninjured wing as he whirled to locate this new voice. They had him cornered. He couldn't fly away, couldn't even run. His only option was to abandon the merlin's body, to cut his losses and run, to try to recoup what he could—

Unless . . .

Michael bore down on his mind, willed himself to change form.

Ignore the injury.

Change!

Now!

Presto-damn-changeo!

"He's shifting!" he heard Eleanor call wildly. "Shoot him!"

Michael didn't wait for the transformation to complete itself. He scrabbled sideways into the tall grass on the incomplete muscles of a forming belly. Pain rippled along his shifting shape—rippled, rippled, *rippled* . . .

He ignored it.

Pain was a sign of life.

As long as he hurt, he still had a chance.

Fireworks flashed golden in the dense fog. Twin concussions rocked the earth, socked the thick air, rolled off into silence.

Still Michael writhed sideways through the grass, his scrabbling, ungainly, creeping movements shifting to the fluid, rippling motion of his new species.

The transformation completed itself as he fled, shifting from noble hawk to sleek, smooth-scaled serpent. Dark, slitted eyes picked out the path of least resistance through the thick grass. Undulant muscles did his bidding, shoved him forward with a rippling gait that compensated for the injured muscles along a portion of the serpent's back.

Another blast ripped the air, *whumped* into the nearby earth, and scattered shards of dirt in all directions.

"He's fleeing!"

"I sense him!"

"How can he? I felt the damage. He was too far gone." This from Eleanor.

"He has become a snake."

"Goddamn him!"

Mahafed's voice contained less fever. "Yes. Goddamn him is right."

Michael slithered beneath a bridge of tall grass, zig-zagged off in a different direction, swerved around a rock, then suddenly spotted the graybound form of a carnival pickup truck.

He rippled straight forward now, his body and course angled slightly for greatest speed.

One . . . two . . . three shotgun blasts *whacked* the hard-packed grasses, scoring Michael's path with heated and ragged spots of raw earth.

In another second he was out of sight beneath the truck.

"Circle it," he heard Eleanor command, her voice low, nearly a hiss. "Make sure it doesn't escape. We'll burn the bastard."

Michael scanned the undercarriage of the truck. Spotting the long crankshaft, he raised his hooded cobra head and entwined himself about the long cylinder. Once secure, certain that he had purchased the precious moments he needed, Michael let his mind float free of the wounded cobra's body.

He sought Dragon I's body, entered it, and energized it.
Move!

Dragon I moved, broke into a spring that carried Michael around several of the gaunt, silent, staring tents. Voices spilled out of opened doors somewhere in the befuddling haze. The carneys were awake and moving now, wondering what the commotion was, angered that intruders were among their wagons and equipment.

Michael crouched, slipped up close to the line of damp tents ringing the pickup truck under which Dragon II's weakened form cowered. Michael dropped to a knee, concentrated on the small, level area in front of him. He could barely see the hulking shape of the pickup through the thick fog, a fog that was beginning to glow golden with morning sunshine reflected off trillions of floating drops of moisture, a shifting, billowing fog as thick as any he had ever experienced.

He sensed Mahafed and Eleanor near the pickup, felt Eleanor bending, heard the muffled blast of her shotgun as she fired at the undercarriage of the truck, at the telltale life force hiding there.

Another muted blast was followed by the ringing of pellets on metal. Sparks flashed beneath the pickup, followed by an instantaneous hollowness that stilled the air ... a sudden vacuum filled almost immediately by the rush of wind and the heat of a gigantic fireball that boosted the rear of the pickup well off the ground and spun it over on its side.

The early-morning air reverberated with the thundering explosion.

Spurting flames outlined the two mysterious figures nearby.

Shouts and cries of distress scuttled through the orange-hued mist as more carneys were jerked awake and began spilling out of their motor homes and into the dense and timeless world that surrounded them. Sparks and flaming debris from the exploding truck ignited small fires on several nearby tents. The tiny flames, scattered across the sloping roof of the nearest tent, re-

sembled glittering candles on a cake. The mists glimmered with haloed spots of brightness.

Michael focused his mind on running forms nearby,
formed an image of a man and woman carrying torches,
setting fire to anything they drew near, drilled the image
into the minds of those nearby.

"Hey, someone's setting the goddamn fires!" a voice
shouted.

"By the generator!" another voice shouted.

The dull pounding of dozens of pairs of feet rumbled
beneath the fog, out of sight. Michael focused on Mahafed
and Eleanor. He sensed them trying to throw a fence of
pain around themselves, a wall of invisibility.

He tore it down, felt Mahafed and Eleanor's stunned
surprise when he sent his power so directly against theirs.

The running forms of angered carneys thundered toward
the burning pickup.

"They're over here! By Finnigan's pickup!"

"Someone grab a gun!"

Michael concentrated, felt the still-living force of
Dragon II slithering toward the safety of one of the nearby
tents. He shifted his attention toward Mahafed and
Eleanor.

Eleanor...

He couldn't detect her.

Searched.

Found nothing.

She'd vanished.

She was by far the stronger of the two.

Mahafed was running toward another tent. Michael
sensed the man's aura, homed on it, followed, pausing now
and then to avoid the rushing, fog-blind carneys scram-
bling to save their burning livelihood.

Another tent was afire. That made three now, three
burning tents ringing the small open area within which the
pickup's skeleton writhed. The flames danced their wondrous magic in indistinct patterns seen through the hazy
screen of the mist. The fog was thicker now, rolling and
bumping across the burning carnival ground like the floating plumes of some monstrous and evil bird.

"One of the animal tents is on fire!" someone screamed.

"Where are those goddamn hoses?"

"Someone call the fire crew!"

"Where are those *goddamn* hoses?"

Mahafed hurried away from the fires, buried himself in the fog. Michael followed, his senses sweeping the grounds around himself like radar. He sidestepped more running carneys, hid behind a stack of wooden crates as the men and women scrambled past, puffing and talking in angered and anxious breathlessness, heading pell-mell for the writhing golden dome near the center of their encampment.

Michael sensed Mahafed trying to divert the running carneys, trying to insinuate an image of Michael into their minds.

Michael slammed his mind into Mahafed's brains.

Mahafed reeled.

He cried out in pain, then slipped into a sudden darkness.

Michael sensed the change somewhere ahead of him in the mists.

Darkness.

Michael fired his senses into the heart of that darkness, into the depths of Mahafed's mind.

He felt a shocked resistance and tore his way madly through it.

For an instant he saw what Mahafed saw, felt what the other felt, heard with the other's ears.

Mahafed was inside one of the untouched tents. Heavy, ruffling canvas sheltered him from the dampness, muffled the shouts and cries from the struggling carneys, dimmed the already weak, fogbound light of morning.

Mahafed's defenses drove Michael's consciousness back. Searing, blistering pain caught him unaware and made him reel. He closed his mind off to Mahafed's retaliation, returned full awareness to Dragon I's body.

He paused a moment, recuperating from Mahafed's attack on his senses. His breathing came in shallow, nervous drafts.

He still couldn't locate Eleanor.

The hair on the back of his neck rose vertically.

He turned, stared into the fog behind him.

No Eleanor.

Not the slightest hint of her existence.

Michael felt surrounded, felt as if Eleanor could drop on him from anywhere and peel his skin off as easily as if he were a banana. He felt helpless—and stunned.

He couldn't locate her.

He had been convinced that his abilities would allow him to know where she was, would keep her located if she were as close as he *knew* she must be. He had been convinced that his powers were stronger—that he was heir to something far greater than either Mahafed or Eleanor could ever know. . . .

And now. . .

Now nothing.

He sensed nothing of her.

He sniffed the wind, as if that could help.

Nothing.

Nada.

Zip.

It was as if she had vanished from the face of the earth.

The hairs on the back of his neck refused to lay down.

Goddamn the woman.

And Mahafed.

So much for confidence.

Michael sent his consciousness across the compound, slipped into the chill form of Dragon II.

Snake eyes made more sense of the morning mist than did human eyes. Michael closed the serpent's eyes, commanded wounded flesh to heal. The shotgun blast that had nearly severed the merlin's wing was a mere pain in the back to the cobra. The long, ragged gash that cut diagonally across the serpent's back began to stretch and writhe. It felt warm, tingly, electrified. Michael concentrated on bringing scaly flesh together, on making it whole and smooth and slick-shiny perfect once again.

The snake's flesh crawled over itself, slithered, wriggled, and merged. The flesh fizzled like fresh 7-Up, like low-grade electricity, tingled and tickled, and . . .

In seconds, the wound was no more.

Michael willed the serpent on its way, guided its path through the coarse grass, then let his consciousness ride the breezes back to Dragon I and his human perspective.

Mahafed's sanctuary lay just ahead.

Michael walked softly toward it.

Behind him, the cries of the fire-fighting carneys meant less to him at that moment than the mournful cawings of a multitude of unseen blackbirds disturbed from their roosts. He let the fog close about the humans.

The hair on the nape of his neck still trembled erect.

But he couldn't locate Eleanor, so to hell with her, for now.

The first thing he had to do was take out Mahafed.

Michael's teeth showed in an expression of neither smile nor grimace.

He had work to do.

Nothing more.

This was a distasteful part of being a sorcerer, but part of the work, nonetheless.

Keeping the world in balance.

And Mahafed threatened that balance.

This was work.

Michael's eyes picked out the elephantine outline of the dark tent. Curtains of vapor swirled about the tent.

Michael felt Mahafed's tentative psychic feelers.

Michael blanked himself, shut down as much of his being as he could, as he imagined Eleanor had done.

Had Mahafed located him?

Did the other bastard know where he was?

It didn't matter, Michael told himself.

He had a job to do.

He made his steps silent.

This was his work now.

This was work.

He wasn't doing this for fun.

This wasn't something he did by choice.

He had no choice anymore.

It was *this* or oblivion.

For himself.

For Jenny.

And for . . . Carol.

This was nothing more than necessary work.

It had to be done.

But those goddamn neck hairs wouldn't stop quivering.

—————————— *27*——————————

Michael dropped to his stomach on the wet grass and rolled under the skirt of the tent. He came immediately to his knees in the darkness.

He let his mind search the nearby darkness and its myriad of strange shapes.

Mahafed was in here, but not near.

And Eleanor?

Nowhere.

Forget her. Take out Mahafed. Then worry about her.

"So, you came for me."

The voice, with its Middle Eastern accent, seemed to float down from the overhead rigging. Instinctively, Michael glanced upward, toward the rigging twenty feet above the floor of the tent. It would be a good place to hide, he thought, a surprising place for death to drop from.

But the rigging was empty.

"You leave me no choice," Michael said, willing his voice, likewise, to fall from the soaring heights of the tent. No sense giving his position away.

"I pity you, Michael Dragon. You have tasted the magic of sorcery, but you will never finish your first meal."

Michael didn't answer.

He started to move.

He needed to know what this tent was all about.

He brushed dirt off his shirt front. The enclosed space

smelled of wax and steel, of damp canvas and wet grass. It
was not unlike the smells in a hayloft. His eyes adjusted to
the darkness. He could see, but not perfectly. He'd made a
mistake by splitting himself. His senses had been sharper
when he was whole, undivided.

But it was too late to berate himself for that.

He was here, as he was.

He had to do what he could with what he had.

"You might be moving into a trap, Dragon." Mahafed's
voice echoed out of the dimness, directionless, like the
voice of God teasing mankind for its frailties.

Michael continued moving.

He was in a storage area, he realized, beneath slatted
bleachers. He shoved his way gently past wooden crates
and peered through the bleacher steps. Beyond him lay a
U-shaped arena. Bleachers stretched up nearly to the eaves
of the tent, forming a perfect U around the arena. Low
tables stood at the inner curve of the U, while a broad wall
blocked the end of the U.

Bull's-eye targets of varying sizes decorated the wall,
while in the center of the wall, the outline of a woman had
been painted on what appeared to be a spinning target
bearing ankle and wrist straps. The target was still at the
moment.

"It's an archery show," Mahafed said.

Michael ducked.

Mahafed's laugh sprinkled from above like a malevolent
rain.

Michael moved off in a crouch, keeping his head low,
avoiding the struts of the bleachers, circling the bend of the
U-shaped arena now, searching for Mahafed's presence
ahead of him, behind him, above . . .

"You have no weapon, Dragon. What are you going to
do, kill me with sorcery?"

Michael paused to ponder the question.

Mahafed didn't give him time.

"Sorcery is not the only way by which we survive," Mahafed said. "It works wonders when you are duping the
innocent or controlling mobs, but against one of your own

kind, the illusions are usually all too evident. More often than not—useless. As you've no doubt learned."

Michael waited, crouched low, wondering what point Mahafed was making.

Wood splinters suddenly exploded inches from Michael's face. He whirled away, sprawling into the dirt on all fours. He scrabbled forward, blinking slivers of biting wood away with a copious flood of tears.

The high-powered rifle bullet had nearly taken his head off.

"Reality, Mr. Dragon. Reality! It is often more powerful than the wildest fantasy."

Michael rubbed at his eyes, pinched out a half inch of hardwood needle. Mahafed was right about the illusions not working. But Mahafed had obviously missed something at Tor House.

Dirt puffed up in front of Michael, and the earth quivered. The bullet ricocheted, slapped a nearby flap of canvas, and hissed away like an angry wasp.

Michael heard no retort, only the soft *ppffftt* of a silenced weapon.

The sound of a fart—carrying death.

There was no time even to grin at his own sardonic thoughts.

He hurried forward, blocking off as much of his energies as he could under the circumstances. Mahafed seemed to know his every move. He needed cover, but also needed to locate Mahafed, needed to figure out how best to reach the other sorcerer.

Michael paused on one knee, ready to sprint forward at the snap of a nerve. Beyond the bleachers, he spotted the low tables in the arena. Bows and dozens of neatly aligned hunting-tipped arrows covered the table. Three bows. Three bunches of vivid, fluorescent-colored arrows. Yellow. Pink. And neon red. The tools of the archer's trade set and ready for the first show of the day. Or ready for early-morning practice.

The different colors for different tricks?

Bow and arrow against a high-powered rifle?

Michael knew nothing of archery. He'd only been exposed to the damn things in phys ed class as a kid. He remembered the embarrassment he'd suffered when he'd first drawn a bow. The damn thing had slipped from his fingers and slapped back in his face. He'd worn the resulting black eye as a bandage of klutziness for the next ten days and been open to ridicule from his classmates the entire time.

No, he couldn't fight Mahafed with a bow *and* arrows.

But he knew what he needed to do now.

He shuffled off, still beneath the bleachers, but not as quiet as he'd been moving a moment before. He kept his senses peeled, his eyes scanning the opposite side of the arena, waiting, waiting, biding his time for the telltale spit of blue flame he knew had to be there when Mahafed's rifle farted again.

Ppffftt.

Michael stiffened as the bullet *splanged* off a bleacher stanchion and *whizzed* into oblivion.

He directed his senses toward the spot where he'd seen the deep gas-blue flame spurt from the muzzle of Mahafed's rifle.

Mahafed was there, hiding in a cloak of his own making, blocking his aura, but detectable because of the very emptiness and blackness in which he was hiding. Michael stared at the spot across the arena, stared at the darker blackness beyond and beneath the horizontal slats of the bleachers. Concentrating on that one splotch of unseen humanity, he locked its location into his mind before shifting his attention to the low tables halfway across the dim arena.

The broadheads on the bunched dozens of neon red hunting arrows glimmered in Michael's vision. They became the center of his attention. He focused on them, forming a vivid picture of what he wanted them to do. The brilliant, fluorescent shafts and bright feathers wavered before his eyes, then shimmered and trembled under an unseen psychic wind building beneath them.

Another bullet whined across the arena.

And another.

One of them tore into the bleacher seat in front of Michael's face and flecked his face with sharp splinters.

Michael ignored the quick flow of blood springing from the superficial wounds.

He was a man in a trance—a sorcerer beyond the boundaries of reality. His senses were totally attuned to one task, and one task only.

Another bullet smashed into a nearby metal strut and *clanged* a sharp echo throughout the still, dark tent.

Mahafed sensed something happening, something beyond his understanding.

He fired again.

And again.

And again.

Centering on Michael's whereabouts but unable to locate the center of Michael's fevered aura.

Michael heard none of the deadly whispers, registered none of the near misses, didn't even respond to the one single bullet that tugged at his shirt and scoured a deep path across his shoulder.

His mind had one goal, was intent on one act, was generating a psychic wind the likes of which he had never tried to muster before.

Another bullet *whined* past, slapped canvas, and died.

But now it was Michael's turn to return fire.

With an explosive release of breath and energy, Michael mentally thrust the red neon arrows at the darkness hiding beneath the far bleachers.

He watched in a stuporous trance as two dozen fluorescent arrows clattered raggedly into flight, whizzed low across the open darkness of the empty arena, and spread into a pattern twice the size of a man. The darkness of the arena centered on the brilliant, flickering, shifting shafts of neon brightness as they sliced the silent air.

Michael felt Mahafed's silent psychic scream before he heard it with his ears.

Mahafed screamed even before the arrows reached him.

Screamed and dived aside.

But too late to avoid the entire fusillade.

Two dozen blood-red, glimmering arrows *snapped,*

splanged, whacked, and rattled into the bleachers and the shifting, insubstantial darkness beneath. A handful of them found living flesh to slice, or bone to smash.

Michael felt himself jolted back to reality. His head throbbed. His vision swam. He felt exhausted, reached out to hold on to a bleacher strut to keep from toppling over dizzily.

At the same time, he sensed Mahafed's pain. Weakly, he cast his senses across the arena, felt for Mahafed's being, and knew that Mahafed had taken enough arrows to kill him—unless he had time to slink off and lick his wounds.

Already, the other sorcerer was responding to the emergency, blocking off blood flow, commanding wounded cells to reunite, to rebuild that which had been destroyed.

Mahafed was responding, but he was stunned, Michael realized. Shocked by what had brought him down.

Inanimate reality as a tool of fantasy.

Michael forced himself to move. He came to his feet and began running beneath the bleachers, around the curved end, closing the distance with Mahafed. Boxes, stacks of equipment, and racks of sequined clothing blocked his way. He stumbled through them, willing Mahafed to sense his coming, to forget about the bleeding, to panic and flee and bleed to death and end this madness.

He saw Mahafed.

The Arab was on his knees, his large eyes staring through the dimness beneath the skeletal bleachers.

Michael stopped.

"You . . ." Mahafed said, slowly rising.

Several bent and broken aluminum arrows lay at Mahafed's feet in the damp, blood-stained dirt. Two glimmering arrows still protruded from the man's right side. One had pierced through his right thigh and was sticking out on both sides. Surprisingly, there was little blood flowing.

Mahafed was backing up now.

Michael willed the man to stop, to let go of that insatiable will to live he sensed within Mahafed.

Mahafed stumbled, crouched, reached out for his rifle.

Michael concentrated on the rifle, mentally kicked it away from Mahafed's outstretched hand. The rifle skidded farther under the bleachers, came to rest half under the foremost row of bleacher seats, its barrel protruding into the arena.

"You can't—you can't do that." Mahafed's voice was a weak whisper of fear. He turned and stumbled through the crisscross stanchions of the bleachers, seeking his escape near the end of the U-shaped skeletal framework. The three arrow shafts rattled off metal struts; their feathered ends wobbled and dripped blood.

Michael followed, blocking the other sorcerer's efforts to stop his own bleeding. The stains on Mahafed's back spread, glistened wetly.

The other sorcerer broke from the end of the bleachers, staggered into the open end of the arena. He held a hand out toward Michael now, as if trying ineffectually to block Michael's power by that simply physical and very human gesture.

Michael stepped from the spider-webbed bleacher supports and stopped. Mahafed foundered several steps farther away. Then he, too, stopped. He stood at the head of the arena. Behind him, the numerous bull's-eye targets formed a strange backdrop in the dimness. They looked like huge eyes staring out of the blackness, the eyes of unfeeling gods watching the necessary demise of a pretender.

Blood welled from Mahafed's mouth.

He wiped it away with the back of his arm and stared at the redness in disbelief.

"It's not illusion," Michael said.

Mahafed shook his head weakly. He tried to concentrate on his wounds, to stanch the flow of his life's blood.

Michael blocked the other's thought process with a bolt of numbing pain.

Mahafed pitched backward, came to rest against one of the largest bull's-eyes. His knees were buckling.

"So," he said wetly, "you think you've won, heh?"

Michael stood silent, unmoving.

His shoulder burned where Mahafed's bullet had ripped his flesh open.

He ignored the pain.

He had something to finish before he paid attention to his own pain.

He was killing this man.

He didn't like it.

But he had no choice.

Again, he blocked Mahafed's efforts to stop bleeding.

Mahafed coughed blood. "Your woman and daughter aren't safe," Mahafed said then.

Michael glared at the dying man. Mahafed didn't look like a sorcerer now. He looked like the frail, helpless prelude to oblivion that all dying people came to resemble. He was pitiable.

The Arab sneered something close to a smile—a smile stained with red. "They were coming for you." His laugh was short, thick with blood. "True love," he said. "The fools. Rushing to Glastonbury to be with you—to share your danger. Eleanor sensed them. She has them, Dragon." He tried to laugh. He didn't make it this time —didn't make it at all. It denegerated in the first paroxysm into a weak and bloody cough. "You . . . you may have the powers of Merlin and the *missing one* . . . but you will lose your loved ones if you try to fight Eleanor. You will carry the guilt of their deaths for centuries if you resist her." He coughed again, lost his balance, and slipped along the slick surface of the target behind him. His back painted a broad red stain across the huge target. He caught himself on trembling legs, locked his eyes on Michael's. "I would try to make a truce with her," Mahafed said very softly, "if she will. . . . She is not someone you want to fight. She is not a nice lady."

Mahafed sucked air and straightened himself against the target. This time his sad laugh did manage to make itself heard as he intended.

"If I must die," he said, "do it now. Quickly."

Michael considered Mahafed's request.

"Do it the way I could never have done. Finish it the

way you intended. With your strange blend of illusion and reality."

Michael nodded. He stepped away from the bleachers. "Good-bye, Mahafed."

"Remember me," Mahafed said. "Write well of me in the book."

Michael eyed the archer's table at the far end of the room, concentrated, and quickly unleashed the power he needed to send the arrows on their way. Twin bunches of fluorescent arrows burst off the table in a rustle of feathers and the soft rattle of shafts. They merged into one glimmering flight of gold and pink shafts.

Michael watched their flight until just before their impact, then turned away.

The dozens of arrows slapped into Mahafed with the sudden impact of a hard-driven rain.

Michael heard a soft sigh, then silence.

He knew what Mahafed's riddled body would look like nailed to the target, and did not want to turn and see it. But he was remembering Caine's admonition about taking another life's force, and thinking about Eleanor.

Eleanor——with Carol and Jenny in her hands.

An Eleanor who cared nothing for innocent lives.

He turned then, ready to ignore the horror of Mahafed's death, ready to take what life energy he could to help himself against Eleanor, but unready for the blow that picked him and lifted him away from the bleachers, unready for the explosion that reverberated around him as he spun into the dirt and sawdust on the arena floor.

His mouth hung open, slack and stupid. He tasted dirt, felt grit between his teeth, tried to rise, but couldn't. The world had been turned topsy-turvy. The soaring heights of the tent reared above him. Painfully, he twisted himself onto his back, turned his head around, feeling dizzy, trembling feebly. His gaze swept back under the bleachers, down the long, skeletal corridors of struts and shadows, slats and darkness.

He saw her then . . .

A shadow figure.

Eleanor.

Large-bore shotgun pointed straight at him.

A scant fifty feet away.

She'd shot him in the back.

He felt his life seeping away.

Felt bruised.

Beaten.

Defeated.

Humiliated.

"You should have an audience for your death," Eleanor said. Her commanding voice echoed through the tent.

A tumultuous clap of laughter burst forth, accompanied by blinding light and the smell of popcorn. Michael blinked. The archery arena was filled with people. They were all gawking at him, smiling, munching on popcorn, their faces hidden behind cotton candy balls, their children pointing at him.

Illusion.

He willed it away.

It hurt, but the brightness faded to darkness, the laughter echoed off into silence. The arena was once again empty, dead.

"You need an audience," Eleanor said. Her voice was closer. She was approaching him, stepping slowly along the corridor of steel struts.

The tent lights flashed back on, the crowd jeered, children laughed, clowns danced by waving, smiling, making faces at him.

"Make him die, Mommy," some little girl squealed.

"Cut him up."

"After he's dead, Daddy, can I have one of his ears?"

Michael ignored the jeering and laughter. He tried to seal off the bleeding flesh of his back, to repair the damaged organs, to close down the flow of blood pouring out onto the ground.

Eleanor blocked his thoughts. Cut him off from himself. Gave him pain. Did to him that which he'd done to Mahafed scant seconds earlier. He glared at her. She smiled back at him. He turned away from her.

Something about Eleanor made him shift his attention back to her. She was leading someone behind her, someone in handcuffs, someone with flowing long hair, someone having difficulty staggering through the maze of stanchions and crossbars, someone who walked as if she were . . . blind.

"Carol!"

The figure behind Eleanor stiffened, straightened. Her voice, which echoed oddly beneath the bleachers, was unmistakable. "Michael . . ."

"Would you like to see him die?" Eleanor asked.

The two women paused just steps from the end of the bleachers. The dazzling carnival lights, falling on them through the bleachers, painted them with writhing, horizontal lines. The skeletal struts of the bleachers appeared to writhe, too, to shift and twine about each other, as if they were alive. Michael couldn't trust his eyes anymore. He was certain that part of the bleacher struts was moving. Eleanor stepped sideways and thrust Carol forward. Michael sensed Carol's shock as the other sorcerer created an image for Carol to see, an image of her dying love, a cruel way to play with her blindness.

He sensed Eleanor's satisfaction . . . and her distraction.

She was enjoying his death.

And if anything about his death was good, *that was*.

Because it entertained her and kept her mind off the writhing form in the bleachers above her.

The crowd created by Eleanor cheered.

Michael let a small smile trace his mouth as he let go of the body within which he existed. It was like a small death, this leaving. The body was dying, he knew, but he had other places to live.

Such as in the living part of the bleacher crossbars, the entwined body of the serpent dangling so sweetly above Eleanor's unwitting head.

He settled into the cobra's body and immediately released its coils.

He dropped like a soft, meaty rope.

The crowd stopped cheering. The smell of popcorn evaporated. Clowns disappeared. The lights went out.

And Eleanor screamed.

Too late.

Too lusciously late.

Oh, sweet Jesus, too fucking late!

Michael felt his substantial weight *thunk* onto Eleanor's back. In the next instant he sank his long, venomous fangs deep into the base of her neck. He felt her buck beneath his weight, struggle to jerk his long, fluid body off hers, to free her neck from those fangs, but she was too late, too fucking late because he felt his venom sacks emptying themselves already, felt his teeth grating on her spine, felt her losing her balance, falling, stumbling, tumbling to the grass and dirt beneath the bleachers, sniveling and crying and begging and fading out that quickly, as rich poison swam through her bloodstream and almost immediately started killing cells in her ancient brain. He held on through her shivering, quaking death, through her screams and wails and convulsive snapping, though her swearing and rolling and bucking and begging and damning, hung on through her final collapse. Then he released himself, let his long fangs slip as easily from her flesh as a vaccination needle from your arm. He languidly twined himself around her smooth neck, past her ear, across her pale cheek, and gently insinuated himself into her mouth, where he inhaled with all his strength and willed her life's energy out of her dead body and into his.

He drew in every bit of energy he could find, then slid free and lay, satiated, upon Eleanor's ancient and still back. He had won. He felt his tense muscles relaxing, going slack. He let his majestic cobra hood settle against his body. His eyes drooped.

It was hard to believe that his battle was over.

In the distance, he heard the muffled shouts of men and women fighting the tent fires.

It was hard to imagine that so much had happened in such a brief time. Time had lost meaning.

Michael glanced around.

Across from him he saw the figure of his human self, the other Dragon, lying on its back, one arm outflung in death.

He should feed on his energy, too, he told himself, on his own energy. He needed to regain his full strength.

Beyond the dead body that had once been himself, he saw Carol. He should really change—

He heard a soft hiss and felt the air parting above him.

He writhed viciously to the side, instinctively realizing that he had been fooled, knowing in his guts that one of his enemies had tricked him—*somehow, some way*—

He wasn't fast enough to avoid the very real blade swung from above with such force. He saw the blade's shadow moving across the ground—held in the crooked shadow of a strong arm.

A machete's blade.

A man's arm.

The blade sliced through the last inches of Michael's snake body and *thwacked* into Eleanor's lifeless body beneath him.

Michael writhed in pain and readiness. He convulsed off Eleanor's body and slithered away as fast as he could move, rippling away, feeling his life's juices flowing out behind him. There was only one of him now, only one left to die, and someone was intent on giving him that oblivion—now.

28

Michael jerked first into the safety of the low bleachers, then swung away from the arena, slithered between boxes and wheeled carts, heading for the chill, damp fog beyond the tent skirt.

He needed time to heal, to seal off the dripping, oozing wound at his rear.

Something grabbed him and tossed him into the air.

Mongoose!

Christ! A natural snake-killer.

Landing on his back, stunned, Michael twisted away from the furry streak of toothed lightning and crammed himself into a space between crates too small for the mongoose to enter. Pain shot the length of Michael's body. He saw the mongoose dancing just beyond the opening between the crates and willed it away. The mongoose disappeared.

Blink, and it was gone.

Illusion.

But so real. Oh, Christ, so real! He'd felt the teeth sink into the flesh of his back.

Michael concentrated on his tail, on vanquishing the wound. This was not so simple. The missing inches were a reality. The machete had been real, as had the arm wielding it.

He concentrated on his wound, on sealing off the flow of blood and—

He heard footsteps.

Human footsteps.

Strong, confident footsteps.

He slithered backward, deeper into the shadows.

A shotgun barrel insinuated itself between the boxes.

Michael writhed backward, reared up, and twisted around the corner of the box. The corner of wood erupted into a spray of splinters.

Michael writhed away under the nearby tent skirt, twisted a crooked and painful path through the wet grass and the thick fog.

The sounds of fire fighting reached his ears, the crackle of flames.

He twisted an oozing path away from those sounds, away from the rush of angry and anxious humanity.

Another tent.

More darkness.

He slithered in, found shelter between two large cages. The first thing to register was the smell. Heavy musk and urine, the stench of disinfectant losing a battle against years and years of animal droppings. He was in one of the animal tents, he realized. Someone was nearby, calming the animals, who were pacing their cages, on the verge of hysteria because of the nearby fire, the scent of smoke and flame in the air.

"Now, now, Daisy, take it easy, there. All's fine with the world, girl. It's me myself here with you."

Soothing words for a tiger; sweet nothings for a lioness; soft reassurance for a lumbering, angry bear. The animals were tense and edgy. Their fear formed a palpable stench, which mingled with the other strong scents in the tent.

Michael couldn't see the animal-trainer, could only hear the man's gentle, reassuring voice as he made his rounds, heard the soft rattle of cages all around the dark room as large animals shifted position, *whuffed,* yawned, and shifted again.

"There's no danger to you, Sam. No danger, 'tall. Here, Bess, have a bite of your favorite."

More cage rattles. A whimper. A soft, tentative purr from the depths of some giant throat, the sound as loud as a smooth-running motor.

Michael ignored it all, went inward, sealed off his damaged tail. His needed time to regenerate the portion lost to the machete—needed to shift shape to something more capable of dealing with the loss of—

"Hey, who're you?"

Michael heard the soft rustle of the animal-trainer reaching for some kind of weapon.

"What the 'ell you doin' in this tent?"

Michael bent his mind inward, forced himself to shift shape again, this time faster than last, shifting this time back to that of his human form.

Michael Dragon emerged from the snakeskin and lay on the raw earth floor, wet and naked, as if from a new birthing.

His left ankle hurt.

Glancing down, he realized that his left foot was gone. Sealed off, but certainly missing. If he became a bird again, a hawk, he could escape, fly away, and take time to—

He heard a gasp of fear, a gentle cry of anguish, and then the unmistakable crumpling fall of a body dropping to the ground.

Then silence.

An unreal silence.

Michael let his mind reach out tentatively to touch at that silence.

Hello, again, my son!

Michael recoiled.

It was *Caine*.

But Caine was dead.

He'd burned the man's remains himself.

"You burned an illusion," Caine said, this time in quite a normal voice. "You forgot your first lesson, Dragon: Nothing is what it seems. Reality is only a branch of fantasy."

The big animals reacted to the new voice in their midst. Michael could smell their fear escalating.

"You might as well step out here, Michael Dragon. I know where you are."

Michael stayed where he was, between the cage of a large bear and that of a lithe yet huge tigress.

"Have it your way, Dragon."

"It was *you* all along," Michael said. "*You* were out to take over from the others. *You* started the battle with Eleanor and Mahafed."

"How perceptive of you."

There was no laugh. The derision was purely sarcastic.

"You used me and your other children. You sacrificed us for your own ends."

"The ways of power are seldom understood by the weak."

Caine's voice filled the tent, yet did so softly. It came from nowhere, from everywhere, from the mouths of the animals, from beneath their cages, from the darkness overhead, from the earth underfoot.

"Why don't you come out, Dragon. We can make this very short and painless."

"Make *what* short and painless?"

"Your death, of course."

"Why do I need to die?"

"Need you ask?"

Michael was silent for a moment.

"With me gone, the world is yours to play with as you wish."

"That's a very simplistic way to put it. But I'll accept that. The time has come to end the charades."

"What makes you think I'll be any easier for you to kill than I was for Eleanor or Mahafed? Or for Drew Garrett or Lea Frazzetti, for that matter?"

"I'm no fool, Dragon. I know you don't want to die. I also know that you are much more powerful than I suspected at first—certainly much more resourceful than Eleanor or Mahafed thought possible. You were a fine weapon to use against them. In the end, I thought Eleanor had ended things for you. I thought I would have to step in and finish Eleanor myself, but you surprised me with your resourcefulness. You *really are* very good, you know. But your wishes and your powers will do little for you now. I've taken your measure, Dragon, and I know you. You might as well stand and see what I'm talking about."

Michael considered his options.

He didn't stand.

He let his mind reach out and search the area between the ages. Caine was standing in the open, bookended by two feminine forms.

"Certainly you recognize your lady loves," Caine said, gloating. "Our friend Eleanor was kind enough to bring them to this place for just this kind of showdown. But you outsmarted her."

Painfully, Michael rose to his feet.

Caine was right.

It was time to end the charades.

Caine stood there, between Carol and Jenny, who were cuffed together. The three of them were flanked by twin rows of cages, behind one of which Michael was standing. Naked bulbs burned overhead, throwing a stark, shadow-harsh light through the tent. Caine held the two-and-a-half foot blade of the machete at Jenny's throat. One move by either Carol or Jenny would draw the big knife across Jenny's throat.

The big animals moved restlessly in their cages. Bars rattled. Metal bases creaked with hundreds of pounds of shifting, pacing weight. The sound of fearful panting formed a strange backdrop to the scene being acted out in the center floor.

"No tricks, Dragon, or your daughter dies before you have time to apologize. And I assure you that I am not as easily fooled as Eleanor."

Michael stared coldly at the man who was his father. He knew Caine would stop at nothing. He felt it in his bones, and thought, *I should have realized it all along.* Under different circumstances, he would have wanted to get to know Caine, not as a friend, not out of any sense of caring, but more as a particularly crazy patient, the epitome of sociopathy, something to put under glass and study.

"What do you expect of me?" Michael asked, his voice flat, emotionless.

"Suicide," Caine said. "Your life for theirs."

Michael stared at Caine, met the other's cold eyes with eyes grown just as cold.

"And if I don't agree?"

"There's no question of that," Caine said.

"You're that sure of me?"

Caine nodded. "You *care*, Dragon. You're not like me. Not like the others. You're very good, perhaps the best in centuries, but you lack something in your makeup. You lack the ability to be objective, to make decisions based on what *must* be rather than on what you want things to be." He shook his head. "No, Dragon, I know you too well. Your life for theirs. You're cornered, and you know it. You have only one choice."

"How do I know you won't harm them after I'm dead?"

"You don't, although I give my word on it. They're of little consequence to me once you're dead." Caine cocked his gray head. "But then, if you fight me, they'll both be certain to die. So, once again, what choice have you?"

"And if I comply, I suppose you have a special way for me to die?"

Caine smiled. "No. Any way will do. Just so you do it quickly. Before we leave this tent."

"Don't listen to him, Daddy," Jenny said. "You don't want him to be the only one left."

Michael considered a feint toward Caine, began to think of a way to block Caine's thoughts for a moment, but stopped when Caine dug the razor-sharp machete blade deeper into Jenny's throat. Michael saw the trickle of blood form, trickle down the blade and spill to the packed grass on the floor of the tent.

"The slightest trick on your part, Dragon, and I warn you: she'll die. Right in front of you. Horribly. *Reality,* dear boy. I assure you. *A knife blade is grim reality, indeed.*"

Michael smiled sadly. "So this is it. I choose the method—"

"And you do it. Now. Without any more dallying."

Michael nodded.

"First let me show you this," he said.

He glared at the floor in front of Caine.

The floor split, parted, as if it were the tender skin of some huge fruit. Steam issued from the parting flesh of the earth. From someplace deep in the world's guts, hot lava bubbled up and spilled onto the floor.

The animals went wild.

"What the hell are you doing?" Caine demanded, a note of nervous caution in his voice now. "I said, 'no illusions.'"

Michael smiled.

"Blink it away," he said.

Caine eyed him oddly, then glanced at the thick, frothing, fiery lava. Caine blinked.

The lava continued to flow slowly from the narrow crack in the earth. It made odd little clinking sounds as rocks heated and cracked.

Caine's eyes suddenly locked on Michael's face.

"It's not illusion," was all he said.

Michael shook his head calmly. "Not at all," he said.

"It's just an illustration of how badly you've misjudged me, Caine."

Perspiration flecked Caine's forehead. He drew the long machete blade deeper into Jenny's soft, white throat.

Michael willed the lava pit closed.

The earth trembled, sealed itself off. The last steam evaporated in the still air.

Caine was shook.

"Even if you can control the elements," he said, "I can kill your daughter before you have a chance to stop me. If you resist me, she dies."

Michael only stared coldly at Caine. It was the man's cold-bloodedness that made him unbearable.

"I could stop you," Michael said.

"No."

"I could." He lifted a shoulder, aware of the chill in the air and the fact that he was still naked. "But perhaps you need to kill Jenny. Maybe you'd do it no matter what I did. I think you intend to kill her. And Carol. No matter what."

"It's not true, Dragon." Caine was sweating now, the machete blade trembling. "I give my word. You take your life, and they live."

Michael only stared at the other man, the man whose genes so dominated his own being.

"Do it, Dragon. Do it now."

Caine was growing desperate.

"How's this?" Michael asked.

Michael bore down with all his ability, concentrated, then stared down the line of cages. The lock on the far cage exploded with a metallic crackle, and the cage door popped open. A startled grizzly bear lunged forward into the open walkway, then stopped, sniffing the air, with one paw raised in Caine's direction.

"What the hell are you doing, Dragon?"

Michael sensed the poisonous worm of fear in Caine's mind.

"Finishing the charade," Michael said. "Let's have a good death."

He concentrated on the next cage.

The lock exploded, patted to the ground. The cage door swayed open, creaking softly.

The next lock crackled, fell apart.

And the next.

Followed by another and another and another.

The tiny explosions moved down the line of cages, then returned up the other side of the service lane.

A tiger inched its way into the lane.

A full-maned, yawning lion.

Followed by his mate.

And a tawny puma.

And others.

Moving now with cautious deliberation.

Caine backed off, forcing Jenny and Carol to follow him.

One of the tigers padded forward suddenly, to within a yard of Jenny and Carol before pausing, neck outstretched, to sniff them.

Michael felt Caine's mind reaching out to block the tiger's senses. He smashed his mind at Caine's evolving illusion, destroyed it, shoved his own illusion down the other sorcerer's psychic throat.

Caine reeled backward in agony. His face was contorted in confusion and pain. "You're going to kill your own daughter," he said with a gasp, "and the woman you love."

Michael waited, watched, said nothing.

The animals were moving now, inexorably driving Caine into a corner.

The puma started forward suddenly.

Caine's mind blocked the animal's lunge, frightened the puma, drove it back.

The old man was sweating.

"When I choose to block your thoughts," Michael said, "you're a dead man."

"You'll kill your daughter," Caine said in a controlled whisper.

Michael shook his head. "The animals won't."

"Then I will," Caine said. "And if you don't help me out of here and do as I say, then your lady love dies next."

"Followed by you," Michael said. He let a thin smile form on his face. "I'm stronger than you, Caine. And you know that now."

"But I have the trump cards." For emphasis, Caine jerked Jenny backward. More blood flowed down the machete blade, staining Jenny's neck now with crimson.

One of the dark, lumbering bears moved in on Caine, Jenny, and Carol.

"Use your trumps," Michael said. "Or the game is over."

The expression on Caine's face shifted rapidly from shock to anger. "I misjudged you," he said.

"And it's going to cost you your life," Michael said.

"And you your loves."

With that, Caine jerked the machete in toward his breast and pulled it forcibly across Jenny's throat. Blood burst forth from Jenny's creamy throat in a bubbling freshet. Her head lolled loosely.

Caine dropped her and grabbed a handful of Carol's hair. "She's next, Dragon. Do you want both of them dead?"

"No," Michael said, "just you."

With that, Michael released a tiny thread of control from deep within his mind. The hair in Caine's hand dissolved, the bleeding girl at Caine's feet disappeared. Carol and Jenny both vanished.

Caine stared.

"Illusion," Caine said. "I . . . I couldn't tell the diff——"

"Better than illusion," Michael said. "Much better."

The carnival animals were reacting to the sudden disappearances in front of them. A tension was growing among them, a controlled waiting-to-explode frenzy.

"You win," Caine said.

"And you die," Michael said. "Good-bye, Caine. Good-bye forever."

Michael nodded toward the animals, tossing the image of a wounded lamb their way, an image superimposed over Caine's being. Caine screamed.

The animals moved in a tumultuous, breaking wave.

Michael rubbed clothes onto himself, paused to regenerate his missing foot, and walked away from the rattling struggle, away from the wet sounds and the snarls,

away from the past he was only beginning to comprehend and toward a future that had been thrust on him
without choice.

The morning fog was thinning, finally. Only one tent
was still burning. Two others were smoldering. With little
effort, Michael wended his way through the crush of
sweating, smoke-stained carneys. They took no notice of
him, didn't even see him.

He was heading home.

Back to London.

But first to the Lake District.

First to Jenny.

And Carol.

From overhead, the first clear rays of sunshine fell
warmly on his head.

29

The sun was bright, the day as warm as days ever got in
England. Michael walked around the base of the Tor, arm
in arm with Carol. Jenny ran ahead, scampering over tufts
and hillocks of grass. Gamboling, without paying attention, she was in danger of slipping off the edge of a craggy
piece of rock.

"Watch out, Jenny," Carol called.

Michael glanced at Carol's sparkling green eyes. Her
gaze met his. She smiled, then quickly kissed him on the
cheek.

Such a little gift, Michael thought.

Sight.

Most of us took it so for granted.

But not Carol.

She reveled in it, feasted on colors, thrived on the tiniest flower, the simplest lichen, soared with the birds above them. For weeks now they'd been joking about how she stared at the food on her plate, or the guttering of candles, or the gentle fall of a leaf.

She seemed insatiable, as if she would never stop her visual gluttony.

"You're laughing at me," she said, teasing.

"*With* you," Michael said. "Laughing *with* you. I like what you see." He smiled at her. "I also like what I see."

She took his hand. There was really nothing she needed to say.

They walked quietly along the uneven ground for nearly another hundred yards before either of them spoke.

"It's near here," Michael said.

Carol paused, her brow furrowed. "I don't feel anything."

"There's a cave under this hill," Michael said. "I can feel it vividly."

He glanced around the steep side of the hill, searching for the slightest indication of where there might be an opening into the hill. He concentrated, picking up decayed, old-age sensations, feeling the last steps of an old man, as vivid as if they were his own steps. Carrying an armload of scrolls, moving up the hill, across a slight diagonal incline, then stooping, touching a rock, rolling it aside, and slipping into darkness for all eternity.

Merlin.

His final journey.

Into darkness.

And legend.

Michael opened his eyes. He clenched his fists. He was humming with tension. The sensation was so frustratingly clear, yet the images so inexact.

A rock.

Something—a depression, a hole, a crawl space, something large enough to admit a man into the heart of the hill.

His eyes scoured the hillside.

"Damn. I know there's an entrance near here."

Carol lifted his hand to her lips, kissed it. "You'll find it."

Michael let his tension go. He knew he would. It was only a matter of time. They'd only returned to Glastonbury the day before. This was only their second trip to the Tor, and already he was certain he'd located the area of Merlin's entrance. He could rip the hill open if he wanted, but he couldn't predict what damage that might cause in the secret caverns within the hill. It was better to take it easy, to take his time.

When Merlin wanted his secrets revealed, Michael was certain the entrance would be found, and not before.

It was only a matter of time.

"Daddy, look!" Jenny was pointing to a ragged tuft of turf jutting from a nearly perpendicular section of hillside. "I just saw a rabbit go in here, and I can hear things echoing inside."

Michael scrambled to his daughter's side. He rested a hand on her very real shoulder and knelt beside the tiny section of rock seen beneath the turf. Dank air issued in a soft breeze from the belly of the hill, air rich with the scent of time and timelessness.

The sensations were strong now.

Very strong.

Images flooded Michael's mind. Images of ancient battles and fallen heros. Images of dark, stone-walled rooms and hushed, torchlit meetings. Images of giant dancing stones floating across storm-tossed seas to stand erect in forlorn fields and defy centuries of wind and rain and the deprivations of man. Images of deception and love, the birth of a king, and the trails of greatness. Camelot and Lancelot. Mordred and Morgana. And behind it all, the machinations of one man—a man who was more than a man—a man who was a sorcerer.

The only sorcerer of his time.

Merlin.

The sorcerer.

Michael rose to his feet as Carol joined him and Jenny.

"They're in there," Michael said softly. "The scrolls. Merlin's legacy."

"They're yours now," Carol said.

Michael nodded, then stared off into the distance, lost in thought. What did it mean? To what purpose had he been brought to this place? Given the abilities he possessed?

Why?

He was the only one now.

As Merlin had been in his time.

And, as with Merlin, he knew the answers would come when their time was right. Fate had its own way of working, and he was nothing but Fate's implement.

Once again, there was only one . . .

One who could bide his time for centuries.

Until needed.

One . . .

Sorcerer.